Liv bristled. "I don't need someone to protect me."

"No one can watch their own back," Hawkeye said. "As a member of the armed forces, I know what it means to trust the guys behind me."

"Who did you have in mind?"

He smiled. "Me."

A thrill of something she hadn't felt in a long time—if she didn't count the kiss—rippled through Liv. Taking on Hawkeye could prove to be a big mistake in more ways than one. "What choice do I have?"

"None," Hawkeye said, his tone firm and final.

For however long it took to find her father's murderer and stop this insanity going on in her community, she was stuck with Hawkeye. And despite her initial resistance, she had to admit to herself she might just need him.

D0756000

HOT ZONE

BY
ELLE JAMES

First Published in Great Britain 2017
By Mills & Boon, an imprint of HarperCollins*Publishers*
1 London Bridge Street, London, SE1 9GF

© 2017 Mary Jernigan

ISBN: 978-0-263-92890-7

46-0617

Our policy is to use papers that are natural, renewable and recyclable products and made from wood grown in sustainable forests. The logging and manufacturing processes conform to the legal environmental regulations of the country of origin.

Printed and bound in Spain
by CPI, Barcelona

Elle James, a *New York Times* bestselling author, started writing when her sister challenged her to write a romance novel. She has managed a full-time job and raised three wonderful children, and she and her husband even tried ranching exotic birds (ostriches, emus and rheas). Ask her, and she'll tell you what it's like to go toe-to-toe with an angry three-hundred-and-fifty-pound bird! Elle loves to hear from fans at ellejames@earthlink.net or www.ellejames.com.

This book is dedicated to my daughters, who chose to give back to their country by joining the military. Thank you for following in your mother's footsteps! Love you both so much!

Chapter One

Trace "Hawkeye" Walsh checked the coordinates he'd been given by Transcontinental Pipeline Inspection, Inc., and glanced down at the display on the four-wheeler's built-in GPS guidance device. He'd arrived at checkpoint number four. He switched off the engine, climbed off the ATV and unfolded the contour map across the seat.

As with the first three checkpoints, he wasn't exactly sure what he was looking for at the location. He wasn't a pipeline inspector, and he didn't have the tools and devices used by one, but he scanned the area anyway.

Tracing his finger along the line drawn in pencil across the page, he paused. He should be getting close to the point at which RJ Khalig had been murdered. Based on the tight contour lines on the map, he would find the spot over the top of the next ridgeline and down in the valley.

Hawkeye glanced upward. Treacherous terrain had slowed him down. In order to reach some of the points on the map, he'd had to follow old mining trails and bypass canyons. He shrugged. It wasn't a war zone, he wasn't fighting the Taliban or ISIS, and it beat the hell out of being in an office job any day of the week.

That morning, his temporary boss, Kevin Garner, had given him the assignment of following the pipeline through some of the most rugged terrain he'd ever been in, even considering the foothills of Afghanistan. He was game. If he had to be working with the Department of Homeland Security in the Beartooth Mountains of Wyoming, he was happy to be out in the backwoods, rather than chasing wild geese, empty leads and the unhappy residents of the tiny town of Grizzly Pass.

In the two weeks he'd been in the small town of Grizzly Pass, they'd had two murders, a busload of kids taken hostage and two people hunted down like wild game. When he'd agreed to the assignment, he'd been looking forward to some fresh mountain air and a slowdown to his normal combat-heavy assignments. He needed the time to determine whether or not he would stay the full twenty years to retirement in the US Army Rangers or get out and dare to try something different.

Two gunshot and multiple shrapnel wounds, one broken arm, a couple of concussions and six near-fatal misses started to wear on a body and soul. In the last battle he'd been a part of, his best friend hadn't been as lucky. The gunshot wound had been nothing compared to the violent explosion Mac had been smack-dab in the middle of. Yeah, Hawkeye had lost his best friend and battle buddy, a man who'd had his back since they'd been rangers in training.

Without Mac, he wasn't sure he wanted to continue to deploy to the most godforsaken, war-torn countries in the world. He wasn't sure he'd survive. And maybe that wasn't a bad thing. At least he'd die like Mac, defending his country.

He'd hoped this temporary assignment would give him the opportunity to think about his next steps in life. Should he continue his military career? His enlistment was up in a month. He had to decide whether to reenlist or get out.

So far, since he'd been in Grizzly Pass, he hadn't had the time to ponder his future. Hell, he'd already been in a shoot-out and had to rescue one of his new team members. For a place with such a small population, it was a hot zone of trouble. No wonder Garner had requested combat veterans to assist him in figuring out what the hell was going on.

Thankfully, today was just a fact-finding mission. He was to traverse the line Khalig had been inspecting when he'd met with his untimely demise. He was to look for any clues as to why someone would have paid Wayne Batson to assassinate him. Since Batson was dead, they couldn't ask him. And he hadn't been forthcoming with a name before he took his final breath.

Which meant whoever had hired him was still out there, having gotten away with murder.

Hawkeye double-checked the map, oriented with the antique compass his grandfather had given him when he'd joined the army and cross-checked with the GPS. Sure of his directions, he folded the map, pocketed his compass, climbed onto the ATV and took off.

At the top of the ridge, he paused and glanced around, looking for other vehicles or people on the opposite ridge. He didn't want to get caught like Khalig at the bottom of the valley with a sniper itching to pick him off. Out of the corner of his eye, he detected movement in the valley below.

A man squatted beside another four-wheeler. He had something in his hands and seemed to be burying it in the dirt.

Hawkeye goosed the throttle, sending his four-wheeler over the edge, descending the winding trail.

The man at the bottom glanced up. When he spotted Hawkeye descending the trail on the side of the hill, he dropped what he'd been holding, leaped onto his ATV and raced up an old mining road on the other side of the ridge.

Hopping off the trail, Hawkeye took the more direct route to the bottom, bouncing over large rock stumps and fallen branches of weathered trees. By the time Hawkeye arrived at the base, the man who'd sped away was already halfway up the hill in front of him.

Hawkeye paused long enough to look at what the man had dropped, and his blood ran cold. A stick of dynamite jutted out of the ground with a long fuse coiled in the dirt beside it.

Thumbing the throttle lever, Hawkeye zoomed after the disappearing rider, who had apparently been about to sabotage the oil pipeline. Had he succeeded, he would have had the entire state in an uproar over the spillage and damage to the environment.

Not to mention, he might be the key to who had contracted Batson to kill Khalig.

At the top of the hill where the mining road wrapped

around the side of a bluff, Hawkeye slowed in case the pursued had stopped to attack his pursuer.

Easing around the corner, he noted the path was clear and spied the rider heading down a trail Hawkeye could see from his vantage point would lead back to a dirt road and ultimately to the highway. With as much of a lead as he had, Dynamite Man could conceivably reach the highway and get away before Hawkeye caught up.

Hawkeye refused to let the guy off the hook. Goosing the accelerator, he shot forward and hurtled down the narrow mining road to the base of the mountain. At several points along the path, he skidded sideways, the rear wheels of the four-wheeler sliding dangerously close to the edge of deadly drop-offs. But he didn't slow his descent, pushing his speed faster than was prudent on the rugged terrain.

By the time he reached the bottom of the mountain, Hawkeye was within fifty yards of the man on the other ATV. His quarry wouldn't have enough time to ditch his four-wheeler for another vehicle.

Hawkeye followed the dirt road, occasionally losing sight of the rider in front of him. Eventually, between the trees and bushes, he caught glimpses of the highway ahead. When he broke free into a rare patch of open terrain, he spied the man on the track ahead, about to hit the highway's pavement.

"I'LL BE DAMNED if I sell Stone Oak Ranch to Bryson Rausch. My father would roll over in his grave." At the thought of her father lying in his grave next to her mother, Olivia Dawson's heart clenched in her chest.

Her eyes stung, but anger kept her from shedding another tear.

"You said you couldn't live at the ranch. Not since your father died." Abe Masterson, the Stone Oak Ranch foreman for the past twenty years, turned onto the highway headed toward home.

Liv's throat tightened. Home. She'd wanted to come home since she graduated from college three years ago. But her father had insisted she try city living before she decided whether or not she wanted to come back to the hard work and solitary life of a rancher.

For the three years since she'd left college with a shiny new degree, she'd worked her way up the corporate ladder to a management position. Eight people reported directly to her. She was responsible for their output and their well-being. She'd promised her father she'd give it five years. But that had all changed in the space of one second.

The second her father died in a freak horseback-riding accident six days earlier.

Liv had gotten the word in the middle of the night in Seattle, had hopped into her car and had driven all the way to Grizzly Pass, Wyoming. No amount of hurrying back to her home would have been fast enough to have allowed her to say goodbye to her father.

By the time Abe had found him, he'd been dead for a couple of hours. The coroner estimated the fall had killed him instantly, when he'd struck his head on a rock.

Liv would have given anything to have talked to him one last time. She hadn't spoken to him for over a week before his death. The last time had been on the telephone and had ended in anger. She had wanted to end her time in Seattle and come home. Her father had insisted she finish out her five years.

I'm not going to get married to a city boy. What use would he be on a ranch, anyway? she'd argued.

You don't know where love will take you. Give it a chance, he'd argued right back. *Have you been dating?*

No, Dad. I intimidate most men. They like their women soft and wimpy. I can't do that. It's not me.

Sweetheart, her father had said. *You have to open your heart. Love hits you when you least expect it. Besides, I want to live to see my grandchildren.*

Her throat tightening, Liv shook her head. Her father would never know his grandchildren, and they'd never know the great man he was. The tears welled and threatened to slip out the corners of her eyes.

"If you sell to Rausch, you can be done with ranching and get on with your life. You won't have to stay around, being constantly reminded of your father."

"Maybe I want to be reminded. Maybe I was being too rash when I said I couldn't be around the ranch because it brought back too many painfully happy memories of me and Dad." She sniffed, angry that she wasn't doing a very good job of holding herself together.

"What did Rausch offer you?"

Liv wiped her eyes with her sleeve and swallowed the lump in her throat before she could force words out. "A quarter of what the ranch is worth. A quarter!" She laughed, the sound ending in a sob. "I'll die herding cattle before I sell to that man."

"Yeah, well, you could die a lot sooner if you go like your father."

Liv clenched her fist in her lap. "It's physically demanding, ranching in the foothills of the Beartooth Mountains. Falling off your horse and hitting your head on a rock could happen to anyone around here." She shot a glance at Abe. "Right?"

He nodded, his voice dropping to little more than a whisper. "Yeah, but I would bet my best rodeo buckle your father had some help falling off that horse."

"What do you mean?"

"Just that we'd had some trouble on the ranch, leading up to that day."

"Trouble?"

Abe shrugged. "There've been a whole lot of strange things going on in Grizzly Pass in the past couple months."

"Dad never said a word."

"He didn't want to worry you."

Liv snorted and then sniffed. He was a little late on that account. She swiveled in her seat, directing her attention to the older man. "Tell me."

"You know about the kids on the hijacked bus, right?"

She nodded. "I heard about it on the national news. I couldn't believe the Vanderses went off the deep end. But what does that have to do with my father and the ranch?"

Abe lifted a hand and scratched his wiry brown hair with streaks of silver dominating his temples. "That's only part of the problem. I hear there's a group called Free America stirring up trouble."

"What kind of trouble?"

"Nothing anyone can put a finger on, but rumor has it they're meeting regularly, training in combat tactics."

"Doesn't the local law enforcement have a handle on them?"

Abe shook his head. "No one on the inside is owning up to being a part of it, and folks on the outside are only guessing. It's breeding a whole lot of distrust among the locals."

"So they're training for combat. People have a right to protect themselves." She didn't like that it was splitting a once close-knit community.

"Yeah, but what if they put that combat training to use and try to take over the government?"

Liv smiled and leaned back in her seat. "They'd have to have a lot more people than the population of Grizzly Pass to take over the government."

"Maybe so, but they could do a lot of damage and terrorize a community if they tried anything locally. Just look at the trouble Vanders and his boys stirred up when they killed a bus driver and threatened to bury a bunch of little kids in one of the old mines."

"You have a point." Liv chewed on her lower lip, her brows drawing together. She could only imagine the horror those children had to face and the families standing by, praying for their release. "We used to be a caring, cohesive community. We had semiannual picnics where everyone came out and visited with each other. What's happening?"

"With the shutdown of the pipeline, a lot of folks are out of work. The government upped the fees for grazing cattle on federal land and there isn't much more than ranching in this area. People are moving to the cities, looking for work. Others are holding on by their fingernails."

Her heart ached for her hometown. "I didn't realize it was that bad."

"Yeah, I almost think you need to take Rausch's offer and get out of here while you can."

Her lips firmed into a thin line. "He was insulting, acting like I didn't know the business end of a horse. Hell, he doesn't know the first thing about ranching."

"Which leads me to wonder—"

Something flashed in front of the speeding truck. A rider on a four-wheeler.

Abe jerked the steering wheel to avoid hitting him and sent the truck careening over the shoulder of the road, down a steep slope, crashing into bushes and bumping over huge rocks.

Despite the safety belt across her chest, Liv was tossed about like a shaken rag doll.

"Hold on!" Abe cried out.

With a death grip on the armrest, Liv braced herself.

The truck slammed into a tree.

Liv was thrown forward, hitting her head on the dash. For a moment gray haze and sparkling stars swam in her vision.

A groan from the man next to her brought her out of the fog and back to the front seat of the pickup. She blinked several times and turned her head.

A sharp stab of pain slashed through her forehead and warm thick liquid dripped from her forehead into her eyes. She wiped the fluid away only to discover it was blood. Her blood.

Another moan took her mind off her own injuries.

She blinked to clear her vision and noticed Abe hunched over the steering wheel, the front of the truck pushed into the cab pressing in around his legs.

The pungent scent of gasoline stung her nostrils, sending warning signals through her stunned brain. "Abe?" She touched his shoulder.

His head lolled back, his eyes closed.

"Abe!" Liv struggled with her seat belt, the buckle refusing to release when she pressed the button. "Abe!" She gave up for a moment and shook her foreman. "We have to get out of the truck. I smell gas."

He moaned again, but his eyes fluttered open. "I can't move," he said, his voice weak. "I think my leg is broken."

"I don't care if both of your legs are broken—we have to get you out of the truck. Now!" She punched at her own safety belt, this time managing to disengage the locking mechanism. Flinging it aside, she reached for Abe's and released it. Then she pushed open her door and slid out of the front seat.

When her feet touched the ground, her knees buckled. She grabbed hold of the door and held on to steady herself. The scent of gasoline was so strong now it was overpowering, and smoke rose from beneath the crumpled hood.

Straightening, Liv willed herself to be strong and

get her foreman out of the truck before the vehicle burst into flames. She'd already lost her father. Abe was the only family she had left. She'd be damned if she lost him, too.

With tears threatening, she staggered around the rear of the truck, her feet slipping on loose gravel and stones. When she tried to open the driver's door, it wouldn't budge.

She pounded on it, getting more desperate by the minute. "Abe, you have to help me. Unlock the door. I have to get you out."

Rather than dissipating, the cloud of smoke grew. The wind shifted, sending the smoke into Liv's face. "Damn it, Abe. Unlock the door!"

A loud click sounded and Liv pulled the door handle, willing it to open. It didn't.

Her eyes stinging and the smoke scratching at her throat with every breath she took, Liv realized she didn't have much time.

She braced her foot on the side panel of the truck and pulled hard on the door handle. Metal scraped on metal and the door budged, but hung, having been damaged when the truck wrapped around the tree.

Hands curled around her shoulders, lifted her off her feet and set her to the side.

Then a hulk of a man with broad shoulders, big hands and a strong back ripped the door open, grabbed Abe beneath the arms, hauled him out of the smoldering cab and carried him all of the way up the hill to the paved road.

Her tears falling in earnest now, Liv followed, stumbling over the uneven ground, dropping to her knees every other step. When she reached the top, she sagged to the ground beside Abe on the shoulder of the road. "Abe? Please tell me you're okay. Please."

With his eyes still closed, he moaned. Then he lifted his eyelids and opened his mouth. "I'm okay," he muttered. "But I think my leg's broken."

"Oh, jeez, Abe." She laughed, albeit shakily. "A leg we can get fixed. I'm just glad you're alive."

"Take a lot more than a tree to do me in." Abe grabbed her arm. "I'm sorry, Liv. If it's messed up, I won't be able to take care of the place until it's healed."

"Oh, for Pete's sake, Abe. Working for me is the last thing you should be worrying about. I'll manage fine on my own." She rested her hand on her foreman's shoulder, amazed that the man could worry about her when his face was gray with pain. "What's more important is getting you to a hospital." She glanced around, looking for the man who'd pulled Abe from the wreckage.

He stood on the pavement, waving at a passing truck.

The truck slowed to a stop, and her rescuer rounded to the driver's door and spoke with the man behind the wheel. The driver pulled to the side of the road, got out and hurried down to where Liv waited with Abe.

"Jonah? That you?" Abe glanced up, shading his eyes from the sun.

"Yup." Jonah dropped to his haunches beside Abe. "How'd you end up in a ditch?"

Abe shook his head and winced. "A man on a four-wheeler darted out in front of me. I swerved to miss him." He nodded toward Liv. "You remember Olivia Dawson?"

Jonah squinted, staring across Abe to Liv. "I remember a much smaller version of the Dawson girl." He held out his hand. "Sorry to hear about your father's accident."

Liv took the man's hand, stunned that they were making introductions when Abe was in pain. "Thank you. Seems accidents are going around." Liv stared from Abe to Jonah's vehicle above. "Think between the three of us we could get Abe up to your truck? He won't admit it, but I'll bet he's hurting pretty badly."

"It's just a little sore," Abe countered and then grimaced.

Liv snorted. "Liar."

"We can get him up there," the stranger said.

"Yes, we can," Jonah agreed. "But should we? I could drive back to town and notify the fire department. They could have an ambulance out here in no time."

"I don't need an ambulance to get me to town." Abe tried to get up. The movement made him cry out and his face turn white. He sagged back against the ground.

"If you don't want an ambulance, then you'll have to put up with us jostling you around getting you up the hill," the stranger said.

"Better than being paraded through Grizzly Pass in the back of an ambulance." Abe gritted his teeth. "Everyone knows ambulances are for sick folk."

"Or injured people," Liv said. "And you have a major injury."

"Probably just a bruise. Give me a minute and I'll be

up and running circles around all of you." Abe caught Liv's stare and sighed. "Okay, okay. I could use a hand getting up the hill."

The stranger shot a glance at Jonah. "Let's do this."

Jonah looped one of Abe's arms around his neck, bent and slid an arm beneath one of Abe's legs.

The stranger stepped between Liv and Abe, draped one of Abe's arms over his shoulder and glanced across at Jonah. "On three." He slipped his hand beneath Abe.

Jonah nodded. "One. Two. Three."

They straightened as one.

Abe squeezed his eyes shut and groaned, all of the color draining from his face.

Liv wanted to help, but knew she'd only get in the way. The best thing she could do at that point was to open the truck door before they got there with Abe. She raced up the steep hill, her feet sliding in the gravel. When she reached the top, she flung open the door to the backseat of the truck cab and turned back to watch Abe's progression.

The two men struggled up the hill, being as careful as they could while slipping on loose pebbles.

Liv's glance took in her father's old farm truck, the front wrapped around the tree. Smoke filled the cab and flames shot up from the engine compartment. She was surprised either one of them had lived. If Abe hadn't slammed on his brakes as quickly as he had, the outcome would have been much worse.

Her gaze caught a glimpse of another vehicle on the other side of the truck. A four-wheeler was parked a few feet away.

Anger surged inside Liv. She almost said something to the stranger about how he'd nearly killed two people because of his carelessness. One look at Abe's face made Liv bite down hard on her tongue to keep from yelling at the man who'd nearly caused a fatal accident. Once Abe was taken care of, she'd have words with the man.

Jonah and the stranger made it to the top of the ravine.

The four-wheeler driver nodded to the other man. "I'll take it from here."

"Are you sure?" Jonah asked, frowning. "He's pretty much a deadweight."

Jonah was right. With all the jostling, Abe had completely passed out. Liv studied the stranger. As muscular as he was, he couldn't possibly lift Abe by himself.

"I've got him." The stranger lifted Abe into his arms and slid him onto the backseat of the truck.

Despite her anger at the man's driving skills, Liv recognized sheer, brute strength in the man's arms and broad shoulders. That he could lift a full-size man by himself said a lot about his physical abilities.

But it didn't excuse him from making them crash. She quelled her admiration and focused on getting Abe to a medical facility. If the stranger stuck around after they got Abe situated, Liv would tell him exactly what she thought of him.

Chapter Two

Hawkeye couldn't follow through on his pursuit of the other guy on the ATV. Not after the fleeing man caused the farm-truck driver to crash his vehicle into a tree. He'd had to stop to render assistance and pull the older man out of the cab before the engine caught fire, or he and the woman might have died.

"I'll follow on my four-wheeler," Hawkeye offered.

"No need," the woman said. "We can take it from here."

Hawkeye frowned. Though young and pretty, the auburn-haired Miss Dawson's jaw was set. Her brows drew together over deep-green eyes as she climbed into the back of the cab next to the injured truck driver.

Hawkeye wanted to argue, but he didn't. She was mad at him for something. Then he realized she'd probably only seen one ATV fly out into the road. Hawkeye had been far enough behind the other guy, he hadn't emerged onto the highway until the truck had already gone off the road.

The Dawson woman wouldn't have seen that there were two ATVs. He smiled and turned away, understanding why she was angry, but not feeling the need to explain himself.

He watched as the truck took off. Then he climbed onto his four-wheeler and followed the group back to Grizzly Pass and the only medical facility in a fifty-mile radius.

The clinic was a block from the Blue Moose Tavern—Hawkeye's temporary boss had set up offices in the apartment above the bar. As Hawkeye passed the Blue Moose, Garner stepped out onto the landing and waved at Hawkeye, a perplexed frown pulling his brows low.

Hawkeye nodded briefly, but didn't slow the ATV. Though it was illegal to drive an off-road vehicle on a public road, he held steady, pulled into the clinic driveway and hopped off.

An ambulance had pulled up in the parking lot and EMTs were off-loading a gurney. A sheriff's vehicle was parked nearby.

Olivia Dawson stood beside the truck, talking to Abe and a sheriff's deputy. One of the EMTs shone a light into her eyes.

She pushed his light away. "I'm fine. It's Abe you need to worry about."

"Ma'am, it looks like you hit your head in the accident. You might have a concussion." He insisted on wiping the dried blood from her forehead and applying a small butterfly bandage. "I suggest you see a doctor before you drive yourself anywhere."

"Really, I'm fine." She pushed past him and gripped Abe's hand.

The deputy flipped open a notepad. "Ma'am, could you describe what happened?"

"A four-wheeler darted out in front of us on the highway. We swerved to miss it and crashed into a tree. You might want to send a fire engine to put out the fire and a tow truck to retrieve the truck."

"Will do, ma'am."

"And stop calling me *ma'am*," she said. "I'm not your mother."

The deputy grinned. "No, ma'am. You're not."

Olivia rolled her eyes and turned back to her foreman.

When the EMTs had the stretcher ready, they rolled it over next to her. She stepped out of the way and stood to the side as they loaded a now-conscious Abe.

The man was obviously in a lot of pain. His pale face broke out in a sweat as the EMTs lowered him onto the stretcher. Once he was settled, he held out a hand to Olivia.

She took it. "Don't worry about me. I can handle the ranch."

"No, Liv, you can't. Things aren't the same as when you left. You need help."

Liv shook her head. "I can work the animals better than most men."

Abe chuckled and winced. "You're right, but you can't do this alone. Promise me you'll get help." His gaze shifted to where Hawkeye stood a few feet away. "Make her get help."

Liv frowned. "You can't ask a stranger to do that."

Abe nodded. "I just did." He waved Hawkeye forward.

Not wanting to get into the midst of a family argument, Hawkeye eased forward. "Sir?"

"I'm Abe Masterson, and you are?"

"Trace Walsh, but my friends call me Hawkeye."

"Hawkeye, this is Olivia Dawson. Olivia, Hawkeye." Abe lay back, closing his eyes, the effort having cost him. "There, now you aren't strangers. Please, Hawkeye, make sure Olivia doesn't try to run the Stone Oak Ranch alone. She needs dedicated protection. Something's not right out there."

When Hawkeye hesitated, Abe opened his eyes, his gaze capturing Hawkeye's. "Promise."

To appease the injured man, Hawkeye said, "I promise."

The EMT interrupted. "We really need to get Mr. Masterson to the hospital."

"I'm riding with him," Olivia said.

"No." Abe opened his eyes again. "The horses need to be fed and the cattle need to be checked."

"They can wait. You need someone to go with you as your advocate," she insisted. "You might pass out again."

"I didn't pass out," Abe grumbled. "I just closed my eyes."

"Yeah." Olivia snorted. "That's a bunch of bullsh—"

"Uh-uh," Abe interrupted. "You know how your daddy felt about you cursing."

She glared and crossed her arms over her chest. "I'm not a child."

"No, but you don't have to worry about me. I'm alive and still kicking. I can take care of myself. You can visit me at the hospital, if it makes you feel better. But call first. I have a lady friend in Cody. I'm sure she'll come keep me company and put me up until I can get around on my own."

Liv pulled her lip between her teeth and chewed on it before answering. "Are you sure?"

The pucker of Liv's brow and the worried look in her eyes made Hawkeye want to ease her mind. And pull her into his arms. He suspected she wouldn't appreciate the gesture, no matter how well-intentioned. As far as she was concerned, he was the bad guy in this situation. Hawkeye had yet to set the record straight.

"I'm positive," Abe said. "Now let the EMTs do their job. I'd like to get somewhere with a little pain medication. My leg hurts like hell."

Liv backed up quickly, running into Hawkeye's chest.

He reached out to steady her as the medical technicians rolled Abe's gurney away.

"Do you need a ride back to the ranch, Miss Dawson?" Jonah asked. "I have a few errands to run before I head back your way."

Liv nodded. "How long do you need?"

"No more than thirty minutes. I just need to pick up some feed at the feed store and a few groceries for the missus. You're welcome to wait in the truck."

She looked around as if in a daze. "If it's all the same to you, I'd like to pick up dinner from the tavern. I don't think I'll have time to cook anything."

Jonah nodded. "I'll pick you up at the Blue Moose, then."

Hawkeye bit down on his tongue to keep from offering the woman a ride out to her place. No doubt she'd turn it down, preferring a ride from a friend to one from a stranger she thought had caused the wreck.

After Jonah left in his truck, the only two people left on the street were Hawkeye and Liv.

Liv turned to him and poked a finger at his chest, fire burning in her emerald green eyes. "You!"

He raised his hands in surrender. "Me?"

"Don't lay on the innocent act." Her brows drew into a deep V. "Your reckless driving nearly got Abe killed. Give me one good reason why I shouldn't turn you over to the sheriff." She crossed her arms over her chest.

Hawkeye glanced at the damning ATV. "I didn't drive out in front of your pickup."

"Like hell you didn't." Twin flags of pink flew high on her cheekbones. "You didn't even look left or right before you barreled out onto the highway. What if we had been a van full of children? You could have killed an entire family." She flung her arm out.

"It wasn't me." He shook his head. "I was chasing a guy on another four-wheeler."

"Right. Why should I believe you?" Her finger shot out again and poked him in the chest. "You're a stranger. For that matter, why were you on my property?" She jabbed him again. "You were trespassing. I could have you arrest—"

As a sniper, Hawkeye considered himself a patient man. But the finger in the chest was getting to him, and the woman with the green fire blazing from her eyes was far too pretty for him to slug—not that he would ever hit a woman. But she just wasn't going to listen to him unless he did something drastic.

So he grabbed her finger, yanked her up against his body and clamped an arm around her waist, bringing her body tight against his. Then he slammed his lips down on hers. For the first time in the past five minutes, silence reigned.

With one hand captured in Hawkeye's hand, Liv pressed the other to his chest and gave a pathetic attempt at pushing him away. Hawkeye strengthened his hold.

After a few seconds, she quit pushing against him, her fingers curling into his shirt.

Her lips were soft and full beneath his. Even though he'd stemmed her tirade, Hawkeye was in no hurry to raise his head. Instead, he raised his hand, his fingers sliding up to cup the back of her head.

She gasped, her mouth opening to his.

Taking it as an invitation, Hawkeye swept his tongue past her teeth to claim hers in a long, slow caress.

The tension in her body melted away and she leaned into him, her tongue toying with his, giving as good as he gave.

When he finally broke the kiss, he briefly leaned his cheek against her temple, careful not to disturb the bandage on her forehead, and then he straightened.

Liv touched her fingers to her lips, her eyes glazed. "Why did you do that?"

His lips quirked upward. "I couldn't think of a better way to make you shut up long enough to listen."

Her glaze cleared and her brows met in the middle

the second before her hand snapped out and connected with his face in a hard slap.

She raised her hand again, but he caught it before she could hit him again.

"There was another four-wheeler," he said. "I was chasing him. He was a good fifty yards ahead of me when he reached the road. I would have caught him if I hadn't stopped to render aid." He forced her wrist down to her side. "Now, you can choose to believe me or not. But that's what happened."

Liv rubbed her wrist, her eyes narrowing. "That doesn't explain why you were on my land."

"I started out on government land, up in the hills, when I ran across the other man, planting explosives in a valley. I thought it might be a good idea to ask him why he was doing that."

Liv's breath caught in her throat. "Explosives?"

"Yes."

"Why would someone plant explosives in the hills?" she asked.

"I suspect it has something to do with the oil pipeline cutting through that area."

"But why come through my property?"

"I don't know, but if you have livestock, your fence is down in two places. You should get someone to help you put it back up."

She laughed, the sound seeming to border on hysteria. "That someone was just hauled off in an ambulance."

His brows furrowed. "Don't you have ranch hands?"

Liv's red hair had come loose of its ponytail. She reached up to push it back from her face. "Only during roundup. It was just my father and our foreman managing a herd of about five hundred Brangus cows and twenty horses."

"Then you might want to let your father know about the fences."

Liv couldn't stop the sudden burning in her eyes, nor could she speak past the instant tightening of her vocal cords. She had to swallow twice before she could answer. "That would be hard considering we buried him today."

Hawkeye had been in the process of turning away. He froze, his shoulders stiffening. When he faced her again, he stared at her without any expression on his face.

The big man's lack of emotion and the anger he stirred inside her helped Liv keep it together.

"Who else is with you on your ranch?" Hawkeye asked.

She squared her shoulders. "You're looking at the sum total of ranch hands on the Stone Oak Ranch."

His gaze raked over her from top to toe. "You're serious?"

Lifting her chin, Liv faced him with all the bravado of a prizefighter. "I'm fully capable of mending fences and taking care of livestock. I learned to ride a horse before I learned to walk."

"You're alone." His word wasn't a question. It was more of a statement. "Have you been living in a co-

coon, lady? Are you even aware of what's been happening around your little community of Grizzly Pass?"

Raising her chin a little higher, Liv met the man's
stare. "I haven't been home in the past nine months.
My father didn't let me know about any of this. I just
got back into town when I was notified of his passing.
Now, if you'll excuse me, I have to meet Jonah at the
tavern in a few minutes."

She pushed past him and thought that was the end
of it.

A hand reached out and grabbed her arm, yanking
her back around.

She raised a brow and stared down at Hawkeye's big
fingers. "Let go of me."

"You're not safe out on that ranch by yourself. A man
with access to dynamite passed through your place."

She had already come to the same conclusion, but
knew she didn't have a choice. The ranch couldn't run
itself and she'd be damned if she sold out to that greedy,
bottom-dwelling Mr. Rausch. "I'm fine on my own. I
learned to handle a gun almost as early as I learned to
ride a horse. I'm not afraid of being alone."

"You should be." He sighed and released her arm.
"Look, at least come with me to talk to my boss. He'll
want to hear what's going on out your way."

"Are you crazy?" She shook her head. "I don't know
you from Jack."

He held out his hand again. "At the risk of repeat-
ing myself, my name's Trace Walsh, but my friends
call me—"

She waved away his hand. "Yeah, yeah. They call

you Hawkeye." With a shrug, she stared down Main Street toward the tavern. "Just who is your boss?"

"Kevin Garner, an agent for the Department of Homeland Security."

Her curiosity captured, she returned her attention to Hawkeye. "Is that it? Is that why you were out in the mountains? You work for the DHS?"

Hawkeye shook his head. "Not hardly. I'm an army ranger on loan to the DHS. This is only temporary duty to help Garner and his team. He seems to think there's enough activity going on in this area that he needed a hand."

Liv didn't say anything, just stared at the man with the crisp, black hair and incredibly blue eyes. Perhaps Hawkeye's boss was onto something. Liv had never quite swallowed the idea that her father had fallen off his horse and died instantly. He was a good rider. No, he was the best, and had the rodeo buckles to prove it. The man had ridden broncos when he was younger and still broke wild horses. When he was on a horse, he wasn't just on it—he was a part of it. "I guess it wouldn't hurt to talk to your boss." She raised her finger. "But don't ever try to kiss me again."

Hawkeye raised his hands, a smile tugging at the corners of his lips. Those lips that had awakened a flood of unwanted desire inside Liv. For a stranger, no less. "Don't worry. I like my women willing."

"And quiet."

"Not necessarily." He winked. "Just quiet when they need to be."

"Whatever." She rolled her eyes. "Just don't kiss me. I can do a lot more than slap."

He rubbed the side of his cheek where the red imprint of her hand had just begun to fade. "I'll remember that. Next time we kiss, you'll have to initiate."

"Good. Because that will never happen." She planted her fists on her hips. "So where is your boss? I'd like to get this meeting over with. I have a ride to catch."

"You're in luck. His office is over the Blue Moose Tavern." He flung his leg over the four-wheeler and jerked his head to the rear. "You're welcome to ride with me."

"No, thanks. I'll walk." Liv stepped onto the sidewalk and hurried toward the tavern.

The four-wheeler engine revved behind her. A moment later, Hawkeye pulled up beside her. "Sure you don't want a ride?"

"I'm sure."

He pressed his thumb to the throttle lever and the ATV sped up the street, disappearing around the back of the tavern.

Alone for the rest of the distance to the tavern, Liv had just enough time to think through all that had happened since she'd arrived home. For a moment her predicament threatened to overwhelm her.

Daddy, why did you have to go and die?

She fought to hold back the tears as she came abreast of the building she'd been aiming for.

Hawkeye rounded the corner and tilted his head. "The staircase to Garner's office is over here."

She followed him up a set of wooden stairs to the landing at the top.

Before Hawkeye could knock, the door flew open and a man probably in his midthirties with brown hair and blue eyes stood in the door frame. "Hawkeye, I'm glad you stopped by. The sheriff isn't keen on the folks around here driving their four-wheelers on the main roads."

Hawkeye turned toward Liv. "Kevin, this is Olivia Dawson. Liv, this is Kevin Garner with the DHS."

Garner held out his hand. "Nice to meet you." His eyes narrowed slightly and he stared hard at her. "Are you any relation to Everett Dawson?"

She nodded, her chest tight. "That was my father."

Garner squeezed her hand in his. "I was sorry to hear about his passing. Everything I've heard from the locals indicated he was a good man."

"One of the best," she added, choking on her barely contained emotion. "They told me he died in a horse-back-riding accident."

"That's what we heard from the sheriff. And you think otherwise?" Garner pulled her across the threshold. "Come in. Tell me what you know."

Liv hesitated only a moment before following the man into the interior of what appeared to be more an operations center than an office. Two other men stood beside a large table with maps spread out across its surface.

"If you knew my father, you'd know his being thrown from a horse was highly unlikely."

Garner nodded. "I'd wondered. I understand his ranch butted up against government property."

Liv nodded. "It does."

"Was he having any problems on the ranch? Any evidence of trespassing?"

"I've been away from home for months. He hadn't told me anything and, with funeral arrangements, I haven't had a chance to ride the perimeter." She nodded toward Hawkeye. "I'm told I have a couple of fences down."

"She does. I went through them chasing a man out of the hills on a four-wheeler."

Garner's eyes widened. "Is that why you rode an off-road vehicle on a state highway?"

Hawkeye dipped his head in a brief nod. "I didn't have much of a choice. My truck's back where I parked it at the gravel road leading up to the national forest. While I was following through on the path that pipeline inspector was traveling before he was shot, I ran across a guy planting explosives at the exact location where Khalig was shot and killed."

"What about explosives?" A tall, red-haired man joined Hawkeye and held out his hand to Liv. "Jon Casper. But you can call me Ghost."

She shook his hand, her fingers nearly crushed in his strong grip.

A broad-shouldered man with brown hair and green eyes nudged Ghost aside and held out his hand. "Max Decker. You can call me Caveman."

Yet another man with a high and tight haircut held

out his hand. "Rex Trainor. US Marine Corps. Most people call me T-Rex."

Liv laughed. "Do any of you go by your given names?"

As one, everyone but Garner replied, "No."

"Guess that answers my question." She shook T-Rex's hand. "Are you all like Hawkeye—military on loan to the DHS?"

T-Rex, Ghost and Caveman nodded.

Ghost held up his hand. "Navy."

Caveman nodded. "Delta Force."

Liv frowned. "Are things that bad around here?"

The three men shrugged.

"Better than being in the sandbox of the Middle East," Ghost said.

"Some of the natives are friendly," Caveman said. "And some…not so much."

Liv leaned around the three big military men. "Anyone else I should be aware of?"

"Yo!" A thin, younger man sat with his back to the others, his hands on a computer keyboard in the corner of the room. He raised his hand without turning away from the array of monitors he faced.

"That's Hack," Hawkeye said. "He's our tech support guy."

"While you get to know each other, I'll call in the sheriff and the state bomb squad." Garner pulled his cell phone from his pocket.

"I don't think the bomb squad will be necessary," Hawkeye said. "I interrupted him before he could connect the detonator. I didn't see anything but the explosive and the fuse."

Ghost grabbed a jacket. "I'll check it out. At the very least we need to retrieve the explosives to keep him from blowing the pipeline."

Caveman slung his own jacket over his shoulder. "The sooner the better."

"The trailer's back where I parked the truck at the base of the mountain," Hawkeye reminded them. "If you're going, you'll have to risk driving the ATVs on public roads. I didn't run into the county cops. But that doesn't mean you'll be so lucky."

"We'll take that risk," Ghost said. "We can cut through some of the less traveled streets."

"Be careful," Hawkeye warned. "He might have circled back to finish the job."

Once the other two men had left the room, Liv cornered Garner. "What the hell is going on here?"

Garner motioned toward the table with the maps. "You got a few minutes?"

She glanced at her watch. "I have about ten before my ride gets here."

"I can get you where you want to go," Garner offered.

She shook her head. "This is all too much. I don't know you, and I don't know what to think about all of this." She waved at the map with the red stars marking locations like a military operation. "First my father, then my foreman. And now you say there was a man with explosives trying to blow up the pipeline? Has the entire county gone crazy? This is Grizzly Pass, not some war-torn country on the other side of the world."

Garner's lips thinned, his face grim. "I've been monitoring this area for the past three months. A lot of internet activity indicated something big was brewing."

Liv nodded. "You're right. I'd say an attempt to blow up the pipeline is pretty big."

He shook his head. "Even bigger. I think there is the potential for some kind of takeover, but we've only scratched the surface."

"Takeover?" Liv's heart thundered in her chest. "Are you kidding me? This is America. Land of the free, home of democracy. We change things by electing new representatives."

"Some people don't like what we're getting." Kevin touched the map. "We've already had flare-ups."

Liv sank into a chair. "Flare-ups? Incidents? Takeovers?" She pinched the bridge of her nose, feeling a headache forming. "This can't be. Not in Grizzly Pass. What do we have here to take over?"

"This is the perfect location to build the equivalent of a small army. There's lots of space to hide nefarious activities. Mountains with caves to store a weapons buildup. People who know how to use guns can train in the backwoods where no one knows what they are doing."

"Sweet heaven, and I thought the worst thing about coming home was burying my father," Liv said. "I can't take in any more of this. I have to go through my father's effects, make arrangements with the lawyer and the bank, not to mention the animals to tend and a fence to mend."

Garner's gaze shot to Hawkeye. "Accidental or cut?"

"From what I could tell, cut," Hawkeye answered for

her. "My bet is that the man setting the charges cut the fence to give him access to government land without going the usual route."

"How many acres is the Stone Oak Ranch?" Garner asked.

"Over five thousand."

He stared down at the contour map. "Lots of hills and valleys."

"There are. We're in the foothills of the Beartooth Mountains," Liv said.

Garner glanced up at Hawkeye. "It bears watching."

Liv's belly knotted. She wasn't at all sure she liked the intent look on the DHS man's face. "What do you mean?"

"Your ranch is in a prime location for trouble. Who do you have working there? Do they know how to use a gun? Do you trust them?" Garner asked.

Hawkeye snorted. "You're looking at 'them.' Miss Dawson is the only person left to run the ranch."

"I don't need anyone's help. If I need additional assistance, I'll hire someone." Liv stood. "All this conspiracy-theory talk is just that—talk. I have work to do. If you'll excuse me, I have a ride to catch."

Garner stepped in front of her. "You don't understand. You could be in grave danger."

"I can handle it." She tilted her head. "I really need to go." She stepped around the man and ran into Hawkeye.

"Garner's right. You can't run a ranch and watch your back at the same time."

"Let me assign one of my men to the ranch. Then you'll get some help and we can take our time making certain the group responsible for the recent troubles isn't conducting their business on your property or the neighboring federal land."

Liv shook her head. "I can hire my own help."

"The men on my team are trained combatants. We think the group planning the takeover are training like soldiers. One of their men had a shooting range and training facility on his ranch."

Liv tilted her head and stared at Garner through narrowed eyes. "Sounds to me like you already know who is involved in this coup or whatever it is."

"We've only just begun to scratch the surface. Someone is supplying weapons on a large scale." Garner took her hand. "Someone with money."

Liv's blood chilled. "You're not kidding, are you?"

Garner's lips firmed. "I wish I was."

She pulled her hand from his and pushed her hair back from her face, wishing she had a rubber band to secure it. "Why do you need my ranch?"

"Stone Oak Ranch is right in the middle of everything." Garner pointed to the map. "You said yourself you didn't think your father could have fallen off his horse. He was too good of a rider. What if he didn't fall off his horse?"

Her gut clenched and she tightened her fingers into fists. "What do you mean? Do you think someone killed him?" Dear Lord, what had happened to her father?

Garner lifted his shoulders slightly. "We don't know, but if someone was out there, your father could have run across something that person didn't want to get out."

A sick, sinking feeling settled in the pit of Liv's belly.

"When my father's horse returned without his rider, my foreman went looking for him. He found my father on the far northwest corner of the ranch, where he'd gone to check the fences." Liv swallowed hard on the lump rising in her throat. "That corner of the property borders federal land."

"Olivia, let me position one of my men on your property," Garner pleaded. "He can appear to hire on as a ranch hand and help you mend the fences. It will give him the opportunity to keep an eye out for trouble, while protecting you."

Liv bristled. "I don't need someone to protect me."

"No one can watch his or her own back," Hawkeye said. "As a member of the armed forces, I know what it means to trust the guys behind me. You need a battle buddy."

"I do want to find out if my father was murdered. And who might have done it." Liv chewed on her lip a moment before sighing. "Who did you have in mind?"

Garner smiled. "The only other man still in this room besides me."

A thrill of something she hadn't felt in a long time— if you didn't count the recent kiss—rippled through Liv. Taking on Hawkeye could prove to be a big mistake in more ways than one. "What choice do I have?"

"None," Hawkeye said, his tone firm and final.

For however long it took to find her father's murderer and stop this insanity going on in her community, she was stuck with Hawkeye. And despite her initial reticence, she had to admit to herself she might just need him.

"Don't look so worried. You can trust Hawkeye,"

Garner said with a smile and a wave before he turned to go back to the maps spread across the table.

It wasn't Hawkeye she didn't trust. What bothered her most was the reaction she'd had to his kiss. Hell, she wasn't sure she could trust herself around the rugged army ranger.

Chapter Three

"We'll get that meal you wanted and then we'll head for your place." Hawkeye cupped Liv's elbow and guided her through the loft apartment's door.

For once she didn't argue or pull away.

Hawkeye counted that as progress.

"Damn. The sun's already setting." Olivia shaded her eyes and looked toward the west.

"We can skip the tavern and head right for the ranch," Hawkeye offered.

She shook her head. "You said yourself that your truck is where you left it on a dirt road. By the time we retrieve it and make it back to the ranch, it'll already be dark. We might as well get something to eat and take it with us. I can guarantee there's nothing edible that doesn't have to be cooked at the ranch." She started down the steps ahead of him.

"I'll be down in ten minutes to take you out to Hawkeye's truck." Garner followed them onto the landing. "You'll need it with Liv's farm truck out of commission."

"The sheriff called a tow truck," Olivia said. "The

way it was smoking, I'm sure my dad's old truck is a total loss." Her lips turned downward. "I'll be in the market for a used, *cheap* truck or we won't be able to haul the hay to the barn before winter."

"You can use mine until then," Hawkeye offered.

Instead of nodding, she frowned. "I can't rely on a man who is at best a temporary solution to a much larger problem."

"That being?" Hawkeye asked.

"I need more than a truck out at the ranch. I need my foreman, or at least someone who can do some of the heavy work. Tossing hay bales isn't easy." She chewed on her bottom lip.

The motion made Hawkeye's groin tighten. He wanted to pull that lip into his mouth and kiss her worries away.

Why?

He didn't know. He'd just met the woman. That she was willing to risk her life to pull a full-grown man out of a smoking truck said a lot about her character. Not only was she strong, she was tough and cared about the people around her.

"I'll be at the ranch," Hawkeye said. "While I'm keeping an eye on things, I can help with hay hauling and doing other chores as needed."

Olivia snorted. "Thanks, but you won't be around for long. I'm sure, once Kevin and his team figure out what's going on, you'll be back with your unit. I need a permanent solution. It took both my father and our foreman to manage the ranch with seasonal help. Even if Abe wasn't laid up with a broken leg, I'd have to find more help. The kind that will stick around for the long haul."

Hawkeye raised his hands palms up and smiled. "In the meantime, you have me. Use me while you're advertising for additional staff. What can it hurt? You're getting my services free."

Olivia's stiff shoulders relaxed slightly. "You're right. And thanks."

"Don't sound so ungrateful. Wait until you see what I can do. I'm strong, and I've hauled my share of hay in my younger days." He stopped at the bottom of the staircase and pulled Olivia around to face him. "And I have a special skill." His lips twitched.

Her breath hitched and her gaze dropped to his lips. "Oh yeah?" she said, her voice a whisper.

Hawkeye leaned toward her, as if he might kiss her, his lips passing her mouth and going toward her ear. "I know the difference between a steer and a cow." He leaned back and smiled. Yes, he was flirting with her, but he could tell she needed a little levity in a bad situation. Having lost her father and now with her foreman off the ranch, she had a lot weighing on her shoulders. Hawkeye winked.

Olivia's lips pressed into a tight line.

Not exactly the reaction he was aiming for. For a moment, Hawkeye thought he might have gone too far flirting with the pretty rancher, and she might slap his face again. Just in case, he leaned back a little farther.

A moment passed and Olivia's firm lips loosened and spread into a wry smile. "You don't know how important a skill that is." She stuck out her hand. "For however long you're here, you're hired."

With an accord reached, Hawkeye shook her hand, an electric shock running up his arm and shooting low into his groin. The woman had an effect on him he hadn't counted on. Rather than kissing her, like he wanted to, he turned her toward the tavern entrance and ushered her inside with a hand at the small of her back. With everything going wrong in Grizzly Pass, helping Olivia was the first thing that felt right.

As Hawkeye opened the door, a young man was thrown through. He stumbled, fell and landed on his knees on the sidewalk.

A man with a scruffy beard and unkempt brown hair lurched through the door, his face red and splotchy, his breath reeking of booze. "No damned stepson of mine is going to be a dishwasher in a saloon, carrying out other people's trash." He pointed a finger at the boy. "Get home, where you belong. You have your own chores to do."

Olivia crouched to help the teen to his feet.

Once upright, the young man shrugged off her hands and faced the angry man. "I finished the chores before I came to town."

"Don't talk back to me, boy," the man growled.

Hawkeye recognized the drunk man as one of the men Garner had on his watch list. Ernie Martin. A man who had a gripe with the government over the discontinuance of the subsidies on his livestock.

"Get back to the ranch," Ernie said.

The teen lifted his chin and set his feet slightly apart

as if ready to do battle. "I have a job. I need to be here when I said I would."

"Did your mother tell you that you should get a job?" Ernie snorted. "Is she too lazy to get out and get one for herself and bring a little income home for once?"

The teen's fists clenched. "My mother isn't lazy. She has three small children to raise. She'd never make enough money to pay for child care."

"And whose fault is that? She shouldn't have had all those brats."

The teen's eyes narrowed. "You should have stayed off of her. They're your kids, too. And what are you doing to put food on the table? My mother should never have married you."

"She's lucky to be off the reservation. And you should be thankful I took you in out of the goodness of my own heart."

With a snort, the teen brushed the dust off his jeans. "You didn't do either of us any favors."

Ernie's face flushed even redder. "Why, you ungrateful little brat. That's all the bull crap I'm taking from you." He launched himself at the teen.

Before he'd gone two steps, Hawkeye grabbed Ernie's arm and jerked him around. "Leave the kid alone."

Ernie glared at Hawkeye through glazed eyes, cocked his fist and swung.

Hawkeye caught the fist in his own palm and forced the man's hand down to his side. "Take another swing and I won't go as easy on you." He fished the man's keys out of his pocket and then shoved the man backward, out of range of landing another punch. "You'll have to find a ride home."

Sheriff Scott pulled up in his county sheriff's SUV, parked and got out. "What's going on here?"

Ernie stalked up to the sheriff. "This man stole my keys and threatened me with bodily harm." He pointed at Hawkeye. "Arrest him." The stern tone was offset when the man belched, sending out a vile fog of booze-heavy breath.

"Now, Ernie, I'm sure there's another side to this story," the sheriff said.

"It's cut-and-dried." Ernie pointed at the keys in Hawkeye's hands. "He has my keys."

Sheriff Scott leaned away from Ernie's face. "The man's doing you a favor and keeping you from getting a DUI." He stared at Ernie. "How much have you had to drink?"

"Just one beer," Ernie said. "A man's got a right to drink a beer. Or is our government going to take that right away, too?"

The sheriff crossed his arms over his chest. "Care to take a Breathalyzer test?"

Ernie opened his mouth and had just enough sense left to close it again before his alcohol-soaked brain let his mouth loose.

Hawkeye almost laughed, but knew it would only rile the man more.

"Hop in, Ernie. I'll give you a ride home."

The man folded his arms over his chest and dug his heels into the concrete sidewalk. "Ain't leaving my truck here."

"I'll drive it home," the teen offered.

Ernie shot a narrow-eyed glare at the young man. "You ain't touching my damned truck."

The teen raised his hands. "Okay. I won't drive your truck."

"Don't worry about it, CJ," the sheriff assured him. He turned to Ernie. "I'll have my deputies bring your truck out to your house in the morning, after you've had a chance to sober up. You shouldn't be driving anymore tonight." Sheriff Scott hooked Ernie's elbow and eased him toward the backseat.

Ernie jerked loose of the sheriff's hold and pointed a finger at the teen. "You're done with this job. I didn't approve of it anyway."

The teen stood with his feet braced apart, his jaw set. "I'm going to work."

"Not as a dishwasher, you aren't. I won't have members of this community pointing at you, feeling sorry for poor Ernie Martin's stepson who has to work to support his family."

"I don't care what you call it—I want my sisters and brother to have something to eat. It's either here or somewhere else."

"I provide," Ernie insisted. "And it ain't your place to be telling tales about what goes on at home."

CJ's fists clenched. "I'm going to have a job."

"Not here, you're not," Ernie said with a finality that made CJ blink.

"How about at my place?" Olivia stepped forward. "Mr. Martin, you might not remember me, but I'm Olivia Dawson, Everett Dawson's daughter."

"Yeah. So?" He ignored her outstretched hand. "That doesn't give you the right to butt into a private conversation."

Hawkeye had to stop himself from snorting. The way Ernie had been yelling, the entire town of Grizzly Pass had to have heard his "private" conversation.

Olivia continued. "Since my father passed—" she swallowed hard and pressed on "—my foreman has broken his leg. I could use some help. CJ can work for me out at the ranch. He can make some money to tide you over to better times, or at least pay for his own meals." Olivia caught Ernie's stare and held it. "What do you say? You and my father were friends at one time. He'd be proud to have your stepson help me out."

Ernie bristled. "If you need help, why not me?"

Olivia smiled gently.

Hawkeye could feel himself melt. The woman needed to smile more often. She went from pretty to stunning in less than a second.

"I wouldn't dream of taking you away from your ranch. I know how hard it is to keep things running. Besides, I can't afford to pay much."

"I'll take it," CJ said. He turned to his stepfather. "I'll do my chores before I leave the house and when I get back."

"And how will you get there and back?" Ernie asked, a sneer pulling at one side of his mouth. "You have school starting in a couple weeks."

"I'll manage."

Ernie snorted and turned back to Olivia. "If he steals

something, don't come crying to me. He's been nothing but a pain in my rear since I brought him to the ranch."

CJ's eyes flashed, but he kept his mouth firmly shut. How he put up with Ernie, Hawkeye had no idea. Just standing near the belligerent jerk made Hawkeye itch to shove his fist in the man's face.

"Fine." Ernie waved at Olivia and his stepson. The drunk swayed and practically fell into the backseat of the sheriff's SUV. As he leaned out to close the door, he said, "He's your problem now."

"You got a way home, CJ?" Sheriff Scott asked.

The teen nodded. "Yes, sir." He glanced toward the sheriff's vehicle as if it was the last place he wanted to be.

The sheriff shook his head and slid behind the wheel. A moment later, all Hawkeye could see of Ernie Martin were the taillights of the sheriff's SUV disappearing at the end of Main Street.

Olivia clapped her hands together. "Well, that was lovely. I have the help I needed." She smiled at CJ. "How soon can you start?"

The young man dug his hands into his pockets. "If it's all the same to you, I'd like to start in the morning. Right now, I need to get home." He gazed in the direction his stepfather had gone.

"Do you need a ride?" Hawkeye asked.

CJ shook his head. "No, sir. I'll just let my boss know I can't work here anymore. I have a bicycle. I'll get myself home."

"That's got to be about five miles out of town. And

it's getting dark." Olivia frowned. "Let one of us take you."

The young man shook his head. "I'll need my bike to get to work in the morning."

"I live three miles out of town," Olivia said. "Between you living on one side of Grizzly Pass and me on the other, that's over eight miles several times a day. You need some other way to get there and back."

"I promise." CJ stepped forward. "I can do it. I'm used to riding long distances. It's nothing." He edged toward the tavern. "I really need to get home."

Olivia still frowned, but she stepped out of the youth's way. "Tell you what—don't worry. We'll figure something out."

"Thank you, Miss Dawson. I'll be there in the morning, right after I do my chores." The teen darted into the tavern, leaving Hawkeye and Liv where they'd been when the ruckus started.

"Are you two ready to go?" a voice said behind Hawkeye. Kevin Garner descended to the bottom step of the staircase leading up to the loft apartment.

"Not quite. We had a little delay." Olivia started to reach for the door.

Hawkeye beat her to it and opened it wide for her and Garner. As his boss passed, Hawkeye nodded. "I'll fill you in as we wait for our orders."

Chapter Four

Liv cradled the food containers on her lap in the backseat of Kevin Garner's truck.

The Homeland Security agent dropped them off at Hawkeye's truck where he'd left it parked with the utility trailer. After disconnecting the trailer from his truck, Hawkeye rolled it around to the back of Garner's and dropped it onto the hitch.

Garner helped Liv into Hawkeye's truck and then extended a hand. "Be careful and let me know of anything out of the ordinary, even if it seems inconsequential. All the little pieces add up."

Liv fumbled with the food, but managed to take the man's hand. "I haven't been home in nine months. How am I supposed to know what is out of the ordinary?"

"Anything strange and unusual, just give me a buzz." He squeezed her hand.

Liv snorted. "Things seem to have changed drastically. This used to be a nice, quiet community filled with neighbors who looked out for each other."

"Apparently, trouble has been brewing for years," Garner said. "Antigovernment sentiment isn't new."

"I suppose." Liv sighed. "I loved being on the ranch and working hard. I guess I didn't have time to hang out on the street corners grousing about what I couldn't change."

With one last squeeze, Garner released Liv's hand. "Trust Hawkeye and your own instincts."

Hawkeye slid into the driver's seat and started the engine. "Ready?"

Using the food containers as an excuse not to look Hawkeye in the face, she nodded. "Ready as I'll ever be." For a moment, the events of the past few days threatened to consume her. This was not the homecoming she'd anticipated at the end of her five-year promise.

All through college and the three years following graduation, Liv could think of nothing she wanted more than to come home to Grizzly Pass. Her promise to her father had kept her in Seattle. Now she was back in the county and the thought of going to the home she grew up in nearly tore her apart.

She sat in the passenger seat, a lump the size of her fist blocking her throat, her eyes burning from unshed tears.

"I take it we go out the way we came into town?" Hawkeye cast a glance in her direction.

All Liv could do was nod, afraid if she tried to get a word past her vocal cords, she'd break down and cry. And what good would crying do now? It wouldn't bring her father back. Crying wouldn't unbreak Abe's leg and make everything all right again. Nothing could fix her world. All she could do was to take one day, one hour and one breath at a time. Her father had taught her a long time ago that cowgirls didn't cry.

Damn you, Dad. This one does.

As they neared the gated entrance to Stone Oak Ranch, her chest tightened and she couldn't manage to take that one breath.

When Hawkeye didn't slow, Liv was forced to squeak out, "Turn here!"

Hawkeye jammed his foot on the brake pedal. The truck skidded to a stop in the middle of the highway, several yards past the ranch entrance.

Liv flew forward. The seat belt across her torso snapped tight, keeping her from jettisoning through the windshield.

"You could give me a little more warning next time." Hawkeye shifted into Reverse and backed up several yards. Then he drove up to the gate.

Liv shot out a hand, touching his shoulder.

Again, he hit the brakes and turned to her. "What?"

The relentless pressure on her chest refused to subside. "I can't breathe," she whispered. "I can't breathe."

"What's wrong?" Hawkeye's brows dived toward the bridge of his nose. "Olivia, look at me. Tell me what's wrong." He reached for her.

She shrank from his hands. If he touched her, she'd fall apart. And she couldn't fall apart. Not now. With her father and her foreman gone, she was all that was left of what had once been her small family. Who else would take care of the animals, the fences, the house and the ranch?

No matter how hard she tried, Liv couldn't seem to

get enough air into her starving lungs. She punched the buckle on her seat belt, shoved open her door and dropped down out of the truck. Her legs refused to hold her and she fell to her knees. A sob rose up past the knot in her throat, coming out as a keening wail. Liv clamped a hand over her mouth, praying Hawkeye hadn't heard.

The sound of a truck door opening and closing spurred her to her feet. She didn't want anyone to see her as her composure shattered and she fell apart. Especially not the stranger she'd just met. Hugging her grief to her chest, she ran.

A tear slipped from the corner of her eye, then another and another, until she couldn't do anything to stem the flow. Soon, she couldn't see the road in front of her.

The footsteps pounding behind her made her run faster. "Leave me alone," she cried out. "Just leave me alone."

Hands descended on her shoulders.

Liv jerked free, tripped, regained her footing and took off. Where, she didn't know.

Then something big and heavy hit her from behind, sending her flying forward. She hit the ground hard enough to knock the breath out of her lungs. A heavy mass landed on top of her, pressing her into the dirt and leaves.

She lay still, tears falling and silent sobs racking her body.

The weight on top of her shifted and rolled to the side. Big hands lifted her off the ground and pulled her into a lap and up against a solid wall of muscles.

"Shh, darlin'. Everything's going to be all right."

Hawkeye's deep voice rumbled in his chest where Liv pressed her ear.

"H-how can everything be all right?" She hiccuped and more sobs racked her body. "My father is d-dead. I'm going home to a house where he sh-should be, but isn't. Even Abe is g-gone."

"Abe will be back sooner than you think." Hawkeye held her cradled in his lap, smoothing the hair from her damp cheeks. "I'm sorry about your father. He must have been a good man to have you as his daughter."

"The best." She turned her face into Hawkeye's shirt and leaned her cheek against his chest, breathing in the outdoorsy scent she would forever associate with this man. The tears slowed to a trickle and her breathing began to return to normal. "He would have liked you, I think."

Hawkeye chuckled. "You think? You mean you don't know?"

"He had a great respect for the men and women who served in the armed forces."

For a long moment, Liv sat in Hawkeye's lap, absorbing some of his strength to tide her over when she entered the house she had grown up in, empty now of both of her parents.

Finally, she squared her shoulders and leaned away from Hawkeye. Wiping the remaining tears from her cheeks, she gave him a weak smile. "I'm sorry. I don't normally fall apart like that."

"You're allowed." Hawkeye tucked a strand of her hair behind her ear. "You haven't had the best of days."

He bent and touched his lips to her forehead, avoiding the bandaged area.

God, it felt good. A kiss on her mouth would be even better. A flood of desire washed over her with an awareness of where she was. Seated across Hawkeye's lap, she could feel the hard evidence of his own reaction to her pressing against her bottom.

She swayed toward him, her lips tingling in anticipation of touching his. Everything would be better, all of her pain would be eased, if she just kissed him.

Hawkeye's arms tightened around her, bringing her closer.

When her lips were a mere breath from his, a sound penetrated the deepening dusk. The urgent, distressed bawling of cattle.

"Shh." Liv stiffened, her pulse quickening. "Do you hear that?"

"Yeah." Hawkeye's hands gripped Liv around the waist. He lifted her out of his lap, scrambled to stand and pulled her up beside him.

"Come on." Liv grabbed his hand and ran for the truck.

Hawkeye jumped into the driver's seat.

Liv climbed in on the passenger side and rolled down her window, trying to hear over the rumble of the engine. Again, the sound of cattle mooing reached her. Something was wrong. At dusk cattle settled in for the night, quietly chewing their cud. Wishing she could put her own foot on the accelerator, Liv clenched her fists and willed Hawkeye to go faster.

The driveway up to the ranch house and barn curved

through a stand of trees. Finally, it opened to a rounded knoll, on top of which stood her family home, a two-story colonial with a wide, sweeping wraparound porch.

Liv pushed aside the stabbing sadness, her thoughts on the cattle and horses for which she was now responsible. "Head for the barn at the back of the house," she instructed.

Hawkeye drove around to the barn and shone his headlights at the corral and pasture beyond.

Cattle moved about in a frenzied stirring of dust. A horse whinnied, the muffled sound carrying through the wooden panels of the barn. The sharp crack of hooves kicking at the insides of a stall made Liv jump.

"What the hell's going on?" She jumped down from the truck and ran for the barn.

"Olivia!" Hawkeye shouted behind her.

She didn't wait for him to catch up to her. There was a rifle locked in the tack room inside the barn. If a pack of wolves was stalking the livestock, it wouldn't be long before the wolves cornered one and took it down. Or worse, the entire herd, situated near the barn, could stampede and trample over each other.

Ripping her keys out of her pocket, Liv entered the barn, slapped the switch on the wall…and nothing. No light came on. She felt her way in the dark to the tack-room door, fumbled for a few seconds trying to find the right key and then jammed it into the lock.

Pushing through, she raced for the desk she could see with the limited light from the western horizon shining through the dingy window. She found the box of bullets her father and Abe kept handy. They never knew when they'd need to shoot a rattlesnake or scare off a wolf or bear. Her father had shown her the stash of bullets and the gun a number of times, stressing that waving her arms wouldn't necessarily frighten wolves or bears. She needed a little more assurance the more dangerous predators wouldn't decide to go for her instead of a tasty cow or horse.

Liv tipped the box over, poured bullets on the desk, grabbed a few and stuffed some into her jeans pocket. Then she stretched her arms upward, going for the rifle hanging on hooks over the door. She wasn't quite tall enough to reach it. She jumped, trying to push it off the hooks.

"Need a hand?" Hawkeye appeared in the doorway and, with very little effort, lifted the rifle off the wall and handed it to her.

"Something's out there," she said, though she knew she was stating the obvious.

"I have a gun. Do you want me to fire off a round?" He held up a nine-millimeter handgun she could just make out in the dim light from the window.

"Not yet." She grabbed the spotlight they kept plugged into a wall socket and shoved it toward the man. "See if that works while I load this rifle."

Hawkeye clicked a button and the room lit up.

With the light on, Liv was able to load the rifle quickly. As soon as she shot the bolt home, she slipped past Hawkeye and into the barn.

A horse whinnied and kicked the side of his stall.

"Shh, Stormy. I'll be back in a minute," Liv said and stepped outside into the barnyard.

The livestock continued to move, churning up a cloud of dust.

Liv coughed and pulled her shirt up over her mouth and nose. "I can't see a damned thing. I'll have to go out there."

"No way," Hawkeye responded. "You'll be trampled."

"I have to get upwind of them to see what's causing them to be so nervous. If you don't want to risk it, stay here." She didn't wait for his response. Instead, she ran along the split-rail fence away from the bulk of the herd. Soon the dust thinned and the first stars of the night twinkled above.

Liv climbed to the top of the rail, swung her leg over and would have dropped down, but for the hand holding her back.

"Let go," she said. "There might be a bear or a pack of wolves out there."

"Exactly." He shook his head, shining his light toward the cloud of dust that was the herd. "You can't handle it on your own."

"The hell I can't." Liv held up her rifle.

"Trust me, wolves will see you before you see them. If it's a bear, one or two bullets might not be enough to stop him and he won't give you time to reload."

"I can't stay here and do nothing. So either you come with me or let go of my arm so I can do this alone."

Hawkeye hesitated a moment and then let go of her arm.

Liv swallowed her disappointment. She couldn't expect him to step into harm's way over a bunch of cattle that didn't belong to him. She dropped to the ground and started toward the herd.

The spotlight bounced several times across the herd and jerked toward the heavens. The sound of something landing on the ground behind her made her turn.

Hawkeye hurried toward her. "Anyone ever tell you that you're stubborn?" He moved past her, wielding the flashlight in one hand and his pistol in the other.

"More times than I can count." The corners of Liv's lips quirked upward and she followed this stranger who'd volunteered to walk into a potential stampede. Perhaps he wasn't a lost cause after all. "Anyone ever tell you a nine-millimeter bullet won't down a bear unless you're within kissing distance?"

HAWKEYE'S HEART SKIPPED a few beats and then hammered on. "I'll save my kisses for pretty ranchers with a lot of chutzpah and attitude. Now shut up and look for what's bothering your livestock." Based on her earlier reaction to his kiss and him holding her in his arms, he'd bet his favorite weapon Liv was feeling some of the same attraction he was.

As he hurried toward the herd of cattle, shining the spotlight around the periphery of the clump of dust and the bovines, he couldn't help but wonder if getting involved with Liv would be a big mistake.

Sure, she was pretty, strong and interesting. And, yeah, she fit in his arms like no other woman he'd held in his past. But what happened when the Grizzly Pass troubles were over? He'd be back with his unit several states away. She'd be on this ranch, fighting against wolves and bears alone.

His chest tightened. The thought of one lone woman defending her livelihood with no backup bothered him. The teenager would assist, but he'd be back in school as soon as summer was over. Who would help her then? And how much could a teen do when things got really bad? Predatory animals usually attacked at night. CJ would be back at his home. Olivia would be alone again.

Her best bet would be to hire more help or sell the ranch. One person, man or woman, couldn't single-handedly run a place the size of Stone Oak Ranch.

It had been years since Hawkeye had lived on a ranch. He'd grown up as the foreman's son, not the owner. He'd learned how to rope, brand, vaccinate, castrate and tag steers almost before he could ride a bicycle. He'd planned to spend his life working on a ranch.

All that had changed when he was sixteen. That summer he'd lost his love for ranching when his little sister had died. So many things changed with Sarah's passing.

Yet here he was on a ranch, standing in a field full of restless cows in the murky darkness.

He hefted the flashlight in his hand and panned the pasture, searching for whatever had spooked the livestock.

A shadowy movement caught his attention and made his pulse leap. When he swung the light back toward it, cattle leaped and darted back the opposite direction. If something was there, it couldn't be seen through the milling jumble of crazed animals.

What had him more concerned was that the cattle

had completely changed direction and were now headed straight for him and Olivia.

"Get back to the fence!" he shouted.

"Not until we find out what's spooking them," Olivia argued.

"They're coming this way. Run!" Hawkeye aimed his pistol into the air and fired off a round.

The herd didn't veer off course. They charged forward, increasing their speed.

Short of shooting every last one of them, Hawkeye wasn't going to stop the beasts' forward momentum. No amount of waving his arms and shouting would detour them to another direction.

Knowing they had only seconds to spare, Hawkeye spun and ran toward Olivia. "Go! Go! Go!" With his arm holding the flashlight, he circled her back and propelled her toward the fence.

Olivia ran several steps, tripped and fell to her knees.

Flinging the spotlight as far from himself as possible, Hawkeye scooped his arms beneath Olivia's legs, flung her over his shoulder, firefighter style, and sprinted for the nearest split-rail fence.

When he reached it, he dropped Olivia onto her feet on the other side and leaped up onto the rail as the stampede bore down on him. He was able to pull his legs over the top, just in time to avoid being speared by a wayward horn, flung to the ground and trampled to death.

Hawkeye lowered himself to the ground beside Olivia and bent over, sucking in huge, gulping breaths.

Olivia ran to the fence and watched as the cattle

raced by, bumping into the rails in their desperate attempt to get away from whatever had frightened them. She coughed and rubbed her eyes, shaking her head. "I can't see anything."

Dust swirled around them so thickly, they could barely see each other, much less the cattle, but they could hear them as they moved past.

When the thunder of hooves faded into the far corner of the pasture, Olivia climbed the fence again.

"Where do you think you're going?" Hawkeye asked.

"I have to see what was after them."

He caught her around the waist and pulled her down in front of him, his hands resting on her hips. "You can't until the dust settles."

"But someone has to."

He waved his hand out to the side. "You can barely see your hand in front of your face. As soon as you get out into that dust, you won't be able to tell left from right and you won't be able to find your way back to the fence or the barn."

"It won't be dusty forever."

"Exactly. We'll wait until it settles."

"But—"

"If you got out there in that fog of dirt, and the herd came back in your direction, you wouldn't know which way to run. You'll have lost sight of the fence and be unable to get out of their way this time." He shook his head. "I can't let you go."

Her eyes narrowed. "You can't keep me here."

He released her. "You're right. I can't keep you here.

But if you go out there, not only are you risking your life, you're risking mine, as well."

She placed her foot on the bottom rail of the fence. "Not if you don't come with me."

"If you go, I'll go. If we both die, my death will be on your hands."

She lowered her foot and stared up at him. "I'd be dead, so I wouldn't know any better."

"What if I died trying to rescue you, and by some miracle you survived?"

She chewed on that confounded lip again, making Hawkeye want to suck it into his mouth and kiss her. Even though she was covered from head to toe in a fine layer of dust, and looked like a dark specter in the night, she still had a way of making him want to shake her and kiss her all at once.

He reached for her hand. "Come on, admit it. You'd feel bad, if this adorable face was crushed in a stampede." He smiled, figuring if he was as dirty as she was, all she'd see was the white of his teeth shining in the darkness.

"Maybe."

"You'd miss your chance to kiss me again."

She glanced away. "I didn't say I *wanted* to kiss you again."

"Sweetheart, you didn't have to say it." With a finger pressed to her chin, he turned her to face him.

As the dust slowly drifted toward the earth, the moon climbed into the sky, transforming the remaining particles of dirt into sparkling diamond dust swirling around her in the darkness.

Olivia opened her mouth—probably to tell him he was wrong, he assumed. Instead she asked, "Big claim for a man who's covered in dirt." Her words came out in a breathy kind of whisper, as if she didn't have quite enough air in her lungs.

"Darlin', you're covered in the same blanket of dust and it doesn't make me want to kiss you any less."

She lifted her chin. "You're insane."

"You're beautiful." He pulled her close and settled his hands on her hips.

"You realize this will never work." Olivia rested her palms on his chest.

"Honey, how difficult can this be? All it takes is two sets of lips with two willing individuals."

"I'm not willing," she insisted.

"Oh no?" He bent to her, his mouth hovering over hers. "Tell me you're not willing again, and I'll forget this kiss."

She stood still, her body tense. What little resistance she'd first exerted changed as her fingers curled into his shirt.

For a moment, Hawkeye thought she might tell him she wasn't willing again and he'd have to end the night frustrated and even more determined to win a kiss from her full, luscious, albeit dusty, lips.

"Afraid?" he whispered, his mouth so close to hers he could feel the warmth of her breath.

Then she tipped upward on her toes and closed the distance in a brief meeting of mouths.

She might have moved away, if Hawkeye had let her, but his hands clasped her hips tightly and he dragged her body against his. He slid his fingers up her back, threading them into her thick auburn hair, disturbing the fine layer of dust. "You call that a kiss?"

She leaned her head back and stared up into his eyes. "I call it insanity."

"Let me show you how it's done." He claimed her mouth in a long, sensuous kiss that sucked the air from his lungs and the starch from his knees.

She opened to him, her lips parting on a gasp.

Before she could change her mind and withdraw from the kiss, he swept in and tasted her tongue, caressing it with his own in a long, sensuous glide.

She might have resisted at first, but her tongue met his in her own dance, tangling and teasing until they finally broke apart, breathless, the cool night air doing nothing to chill the heat building between them.

A distant howl pierced the night sky, answered by the restless moos of the herd on the far side of the pasture.

"I guess I'd better find my rifle and bed down under the stars."

"You're kidding, right?" He thumbed a path through the dust on her cheek. "You can't sleep out here."

"I can and will." Olivia chuckled, the sound tugging at Hawkeye's insides. "What? Are you afraid of the dark?"

"Not hardly. Just what's in it."

"I'm not leaving the livestock to fend for themselves. If that howl was any indication, wolves were behind this little midnight raid. I'm not letting them steal even one calf."

Hawkeye kissed her briefly and turned her toward

the house. "Then you'd better get your shower first. I have a sleeping bag in my truck that will fit both of us, but I'd rather not fill it with dust."

"Not to worry." Olivia stepped back and brushed at the dust on her jeans. "I have my own bag."

"It gets downright cold here at night." He tilted his head. Yeah, he'd just met her. Yeah, he was pushing the envelope, but hopefully his flirting would help her forget about the bad stuff. If only for a few minutes. "Sure you don't want to share mine?"

"Not a chance."

"Then go make some mud in the shower. I'll keep an eye on things out here."

She pointed to the barn. "There's a shower in the barn, if you want to get one, too."

"I'll do that. Now go, before I'm tempted to kiss you again."

Chapter Five

Olivia turned and ran toward the house, her footsteps slowing as she neared the structure. Memories crowded in on her as she stepped up onto the porch. Her mother and father had sat with her in that swing when she was a little girl. It had taken her years before she'd sat in it again without wanting to cry over the loss of her mother to cancer.

Not until she stood at the back door did she realize she'd left the keys in the door lock of the tack room. Then she remembered the spare key. Liv lifted the flower on the porch and retrieved the key taped to the bottom where her father had always left it. Some things never changed.

And some things changed forever.

She slipped the key in the lock and turned the knob at the same time. The door swung open, and the scent of home wrapped around her, threatening to drag her to her knees. She didn't have time to wallow in grief. Hawkeye waited outside for her return.

Squaring her shoulders, she entered the kitchen and hurried through the house to her bedroom. Once there, she rifled through her drawers, pulling out fresh underwear, jeans and a sweatshirt. The nights got cold in the high country, even in the summer. Armed with her clothes, careful not to let them brush against her dust-covered body, she crossed the hallway to the bathroom.

Liv refused to look toward her father's bedroom. It could only start the tears flowing all over again. She'd cried enough for one day. With cattle in danger of a wolf attack, she couldn't spare the time and emotional energy it sapped out of her.

Hawkeye's strong arms around her had stemmed the last flow. She couldn't rely on him to be there to hold her every time she thought about her father and the fact she had no family left.

"Abe is family," she reminded herself aloud as she stepped into the bathroom and closed the door behind her.

A few minutes later, she stood beneath the shower, dark streaks of water making trails down the drain. Liv wondered if Hawkeye had found the shower in the barn or if he would wait until she finished before washing the dirt off his body. She also wondered what it would be like to share a shower with the man.

Her belly tightened and an ache grew between her thighs. How long had it been since a man had held her in his arms? She'd been too wrapped up in her studies in college to date much. And most of the boys hadn't been interested in intellectual conversations. They'd wanted only one thing. Now that she'd kissed the ruggedly handsome army ranger, Liv could understand fixating on getting naked with another person.

Standing beneath the warm water sluicing over her shoulders, she could imagine Hawkeye sharing the space with her, his broad shoulders filling the shower. She tried to tell herself it was wrong to think about him naked, but it beat the heck out of thinking about her grief.

So, standing naked in the shower spray, Liv let her thoughts go to the ranger and something inside blossomed and grew more intense, spreading all the way out to her fingertips.

She closed her eyes and imagined the man lathering the bar of soap and slathering it along the column of her throat, over the swells of her breasts and down her torso to the juncture of her thighs. She gasped and turned toward the spray, her breathing ragged, her blood on fire and pumping hard and fast through her veins.

Reaching down, she turned the handle, reducing the heat until cool water chilled her skin. But nothing could quench the flames raging inside.

At last, she shut off the water, reached for a towel and dried herself quickly. The sooner she dressed, the sooner she'd stop thinking of Hawkeye naked.

Or so she thought. Wearing clean jeans, thick socks, cowboy boots and the sweatshirt, she assumed any lusty inclinations would be thoroughly squelched. Not so. She'd forgone wearing a bra, reasoning the sweatshirt was enough. Only the inside of the shirt brushed against her nipples, making them bead into tight little nubs.

Having been gone from the herd long enough, Liv threw on a jacket and hurried through the house and out onto the porch. Then she thought about the shower in the barn. How long had it been since someone had taken fresh towels out there? She ran back inside to the linen closet, retrieved a large, fluffy towel and returned to the barn.

She listened for the sounds of wolves or livestock in distress. Silence reigned, except for the chirping of crickets and the occasional owl hooting in the distance.

Hawkeye was nowhere to be seen.

For a moment, Liv panicked. Had he left? She spun to find his truck sitting where he'd parked it. Relief washed over her and she entered the barn, going to the tack room that doubled as the foreman's office. Her father had installed a shower at the rear of the tack room on her mother's insistence. She wouldn't let him into the house while he was covered in dust, claiming he left a muddy trail when he did. Rather than hose down in the yard, he'd built the shower, complete with a small hot water heater. It had saved him from a freezing shower on more than one occasion.

Outside the bathroom door, Liv paused, listening for the sound of the water hitting the stall doors and floor, verifying that Hawkeye was inside, probably naked, his hands and body covered in soapsuds.

Liv raised her hand to knock, thought better of it and lowered it. He wouldn't hear her knock, and if he did, he might slip on the bathroom floor trying to get to the door.

Liv figured there wouldn't be any clean towels in the bathroom, which meant Hawkeye would have to drip dry unless she could get the towel to him before he finished his shower.

If the door wasn't locked, she could slip in, drop the towel on the counter and exit with Hawkeye none the wiser.

She twisted the handle and the door opened.

Her heart hammering against her ribs, Liv eased into the small room, laid the towel on the counter and turned to leave.

That was when she noticed the sheerness of the shower curtain and the explicitly defined silhouette of Hawkeye's form behind the milk-white, plastic sheath.

Liv froze, her gaze raking over the thick forearms and biceps, the narrow waist and the thighs. Sweet heaven, the man was built like a gladiator, all muscles and sinew from his thick neck to his tight, well-defined calves.

The water ceased spraying and the curtain jerked back. Hawkeye stared out at her, a quirky smile curling the corners of his mouth. "Like what you see?"

For half a second, she froze, her gaze not connecting with his eyes, but running the length of his lean, sexy body all the way down to his...

Liv jerked her eyes back up to connect with his, red-hot heat rising up her neck into her cheeks, burning its way out to her ears. "A towel," she blathered. "I brought you a towel."

Still her flight instinct wouldn't kick in.

"Thank you. I'd anticipated dripping dry." He stepped out on the cool tile floor, his grin spreading as he reached for the towel. "Are you going to help me dry off?"

"No. I...uh...was just leaving." Finally, her legs

moved and she ran out the door, slamming it behind her. She would have run all the way out to the barnyard, but the horse in the stall whinnied, the sound just loud enough to penetrate her quivering brain cells.

Stormy, her gray quarter-horse gelding, pawed at the stall door, bringing her focus to the animal anxious to get her attention. She remembered then that he hadn't been fed that evening. Abe usually performed all of the chores before supper. His hunger and the nervous energy from the ruckus outside made for an unhappy horse. And he wasn't the only one. Three other horses were stabled in the barn, all stamping their hooves, ready for hay and grain.

Liv had to suck up her embarrassment and get to work feeding the animals. They didn't have to suffer because she'd made a fool of herself.

She scooped a couple of coffee cans full of sweet feed and dumped them into buckets.

Stormy whickered again.

"I hear you. You'll get yours first, since you're the loudest." She carried the bucket to the stall and hefted it over the top, hanging it on the hook on the other side. Stormy immediately buried his nose in the feed and quieted down.

"How much hay do you give each?" Hawkeye's voice made her jump.

Pulling herself together, she turned with as much dignity as she could muster after seeing the man completely naked. "A section each." As her gaze met his, heat rushed up into her cheeks. She ducked her head and hurried over to the next stall, hanging the second bucket over the side. The bay mare in the stall nodded her head as if in approval and dug into her meal.

One more trip to the feed bins and she was finished with the sweet feed.

Hawkeye had placed sections of hay in all of the occupied stalls and started filling water troughs.

Liv took a deep breath and launched into sleeping arrangements. "You can have the spare bedroom in the house. It has clean sheets on the bed."

"We've already discussed this. I'm staying outside with you."

"I'll have my gun, and I'll build a fire," she said. "I've done it before." She gave him a tight smile. "I'm not afraid of the dark."

"Not alone," he repeated. "I'll bed down outside with you." He finished filling the troughs.

Liv turned off the water and wiped her hands on her jeans. "I'll get some firewood and tinder."

"Do you mind if I break up a bale of hay for a pallet?"

"Knock yourself out." Liv hurried to the stack of wood her father and Abe had cut for the huge fireplace in the house. She selected three logs and some kindling and hurried back to the barnyard close to the pasture fence where the cattle had settled in for the night.

The sky had turned black, the stars and moon illuminating the landscape enough that Liv didn't need a flashlight to see. She made another trip for more logs and dropped them beside the first load. "I'll be back."

Liv returned to the house. This time her mind was on the man she'd be lying beside under the blanket of stars. The ache of memories wasn't quite as powerful when she entered through the kitchen. She was able to retrieve the sleeping bag from the closet and get out without shedding another tear. Liv considered that a significant accomplishment.

In the couple of minutes it took Liv to get her bag, Hawkeye had arranged a straw pallet by the fence, spread a sleeping bag over it and was in the process of starting a fire.

"Well, you're a regular Boy Scout," she commented as she laid her bag on the ground nearby and sat cross-legged. "Did you rub two sticks together to get that started?"

"I found matches in the desk in the tack room." He blew a steady stream of air onto the flaming tinder to get the fire burning brightly. In a few minutes, the flames climbed onto the logs and Hawkeye sat back.

He frowned when he turned toward her. "I put the hay out for both of us. No use sleeping on the hard ground."

She shrugged, not wanting to get too close to him. Whenever she did, sparks flew. Not the mad and angry kind, but the lusty, sexy ones. "I'm fine where I am."

"Look, I promise not to touch you." His lips quirked into a smile. "Unless you want me to."

She wasn't so worried about him touching *her*, as she was about her own desire to touch *him*. But she would get little sleep on the hard ground. Liv picked up her sleeping bag and spread it out next to Hawkeye's on the side closest to the fire. Her pulse quickened and her insides heated. She sat on the bag and raised her hand to the warm fire, glad for the sweatshirt and jacket. The temperature would dive to near freezing by morning.

Rather than stare at him, she shifted her gaze to the silhouettes of the cattle in the pasture. "Any more signs of the wolves?"

"None. And the livestock have settled in for the night. You don't have to sleep out here, if you don't want to. I can keep an eye on the herd."

"Thanks. But I don't want to rely on anyone. If I'm going to stay, I need to be able to handle things on my own when the need calls for it."

"If?" He sat beside her, staring into the fire. "Was there any question of your staying?"

She wrapped her arms around her legs and rested her head on her knees. "The ranch doesn't feel right without my dad."

"I take it you grew up here?"

She tipped her head toward her home. "My mother gave birth to me on this ranch. They couldn't get to the hospital in time, so my father delivered me in the house he built for her." She smiled, staring into the fire, the few memories of her mother crowding into her thoughts. "She was pretty, with blond hair and blue eyes. I don't look anything like her. I get my red hair and green eyes from my dad."

"Where is your mother?"

Liv sighed. Her chest tightened. Even though her mother had been gone a long time, she still missed her. "She died of a cancer when I was twelve."

For a long moment Hawkeye remained quiet. "I'm sorry. It had to be rough on you as a little girl."

"Yeah. I didn't have her around for a lot of things girls share with their mothers. But my father tried to make up for it." She laughed and nearly choked on a sob. "He even learned to French braid my hair. He was determined to be a great father and a substitute mother all wrapped up in one person."

"And run a ranch."

"Thankfully, I wasn't much of a girlie-girl to begin with. I loved ranching as much as my father."

"But you lived in Seattle for how long?"

"Seven years. Through college and three years following."

"Why didn't you come back after college?"

"My father made me promise to give city life a shot before coming home to Grizzly Pass. I was three years into the five years when I got the call." Again, her throat tightened, threatening to cut off her air.

Hawkeye slipped an arm around her waist and pulled her up against him.

"You said you wouldn't touch me," she said, though she didn't push him away. It felt good to have someone to lean on, especially when the main man in her life couldn't be there anymore.

"I said I wouldn't unless you wanted me to." His arm tightened around her waist. "I figured you could use a shoulder to lean on about now."

"Thanks." She leaned her head into the crook of his arm and inhaled the woodsy, smoky scent of a man used to the outdoors.

"So that leaves you and Abe to run the ranch. Wouldn't it be easier just to sell it?"

She stiffened. "That's what Mr. Rausch tried to tell me. I'll be damned if I fire-sale this place to him. He owns enough of Grizzly Pass without owning my family ranch. Besides, he'd probably turn it into a big-game-hunting place where they raise prize elk and buffalo for rich folks to come slaughter as they stand at the feeders." Liv shook her head. "I can't let that happen."

"I take it you have a job in Seattle. Won't they expect you to come back to work soon?"

She nodded. "I took a leave of absence. I haven't completely quit."

"Do you want to go back?" Hawkeye asked.

She shrugged. "For the past seven years, all I wanted was to come home to Grizzly Pass and Stone Oak Ranch."

"And now?"

She leaned into him, glad for his warmth and strength. "I don't know. I'm having a hard time imagining this place without my dad." Liv's eyes stung with ready tears every time she thought of her father. "I don't know," she whispered past the knot around her vocal cords.

"Well, for a little while you won't have to make that decision. While I'm here, I'll help with chores, feeding and taking care of the livestock. But you should consider hiring more help."

"I know. CJ won't be around all the time and I need full-time help." She lifted her head and looked up at his face. "Enough about me. My life right now is too depressing. Tell me about you."

HAWKEYE SHRUGGED. "THERE'S not much to tell." He didn't like talking about himself. Most of his recent memories were of war and fighting. Coming back to the States had left him feeling itchy and uncomfortable. But in the grand scheme of world events, his feelings didn't amount to a hill of beans.

"Where did you grow up?" Olivia persisted.

Knowing the woman wouldn't give up unless he gave her a little of his background, he sighed. "On a ranch in the Texas Panhandle."

"See? That didn't hurt so much, now, did it?" She shifted her gaze back to the fire. "I should have known. You were right at home, feeding animals. Did your family own the ranch?"

Here was the huge difference between Hawkeye and Olivia. He was from humbler beginnings. His family never owned any acreage. Especially not in the magnitude of what Olivia's father owned. "My father was the foreman. My mother helped out as the cook in the ranch house."

"They must have been great role models. After living in the city where most people have never been up close and personal with a horse or a cow, it made me appreciate all of the hard work Abe and my father put into this place." She snuggled closer. "Is it me, or is it getting colder?"

"Colder," Hawkeye said, his side warming where she pressed against it. She fit perfectly under his arm. He had to fight the urge to kiss her temple.

"I assume you ride," she said, her voice soft in the darkness.

"Four-wheelers."

Again, Olivia glanced up at him. "You can't tell me

you grew up on a ranch in Texas and never learned to ride. I won't believe it."

Hawkeye pressed his lips together, memories flooding into his head. "My sister and I learned to ride bareback before we learned to walk. I did a little junior rodeoing, but not for long."

"But you don't ride now?" The starlight and the three-quarter moon reflected off her eyes, making them sparkling diamonds in the night.

"No," he said. "I don't ride now."

When she opened her mouth to ask why, he shook his head. "Please. Don't ask."

She closed her mouth, her gaze scanning his face, as if searching for clues. Finally, she looked back to the fire. "I always wanted a sibling." Olivia sighed. "My parents tried for more children, but it just didn't happen. I think my father would have liked a boy to take hunting and fishing."

Off the subject of horseback riding, Hawkeye relaxed and let the warmth of the fire and the flickering flames calm him. "I can't imagine you staying home. Surely you went with him?"

Olivia chuckled. "Much to my mother's chagrin, I tagged along with my father, dressed in camouflage or hunter orange. She couldn't get me into a dress except on Sundays. I got my first deer when I was nine."

"I bet your dad was just as proud of you, even if you weren't a boy."

"I know he was. But my parents would have liked more children. It made my mother sad that she couldn't get pregnant again." Olivia yawned. "Tell me about your family."

Again, Hawkeye tensed. "Do you always talk this much?"

Olivia yawned again. "Only when I'm trying to stay awake at the same time as I'm trying not to think about my dad and the fact he isn't coming home ever again."

Hawkeye's chest tightened. He knew what it was like to lose someone you cared about. Yes, his parents were alive and still lived on the ranch in Texas. But he'd lost a number of friends in the war. Friends he considered his brothers. And then there was Sarah.

"What is your sister like?"

The dull ache that had been with him most of his life intensified.

"Sarah was everything I wasn't—pretty, delicate, blond-haired and blue-eyed like my mother. She laughed all the time. Life was a joy to her, and she was a joy to everyone whose life she touched."

Olivia rested her hand on his and squeezed. "What happened to her?"

The horror of that day replayed in Hawkeye's mind like a video. "Sarah loved riding her horse, Socks. We raced often, thundering across the pasture toward the barn or to our favorite swimming hole. On her birthday, we were racing. Her horse wasn't quite as fast as mine, so I slowed to let her win, to make her day even more special. Socks galloped ahead. They went down into a gully and, on their way back up, Socks reared unexpectedly. Sarah was thrown. She landed on her head, snapping her neck. She died instantly."

"How old was she?"

"Ten."

"And you?" Her hand tightened on his.

"Fifteen. Almost sixteen."

"Wow. I imagine that was hard on you."

He'd jumped off his horse and run to his sister, but nothing he could have done would have changed the outcome. The two horses were spooked and took off back to the barn. Hawkeye had been torn between staying with his sister and going for help. Finally, he'd left her and run all the way back to the house to get his father.

"Sarah was everything to my parents," he said softly.

His mother had ridden in the truck beside his father all the way back to where Sarah lay. For a few minutes, Hawkeye hadn't been able to remember exactly where she'd been. When they finally found her, her face had been pale, the light drained out of a bright and happy human being.

"I'm sorry," Olivia said. "I would like to have met her. She sounds like she was amazing."

"She was." Hawkeye didn't pull his hand free of Olivia's. Her touch seemed to ease the pain he'd lived with for so long.

"You felt responsible, didn't you?" Olivia said.

"As an adult, I can reason with myself, but I still come back to the same 'if only' scenarios," he said.

"What do you mean?"

"If only we hadn't gone riding that day, she'd still be with us."

"You don't know that," Olivia countered.

"If only I hadn't challenged her to that race."

Olivia's hand stroked his. "Are you sure she didn't challenge you?"

"Even if she did, I didn't have to take her up on the challenge." A number of times Hawkeye had wished he could go back and do that entire day over. Anything to get Sarah back.

Olivia turned in his arms. "So you stopped riding horses to punish yourself?"

"It's more complicated." Hawkeye stared off at the bright moon rising above the mountaintops. "My mother was devastated by Sarah's death. She quit caring about anything, stopped eating and sank into a deep depression. My father had a job to do. He couldn't stay at home and take care of her."

"You were her only other child?"

Hawkeye nodded. "I never knew someone could be that depressed or how debilitating it could be. I'd lost my sister, but I was losing my mother, too. So I promised her I'd never ride again."

"And you felt like it was all your fault."

"Yeah." He looked at her for a moment and then back at the moon.

"Looking back, I'm sure you realize it wasn't."

He nodded. "But I was older than Sarah. I should have done something to prevent it from happening."

"Like?"

He shook his head. "I tell myself that I should have stayed at home. Then Sarah wouldn't have been on that horse to begin with."

"Should have, could have, would have, doesn't

change anything." Olivia touched his cheek with her fingers.

Hawkeye leaned into her palm. "I know."

"You did everything you could have done."

"Except save her."

"I'm sorry," Olivia repeated and leaned up, pressing her lips to his.

He raised his arms around her and held her tightly against his body, his mouth crashing down on hers. God, he wanted this woman who'd lost her father so recently. She needed the shoulder to lean on more than Hawkeye. Instead she gave him the opportunity to share his deepest regrets, offering her sympathy for his loss from over sixteen years ago.

Olivia deserved to mourn her father, not listen to his sad story. Hawkeye gripped her arms, pressed Liv away from him and dropped his hands to his sides. "We should get some sleep. Tomorrow could prove as challenging as today."

"Nothing could be as challenging as burying your father," she whispered.

She was probably right. But Hawkeye's current challenge was to keep from taking this woman he'd only met a few hours ago and making sweet love to her under the star-filled sky.

Olivia stared up into his eyes, her own glazed, her lips swollen from his kiss.

Rather than kiss her again and compound his error, Hawkeye turned away, closed his eyes and listened for sounds of wolves or mooing cattle. Silence soothed the darkness, marred only by the occasional hoot of an owl.

Hawkeye lay on his side, facing away from Olivia, making it clear he didn't want to interfere in her space or she in his, though interfering was all he could think about.

Eventually, she settled behind him, leaving him in silence, with his burgeoning desire keeping him awake into the small hours of the morning. This mission could prove to be one of the hardest he'd ever undertaken, if he planned to keep his hands off the pretty ranch owner.

Chapter Six

Liv lay very still for a long time after that kiss.

That kiss.

Never in all her twenty-five years had she had a kiss that left her as shaken and as hungry for more. Liv liked being in control of her life, her emotions and her destiny. In one kiss, Hawkeye had shown her just how out of control her heart could be.

She lay staring up at the stars and the moon well into the night. When she finally fell asleep, she dreamed of lying naked with Hawkeye in a soft bed, his arms wrapped around her from behind, his lips nuzzling the sensitive skin of her neck.

Liv woke with a start, forcing herself out of the dream. He'd made it clear he didn't need her kisses by breaking it off and turning away. Why would she dream about him holding her when it wasn't going to happen? He was there as part of his job. She was a means to an end, giving him access to her property to look out for whoever might have killed her father or was stirring up trouble in the area.

Liv blinked her eyes up at the stars. The chill night

air cooled her face, but not her body snuggly wrapped in the sleeping bag. Though the sleeping bag was considerably heavier than usual. She shifted onto her back, only to realize the bag wasn't what was heavy.

Hawkeye's arm lay across her middle, tucked beneath her breasts. He'd spooned her body with his, sharing his warmth.

Liv smiled. Yeah, he could turn off his desire, but he must have felt something or he wouldn't have snuggled up to her in the night, laying his arm across her to keep her warm.

Rolling back to her side, she pressed her back to Hawkeye's front and nestled in his embrace, her eyes drifting closed again. Morning would come soon, and with it, she'd be forced to sort out her feelings and get on with the task of taking care of a ranch. But for now, she had the strength of Hawkeye's arm and body beside her. That was enough to get her through the night.

As the first hint of morning lightened the sky, Liv woke, strangely pleased that Hawkeye's arm was still around her, his body pressed firmly to her back. Feeling a little on the shy side, she inched her way from beneath that arm and rolled herself and her sleeping bag away from him before sitting up.

Hawkeye slept on, his chest rising and falling in a steady pattern.

In the gray light of dawn, Liv studied his face, softened by slumber. Tanned and rugged, Hawkeye appeared more gentle and vulnerable in his sleep. With his eyes closed, his long, dark lashes made shadowy crescents on his cheeks. Any woman would give her eye teeth for lashes like that. Hawkeye would sire beautiful children with his dark hair and blue eyes.

Liv's chest tightened. She'd always imagined herself having kids, even dreamed about them. Somehow, she'd never pictured the face of a husband in the dreams. Perhaps because she hadn't met Hawkeye.

Now she could imagine dreaming about a man with dark hair and blue eyes and a little girl of the same coloring.

Holy hell, what was she thinking? Hawkeye wasn't going to be there after the mystery of her father's death was resolved and the people responsible for the troubles in the area were revealed.

She stared at his rugged face for a while longer, attracted to the rough stubble on his chin and the fullness of his lips. Before she could think her way out of doing it, she leaned over and brushed those lips with her own.

When she realized what she'd done, she held her breath, fully expecting his eyes to open. They didn't, and his breathing continued slow and steady. Liv let go of the breath she held and rose to her feet. She had a lot of things to do that day and kissing a sleeping man wasn't one of them.

For a moment, she thought his eyes opened slightly, but he didn't move from his original position.

Quickly, before she changed her mind and slipped back beneath his arm, Liv ran for the house, up the steps and into the home she'd grown up in.

With light edging through the windows, Liv was able to make her way to the bathroom without flipping any electrical switches. Once in the bathroom, she closed the door and leaned against it, willing her breathing to return to normal. Who was she running from, anyway? Not Hawkeye. He hadn't come after her. And it wasn't Hawkeye she was afraid of. He'd been there for her by saving Abe from a flaming truck and her from a stampede. Then why had she run all the way up to the house?

If she was being honest with herself, she'd admit she was afraid of the way she was feeling toward the man she'd only met the day before. Was she subconsciously clinging to him because of the loss of her father? Was Hawkeye the father figure she wished she hadn't lost?

Her lips tingled at the memory of the kisses.

Liv smothered a nervous laugh. No way in hell a kiss like the one last night was fatherly. She didn't think of Hawkeye as a father figure. Far from it. Her body burned with the warmth she'd felt with her back pressed against his front even with the thickness of two sleeping bags between them.

Dragging in a deep, steadying breath, she pushed away from the door, splashed water on her face, brushed her teeth and pulled her hair back into a neat ponytail. Feeling a little more in control of herself and her situation, she peeked out into the hallway, half expecting to see Hawkeye waiting outside.

Disappointment flashed through her. Apparently, she was the only one thinking about the other person in this case. Hawkeye was probably sound asleep on the ground outside where she'd left him, not a single thought about her floating through his dreams.

Shoving her sleeves up her arms, she marched into the kitchen and started breakfast. God, she hated cooking. Her father and Abe had alternated kitchen duties. When Liv was home, they continued their routine and she helped out by washing dishes, cleaning the house and bathrooms as well as taking care of the livestock.

Cooking was not her strong suit. She burned everything.

Well, not today.

She dug the frying pans out of the cabinet and bacon and eggs from the refrigerator. Soon she had bacon popping in the frying pan and had poured eight scrambled eggs into another skillet.

"I've got this." Her confidence growing, she reached for the loaf of bread and popped four slices into the toaster. Then she thought about the coffee that she should have started brewing before anything else. Turning her attention to the coffeemaker, she poured several scoops of grounds into the filter and dumped a carafe of water over it.

By the time she turned back to the stovetop, smoke was roiling from the bacon pan.

"Shoot! Shoot! Shoot!" She ripped the pan from the fire. Hot bacon grease sloshed onto her hand. Liv let loose a string of curses, slammed the pan back on the stove and dived for the sink, her hand stinging where the grease had landed.

"Need some help?"

"No," she responded automatically. She turned on the cold water and jammed her hand beneath it.

Hawkeye trotted across the kitchen and turned off the burner beneath the smoking bacon. "Do you always burn the kitchen down when you cook breakfast?"

"No," she said, her voice a little harsh, the pain diminishing as the grease was removed from her skin. No doubt, she'd have a blister there. "Well, yes, actually. I'm a bit hopeless as a cook."

"And you lived on your own for how many years?"

"Long enough to figure out a microwave and frozen dinners."

"For breakfast?" Hawkeye pushed a spatula through the scrambled eggs and raised his brows when the eggs stuck to the bottom of the pan. "We might want to start over."

Liv inhaled and let go of a deep breath, her eyes stinging. "Abe and my father were in charge of cooking. The only culinary delights I ever managed were hot dogs on the grill." She stared down at the red spot on her hand. "And I can make a decent cup of coffee."

"At least you have your priorities straight. How about you butter the toast and pour us a cup of coffee while I scrape these eggs out of the pan and put on a fresh batch?"

"I really had every intention of having a decent breakfast on the table. I figured, since I'm getting your services free, the least I could do was provide decent meals." She sighed. "I'm sorry."

"Don't be. Not everyone is born with the knack for cooking."

"Sometimes I wish I was more like my mother. She was a wonderful cook."

"I'm sure you made up for it in other ways."

Liv nodded. "I'm pretty good at everything to do with ranching."

"There you go." He finished cleaning the pan, dropped butter to melt across the slick surface and cracked nine eggs onto it. Soon he was scooping fluffy yellow eggs onto three plates, adding the salvaged bacon and buttered toast.

Liv sat at the table, thankful for Hawkeye's sure hand at cooking and the hot steaming cup of java in her hand. "Three plates?"

"CJ should be here anytime."

A knock on the front door of the house made Liv start.

Before Liv could rise from her chair, Hawkeye held up a hand. "Stay. I'll get it."

Liv sank back down and lifted her fork, pretending interest in the light and fluffy eggs Hawkeye had whipped up, when in fact she was more attuned to the way his hips swayed in the faded blue jeans he wore.

Liv's pulse quickened. She had to force her gaze back to her plate full of scrambled eggs and slightly burned bacon.

A few moments later, CJ entered the room, a battered straw cowboy hat in his hand, a ruddy pink flush building in his dark-skinned cheeks. His raven hair was shaggy, hanging down around his ears and on his collar, like he hadn't had a haircut in a month or two. "Sorry to bother you at breakfast, Miss Dawson."

"Not at all. In fact, I believe Mr. Walsh made enough breakfast for you. Have a seat."

He straightened. "I'm here to work, ma'am. If you could tell me where to start, I'll get to it."

Liv shook her head. "You can start at the breakfast

table and load up on enough protein to keep you working hard through the day. Then you can do the dishes."

CJ shot a glance at Hawkeye.

"She's the boss. I'd do what she says." When CJ glanced back at Liv, Hawkeye winked.

"I don't feel right eating your food. I came to work."

"I understand. But I plan on leaving you here while I go to town for feed and supplies. I need to know you won't pass out because you haven't had a decent meal."

"I won't pass out." The teen stood tall, his shoulders back. "I'm strong."

Hawkeye pulled out the chair in front of his untouched plate of food and pressed CJ into it. "Eat, or we'll never hear the end of it."

Liv ducked her head to hide the smile pulling at her lips.

Hawkeye retrieved the third plate and sat in the seat beside CJ.

Soon they were all tucking into a hearty breakfast.

When Liv had almost cleaned her plate she caught Hawkeye's gaze.

"What's this about going into town?" he asked.

"I need to replace the feed and supplies we lost in the crash yesterday. We're down to the bottom of the grain barrel for the horses and I need barbed wire and staples for the fence repairs we'll be doing later." She drew in a deep breath.

"Which brings us to the question of transportation," Hawkeye said. "Do you have another ranch truck?"

Liv shook her head. "Sorry, that old truck was the only one we had. I'll have to find a good used one to replace it. But that will take some searching. In the meantime, I can use my SUV. It'll carry the bags of feed and barbed wire."

Hawkeye shook his head. "We'll take my truck."

"I don't want to take advantage of you and your truck. Ranching can be harsh on vehicles."

"I bought it to be a work truck."

"Yeah, but—"

"We'll take my truck."

Liv wasn't sure she liked being overruled on her own ranch, but it would be easier to load and unload fifty-pound bags of feed into an open pickup bed than to slide them in and out of the back of her SUV. She'd have to search the internet that night to find a good used four-wheel-drive pickup. Winters in Wyoming could be harsh, cold and snowy. Whatever she got had to be able to climb slippery dirt roads in all weather conditions.

"Okay." She pushed back from the table and focused on her new hired hand. "CJ, are you ready to learn the ropes?"

He set his fork on his plate. "Yes, ma'am. But I need to do the dishes."

"You could do them at noon when you come inside to make a sandwich for lunch. Right now, I want to show you what needs to be done so that I can get into town and back before it gets late."

"Yes, ma'am." CJ piled his plate on Liv's and Hawkeye's and carried them to the sink. Then he hurried for the back door, opened it and held it for Liv.

She smiled as she walked out onto the porch. If the teen worked as hard at doing his chores right as he worked at being polite, he'd be a real asset to the ranch in Abe's absence.

After showing CJ what stalls needed to be cleaned and which horses needed to be exercised and fed, she left the teen, grabbed her purse and climbed into the passenger seat of Hawkeye's truck. "Do you think he'll be all right?"

"He seems to know his way around livestock." Hawkeye shifted into Reverse, backed up and turned the truck around. "He'll be fine."

"We won't be gone long," Liv reasoned. "Hopefully we'll be back before lunch."

"I'm counting on it. I want to get out to check on the downed fences."

Liv snorted. "You and me both. Cows seem to know when a fence is down and are drawn to the holes like magnets."

Hawkeye nodded. "I remember. My father worked on a ten-thousand-acre ranch in Texas. A tree could fall on the farthest fence in the most remote corner of the property and the cattle would find it, exit and wander onto another rancher's land. Thankfully, all of the steers were tagged for just that reason. We were forever trading livestock with the neighbors."

Liv smiled. "We have the added complication of grazing cattle on government land. Just *finding* your animals can be a challenge. We train them to come to the honking of a horn."

"Seems to be a universal cattle call." Hawkeye glanced across at her. "With your father gone, are you sure you want to take over the reins of a cattle ranch on your own?"

Liv stared out the window, her heart tightening in her chest. She was hit all over again that her father wouldn't be coming home to handle the myriad problems that came up on a daily basis when managing a cattle ranch.

"All the years I've been away from home, I dreamed of returning and helping my father with the ranch. I love working with the animals, riding horses and getting dirty." She gave him a sheepish grin. "I guess you've noticed I'm not much of a girlie-girl."

Hawkeye's gaze connected with hers, the heat in his look warming Liv all over. "I hadn't noticed. To me, you're all female. Through and through. With the added advantage…you aren't squeamish and you aren't afraid of anything."

Liv dragged her gaze away from his, afraid she would lose herself in it. "Most men would find that intimidating."

"Then most men are fools."

She looked back in time to see Hawkeye's lips quirk upward. "As an army ranger, I take it you aren't intimidated by much?"

"Oh, I wouldn't say that. I can be scared by a howitzer if it's pointed directly at me."

Liv nodded. "That would have me shaking in my boots. Have you had a howitzer pointed at you?"

"No, but I've had a live machine gun pointed at me and my team, and explosives detonate within ten feet of where I was standing." His words faded into silence.

Liv's chest tightened again. All the while she'd been

mourning her father's death, she hadn't stopped to consider Hawkeye's losses. Yeah, he'd lost his little sister a long time ago, but what about more recently? "Do you miss your work with the army?"

He nodded. "I miss the men who were part of my team."

She lowered her voice and asked, "Were they also the target of that machine gun?"

For a long moment, he remained silent.

Liv thought he preferred to avoid the question altogether. She turned toward the road ahead, accepting that he had a right to his silence.

"Yes. But it was the grenade that went off in the middle of them that did the most damage. I lost my battle buddy that day."

Liv's eyes stung at the hollowness in Hawkeye's tone. She swallowed hard and remained silent for a full minute before responding. "I'm sorry. He must have meant a lot to you."

His lips pressed together. "Mac was the brother I never had. We'd been through a lot together. He had my back."

And Liv would bet Hawkeye blamed himself for not protecting his buddy, like he'd blamed himself for not saving his sister. Her heart hurt for Hawkeye.

"If you're like me," Liv said, "you wander around in a bit of a haze, wondering if he'd still be here if you'd done something different. I keep wondering if I'd broken my promise to my father and come home when I'd wanted, would he still be alive?"

"You can't undo what's done. No amount of what-ifs

will bring them back," Hawkeye said, his tone harsh, his jaw tight.

"I know that, but it doesn't stop my mind from going through alternate endings." Liv pushed the loose hairs out of her face, tucking them behind her ears. "It's hard for me to think of life without my father in it. I keep thinking it's all a bad dream and I'll wake up to find him out in the barn, mucking a stall, or sitting in his lounge chair watching his favorite team play football."

"I keep thinking I'll get a text from Mac asking where the hell I am. Why am I not at the gym working out, or eating pizza with the team?" Hawkeye's grip tightened on the steering wheel until his knuckles turned white.

About that time, they arrived on the edge of town.

"Sheriff Scott said my truck would be towed to Roy Taylor's body shop in town. I'd like to stop by and see if any of the feed bags that were in the back of the truck are still intact."

"Point the way," Hawkeye said.

"Right turn at the next street."

Hawkeye turned where she'd indicated and pulled into the gravel parking lot of the body shop.

The damaged truck was parked at the side of the building, the front end smashed with clumps of dirt clinging to the fenders.

Liv hopped out of the passenger seat and hurried over to the truck. As she suspected, the bags of feed had been thrown clear of the truck or were busted, with grain scattered across the truck bed. Not one of the bags were salvageable. And the roll of barbed wire was missing.

"Hey, Liv." A man walked out of the open overhead door, wiping his hands on a greasy rag.

"Hi, Roy." She nodded toward the truck. "Any chance you can fix her?"

He shook his head. "I'm afraid it'll cost more than the truck is worth. Do you have collision coverage on it?"

Liv shrugged. "Knowing my father and how old that truck is, I'm betting he only had liability insurance coverage."

Roy tipped his head. "It's up to you, but if it were me, I'd haul it off to the junkyard for scrap and find a newer truck."

Liv nodded. "I'd come to the same conclusion, but it's good to know you agree."

"Sorry about your father. He was a good man." Roy dipped his head. "I'll take care of hauling your truck off to the junkyard."

"Send the tow-truck bill to me. I'll make sure it gets paid," Liv said.

"No charge. Your dad helped me out on several occasions."

"Thanks, Roy." She hugged him, fighting back unwanted tears, and hurried back to Hawkeye's truck. She jumped in and stared straight ahead.

Hawkeye slid behind the wheel and twisted the key. The engine leaped to life, but he paused before shifting into gear. "Everything all right?"

"Yes. Just go." She leaned her head back and closed her eyes, a teardrop escaping as she did. "Why does everything have to remind me of him?"

"This is a small town. Every life touches another."
She gave a shaky sigh. "And the only way to get away
from that is to leave. What if I'm not ready to leave?"

Chapter Seven

Hawkeye shifted into gear and pulled out of the parking lot of the body shop. He knew exactly what Olivia was going through. When he'd recovered enough to return to the apartment complex where he and Mac had lived, he'd been haunted by every little reminder of his friend.

No sooner had Mac's parents moved his things out of his apartment than another tenant moved in. Hawkeye had wanted to pound on the door and tell them to get out. Mac was supposed to live there. When he went to the gym on post, people would stop and ask about Mac. People who didn't know Mac hadn't made it back from the war. It was all Hawkeye could do not to slug one of them in the face. Not because they were being disrespectful. But because they were alive and Mac wasn't.

He'd jumped at the opportunity to leave everything he knew in order to get away from the memories of Mac and the other members of his team he'd lost in that last firefight. Far from Fort Bragg, far from his unit and his life as an army ranger, he'd hoped to get his life back on track.

Instead he was paired with a woman who'd lost her

father and was in the first stages of grief. What did he have to offer her when he couldn't get his own life together?

"Where to?" he asked. The sixty-four-million-dollar question he'd yet to answer. Where was he going?

Olivia had the answer, even if he didn't. "The feed store."

Hawkeye pulled onto Main Street and drove down to the only feed store in town. He backed into the loading dock at the front of the store.

A small crowd had gathered around the raised front porch of the store, and a white van displaying a local news station logo on the side was parked nearby. A man was setting up a camera on a tripod, aiming it at the porch of the feed store.

"What's going on?" Hawkeye asked.

"Because the feed-store porch makes a great raised stage, any town meeting or political campaigning is usually conducted here. Based on the placards leaning against the porch, I'd say a political candidate is about to give a speech." She pushed open her door. "We'd better get our feed and get out before we are surrounded by spectators."

Hawkeye dropped down from the truck and followed Olivia up the steps and into the feed store.

People milled around, pretending to shop for tack and horse liniment. Hawkeye suspected they were waiting for the show to begin.

Olivia made for the counter and waited her turn in line. Once there, she placed her order for feed, staples and a roll of barbed wire.

The man behind the counter rang up her purchases and took her credit card. When he handed it back with the slip for her to sign, he said, "Sorry about what happened to your father, Liv."

"Thanks, Mr. Nelson." Olivia signed the slip and replaced her card in her wallet.

"Don!" Mr. Nelson held up the printout of Olivia's purchases. "Help Miss Dawson with her order."

A big man with heavy brows and a deep tan emerged from a back room, snatched the paper from Mr. Nelson, shot a narrow-eyed glare at Olivia and walked back into what appeared to be a warehouse in the back of the main store. A few minutes later, he wheeled out a cart loaded with eight bags of feed, a bucket of staples and a roll of barbed wire. He headed straight for the loading dock without saying a word to Olivia.

Hawkeye studied the man. Something about his bearing gave him away as prior military. As he loaded the bags of feed into the back of the truck, Hawkeye noticed the tattoos on the man's arm. One was a US Marine Corps symbol with a skull and crossbones positioned above it.

When the man finished loading the supplies into the truck he turned to leave.

Hawkeye stuck out his hand. "Name's Trace Walsh. I notice you have a Marine Corps tattoo. Prior service?"

The man looked sideways at Hawkeye through narrowed eyes and didn't take the proffered hand. "Yeah. What's it to you?"

"It's just nice to meet another veteran. I'm army."

The man's lip curled into a sneer. "Yeah, well, I have work to do."

"I'm sorry but I didn't catch your name," Hawkeye persisted.

"Sweeney. Not that it's any of your business." He turned and left them standing on the dock.

Hawkeye nodded toward the retreating man. "Someone you know?"

Olivia shook her head. "He looks older than me. I don't remember him from high school. However, I do recognize his name. The Sweeneys own the ranch next to mine." She shivered. "He looked positively angry."

"I wonder why." Hawkeye closed the tailgate of his truck and placed his hand at the small of Olivia's back. "Not someone you'd want to run into on a dark night."

"No." Olivia started for the staircase leading off the dock to the parking lot.

Before she reached the top step to descend, a voice behind them said, "Miss Dawson."

Olivia stopped and turned toward the man who'd called out her name.

Hawkeye stood partially between them.

"Miss Dawson." He wore khaki slacks and a black windbreaker with LF Enterprises embroidered on the left breast.

"That's me," Olivia said, taking the man's hand.

"Leo Fratiani."

She raised her brows. "Nice to meet you, Mr. Fratiani. Should I know you?"

He smiled. "No, no. I'm new in town. I understand you own the Stone Oak Ranch. Is that right?"

Hawkeye could see the muscles working in Olivia's throat as she swallowed hard before answering.

"Yes, that would be correct," she said, though her voice was strained.

Hawkeye's fingers curled into a fist, ready to take on this man who was causing Olivia pain.

Leo pulled a card from his pocket and handed it to her. "I represent a client interested in purchasing your ranch. Do you have time to talk?"

She dropped the man's hand. Color rose in her cheeks and her lips thinned into a straight line.

Hawkeye almost felt sorry for the man. But not quite. The woman's father wasn't even cold in his grave and already scavengers were feeding on what was left behind.

Fratiani stepped forward. "I only need a few minutes of your time. Then we could set up a better time to go over my client's offer."

Hawkeye stepped between Olivia and the land agent. "I'm sorry, but Miss Dawson has a prior commitment."

He circled her waist with his arm and led her toward the stairs.

"Would another time be better?" Fratiani called out behind them.

"No," Olivia said through clenched teeth. She descended the stairs and waited while Hawkeye opened the passenger door for her.

With her hand on the door's armrest, she paused before climbing in and glanced up at Hawkeye. "Why does everyone assume I'll sell the ranch? Why can't they just leave me alone?"

Hawkeye pulled her into his arms and held her for a moment. "Don't let him get to you."

"I shouldn't. But I can't help it. It makes me so angry."

"And it should. You have a right to be mad at people like Fratiani coming at you so soon after your father's passing." Hawkeye kissed her temple and would have handed her up into the truck, but a shout went up behind him.

"There he is!"

Hawkeye and Olivia turned toward the sound.

In the short time they'd been inside the store, the crowd had thickened. A limousine pulled up at the edge of the gathering and a man dressed in a pair of neatly ironed blue jeans and a tailored white button-down dress shirt stepped out. He'd rolled the sleeves a third of the way up his arms, giving the appearance of a man about to go to work on something.

Hawkeye got the impression it was a staged look and the man was a politician, with his perfectly combed hair and manicured hands, and his entourage climbing out of the car with him.

Someone held up one of the campaign signs and started a chant. "We want Morris!"

Olivia muttered a curse word.

Hawkeye glanced her way. "Someone you know?"

"Grady Morris." She climbed into the truck. "Let's go."

Hawkeye turned back to the politician, studying him. "You don't want to hear what he has to say?"

"Not really," Olivia responded.

The man climbed to the porch and waved at the crowd. "Thank you for coming to my campaign kick-off. I couldn't start a campaign without the support of the good people of Grizzly Pass."

Hawkeye walked slowly around the truck, climbed in and rolled down his window.

"I want you all to know that I will represent the people of Wyoming in Washington. You will not be forgotten."

"What about the Native Americans?" someone shouted.

Morris nodded. "I will do my best to represent the interests of the people who were here first in this great nation."

"How will you help bring jobs back to our state?" another voice questioned loud enough to be heard over the others.

Morris raised his hand as if swearing on a stack of Bibles. "I will work in Washington to help keep our manufacturing jobs from going to foreign countries, and make it more difficult for foreign products to be sold in the States by increasing tariffs on imports."

"And the oil industry?" another man shouted. "What will you do to bring the pipeline back so that we can have our jobs back?"

"No!" a Native American cried. "No to the pipeline crossing our sacred grounds and poisoning our water. Find another way."

"Fine, then how about crossing other grounds?" asked the man who'd asked about bringing the pipe-line back. "We need to quit relying on foreign oil and build the infrastructure to get our own oil out of the ground and across the country."

"As your congressman," Morris said, "I promise to address the issues with the oil companies to bring jobs and prosperity back to our state."

"What about reducing the fees for grazing on government land?" a rancher asked.

"I'll work on that, as well." Morris pressed his hand over his heart. "I'll be your voice. Your advocate."

"If you can do all of that, I'll vote for you," someone encouraged.

Another added his approval. "Yeah, me, too."

A woman holding a baby on her hip raised her voice above the others. "How do we know you're not lying? That your promises aren't empty like every other politician's?"

"That's the big question," Olivia muttered. "My father always swore that man was only out for himself. Everything he did was for the almighty dollars that would line his pocket."

"Do you know why your father would have said that? Did he have proof?" Hawkeye asked.

"Morris has always been involved in every deal that could make him money in this state. He's in bed with all of the big corporations and he's willing to do anything it takes to make a profit."

"So he's a businessman. Does that make him untrustworthy?"

"I trusted my father's judgment." Olivia clenched her hands in her lap. "Morris is no better than Fratiani or Bryson Rausch. They want something for nothing. Rausch offered to buy my land, yesterday." Olivia snorted. "He said it would be too hard for a lone woman to run a place as big as Stone Oak Ranch. He'd help me out by taking it off my hands for a quarter of what it's worth."

Hawkeye's lips twitched. He could imagine her reaction to those words. But he held in his smile. "What did you tell him?"

"Hell no." She crossed her arms over her chest. "I didn't appreciate the man's condescending attitude about my ability to run a ranch on my own. I know more about ranching than he knows about good business practices."

Hawkeye released the tension on his lips and allowed his smile to spread across his face. "Good for you." He really liked this woman's spunk.

"I haven't had time to think about *now*, much less my *future*. You'd think people would give me a few days before they descend on me like maggots on roadkill."

Hawkeye cringed. "That's a bit graphic."

She shrugged, her lips twisting into a wry grin. "Yeah, I guess it is, even for me. But Rausch is as low as they come."

"I'll take your word for it." Hawkeye shifted into Drive, but kept his foot on the brake. "Ready to go?"

"More than ready." She cast another glance toward the candidate, her chin tilting upward as they passed Grady Morris. "Just because I'm a woman doesn't disqualify me as a ranch owner. I am my father's daughter. The son he never had."

Hawkeye's lips parted in a smile. "I like that about

you. You stand up for yourself and what matters most. You won't let people walk all over you."

"Darn right."

He eased forward, skimming the side of the crowd, careful not to run over anyone. Morris had just concluded his speech and was walking toward his limousine when he caught sight of Olivia in the passenger seat. His gaze followed her the entire time it took for Hawkeye to drive past.

Out of the corner of his view, Hawkeye caught a glimpse of Don Sweeney standing on the loading dock, his narrow-eyed gaze also on Hawkeye's truck. On the porch Morris had just vacated stood Leo Fratiani, leaning against a column, his gaze first on Morris and then switching to Hawkeye's truck.

Interesting. Hawkeye focused on the road ahead. "I'd like to make a stop at the tavern for just a few minutes."

"Are you hungry?" she asked.

"No. I want to meet with Garner and the team."

She glanced his way, her eyes narrowing. "Got anything? Because if you do, I completely missed it."

"Not much. But every clue should be investigated."

Olivia nodded. "Agreed."

Hawkeye drove the three blocks to the tavern and parked at the side close to the stairs up to the loft apartment. Hawkeye dropped down from the vehicle and hurried around to open Olivia's door.

She was already on the ground.

"Do you ever let a man open a door for you?"

She gave him a half smile and shrugged. "I tend to be impatient."

"Noted." Hawkeye waved her by. "After you."

Olivia passed him and climbed the stairs to the apartment.

Garner met them at the door. "Oh, good. I'm glad you came by. What do you have for us?"

"Four names we need you to look into." Hawkeye ushered Olivia into the room. Garner and Hack were the only people present. The other members of the team were nowhere to be seen.

Garner chuckled. "I think we have just about everyone in Grizzly Pass on our list of suspects involved in either murder or plots to overthrow the government or both." Garner sobered. "Seriously, this town isn't that big."

"Check into Don Sweeney," Hawkeye started.

"Wait. Let me get a pen to write with." Garner grabbed a pen from the desk and a pad of paper. "Shoot."

"Do a background check on Don Sweeney, Leo Fratiani, Grady Morris and Bryson Rausch."

Garner's pen stopped midstroke. "Bryson Rausch? As in the pillar of the community, Bryson Rausch? And isn't Grady Morris the man who is running for the US House of Representatives for the state of Wyoming? Have you met them?"

"No." Hawkeye shook his head. "But I saw Morris give his campaign speech in front of the local feed store."

"And something he said set you off?" Garner held up his hand. "Don't get me wrong. I trust your judgment. I'm just curious."

"As a candidate, having upheaval in your state can

make you more appealing than the incumbent," Hawk-eye said.

Olivia gasped. "Do you think Morris could have killed my father?"

"Right now, I don't know who killed your father." Hawkeye stroked her arm and took her hand in his, squeezing gently. "I'm sure if Morris had killed him, he'd have an ironclad alibi for the day your father died."

"Then why do you want Morris's background checked?" Garner asked.

"He's in a tenuous position. He probably has some ghosts in his closet he doesn't want exposed." Hawkeye turned to Hack. "Can you get into his personal accounts, email, texts, et cetera, and see if anything comes up? I'm not saying he's guilty of anything, but it wouldn't hurt to check him out."

Hack gave Hawkeye a mock salute. "Will do."

"What about Don Sweeney and Leo Fratiani?" Garner asked.

"Sweeney is prior service. A marine with the tattoos to prove it and a boatload of attitude. I'd like to know why he left the military."

"A lot of people leave the military after their enlistment is up," Garner said.

"Yeah, but something tells me Sweeney might not have left voluntarily. He had the Marine Corps emblem tattoo with a skull and crossbones over it. Most marines are proud of their service and wouldn't sully the emblem with anything else."

"Check." Garner nodded. "And Fratiani?"

Hawkeye tipped his head toward Olivia and gave her the opportunity to fill in Garner.

"He hit me up with an offer to purchase my ranch," she said, rubbing her hands over her arms, as if the air in the loft apartment had suddenly chilled. "He wasn't the only one. Rausch offered yesterday. I turned down both of them. My ranch isn't for sale."

Garner's eyes narrowed and they fixed on Olivia. "You do realize that if your father was murdered, it could be in connection with his ranch. Someone might want it badly enough to kill to own it. If that's the case, you really are in danger."

"I don't care." Her lips thinned. "I'm not selling."

Garner grinned. "I didn't say you should. But you need to be extra careful. You could be the next target."

"All the more reason for me to stay with her at the Stone Oak Ranch." Hawkeye squeezed Olivia's hand. If he had anything to say about it, he'd protect Olivia with his own life. "If someone makes an attempt on Olivia, someone needs to be there to give her some protection and maybe even bring down the perpetrator."

"And if you manage to take him alive, all the better." Garner clapped his hands and rubbed them together. "We really need a live witness to help us pinpoint the kingpin of the Free America movement and put an end to the threat to overthrow the government."

"I'd rather Olivia wasn't a target," Hawkeye said.

Olivia pulled her hand from his and squared her shoulders. "I don't plan on dying anytime soon. You can bet that if someone takes a crack at me, we'll bring him in for investigation."

Garner grinned. "I like your pluck, Miss Dawson."

"Call me Liv," she said.

"Liv it is." Garner smiled. "If you ever need anything, don't hesitate to ask."

"Thank you," Olivia said.

If Hawkeye wasn't mistaken, the ranch owner's eyes filled with tears, and she'd probably rather die than let them fall.

Blinking them back, she squared her shoulders again. "Now, if we're done here, we have a lot of work to do before sundown."

"We'll get to work on those names." Garner clapped a hand on Hawkeye's shoulder. "Be sure to yell if you need backup."

"You bet I will," Hawkeye promised. He'd seen how quickly events could escalate by the two incidents that had already occurred in the Grizzly Pass area. The kidnapping of a busload of children had happened so quickly, no one had anticipated the horror. It had taken their entire team and additional help from the sheriff's department and Homeland Security to get that disaster under control.

And the team had been mobilized again to bring one of their members out of a hunt where he and a local female had been the targets.

Damn right he'd call for backup if he smelled even a hint of trouble.

He prayed that Olivia's misfortune wouldn't continue. But he wouldn't place bets on peace and tranquillity. Not now. Not until they found the man responsible and fully understood his motivation for killing her father.

Chapter Eight

Liv settled back in her seat, her mind moving a hundred times faster than the speed of the truck. "When I came back to Grizzly Pass, I thought my father had died due to an accident. That was hard enough to accept. But now…" She shook her head. "If someone killed him for his land…" Her fists clenched in her lap and she ground her teeth together. The injustice burned like a fire in her belly.

"We don't know that for sure yet."

"But you and Garner seem to think it has something to do with the ranch and maybe even the man you were chasing yesterday. Didn't you say he was trying to blow up the pipeline?"

"It appeared to be his goal."

"And he crossed onto my property to escape, as if he'd been across my land before and knew his way. It's easy to get lost in the hills. He had to know how to get back to the road across that corner of the ranch."

Hawkeye nodded. "That would be my assumption. I had a contour map to get around with, and it was slow going because I didn't know the existing trails and paths. The man I chased out of the hills knew the way."

"Through my property." Olivia clamped her teeth together, anger simmering. What was important enough to kill a man who'd done nothing to anyone? A man who'd spent his life working with his land and livestock? Again, her heart pinched in her chest. If she found out who'd done this, she'd…she'd…

Hell, she wanted to kill the one responsible. But if she did, would she be any better than him? Would her father want her to risk going to jail for killing a man who'd taken his life?

Still the anger roiled.

By the time they'd entered the gate to Stone Oak Ranch, Liv was ready to jump out of the truck and run all the way up the driveway to the barn. Her pent-up rage and energy were ready to explode into action. Holding them back challenged her patience like nothing before. But she did hold them back. All the way to the barn, where Hawkeye pulled his truck to a stop.

She was out of the truck and lowering the tailgate before Hawkeye had time to shift into Park and turn off the engine.

CJ emerged from the barn, sweat-soaked and pushing a full wheelbarrow of straw and horse dung. He parked the wheelbarrow to the side and hurried over to grab a sack of feed. The teen didn't look strong enough to carry the fifty-pound bag, but he slung it over his shoulder like a pro and carried it into the barn without being asked or told to help.

Liv smiled across the bed of the truck at Hawkeye. "I like him already."

Hawkeye nodded. "Me, too." He gathered two bags, lifting them to his shoulder.

Liv loaded a feed bag onto her own shoulder and followed the ranger into the barn, admiring his strength and stamina. She could sure use someone like him on the ranch.

As soon as the thought emerged, she squashed it. The man was all about his military connection. He'd want to return to his unit as soon as his assignment was up in Grizzly Pass.

Liv couldn't get used to having him around. She'd really have to get onto the task of hiring a ranch hand soon. Abe wouldn't be able to help for weeks and CJ's school would be back in session soon, leaving her to handle everything by herself.

She wanted to keep the ranch, but she knew her limitations. It took her father and Abe working full-time and then some to keep up. And they hired additional ranch hands at roundup to work the ranch, tag, vaccinate, deworm and castrate the young steers. It was a huge effort, requiring veterinary, management and accounting skills to run a place like Stone Oak Ranch. Liv couldn't do it on her own. But maybe if she had at least one really good ranch hand, Abe could manage the books while he recuperated.

Once the feed bags were stacked and two had been poured into bins, Liv inspected CJ's work in the stalls. He'd done as good a job, if not a better one, mucking stalls as Liv would have. "Great work, CJ."

The teen's cheeks turned a ruddy red. "Thank you, ma'am."

"Call me Liv. *Ma'am* makes me feel old," she said with a smile.

"Yes, ma'am— Sorry, Miss Liv." Again the blush rose in his cheeks.

Liv flattened her smile, not wanting to embarrass the youth any more than she already had.

"I had planned on cleaning the horses' hooves and exercising them this afternoon," CJ said. "Unless there's something else you'd like me to work on."

"No. That will be perfect." Liv studied the teen. "You have cared for horses' hooves before?"

His eyes widened. "Oh, yes, ma'am—er—Miss Liv. My stepfather has four horses at home. I usually take care of them. I learned from the farrier how to do it when I was eight. I've been doing it ever since."

Eight? Liv was amazed at this young man who seemed older than his sixteen years. "Just be careful not to dig too deep."

The teen nodded. "I'll be very careful. I love to work with horses and they seem to like me."

"I'll be out this afternoon checking fences with Mr. Walsh. If you need anything, I won't be much help. If you get into any trouble, call the sheriff. It's near lunchtime now. You're welcome to make yourself at home in the kitchen. There's peanut butter and jelly and a loaf of bread."

"Thank you, Miss Liv." He ducked his head. "I really appreciate the job."

She couldn't help herself. Liv leaned close and

hugged the teen's bony shoulders. "And I appreciate the help."

"What time do you expect to be back?" CJ asked.

"Before the sun sets," she answered. "But if we're not back by then, don't worry. We'll be okay."

"I have to be home an hour before dark to take care of my chores. Do you want me to stay until you get back?"

"No, but there is something you can do this afternoon before you leave." Liv tipped her head. "Follow me," she called over her shoulder. "You can come too, Mr. Walsh."

CJ and Hawkeye followed her to a separate garage behind the house. Inside was a collection of dusty antique furniture, car parts and tool chests. In the far corner was something under a faded and dusty tarp.

Liv suppressed her smile as she pulled the tarp off, sending a cloud of dust flying into the air.

When the cloud cleared, she could see her old scooter. "I used this scooter through college in Seattle. It got me around great, although I don't recommend driving it in the snow and ice."

CJ shook his head and looked from the scooter to Liv. "I don't understand. Do you want me to fix it for you? Fix it to sell?"

"It should be in good working condition. My father was pretty consistent about cranking it up at least once or twice a year. He'd change the oil, even if he didn't use it." She inhaled and let out the breath in a long steady stream. "It's yours if you want it."

CJ's eyes widened and he shook his head. "I can't accept it."

"Of course you can. I want an employee who can get here on time every day. Again, I don't expect you to drive it on icy roads. In fact, I don't want you to drive it in the winter at all." She touched his arm. "Promise you won't drive it on icy roads. I'd never be able to live with myself if something happened to you on this contraption."

CJ continued to shake his head. "I can't accept it."

"Why not? It's either that or it goes back under the tarp and deteriorates until it's no longer any good for anyone."

Despite her efforts to convince him, Liv couldn't get him to quit shaking his head.

"If I take this home, my stepfather will claim it as his. He says that anything he finds on his property is his."

"Then park it just off his property and walk in."

The teen's face brightened and then he chewed on his lip. "I suppose I could hide it in the woods by the road. Ernie doesn't have to know."

Liv didn't like setting the kid up to lie to his stepfather, but Ernie was just mean enough to take CJ's only method of transportation, forcing the teen to use his rusty bicycle or walk the ten miles to Stone Oak Ranch.

CJ walked forward and ran his hand across the vinyl seat. "Why are you doing this for me?" he whispered.

"I'm not doing it so much for you as for me," Liv said. "I need to know you won't have problems getting here, and I need to know you won't be too tired to work."

The teen shot a glance back at Liv. "May I sit on it?"

"You bet. I hope you can get it going before you leave."

CJ swung his leg over the seat and sat on the smooth faux leather. "I'll work on it after I take care of the horses."

"Good. Try not to do anything that will cause you injury, since no one will be here as your backup."

"I'm used to working on my own," CJ said. "And you don't have to pay me at all. I'll work off the cost of the scooter. I could never repay you for your generosity." He twisted the throttle handle.

"Repaying me isn't necessary, and I intend to pay you for your work. But you'll have to get your mother's permission to ride the scooter."

"She'll let me."

"And your stepfather?"

"What he doesn't know won't hurt me." The teen's face hardened. "As long as I have my mother's permission, it shouldn't be a problem."

"Thank you for helping out. With my foreman in the hospital, I wasn't sure how I would manage." Liv smiled. "Now I have to get to work mending fences."

"I could help with the fences," CJ said, his tone eager, his enthusiasm contagious. "I know how to stretch wire and I'm pretty handy with a hammer."

"I really need you to take care of the animals around here. I'm sure I'll take you up on that offer another time." Liv cast a glance toward Hawkeye. "Ready?"

"You bet." He followed her out into the open. "You made that kid's day."

"I just hope I don't cause more problems between him and his stepfather."

"I'm sure that comes with the territory for CJ. I don't think there's much love lost between Ernie and the kid." Hawkeye glanced around. "We're taking my truck?"

She shook her head and walked toward the pasture. "No. The trails are too narrow for a full-size truck to make it safely onto the back end of the property in the hills." She stood at the gate to the pasture and gave a shrill whistle.

Her gray gelding trotted up to the fence and nuzzled her hand. "I'm taking Stormy. You can choose any horse you might like to ride. They're all trained for ranch work and are familiar with trail riding."

HAWKEYE SHOOK HIS HEAD. As tempted as he was, a promise was a promise. "I'll pass."

"You're missing out. Riding horses up into the hills is much more serene than taking loud, motorized vehicles." Liv caught Stormy's bridle and snapped a lead onto one of the metal rings. She turned to Hawkeye. "There are two four-wheelers in the back of the barn. You're welcome to take one of them. You can carry the barbed wire and fence staples."

Hawkeye reached out to rub the gelding's nose. "Thank you for understanding."

Liv led the horse toward the barn. "I understand, but I'm sure your mother wouldn't hold you to a promise you made when you were a kid. Especially since you've been to war and faced much worse circumstances than being tossed from a horse."

He nodded. "True. And someday, I might change my mind, but for now, I'd rather not ride a horse."

"I respect that, but you'll have to stay back a ways so that you don't spook my horse on some of the more difficult trails."

"Are you sure you don't want to ride a four-wheeler?" Hawkeye suggested. "You said you had two."

"I prefer horseback." She led her horse into the barn and tied him to a post. "I only take the motorized vehicles when I have to carry fence posts or other large items that would be too bulky on horseback."

"Like rolls of barbed wire?"

She nodded, her lips turning up slightly at the corners. As he suspected, she'd planned on him taking the four-wheeler all along. If he didn't have to carry the barbed wire and staples, he'd be tempted to break his promise and ride a horse, just to prove to her that he wasn't afraid. But not today. They had real work to do and would need the tools and supplies to accomplish the job.

"Fair enough," he said. "While you saddle up, I'll check the status of my transportation."

Grabbing the roll of barbed wire and the bucket of staples, Hawkeye walked to the back of the barn and found two four-wheelers tucked beneath the ladder leading up to the loft. Neither vehicle was new, and both had been scuffed enough to indicate they'd been used on rough terrain. Each ATV had metal mesh racks on the front and back and a rifle scabbard mounted on the right side.

Hawkeye dropped the bucket of fence staples and the

roll of barbed wire in the back rack and secured them with bungee cords and metal ties. He found a couple of hammers in the tack room and a come-along hanging on the wall.

As part of his upbringing on the ranch, he'd learned many skills, including proper fence building and mending. He'd need to bring every tool necessary with him or the project would end before it started. Once they were up in the mountains, it wouldn't be so easy to run back to the barn for supplies or equipment.

Once he had everything loaded and tied down, he shifted the ATV to Neutral and pushed it out the back door of the barn before twisting the key in the ignition.

The engine leaped to life, blowing very little smoke. Olivia's father and foreman had kept the ATVs in good working order.

Hawkeye mounted and revved the accelerator while still in Neutral before shifting it into gear and driving it around to the front of the barn.

Olivia stood with the saddled gray, the reins draped over her gloved hands. "I'll get the gate." She led the horse to the fence, pulled back the bar and let the gate swing open.

Hawkeye drove past her and waited on the other side of the fence for Olivia to lead her horse through, close the gate and mount. She took off at a trot across the pasture and up into the hills, following a broad trail that was wide enough for his truck. That trail started to narrow to barely the width of the four-wheeler's tires.

Hawkeye trailed fifty feet behind, careful not to get too close and spook Stormy. He lost sight of Olivia at several sharp bends in the path, but would soon spot her ahead. Every time she slipped from his view, his heart pounded and he instinctively goosed the accelerator, kicking up gravel and rocks beneath his tires. He could see the benefit of riding a horse in that the only sound would be the clip-clop of the animal's hooves on the stones.

The roar of the ATV engine drowned out all other sounds around Hawkeye, a fact he regretted. If Olivia were to scream, he probably wouldn't hear it until it was too late. If she'd driven another four-wheeler, at least he could have followed her more closely, keeping her within his line of sight at all times.

Surely the promise he'd made to his mother had reached its statute of limitations. Given the severity of the situation on Stone Oak Ranch, Hawkeye needed every advantage he could get. Hearing the enemy before he saw them would be a major advantage. One he currently couldn't claim. He found himself more than a little frustrated the entire journey to the far northwestern corner of the ranch.

Rounding yet another outcropping of rock, he searched for the woman on horseback and held his breath until he found her. She'd stopped near a fence post where the wire had been cut and the barbed strands lay in big coils several feet away.

Olivia sat on her horse, staring down at the fence. Then she swung her leg over the side and dropped down out of the saddle to the hard, rocky ground. For a long moment, she stared at the rocks, not the destroyed fence. Sunlight glinted off giant tears welling up in her eyes.

Hawkeye pulled his four-wheeler to a stop on the edge of the clearing, shut off the engine and climbed off. "What's wrong?"

Olivia continued to stare at the ground. "This is where he died." Then she looked up, the evidence of her grief clearly written across her face. Big tears slipped over the lower edges of her eyelids, ran down to her chin and dropped into the dirt. She sniffed and wiped at her tears. "I'm sorry. I'm not normally so weepy."

He crossed to her and pulled her into his arms, resting her cheek on his chest. "You have every right to be weepy."

"But it accomplishes nothing. My dad would have told me it's a waste of time and energy." She laughed, choking on a sob. "I never pointed out to him that he'd cried when my mother died. He didn't know I saw him by the barn, bent double, sobbing. My dad cried, too. That made him even more human and caring." She stared up at Hawkeye, tears trembling in her lashes. "I loved him so much."

Hawkeye gathered her closer and kissed her forehead. "I would like to have met him."

"Thanks for putting up with me."

"I wouldn't call it putting up with you. I kind of like holding you." He smoothed the hair back from her forehead and pressed a kiss there.

Liv leaned into him, her fingers curling into his chest. She held on, prolonging the pressure of his lips on her skin.

He loved the way she felt against him and the way

she smelled of the outdoors. But holding her wasn't getting the work done.

She must have come to the same conclusion because she straightened and pushed away from him. "Come on. We have a fence to mend before dark."

"Before we start on the fence, I'd like to cross over onto the other side and explore."

"I could start laying out the barbed wire and tools, while you do your thing on the other side," Olivia offered. "Then, when you get back, I'll show you how quickly I can string wire."

Before she finished speaking, Hawkeye was shaking his head. "You heard Garner. If someone wants this ranch bad enough to hurt your father, you're as much of a target."

She pulled a handgun from beneath her jacket and waved it in the air. "I can protect myself."

Hawkeye touched his finger to the barrel and pushed it away. "I'm sure you can handle yourself, but I'd feel better if you stayed right with me. I didn't even like it when you rode ahead of me on your horse."

She gave him a sassy glance from beneath her lashes. "Maybe next time, you'll ride a horse and we can stay closer."

"Or you can ride the other four-wheeler." He touched a finger to her cheek. "Please. Come with me for a few minutes. I'd like to see if I missed anything when I was chasing Demolition Man yesterday."

"All right. But I doubt anyone would want to hurt me. I haven't stayed here in years." She started for her horse, but Hawkeye grabbed her arm and pulled her short.

"Ride with me," he said, keeping the request low, insistent, a warm entreaty in her ear.

He prayed she couldn't resist the request when he made it seem so personal.

Her eyes flared wider, and her gaze dropped to his lips. She sighed. "Fine. I'll go with you."

"On the back of my four-wheeler," he said.

"I'd rather ride my horse."

"It puts too much distance between the two of us. I don't feel comfortable going off your property into government-controlled land where anyone could be watching or waiting."

"Anyone could be watching and waiting on my property." She swept her hand toward the downed fence.

"You have a point." He tipped his head toward the four-wheeler and gave her his best bone-melting half smile. "You can drive, if you want."

LIV'S HEART FLUTTERED and butterflies erupted in her belly. How could one man have such a hold over her? When he put it that way, with that smile… *Damn.* Who was she kidding? Though she wasn't eager to be in close proximity to the man who made her blood sing every time he got too close, she couldn't resist. But if they were going to ride double on a four-wheeler, she preferred to do the driving. It might be the only thing she had control over. She sure as heck didn't have control over her reactions to the man.

Liv climbed onto the ATV and waited for Hawkeye to get on the back.

When he did, he wrapped his arms around her waist and leaned his body into hers.

Holy hell, she was entirely too aware of the man holding on to her. Perhaps she'd have been better off riding on the back of the ATV. At least then she could have held on to the ATV seat, instead of wrapping her arms around Hawkeye's waist.

She'd let him drive back. At least then she wouldn't have his arms around her waist and she wouldn't be so confused...and...turned on.

Chapter Nine

Hawkeye held on tightly around Olivia's waist. Not only because he liked being close to her, but because she drove like a bat out of hell. If he hadn't held on, she'd have lost him a couple of times going around some of the tighter corners along the trail.

Thankfully, she seemed to know her way. He recognized the shapes of the ridges and the rugged trails down into the gorges. As they neared the trail down into the valley where he'd found the man planting the dynamite near the pipeline, he yelled, "Slow down."

Olivia brought the ATV to a halt on the top of the ridge overlooking the area.

Hawkeye cast a glance around, taking in the other hilltops, searching for any movement. Anyone with a weapon perched on the ridgelines could easily pick off someone at the bottom. His military training made him look at terrain that way. He was glad of that training. Not only had someone tried to plant explosives at this pipeline checkpoint, but a pipeline inspector had been killed there. Shot from one of the surrounding ridges.

Yeah, Hawkeye would do well to treat this as enemy

territory and be prepared for anything. "Let's go to the bottom. I want to check on something."

"Is this the place?" Olivia asked.

His chest tightened and he gave the neighboring hills another once-over with a trained eye. "Yeah."

Olivia thumbed the throttle lever and eased the four-wheeler down the trail into the valley.

Hawkeye had her park it in the shadows of a lodge-pole pine tree. When he got off, he pointed to the tree's trunk. "Stay here. If there is anyone after you, you won't present a decent target hidden in the shadows."

Olivia shook her head. "I'm not hiding from anyone. I have just as much right to be here as anyone else." She started past him.

Hawkeye snagged her arm and pulled her against his chest. "You aren't wearing a bulletproof vest or a Kevlar helmet. If someone takes a shot at you, you're dead. Who will take care of your family's ranch?"

"If I die, who cares? I don't have any family to leave the ranch to." Her lips pressed into a thin line, her shoulders pushing back, displaying an inner strength and a willingness to charge into danger and seek justice. But the mist in Olivia's eyes reminded Hawkeye of just how vulnerable she still was, having lost her father—the only relative she'd had left in the world.

"Yeah, you might not have a family to leave the ranch to, but you have an employee who, if I'm guessing right, is just as much a part of the family as your father. If you die, the ranch will be sold to the highest bidder and Abe will be out of a job. At his age, and still recovering from his broken leg, he'll have difficulty finding work."

Olivia frowned at Hawkeye. "Yeah, hit me where it hurts. Okay, I'll stay close to the shadows and I won't stand in one place very long. How's that? Make you more comfortable being with the walking target?" She gave him a wink, shook off his hand on her arm, strode out into the open and glanced at the disturbed ground where the dynamite had been planted and retrieved.

Hawkeye followed her, staying close, offering his body up as her first line of defense against gunfire.

"Seriously?" She pushed him away. "I don't want you taking a bullet for me. But thanks for the thought." After a quick inspection of the vicinity around the site, she stepped back into the shadows.

Hawkeye's lips quirked at the corners. He made a wider sweep of the area, looking for anything his dynamite-planting bad guy might have dropped. The place was clean.

"Anything else you want to look at while we're on this side of the fence?" Olivia asked, her gaze on the surrounding hills. "The sun drops behind the mountains a good thirty minutes before the scheduled sundown for this area. And from the looks of it, we'll have a cloudy night, which means darkness will come even sooner."

He glanced up at the surrounding hills. "Do you know of any caves around here?"

She nodded. "My dad and I used to explore the caves in the mountains whenever he had time. There are some with cave paintings hundreds of years old."

"Far from here?"

"Not very." She looked around. "It's been years, but I think I can find them. We'd better hurry, or we won't have time to mend the fence and get back to the house before dark."

Hawkeye glanced up at the thick gray clouds rolling in above the ridges. "We'll give it thirty minutes. If we don't find the caves by then, we'll head back."

Olivia nodded. "Deal." She climbed onto the four-wheeler and scooted forward.

Hawkeye hid a grin. He liked that Olivia was no-nonsense and brave. But he also worried she wasn't taking the threat to her life as seriously as he was. Her father was dead. You couldn't undo that. And the woman was growing on him. He'd hate to lose her when he was just getting to know her.

He slipped onto the back of the ATV, wrapped his arms around her narrow waist and inhaled the mix of herbal shampoo and the outdoors. Both scents would forever remind him of Olivia, even when he was back in some hellishly hot desert in the Middle East.

The thought of returning to war sobered him. Being on a ranch had brought back the good memories with the bad. Yeah, he'd lost his little sister, but working with the horses and cattle had always made him feel like his efforts counted. He could see the results of his efforts. Not so much in the army.

As for the horses, it wasn't that he didn't like them. He loved them. And he liked the smell of freshly cut hay and the earthy aroma of manure. Hell, he'd shoveled his share growing up. He could almost feel the straining muscles and the sweat of a hot summer's day working in the hay fields of Texas.

Hawkeye shook himself free of his memories and focused on the hills around him. By letting Olivia drive, he maintained the freedom to study the bluffs, searching for easily accessible caves.

When the day-care children had been kidnapped and trapped in an abandoned mine, their caregivers had discovered empty crates and boxes that had stored a pretty impressive number of AR-15 rifles. Which led them to ask: Who'd had the money to purchase so many? And even more disturbing was the question of where all the semiautomatic rifles had disappeared to.

These hills were riddled with natural caves and abandoned mines from the gold-rush era of the 1800s. There were any number of places someone could have hidden the rifles.

Hell, they could be in someone's barn or in a basement. Unless they discovered a list of the names of all the Free America members, they didn't really have a place to start looking or a chance at a warrant to search premises. So far, they only had a few names of suspected members. A judge wouldn't give a warrant to search based on pure supposition.

But something about this place out in the mountains meant something to someone. Enough for people to be murdered—the pipeline inspector and potentially Olivia's father. And it appeared that someone wanted the valley to be destroyed via dynamite.

Why? What was so important in these hills that people were dying over it?

Olivia shouted over the roar of the engine. "Check it out!" She pointed to the hillside ahead of her.

When the trail would have wound around a bluff to

the right, she slowed to a stop and shut down the engine so they could talk.

"That's one of the caves my father and I explored. I remember because it had a huge boulder in front of it that was shaped like a sitting frog." She smiled sadly. "The last time I was here, I was only fourteen. My dad and I rode horses out here and camped under the stars."

She started the engine and rounded the bend in the trail, curving along the side of the hill until they descended to a grassy glen at the foot of the cave entrance.

Hawkeye hopped off the ATV and held out his hand.

Olivia took it and swung her leg over the seat, dropping to the ground. She smiled. "There's the ring of stones my father put together for a fire." She walked across to the charred stones and frowned. Dropping to her haunches, she pushed aside the charred remains of a log and held her hand over a bed of ashes. "These are a lot more recent than anything from the last time I was here. Based on the residual warmth of the embers beneath the log, I'd say they were from last night." She straightened and glanced around.

Hawkeye stood close, turning his back to her, facing outward to the nearby hills. He didn't like that there were so many vantage points above them. A sniper would have an easy target to aim for. "Let's check out that cave," he said, backing toward her.

Olivia climbed the gravel- and boulder-strewn incline to the cave's entrance. She pulled her pistol from where it was tucked into her waistband and disappeared into the shadows.

His pulse quickening, Hawkeye hurried in after her,

his weapon drawn. It took a moment for his eyesight to adjust to the darkness. When it did, he was amazed at how big the inside of the cave was compared to the narrow entry. The trickle of light was just enough to illuminate the walls closest to the entrance.

"Look." Olivia stood near the side of the cave, staring at the wall in front of her.

Hawkeye studied the interior of the cavern, searching for any movement. The dark abyss of a tunnel gaped like an open maw. Without a flashlight, he didn't have a chance of penetrating its inky depths.

In the limited lighting, he could make out the cave wall and rudimentary drawings in dark red, mustard yellow and black. One was a picture of a bear standing tall in front of a hunter holding a spear. Another painting included two figures sporting clubs in a face-off with what appeared to be a pack of wolves.

"Aren't these beautiful?" Olivia whispered, as if they stood in a library or a museum.

"Incredible." Hawkeye sighed. "I wish I'd thought to bring a flashlight."

"Like this?" A click echoed off the cave walls and a narrow beam of light cut a line through the darkness. Olivia held a small key chain flashlight in her hand. "It's not much, but I carry it in my pocket in case I need it in a pinch."

As he took the light from Olivia's hand, Hawkeye shook his head, leaned in and captured her lips in a quick kiss. "You are an amazing woman."

Hawkeye shone the light around the interior of the cave. The beam didn't go far, but it was far enough to see that the cave wasn't that deep and nothing but the paintings were of interest inside. He returned the beam to its original position and caught Olivia with her fingers touching her lips.

Her cheeks were pink and her eyes narrowed slightly. "You really shouldn't kiss me."

He liked that he'd flustered her. "Why not?"

"Because it makes me want to kiss you back…" she said, her voice trailing off, her eyes widening as he closed the distance between them.

"Does it?" Hawkeye wrapped his arm around her waist and drew her body against his. "Then I should kiss you again." He didn't know why he was pushing the issue, but he knew he couldn't resist another kiss from this strong, beautiful woman. He lowered his head, his lips hovering over hers. "Show me."

Liv's heart fluttered and a deep ache built inside her belly, spreading lower. She leaned up on her toes and pressed her mouth to his.

As soon as they connected, Hawkeye's arm tightened around her, crushing her against him. His tongue drew a line along the seam of her lips.

She opened to him and met his tongue stroke for stroke, loving the taste and feel of him. Until she kissed Hawkeye, Liv had never known a desire so intense that she forgot everything around her.

When her lungs reminded her she needed air, she tore her mouth from his and sucked in ragged, shaky breaths. "What is wrong with me?"

Hawkeye leaned his cheek against her temple. "Nothing. As far as I can tell, you're just about perfect."

She shook her head. "The more I learn about what's been happening around here, the more I'm convinced my father was murdered. And I'm standing in a cave kissing a stranger when I should be out searching for my father's killer." She stared up at him. "I must be a very bad person."

"Or a very good kisser." He brushed a light kiss over her mouth. "But you're right. We should be focusing on what's going on. There will be time for kisses later."

If you're still around. Liv didn't say the words out loud, but she felt them, and it added more sadness to her heart, already breaking over the loss of her father.

As if on cue, they broke apart.

Liv turned toward the back of the cave. "Is there nothing in here of interest?"

"Nothing but the paintings and us." He rested his fingers in the small of her back and led her to the cave entrance. Then he took her hand as they walked and slid down the slippery slope to where they'd parked the four-wheeler in the shade of a bush.

Liv liked the feel of his big hand holding hers. She'd never thought of herself as a girlie-girl, but Hawkeye made her feel delicate and protected. Her chest swelled at his touch, and for a moment she felt some things were right in a world gone wrong.

With her hand on the ATV's grip, Liv was about to throw her leg over the seat when Hawkeye touched her arm. "Do you hear that?"

She was so caught up in her blossoming feelings for

the army ranger, Liv hadn't noticed the buzz of small engines until five ATVs popped up over the top of a ridge and came careening down the hillside straight for where she and Hawkeye were standing. Each of the riders wore a dark helmet and dark clothing, and they didn't appear to be slowing down a bit as they barreled down the side of the hill.

"What the hell?" Liv said.

"Damn, they've got guns," Hawkeye said.

At the same time Hawkeye made note of that fact, Liv saw one of the men aiming a handgun at them. A shot rang out, echoing against the bluffs. Dirt kicked up at Liv's feet, making her jump back.

"Let's get out of here!" Hawkeye jumped on the bike, started the engine and barely waited long enough for Liv to hop on the back and wrap her arms around his middle.

He thumbed the throttle, sending the four-wheeler leaping forward, heading for the trail that had brought them down into the valley.

Liv craned her neck, staring back at the five ATVs rushing toward them. She held on tighter and screamed, "Faster!"

Hawkeye bumped up onto the trail and gunned the accelerator, spinning loose rocks and gravel up in their wake.

The five pursuers didn't slow. They hit the grassy glen and sped up, rocketing across the flat expanse and up onto the trail Liv and Hawkeye were following. It wouldn't be long before they caught up.

They had to find a place to hide or set up a defensive

position. Hell, Liv wasn't the army guy—Hawkeye was. Surely he had a plan.

They rounded a bend in the trail heading back toward her ranch. At the rate the others were racing along, they'd catch up before Liv and Hawkeye made it to the fence. Not that the broken strands of barbed wire would stop the gang. Continuing to run wasn't an option.

The trail curved around a jutting bluff, blocking her view of their pursuers, which meant they couldn't see her and Hawkeye, either. If only they could throw them off.

Think, Liv. Think!

Then she remembered a maze of huge boulders and a line of caves carved out of the rocky hillside in the valley on the other side of the upcoming ridge.

The trail would split ahead. The left fork would take them back to her property.

As they neared the fork in the trail, Liv yelled over the sound of the engine, "Take the right fork."

Already halfway turned toward the left, Hawkeye yanked the handlebar to the right, making them skid sideways. He held on tightly to keep the ATV from tumbling over the edge of the trail and down a steep hill into a stand of trees.

Liv glanced behind them. The dust cloud that plumed behind them was caught in the breeze and blown toward the left fork. If they could round the next bend in the next two seconds, they might succeed in throwing off the gang of bikers behind them.

She held her breath, turned halfway in her seat and

watched for the following vehicles to emerge from behind the bluff outcropping.

Hawkeye spun the four-wheeler around a bend in the trail and still Liv hadn't seen the trailing vehicles. "When you get to the huge boulder at the base of the hill, swing around behind it!" she yelled into Hawkeye's ear.

He nodded without slowing, hurtling around the curves descending into another narrow valley between hilltops.

Liv watched behind them, her heart pounding each time she thought she caught a glimpse of the others behind them. If they could make the boulder-strewn valley before the others, they could lose them in the maze of bus-size boulders and very rough terrain.

At the bottom of the trail, Hawkeye slowed and swung around the back side of the giant boulder Liv remembered from when she was a teen. The ground was littered with larger rocks, making the going a lot more difficult and much slower. But the rocks wouldn't leave tracks. If they could stay hidden from above, they had a chance at making it to one of the caves where they could hide.

Liv held on for dear life, nearly tossed several times as they rumbled across the rocks and clung to the lengthening shadows of the hillside. Soon the sun was completely hidden behind a dark gray pall of clouds and darkness descended on the rocky valley.

When she thought they might have escaped the others, Liv tugged on Hawkeye's arm and pointed to one of the caves hidden behind a huge rocky outcropping. "There."

He aimed the four-wheeler toward the cave and drove up the steep slope through the entrance and cut the engine as soon as they were inside.

Liv and Hawkeye jumped off and pushed the vehicle the rest of the way inside, hiding it in the darkness.

Pulling her mini flashlight from her pocket, Liv shone it into the interior of the cave, praying they hadn't walked into the den of a wolf or a bear. Or worse, that they'd stumbled into a timber rattler's home.

She shivered in the damp coolness of the cavern, clicked off the light when she was certain they were safe from what was inside the space. Then she crept up to the edge of the entrance and stood beside Hawkeye.

"I can still hear their engines," he whispered.

She listened, her heartbeat fluttering. "Me, too. But it's getting dark. I'll bet they're not willing to keep looking when the sun is setting. It's too easy to get lost in the mountains."

Hawkeye snorted. "Tell me about it." He glanced down at her. "I'm going out to perform a little recon to see how close they are."

"I'll go with you," she said.

"No. Two people are easier to spot than one."

"And if you get into trouble?" She raised her brows. "Who has your six?"

"I'll stay out of sight."

"So will I."

"Anyone ever tell you that you're stubborn?"

She nodded. "Many times. I consider it one of my good traits."

He shook his head. "Fine. But if I say get down, do it, immediately."

She gave him a mock salute and followed him out of the cave.

They crept along the base of the rocky bluff stretching the length of the narrow valley until they came close to the stand of boulders blocking their view of the trail.

Liv could hear the rumble of engines close by. Too close.

She laid her hand on Hawkeye's arm. "Let's go back."

He touched a finger across her lips. "Stay here," he whispered. "I want to see if I recognize any of them."

"And get yourself killed?" Liv increased the pressure on his arm. "Don't."

"I'll be okay." He gripped her arms. "But only if you stay put. If you come after me, I'll lose focus and we might both be found." He pressed a firm kiss on her lips. "Promise me you'll stay."

Liv wanted to tell him no. She couldn't promise not to follow him. But the intensity of his gaze made her nod. "Okay. I promise."

"Good girl." He kissed her again. "I'll be right back." Then he slipped away into the shadows of dusk.

Before long, Liv couldn't pick him out from among the boulders. She hunkered down in case someone was watching from above and remained as still as she could, straining to hear what was going on.

The engines had been shut off. Male voices bounced

off the sides of the bluffs, their echoes making them sound like they were closer than they were.

Liv held her breath, waiting for a shout to go up that they'd found Hawkeye. If that happened, all bets were off and she'd come out fighting. She had her pistol. She had at least ten rounds in the magazine.

With her hand on the weapon, she waited, counting to one hundred, then counting to one hundred again. By the time she'd counted backward from one hundred, she had waited as long as she possibly could. Liv bunched her muscles and started to rise.

One of the men's shouts was loud and clear. "Let's go!"

Engines fired to life and took off, heading back the way they'd come. Did they have Hawkeye with them? Was he lying on the ground, bleeding out? Had they crushed his skull?

Scenario after horrible scenario ran through Liv's head. She was on her feet and had taken two steps in the direction Hawkeye had disappeared when he emerged from the shadows and pulled her into his arms.

"Why are you shaking?" he asked, rubbing his hands up and down her back.

"Damn you," she said into his shirt. "You had me so worried." She hadn't realized she was shaking until he'd called attention to the fact. Her teeth were chattering and she was cold.

"We need to get you out of here and back home."

"We can't leave. What if that gang is waiting at the fork in the road, or if they've gone to where the fence is down and are lying in wait to jump out and cut us down?"

Hawkeye sighed. "You're right. But it's too cold to stand out here. Let's go back to the four-wheeler. If the stars and the moon come out tonight, we might be able to find our way home."

Liv nodded, not really ready to step out of Hawkeye's embrace to walk back across the increasingly difficult, ankle-twisting terrain.

The clouds descended on the mountains, cutting off any light from the stars above, making it harder and harder to see. They almost missed the cave, finally finding it when they were nearly past the hidden entrance.

Stumbling inside, Liv stood with her arms wrapped around her middle. "Now what?"

"I'm going to find some firewood."

"We can't light a fire. What if they see us?"

"For later. They won't stay out in the cold if they don't have to. Besides, as well hidden as this cave is, they won't see the glow of the flames."

A fire sounded good. The later it got, the more the air temperature dropped.

"I hope they don't find Stormy," Liv said, through chattering teeth.

"I'm betting your horse is back at the barn by now."

Liv smiled. When Stormy was hungry, there wasn't much that could stop him on his way back to the barn for feed. Her biggest worries for the night were the return of the trigger-happy four-wheeler terrorists and the chilled air.

If they didn't start a fire, they could die of exposure.

It wasn't unusual for the temperatures in the late summer to be in the high eighties during the day and drop into the low fifties, even forties, at night. She'd even seen it snow in the mountains in August.

"I'll help with the firewood," Liv said and walked outside with Hawkeye.

Fortunately, some was close by and they didn't have to go far to gather enough logs and kindling for a decent blaze.

By the time they returned to the cave, what little lingering daylight that had helped them find the cave in the first place had been leached from the sky and replaced by inky blackness.

Liv touched the button for the mini flashlight, which gave them just enough light to arrange some stones in a circle and place the kindling and firewood in the center.

"I don't suppose you have a match or a lighter?" Hawkeye asked.

Liv shone the light toward the four-wheeler. "We used to keep a small survival kit in the storage compartment of each four-wheeler, and in our saddlebags in case we got caught out at night. I can't imagine my dad changing things up." She handed the flashlight to him and rummaged in the small compartment, unearthing a box of matches. She kissed the box. "Thanks, Dad." Then she handed them to Hawkeye and watched as he used only one match and coaxed the tinder into a flame that eventually ignited the logs.

The fire made the inside of the cave glow, giving it a warm and cozy feel.

Liv's body shook for an entirely different reason now.

With just the two of them in the cave, with an intimate fire burning, Liv's imagination went wild.

One glance across the gentle flames into Hawkeye's gaze let her know he might just be thinking along the same lines.

Her heart thundered against her ribs and a fire lit inside her. The night had a whole new set of possibilities.

Chapter Ten

Hawkeye stared across the fire at Olivia, his pulse kicking up several notches.

Her green eyes reflected the flames of the fire burning in the circle. She stood with her hands curled around her elbows. And she was staring at him. Her tongue snaked out to trail across her lower lip.

Holy hell, how was he going to keep his hands off the woman all night long? He'd have to stay awake enough to keep the fire burning, but what he was more concerned about was the desire building like molten lava pressing against the earth's crust. If he didn't find a relief valve soon, that hot lava would erupt and spill all over the interior of the cave and flow right into Olivia.

Somewhere along the way, her long hair had slipped free of the ponytail. Now it lay in wild disarray around her shoulders and down her back. She looked like a wild, untamed Valkyrie, ready to make her stand.

"I don't suppose you kept a stash of nuts or jerky in that compartment, did you?" Not that he was hungry for food. He'd rather feast on the woman standing before him.

Well, damn. He'd promised himself he wouldn't get involved with a woman again while he was on active duty. One-night stands were okay because he refused to make commitments. Unfortunately, Olivia wasn't the one-night-stand kind of woman.

She deserved better. She needed a man who could work alongside her, help her run the ranch and give her an entire houseful of children.

That man wasn't Hawkeye. With a career in the army, children weren't in the cards for him as long as he was on active duty. War took him away too often, for up to fourteen months at a time. He didn't want any kid of his growing up without a father. And he didn't want the mother of his children to have to raise them alone. Not while running a ranch. That would be impossible. If he were killed in battle, where would that leave his wife? Alone and raising kids without help.

Of course, a man could die from being thrown by a horse, or killed in a car wreck. But he was more likely to be thrown into harm's way in the military. It took a special kind of woman to stand by her man while he was away. And it took a special man to make the sacrifices necessary to do right by his wife and children.

And he was back to the fact that stood out most in his mind—Olivia wasn't a one-night-stand kind of woman.

Which meant he had to keep his hands to himself.

But when she looked at him across the fire, with her soft green eyes so wide and trusting and full of...

Lust?

His pulse hammered in his veins, pushing blood low in his groin.

If he explained it to her, she could make the choice. If she said no, that would be the end of it.

"Olivia," he started, his voice catching. He cleared his throat and rounded the fire pit to stand in front of her. "We should talk."

She nodded. "What do you want to talk about?"

He took her hand in his and stared down at her fingers—so small, yet capable.

The first mistake.

As soon as their skin touched, an electric current zipped through him and couldn't be undone. He lifted her fingers to his lips and pressed a kiss to the backs of her knuckles. "You know I'm here on a temporary basis."

She nodded. "I know."

"I have a career with the army."

Her lips curled slightly upward. "I know that, too."

"Whatever it is we're feeling…"

She stepped closer, bringing their joined hands up, sandwiching them between their bodies. "Go on." Her gaze lifted to his, forcing him to face her, to say what came next.

"I find you very attractive."

She chuckled. "Even when I smell like a horse and my hair is a tangled mess?"

"You've never been more beautiful with the flames emphasizing the fiery red highlights in your hair." He reached up and brushed a strand back from her cheek.

"Are you trying to let me down easy?" she asked, her gaze dropping to his mouth. "Before we've been out on even one date?" She shook her head.

"When this assignment is done, I'll be back with my unit, possibly shipping out to another assignment in the Middle East."

"I know." She leaned up on her toes and brushed his lips with hers. "What's your point?"

"I can't make any commitments." There, he'd said it. He'd more or less told her that anything they might have between them wouldn't last. It was her turn to tell him to take a walk. That she wasn't interested.

"Who said I wanted commitment? I have my own life and my own responsibilities. Besides, we barely know each other."

"I know enough about you to realize you deserve a man who can stick around and help you on your ranch."

She spread her fingers across his chest. "I can hire a ranch hand for that."

"You need a man who will be there for you 24/7."

She tilted her head. "Haven't I told you? I can take care of myself."

He smiled. "Yes, you can. But you deserve someone you can depend on when the going gets tough."

"I have Abe," she countered.

"What I'm saying is— Oh, hell." He sighed and pushed a hand through his hair. "I'm only good for a one-night stand. You deserve better."

"Who said I wanted more?" She traced his jawline with the tip of her finger. "What if I have too much on my plate for anything more?"

Hawkeye groaned. "Do you know how much I want to make love to you?"

She pressed her body to his. "I do now."

He dropped his hands to her hips and pulled her against him, loving the feel of her soft belly against his hardness. "This isn't how I pictured making love to you."

She grinned. "So you've been thinking about it?"

He nodded. "You're an amazing woman. You're strong, independent and sit a horse like you belong there."

She leaned up on her toes and kissed his chin. "I thought you didn't like horses." Then she touched her lips to his in the gentlest of brushes.

"I never said I didn't like horses."

She moved her hips, rubbing against that very sensitive and engorged part of his body.

He drew in a steadying breath. "I'm going to go to hell for this."

She laced her hands at the back of his head. "Then take me with you." Pulling his head down to hers, she kissed him, thrusting her tongue past his teeth to parry with his.

He took her mouth, claiming it as his own, his hands roaming over her shoulders, down her back to the curve of her buttocks. She was strong, passionate and his.

For the moment. And he had no intention of missing out on that moment.

Olivia gave as good as she got, thrusting, twisting and tangling with him. But then, in the middle of the kiss, she stiffened and pulled back. "Please tell me you have protection."

He drew his head back and stared down at her, his brain fogged with lust. "What? Protection?" It took him a full second to realize what she was talking about. Then he remembered he still carried his wallet in his back pocket. He fumbled for it, flipped it open and dug inside until his fingers closed around a foil packet.

He held up the treasure. "We're covered."

"Good, because I can't wait much longer." She unzipped her jacket and let it fall to the floor. Then she flicked the buttons loose on her blouse and pushed it over her shoulders.

While Hawkeye slipped the straps of her bra down Olivia's arms, she shoved his jacket over his shoulders and dropped it to the floor.

Her breasts spilled from the cups of her bra into his hands and he bent to kiss the tips of both, one at a time.

Hawkeye straightened, tugged his T-shirt from the waistband of his jeans and ripped it up over his head. He bent to spread his jacket and T-shirt across the smooth surface of the cave, near the fire. Turning to Olivia, he held out his hand.

She took his and walked to him. "You still have time to back out."

He chuckled. "That's my line."

With a shrug, she reached for the button on his jeans. "Just saying. If you aren't feeling it, don't think you have to go through with this."

"Have you changed your mind?" He caught her hands in his, stilling her fingers from tugging his zipper down.

"No. I'm all in on this adventure."

Hawkeye released her hands.

She slid the zipper down and pushed the jeans over his hips and past his thighs.

His patience stretched too thin, Hawkeye shoved them the rest of the way down, toed off his boots and stepped out of the jeans. The cool night air couldn't begin to chill his desire for the woman standing in front of him.

When she reached for the button on her jeans, he brushed her hands aside and took over. In a slow, steady motion, he lowered the zipper and smoothed her jeans down her gorgeous legs to her ankles. There he helped her out of her boots and jeans, and the cute pink bikini panties that surprised him.

"Pink?"

"I might not be a girlie-girl on the outside, but I like pretty underthings." Olivia cupped his cheeks, leaned up to kiss him and then dragged her lips over his chin and down his neck to his collarbone.

"Sweetheart, you're burning a path right through me." He swept her up into his arms and laid her down on the shirt and jacket, pressing a kiss to the pulse beating wildly at the base of her throat. "Promise me you'll have no regrets."

"The only regret I might have is that you're taking it too slow and easy." She captured his face between her palms. "Foreplay can be entirely overrated. Besides, my body is on fire."

"Are you too close to the flames?"

"You could say that. But the heat has nothing to do with the campfire." She wrapped her leg around the back of his, rubbing her sex against his thigh.

With the fire keeping the chill night air at bay and providing a warm, inviting glow, Hawkeye knew he wouldn't last long if he took her fast. He wanted her to enjoy their lovemaking as much as he did. For that to happen, he had to take her there, a little at a time.

He dropped down over her, leaning his weight on one arm, his knee nudging her thighs apart.

She spread them wide enough for him to slip between.

He pressed his erection, pulsing and hard, to her entrance and held it there without penetrating. Once again, he claimed her lips, kissing her long and tender, thrusting his tongue between her teeth, mimicking what their bodies would be doing next. "Woman, do you have any idea how much I want you?"

LIV LAUGHED, THE SOUND echoing off the walls of the cave. "Oh, I have a clue." And she was every bit as turned on as he was. If he didn't get moving soon, she would explode into a thousand little pieces.

Olivia gripped his buttocks and pulled him toward her, trying to get him to consummate their lovemaking. She wanted him. Inside her. Now.

He resisted her insistent grasp, refusing to enter. Instead, he slipped lower, sliding his lips down the long column of her throat to the base where the pulse beat so rapidly she was afraid her heart would spontaneously combust.

Moving lower, Hawkeye skimmed over the swell of her breast and stopped at her right nipple, sucking the beaded tip into his mouth. Pulling hard, he tongued, flicked and nibbled it.

Liv arched her back off the floor of the cave, gripped the back of Hawkeye's head and urged him to take more.

He did, taking half of her breast into his mouth. Then he switched to the other and treated it to the same sensuous delights.

A moan escaped her lips. "Oh, please, don't make me wait. I want you inside me."

"When you're ready," he said, his lips trailing a path down her torso to the tuft of hair covering her sex.

"Honey, any more ready and I'll come apart."

He parted her folds and blew a warm stream of air over her heated flesh.

Liv dug her heels into the ground and lifted her hips. She wanted more. Hell, she *needed* more. "Please," she whispered.

Hawkeye bent his head and tongued her there.

A burst of sensations swept over her, the tension inside building, like a bowstring pulled back until it was so taut it might snap. How much more could she take? Liv felt like she teetered on a precipice, her body no longer under her control.

Hawkeye pressed two fingers into her and swirled his tongue over that most sensitive strip of flesh, sending her flying over the edge, jolts of electricity catapulting her into the stratosphere. She dug her fingers into his scalp and lifted her hips, her back straining, her body so tight she couldn't move as wave after wave washed over her.

She rode it all the way to the shore. When she could

breathe again, she tugged on Hawkeye's hair, grabbed his shoulder and pulled him up her body. "Now. I need you inside me, now!"

He chuckled, his body sliding against hers, his hips dropping down between her thighs. "Are you ready?"

"Oh, yes!" She dug her fingernails into his butt cheeks.

"Will you do the honors?" He handed her the foil packet.

She tore it open and rolled it down over him in less time than it took to say *make love to me*.

Then he was pressing into her, his girth stretching her, filling her. He slid deeper, until he could go no farther. For a long, excruciating moment, he paused, letting her channel adjust to his size.

She pushed his hips away.

He let her guide him in the slow, steady strokes.

Liv raised her hips to match his thrusts with ones of her own.

Soon, he took over, bracing his hands on either side of her. He pumped in and out of her, increasing in speed and intensity until he was slamming in and out of her, again and again.

The same sensations rose inside all over again, exploding in a flash of electrical impulses, tingling from her core all the way out to her fingertips and toes.

Hawkeye thrust one last time, burying himself all the way inside her where he remained, his staff throbbing against her channel, his buttocks tight, his face strained.

At last, he collapsed against her and rolled them both to the side, placing her backside to the fire.

Liv lay there for a long time, loving that they were still intimately connected. Being with Hawkeye gave a whole new meaning to sleeping by the campfire. She could do this again. And again.

With the warmth of the fire behind her and Hawkeye's heat in front, she snuggled close and shut her eyes. "Do you think they will come back and find us tonight?"

"I seriously doubt it. But I'll keep one eye open, just in case."

"Let me know—" she yawned "—if you need another. In the meantime, I'm going to take a little nap. You wore me out."

His chuckle was warm and rich, filling her heart with joy and contentment.

Yeah, she could get used to his laughter and his body cocooning hers. "Thank you."

He laughed again. "You nut. What for?"

"For reminding me why foreplay is so very important."

His still-stiff staff flexed inside her.

Liv draped her leg over his and moved closer. Then she drifted to sleep, not caring that the stone floor of the cave was cold and hard. She was wrapped in the arms of a man who could very easily steal her heart. It was a good thing neither one of them was in the market for commitment. Otherwise, he could also very easily break her heart.

Chapter Eleven

Sunlight filtered in through the cave entrance along with a cool morning breeze. The fire had long since burned out, leaving nothing but fading embers. Gooseflesh made the hairs on Hawkeye's arms stand straight.

He stared down at Olivia, memorizing her straight, perky nose and the swell of her full, sexy lips. Though she wore no makeup, her auburn eyelashes made fiery crescents against her lightly tanned skin as she slept.

He knew that when the time came, he was going to miss this woman who had managed to capture his attention and make a significant chink in the armor he'd erected around his heart.

If only he had more time with her. If only he could take her with him when he left.

But Olivia would hate being an army wife. She'd get tired of following him around the country or world, packing every three or four years, sometimes more often, and moving to places where she wouldn't know anyone.

Finding work was often difficult for wives of service members. Employment opportunities weren't always as available around the posts as they were in less remote locations.

Why was he even contemplating it? He'd only known Olivia for a couple of days.

When you know...you know.

His mother's words echoed in his head. He'd asked her how she'd known his father was the right man for her. She'd smiled and said those words then. She'd loved his father with all of her heart. And she'd loved her children so much, she couldn't live with the knowledge one of them had died. She'd always felt everything more deeply than anyone else.

When you know, you know.

Hawkeye's gaze swept across Olivia's features. She had high cheekbones, smile lines beside her eyes and lips, and a strong chin. And her body...

His own tightened as his gaze traveled over her breasts down to the juncture of her thighs. Even if he wanted to wake her by making love to her, he didn't have any more protection. He refused to risk the odds. Leaving her pregnant with a ranch to run would be a crappy thing to do. She had enough on her hands to worry about.

Hawkeye slipped from beneath her leg draped over his, stood and dressed in his jeans and boots. His shirt and jacket lay beneath Olivia's beautiful body, and he didn't have the heart to wake her yet.

Instead, he walked to the cave entrance and out into the morning light, careful to look for trouble before revealing himself.

There were no signs of the five gunmen from the

evening before. If he and Olivia got going, they could fix that fence and get back in time to have breakfast.

His stomach rumbled loudly as he flexed his arms and back. The hard cave floor had left him stiff and aching.

"Hungry?" a voice called out behind him.

Olivia stood in the opening, her hair rumpled, her jeans and boots pulled on. She worked the buttons on her blouse with her fingers as she blinked in the morning sunlight. "Any sign of them?"

He shook his head. "Not as far as I can tell. We'll have to make our way out of here to see if they're really gone."

"I'm ready when you are." She handed him the T-shirt and jacket he'd worn the day before.

Olivia tucked her shirt into her waistband and finger-combed her hair in an attempt to tame the thick, wavy locks. Finally, she gave up and walked back into the cave.

Hawkeye followed.

She stood next to the four-wheeler. "You can drive. I feel like my arms and legs were pummeled by our ride across the boulders. I'm not sure I can manhandle the handlebars to get us back."

He nodded, certain Olivia could do anything she set her mind to. However, the shadows beneath her eyes told him she hadn't slept any better than he had on the hard ground. He wanted to soothe her aches and make everything all right for her. Hawkeye opened his arms.

For a moment, she hesitated. But then she leaned into

him and rested her cheek against his chest. "I hate that I don't feel safe anymore."

"Stay with me. I'll do my best to protect you."

She shook her head. "I can't get used to having you around. When you leave, I'm on my own again. I might as well get used to it now."

"By then, we will have figured out the problems here. I'm not going anywhere until everything is settled."

She glanced up at him. "What if it takes a long time?"

He brushed his lips across her nose. "Then we will have more time together." His brows furrowed. "Seriously. I'm not leaving until I know you're safe."

She wrapped her arms around his waist. "I'm glad. I'm sure I can take care of myself, but you were right. I like having someone watching my back."

He rested his cheek against her riotous hair. "You've got me, babe." Until he left. The more he thought about that day, the less he liked it. Even if they settled the troubles and figured out who was responsible for the guns and the killings, there could always be another bad guy to take the place of the ones they cleaned up. Olivia would be on her own with only Abe as her backup. And Abe wasn't getting any younger.

For the first time since he'd enlisted in the army, Hawkeye thought about what he'd do if he wasn't a soldier anymore.

He could go back to ranching. It was in his blood. Maybe he could hire on as a ranch hand on the Stone Oak Ranch. Then he could be close enough to Olivia to help her out when she got into a pinch. Or he could hire on with the sheriff's department. He had the skills.

He'd only need to go through the training to learn all of the nuances of local laws. Or he could ask Kevin Garner for a job as a permanent member of his Homeland Security team.

Ah, who was he kidding? It was hard enough adjusting to the civilian world on a temporary assignment. He'd been in the military for so long, he wasn't sure he could transition out of it permanently. He inhaled the scent of Olivia. Although the civilian world had its perks.

Hawkeye's arms tightened around her. "Ready to go?"

"No." She hugged him harder and then sighed, her arms loosening. "If we must. The fence still needs mending and the animals will need to be fed and watered."

"I'd bet my socks CJ has the barn animals under control."

Olivia smiled. "He's a good kid. I just hate that his stepfather is a jerk."

"You and me both." Hawkeye climbed aboard the four-wheeler and waited for Olivia to mount behind him. Then he eased out of the cave entrance and half drove, half slid down the hill to the rocky bottom.

They wove through the big boulders until they reached the trail headed back to the ranch.

Hawkeye paused for a moment and looked back at the many caves lining the bluffs. "I'll have Garner send some of the other team members back this way to check out the other caves. The weapons cache has to be around here somewhere."

The ride back to the mangled fence passed uneventfully.

As soon as they crossed back onto Stone Oak Ranch land, Olivia hopped off the four-wheeler and whistled loudly for her horse. An answering whinny made her smile. She ran toward a stand of bushes where she found Stormy's reins tangled in a thorny briar vine. Stormy stamped his hooves impatiently while Olivia and Hawkeye pulled the leather free of the prickly plant.

Once free, the gelding tossed his head and nuzzled Olivia, searching for a treat.

"Sorry, old boy. We have to fix this fence before we go back to the barn." She tied him to a low-hanging tree branch and joined Hawkeye.

He loved watching her work with animals. She had patience and a true affinity for them. Olivia showed she cared by the way she treated them and the way they responded to her.

Hawkeye tacked the end of the barbed wire to a fence post and unwound a strand long enough to fill the gap where the fence had been cut. Using the come-along, he and Olivia quickly strung fresh barbed wire in four rows and tacked the wire to the fence posts with the staples. The job only took an hour and then they were loaded up and heading back to the ranch house before the sun had fully risen in the sky.

Again, Hawkeye trailed Olivia and her horse, giving the gelding enough room that he wasn't spooked by the noise from the engine.

Next time, Hawkeye vowed to take a horse if Olivia insisted on riding one. At least then he'd be able to hear the sound of engines before the gang riding the ATVs caught them in their sights. Following behind Olivia wasn't all bad. The woman sat her horse beautifully, swaying with every step, as much a part of the animal as the animal itself.

She hadn't mentioned their lovemaking, which made him wonder if she was now regretting it. If that were the case, he'd be disappointed. He'd already envisioned a night with Olivia in a real bed, not on the hard surface of the cave floor. Call him selfish and lacking focus, but Hawkeye couldn't help it. The woman had his libido tied in knots.

LIV'S TENDER PARTS were sore that morning as she eased into the saddle. Having Hawkeye follow her back to the ranch made her hyperaware of his gaze on her backside.

She'd wanted to wake in his arms, but he'd been up and outside before she woke from an uneasy sleep. Liv had hoped they'd pick up where they'd left off the night before. But then she remembered he'd only brought protection for one round.

A trip to town would remedy that shortfall for future encounters with the gorgeous army ranger.

Crap! What if they didn't carry such protection in the grocery store? Would they have them in the feed store? If she had to, she'd drive all the way to Bozeman, Montana, for them.

As long as Hawkeye was in town, she hoped to continue relations with the man. When it came time for him to leave, she'd just have to remind herself she'd agreed to the no-commitment clause.

Her chest tightened at the thought of Hawkeye leaving. Hopefully, his little team would be around for a lot longer. Although she'd like to solve the mystery of who was doing all the killing as soon as possible—before someone else turned up dead.

Liv swung out of the saddle at the gate to the barnyard and unlatched the lock.

"CJ?" she called out as she led Stormy through and waited for Hawkeye to drive the ATV in behind her.

The barn door swung open and CJ emerged carrying the rifle from the tack room. "Oh, thank goodness, it's you two." He lowered the weapon and sighed. "If you hadn't turned up by nine o'clock, I was going to call the sheriff."

"We're all right, but thanks for worrying about us." Liv led Stormy into the barn.

Hawkeye killed the engine on the four-wheeler and pushed it into the barn behind her.

"How long have you been here?" Liv called out over her shoulder.

CJ had ducked into the tack room to hang the rifle on the wall. He rejoined them, stretched and yawned before answering, "All night."

Liv spun. "All night?"

"I left long enough to do my chores at home. As soon as I could, I snuck out and came back to make sure someone watched over the house and barn in case you didn't make it back before dark. I was worried about you."

Liv hugged the teen. "Oh, CJ. I'm sorry. I hope you didn't stay awake all night."

He shrugged. "I can catch up on my sleep later."

"Why were you up all night?" Hawkeye asked.

The boy's brows furrowed. "I was sleeping in the barn, but something woke me in the middle of the night. Sadly, a little late for me to do much about it, but, heck, you'll have to see this for yourself."

Liv tied Stormy to a metal ring on the wall and followed CJ outside and up the hill to the house.

"The horses and cattle out in the pasture were making a lot of noise. I thought maybe a wolf or a bear had found its way into the pens. I grabbed the gun from the tack room thinking I could fire into the air and scare it off. But when I came out of the barn, I saw someone moving around the house."

They'd arrived at the house and swung around to the front.

A chill slithered down the back of Liv's neck. She and Hawkeye had been gone all night. "You didn't try to confront him, did you?" CJ could have been attacked and injured or killed. She glanced over the boy's head to Hawkeye.

The ranger's brows had dropped into a deep frown as he stared toward the house.

Her stomach churning, Olivia's gaze followed Hawkeye's.

There on the front of the house in huge bloodred scrawl across the white paint and the glass of the windows were the words "LEAVE OUR SACRED LANDS."

"I'm sorry I couldn't stop him sooner," CJ said. "I fired off a round. It must have scared whoever it was, because he disappeared down the driveway. I heard the sound of a vehicle engine, but by the time I chased after him, he was gone."

Liv wrapped her arm around the teen. "Oh, CJ, no. You shouldn't have chased him at all. Dear Lord, I would never forgive myself if something bad happened to you."

He stood taller, his shoulders thrown back. "I had the rifle. The shot I fired into the air scared him away."

Hugging the boy again, Olivia felt her stomach knot. What if the man who'd spray painted her house had come after CJ?

"Why would they paint this message?" Hawkeye asked. He turned to Olivia. "Have you had troubles with the local Native American tribes in the past?"

Liv shook her head. "Never. As far back as I can remember, we haven't encountered any disputes over the property. We border the national forest, not a reservation."

Hawkeye crossed his arms over his chest, still studying the scrawled words on the wall as if they might shed more light. "Are there any ancient burial grounds on Stone Oak Ranch?"

"Not that I'm aware of." The warning made no sense. "My father has always had a good relationship with just about everyone in the county and on the nearby reservation. He donated whole steers to them to help feed people during some of the more trying times."

Hawkeye turned away from the house and stared at the yard surrounding it. "Look around. See if you can find the spray can. Maybe we can lift prints from it."

The three of them split up, combing over the lawn, the shrubs and the tree line several yards away.

"I found it!" CJ called out.

"Don't touch it," Hawkeye said.

The two adults converged on CJ and stared down at the empty can of red spray paint.

"I'll get a paper bag from the kitchen." Liv ran around the back of the house and entered through the kitchen door. She dug through the pantry until she found an old paper grocery bag. After grabbing it, she ran back out into the yard.

Hawkeye nudged the can with his foot, pushing it into the paper bag without touching it with his own hands. Once the can was safely inside the bag, he lifted it, folded the top and carried it back to the house.

"I'll call the sheriff." Liv went to the phone and dialed the sheriff's office, reporting the vandalism.

By the time she got off the phone, she could smell bacon cooking in the kitchen. Her stomach rumbled, reminding her she hadn't had anything to eat since breakfast the previous morning.

But more than food, she wanted a shower to wash the scent of the campfire out of her hair and off her skin.

Leaving the men to the kitchen, she sneaked away to her room for fresh clothing and ducked into the bathroom for a shower. A few minutes later she was clean, combed and dressed in freshly laundered jeans and a T-shirt.

When she stepped out of the bathroom, she heard voices coming from the hallway.

Sheriff Scott stood with Hawkeye and CJ. All three turned when she joined them.

"Miss Dawson." Sheriff Scott enveloped her in a bear hug. "I'm sorry about the vandalism to your house. We'll do our best to find out who did this and make him clean it up and hopefully keep him from doing it again." He shook his head. "And about the gang who chased you in the hills… I'll have my deputies do some asking around. Attempted murder is serious business. If you could swing by the office and give me your statement later today, I'd appreciate it."

"You bet, Sheriff." Liv hugged the older man again. "Thank you for all of your help."

"Glad you're back," the sheriff said. "Your dad missed you something fierce." He shook his head. "I was really sorry about his passing. He was a good man."

She drew in a deep breath and lifted her chin a little. "Did anyone suspect his death might not have been an accident?"

The sheriff tilted his head to the side and considered her question. "With so many strange things going on, we haven't ruled it out. But we didn't have any witnesses and the only person we knew to question was Abe, who wasn't anywhere near your father at the time. Don't worry, though. We haven't given up."

Liv nodded. "Thanks, Sheriff. I don't suppose you'd like to join us for breakfast?"

He shook his head. "No, thanks." He patted his belly. "The wife keeps me fat and happy."

After the sheriff left, Liv joined Hawkeye and CJ in the kitchen. She ate the eggs, bacon and toast Hawkeye had whipped up, enjoying every bite. After she'd cleaned her plate, she sat back. "I need to remember to hire someone who can cook as well as you do when I'm looking for a ranch hand."

Hawkeye's jaw tightened, but he didn't respond to her statement. "I'd like to make a trip into town after we finish the chores around here."

"Okay. Are we going to see your boss?"

He nodded. "I'll give him a call with a heads-up on what's been going on. He'll need to know what happened yesterday. It might be connected with your father in some way."

CJ cleared the table of the plates and returned for the glasses. "You know, there's a gang at the res that likes to ride dirt bikes and ATVs all over the place. Sometimes they get into trouble."

Liv pushed her chair away from the table and stood. "Why didn't you tell the sheriff?"

"I wasn't sure it was the gang and I'd hate to get them into trouble if it wasn't." He took the glasses to the sink and rinsed them before loading them into the dishwasher. "I wouldn't want them to know I was the person who ratted them out."

Chapter Twelve

Hawkeye understood CJ's wanting to stay quiet.

Olivia looked at him over the boy's head.

Hawkeye's lips pressed together and he gave her a slight nod. "I'll have Garner ask around. He might have more luck getting information than an officer of the local law enforcement."

CJ faced them. "You won't tell them you got that lead from me?"

Hawkeye smiled. "No. Your secret is safe with us."

"Thanks." He wiped the counter and headed for the door. "I'll work on removing the red paint today, after I finish my chores in the barn."

"Don't worry about it, CJ," Olivia said. "I think I can get it off. If not, my father stored touch-up paint in the basement. And thanks, CJ. I don't know what I'd do without you around."

The teen's cheeks reddened and he ducked out the door.

"If you don't mind, I'll use the phone in the hall-way," Hawkeye said.

"Please. Make yourself at home." She snorted softly.

"Funny, but this house hasn't felt much like home since I returned."

"Your family isn't here," Hawkeye said. "Family is what makes a house a home."

She nodded. "Though I resisted at first, I'm glad you stuck around."

"Why's that?"

Olivia shrugged. "As much as I hate to admit it, you make me feel safer."

"Glad I could help." He would have said more, but he still wasn't sure what good he would be to her once he was gone. Hawkeye left the kitchen, headed for the hall, anxious to report in to Garner.

His temporary boss answered on the first ring. "Garner."

"Hawkeye here. We had a little incident last night."

"Shoot."

After describing the encounter in the valley and their subsequent campout in a cave, minus a few more personal details, Hawkeye paused. "And that's not all. We got back to the Dawson house to some threatening graffiti sprayed on the front of the ranch house. Olivia's ranch hand nearly caught the man in the act, but he got away."

"I thought her ranch hand was in the hospital?"

Hawkeye grinned. "She hired CJ Running Bear to help out while her foreman is laid up."

"Glad she found some help. Wait. Isn't CJ Ernie Martin's stepson? The teen working in the kitchen at the tavern?"

"Not anymore. His stepfather made him quit."

Garner muttered a curse. "Poor kid. I feel for him. Martin has a nasty temper."

"Yeah. We were there when he threw the kid out of the tavern."

"So that's what all of that was about? I heard the scuffle, but it was over by the time I came outside. I'm glad Miss Dawson could use CJ. Ernie Martin is in serious trouble financially. He hawked his house to purchase Angora goats right before the government ceased the subsidies on them. He has no way to pay back the loans and he's not making enough money on his ranch to feed his family."

"All reasons to be angry enough to join a survivalist organization. Is it enough to make him a killer?" Hawkeye couldn't be sure. Though, as mean as Ernie had been to CJ, Hawkeye wouldn't put it past him to take it one step further.

"Hard to say," Garner said. "We'll check into his alibi for the afternoon Dawson died."

"Might be worth looking into," Hawkeye said. "Anything from Hack?"

"As a matter of fact, I was about to call you." Garner spoke as if talking to someone else in the room. "Could you bring me that printout we were discussing?"

Hawkeye waited.

"Hack checked into the names you gave us. Leo Fratiani checks out as a land agent for one of the big oil companies. Hack is still digging, trying to see if he's connected to anything that raises any red flags besides the oil industry, as if that isn't enough. Morris's record is a bit too clean. Hack will be digging much deeper."

"He has to have a fairly clean record to run for Congress." Hawkeye's eyes narrowed. "Is there a way to cleanse your background?"

"If there is," Garner said, "he's found it. I'm talking squeaky clean."

"What about Bryson Rausch? Any skeletons in his closet?" Hawkeye asked.

"Nothing more than the fact he owns about half of the buildings in Grizzly Pass and is always looking for more real estate to gobble up."

Which matched up with Olivia's description of the man.

Garner continued. "Sweeney has us concerned."

The tone of Garner's voice had Hawkeye's attention. "Why?"

"That man's bad news. He was kicked out of the Marine Corps with a dishonorable discharge. Spent some time at Leavenworth before he was discharged for raping an Afghan woman."

A knot of tension settled low in Hawkeye's gut. "Bastard. Does he have to register as a sex offender?"

"You bet he does," Garner said. "That's how Hack found out Sweeney had been kicked out of the Corps. His first hit on the guy was that he'd been marked as a sex offender and has to register in whatever county he lives. Then Hack found his way into the man's military records and discovered his court-martial for the rape of the Afghan woman."

"That's not what I wanted to hear, but it's better to know than not."

"Right," Garner agreed.

"We sent the spray can used to vandalize the Dawson house with the sheriff," Hawkeye said. "He's going to see if he can lift prints. Let us know if you hear anything before we do."

"I'll touch base with the sheriff right now. You two need to grow eyes in the backs of your heads and stay safe."

"Will do." As Hawkeye hung up, Olivia walked into the hallway.

"Has he heard anything about the people you asked him to check up on?" Liv asked.

Hawkeye held out his hand.

Liv placed hers in his and he pulled her up against his body. She fit him perfectly. Leaving her and Grizzly Pass would be really hard when the time came.

"Yeah, he did have some news. Not much on Morris, Rausch or Fratiani."

"What about Don Sweeney?" Liv raised her face to his.

Hawkeye brushed a strand of her hair back behind her ear. "He did say Sweeney had a record."

"Oh?"

He told her what Garner had said about the rape charge and his dishonorable discharge.

Liv's face hardened and her lips thinned into a straight line. "It's men like him we don't want coming back home to live in Grizzly Pass."

"And, yes, he has to register as a sex offender."

"A real piece of work." Liv's gut tightened. "I'll be sure to steer clear of him and let the other women in the county know to stay away."

"One other thing that has come up before in our investigation of what's been going on around the area." Hawkeye paused. "Sweeney along with Ernie Martin and a couple other locals are suspected members of the Free America organization."

"You'd think, with his record, Sweeney wouldn't be allowed to join such an organization." Liv laid her cheek against Hawkeye's chest.

He stroked her hair and down her back, his groin tightening the longer she pressed against him. He was so caught up in what her nearness was doing to his body, Hawkeye almost forgot what Olivia had said.

He pulled his focus back to the issue. "The Free America group is secret. We still don't know who is leading it or is funding its arsenal." He leaned her back far enough to press a gentle kiss to her healing forehead. "I'm worried about you."

She stared up into his eyes. "I'm worried about all of the good people of Grizzly Pass. I always thought this was a good place to live and raise a family. And it used to be just that." Liv shook her head. "And it was that for a very long time."

"It's a shame that a few people can bring chaos to an entire community." He bent to touch his lips to hers. "Part of me is glad it happened."

Liv opened her eyes wider, her lips full and inviting him to kiss them. "What did you say? You're glad?"

"If this part of the country wasn't in trouble, Garner wouldn't have asked for help from the military. I would never have been assigned to assist the Department of Homeland Security."

"And we would never have met," Liv whispered.

"Exactly." This time Hawkeye took her mouth, her tongue and crushed her to him.

Liv wrapped her arms around his neck and returned the gesture, coiling her tongue around his.

Hawkeye lost himself in the kiss, becoming a part of her in the process. When he finally brought his head up, he stared down into her eyes. His heart pounded in his chest, and his desire welled up inside so hot and fast he felt like Old Faithful seconds before it blew. Hawkeye held himself rigid, afraid to move. Afraid he'd take her there in the hallway. "I didn't think it could get any better than making love to you in a cave. But I could be wrong."

"We could test the theory. Now." Olivia tilted her head toward her bedroom. "In a real bed."

"You don't know how much I want that." Hawkeye drew in a deep breath and let it out slowly, shaking his head. "But not without protection."

Olivia sighed. "I hate it when you're right."

So did he. With everything else going on, Olivia couldn't afford to get pregnant. Who would take care of the ranch if she was knocked up?

Telling himself he could wait didn't make him any less anxious to strip her and make love to her. But he had to remain in control. Especially when Olivia was in danger.

She rested her forehead against his chest for a moment, seeming to get a grip on her rising passion. Then she pushed away from him. "So where do we go from here?"

He squared his shoulders and nodded toward the front of the house. "To work."

For the next couple of hours, Olivia scraped graffiti off the windows and applied several coats of paint to cover the dark red lettering on the siding.

Hawkeye banished himself to the barn to help CJ organize the hay in the loft. He came out periodically to check on Olivia's progress, offering to take over and finish the restoration.

Olivia refused, stating this was something she wanted to do herself. "The house, the ranch and everything on it was a source of pride to my father. The least I can do is restore the house to honor him."

A little after noon, Olivia had disappeared inside the house.

Hawkeye laid the last bale of hay in the neat stack they'd made in the corner of the loft and straightened his aching body. The pain in his lower back reminded him how hard work on the ranch could be. But it was also rewarding to see the results of his and CJ's efforts. He clapped a hand to the teen's back. "Good job."

The boy's belly grumbled and he pressed his palm to his midsection.

Hawkeye laughed. "Let's see if Miss Dawson has something in mind for lunch."

CJ shot a narrow-eyed glance at Hawkeye. "I didn't think she could cook. You're always the one making breakfast."

"True. But maybe we underestimate her." He led the way down the steps to the ground floor of the barn and out to the water hose in the barnyard. He turned on the water and ducked his head beneath the stream, washing out the sweat and hay dust.

When he was done, he held out the hose to CJ. "Your turn."

When they were sufficiently washed up, they headed to the back door and knocked.

"Lunch is ready," Olivia called out.

Hawkeye held the door for CJ and he entered.

Olivia had laid sandwiches on the table along with chips and a pitcher of lemonade.

"I told you she could cook." Hawkeye winked at CJ.

"Making a sandwich is not the same as cooking," CJ said, beneath his breath.

Olivia planted her fists on her hips. "I can cook. Just not with a stove." She laughed. "Stoves and I have a love/hate relationship."

"How's that?" Hawkeye asked, holding a chair out for Olivia and then sitting beside her.

CJ took the seat on the opposite side of the table.

Olivia smiled. "I hate using them, but love what others are able to accomplish with them." She waved her hand at the table. "Eat up, unless you want to cook something else. In which case, I'd like to add my order to your efforts."

"Peanut butter and jelly sounds great." CJ lifted his sandwich and took a big bite.

Hawkeye followed suit.

When they'd finished off their lunch, Hawkeye patted his belly and grinned. "Reminds me of summers at home."

CJ licked the jelly off his fingers and glanced up.

"Speaking of home, I need to check in. My mother will be worried that I wasn't there this morning."

"You're welcome to use the telephone and call her."

"Can't." The boy's face was grim. "They cut off our telephone service."

"Cut off?" Olivia frowned.

CJ blushed and looked away. "Ernie didn't pay the bill."

Olivia stood. "If you need an advance on your wages, I can do that."

The teen's cheeks grew even redder. "No. You've done enough just giving me this job." He hopped up from the table and cleared their dishes. Once he had the kitchen clean, he was out the door.

Hawkeye followed Olivia out onto the porch.

She leaned against the rail and waved at CJ driving off on the scooter. "I think I embarrassed him."

"I'd like to help him more."

"Me, too." She sighed and then straightened. "I need a few groceries from town. You don't have to come if you don't want to." For some strange reason, her cheeks turned a rosy pink.

"I'll drive."

"I don't want to put the miles on your truck." She entered the house and grabbed her purse from the counter. "Really, I can do this on my own."

"I don't mind," he insisted, though he could swear she was trying to get rid of him. The way things had been going, he didn't want to let her out of his sight for long. "Give me a minute to shower and I'll be ready."

"Sure. I guess that will be okay. I'll just lock up." With the color high in her cheeks, she sailed past him.

He hurried out to his truck, grabbed his duffel bag and returned. Five minutes in the shower, then dressing in a fresh pair of jeans and a T-shirt, and he was ready.

He found Olivia on the porch, where she stared out at the horses in the pasture.

"Ready?" he said.

She nodded, the color in her cheeks back to normal. They spent the drive into town in silence.

"I'll get the groceries," Olivia said as Hawkeye pulled into the parking lot of the only grocery store in town. "Why don't you check in with your boss? I'll be at least fifteen minutes."

He glanced at the store and then across the street to the tavern. "Are you sure you'll be all right?"

She laughed. "I'll be fine. Nothing's going to happen in broad daylight."

He frowned. "That's what we thought when the kids were hijacked on the bus."

"I'm not a busload of children, and I'll be within shouting distance." Olivia shook her head. "Really, I'll be all right. I want to talk with the store owner in private. She tends to be a wealth of information. If there's gossip, she'll be the first to spread it."

"I've heard that before. Would that be Mrs. Penders?"

Olivia grinned. "The one and only."

He thought about it. What could it hurt? He would be across the street, watching the store from the upstairs apartment window. "Okay. But fifteen minutes and then I'm coming to find you."

She stuck out her hand. "Deal."

He took it and jerked her into his arms. "Seal it with a kiss?"

"I like the way you think." Olivia kissed him hard and long, her tongue dueling with his. She wrapped her hands around the back of his neck and pulled him closer, until the truck console dug into his side.

When she finally let go, he took a ragged breath. "How about we head back to the ranch and finish that kiss?"

She touched his cheek and winked. "After I get the groceries." Then she jumped out of the truck and hustled toward the store entrance.

Hawkeye took a little longer getting out of the vehicle. He had to adjust his jeans to relieve the pressure inside. The woman was making more of an impression on him by the minute. He doubted he would escape Grizzly Pass without feeling like he'd left something important behind.

His thoughts swirling around Olivia and that kiss, Hawkeye crossed the street and climbed the stairs to the loft apartment and knocked once before entering.

Kevin met him at the door and shot a glance over his shoulder. "Where's Miss Dawson?"

"At the grocery store." Where he wanted to be at that moment, pinning her to the door of a giant refrigerator to finish that kiss.

"I just got off the phone with the sheriff. They got a match on those prints."

"Already?"

"They didn't have to go far. The prints belong to Ernie Martin."

A lead weight settled in Hawkeye's gut. As if CJ didn't have enough going wrong with his family. His stepfather would likely get jail time or a heavy fine he couldn't pay, and the man would blame it all on CJ. Hawkeye pushed his hand through his hair and walked to the window to stare down at the store on the other side of the street. "Why do you suppose he painted 'leave our sacred lands'?"

"My bet is he was trying to scare Miss Dawson off the ranch and wants to lay the blame on people from the reservation."

"Why?"

"I don't know." Garner stood beside Hawkeye.

"I also had Ghost check out the gang at the reservation. They had an alibi for yesterday afternoon. They were playing basketball at the recreation center on the res at the time you two were being chased. There were plenty of witnesses."

"If not the reservation gang, who could it have been?"

"My bet is some of the Free America recruits." Garner tapped his fingers on the table. "There's something else you need to know."

Hawkeye turned toward Garner.

"Before he'd gotten the word on the latent prints, the sheriff had one of his deputies go back out to where he suspected the getaway vehicle might have been parked in case the perpetrator dropped any other evidence or left any tire tracks. He found a five-gallon jug of gasoline, lying in the ditch along the highway near the Stone

Oak Ranch gate. It was as if it might have been thrown there. It was still full of gasoline. We got the fingerprints off it, as well."

The heaviness in Hawkeye's gut turned over and twisted his nerves in a knot. Had he intended to burn the house down? No one but the five guys on the four-wheelers would have known Olivia wouldn't be in her house that night. Hawkeye shifted his attention back to the store, feeling more and more like he needed to cross the street early and make sure Olivia was okay. "Ernie again?"

"No."

Hawkeye's gaze shot to Garner. "No?"

"They got a match on Don Sweeney."

"Damn." Hawkeye clenched his fists. "Tell me the sheriff took him into custody."

The Homeland Security agent shook his head. "He disappeared. Same with Ernie Martin."

Hawkeye spun on his heel and sprinted for the door.

"Where are you going?" Garner asked.

"To the store, to check on Olivia."

Chapter Thirteen

Once Olivia entered the store, she couldn't escape the chatty Mrs. Penders.

The gray-haired woman, wearing an apron with the store name embroidered across the left breast, came out from behind the counter and hugged her. "Olivia, darling. I'm so sorry about your father. He was always such a gentleman and did so much for everyone around here."

"Thank you, Mrs. Penders. I appreciate your kind words." Olivia hugged the store owner, her eyes stinging all over again. She'd never get used to the fact her father wouldn't be home when she returned. Most everyone in Grizzly Pass had been so nice to her, but it didn't help ease the pain. She'd rather have her father back than all of the condolences in the state of Wyoming.

Mrs. Penders leaned back and stared into Liv's face. "I still can't believe they called it an accident."

Liv nodded. "My father was one of the best horsemen in the county. He rode broncos in the rodeo before he met my mother."

Mrs. Penders smiled. "He was always such a handsome man." Then she shook her head and her lips thinned. "No. I don't think he fell off his horse. Someone had to have hit him. I just won't accept that a man who could win so much on the rodeo circuit would fall off a horse to his death."

"If everyone loved my father so much, why would someone want to kill him?" Liv asked the woman who heard every rumor in the little community.

Mrs. Penders leaned closer. "I think it has to do with that darned oil pipeline."

"The pipeline has been there for years. Why would it be a problem now?"

"*Because* it's been there for years. It's getting old. They'll want to replace it soon." Mrs. Penders rounded the counter and leaned on the surface. "It's big business. It could mean a lot of money to the company that lands the contract and a lot of jobs to the locals if they start over."

"Why don't they just repair the old pipeline? It would be a lot less expensive."

"Some argue that the old pipeline runs through some of the most unstable land in North America." Mrs. Penders paused for Liv to make the connection.

"Yellowstone?"

The older woman smiled and nodded. "Some people think an explosion on the pipeline would cause the supervolcano beneath Yellowstone National Park to wake up. They think it would be the end of the world, or at least this part of the world, if that should happen."

Liv shook her head. "That's ridiculous. The chances of that happening in our lifetime are really slim."

"There are people who think otherwise."

"So what does all of this have to do with Stone Oak Ranch?" Liv asked.

"It's rumored the new pipeline will be located farther south to avoid much of the Yellowstone Caldera. And if that's the case, it might be headed through Stone Oak Ranch." She leaned even closer. "You could be sitting on a gold mine. You could sell the ranch for ten times more than it's worth if the pipeline goes through."

"I don't want to sell my ranch," Liv said.

"Well, you could sell the part they want and have enough money to retire on."

"You think someone killed my father for the land the oil company *might* build a pipeline on?" Her stomach roiled at the thought. Her father was dead because of someone's greed. All because he stood in the way of a pipeline deal? "None of this makes sense. And what has the Native Americans upset?"

"If they take the pipeline farther south, it will cut across the corner of the reservation. They're afraid a break in the pipeline could contaminate their water supply."

"The old pipeline could do that, too. Those rivers and streams flow across the reservation."

"They want to shut down the pipeline altogether."

Liv's chest tightened. Hawkeye had caught someone trying to set off a stick of dynamite at a point along the pipeline. It could have been someone from the reservation trying to prove a point, or someone wanting the pipeline work to start up again, thus giving locals the jobs they so desperately needed.

Liv's gut clenched and churned. "What a mess."

Mrs. Penders reached for Liv's hand and gave it a squeeze. "Oh, honey. It seems like it's nothing but gloom and doom. But I'm sure it will all work out."

"I'm glad we have optimists like you, Mrs. Penders." Liv smiled and glanced around. "I guess I better get my groceries and let you get back to work."

"Let me know if I can help you with anything."

"Thank you." Liv couldn't imagine Mrs. Penders being any more helpful than she'd already been.

Could Kevin Garner know all about this? As the resident agent for the Department of Homeland Security, he should have his pulse on all of the factions stirring up trouble in the area. Pipeline corporations, activists protesting them, Native Americans in the line of fire and a survivalist organization tired of big government calling the shots. What more could go wrong?

Liv didn't want to tempt fate by asking the question aloud. Instead, she hurried to the pharmaceutical aisle where she found a small selection of what she'd originally come to the store to find. She studied the offerings closely, trying to determine what would be the best brand and the most comfortable for both her and Hawkeye. All the while she felt guilty for thinking about her own pleasure when her home was in the middle of a potential firestorm of warring factions.

"If it helps, I run out of this brand before any of the others."

Olivia jumped back, dropping the box in her hand.

Mrs. Penders stood behind her, pointing at the box Olivia hadn't selected. "But I believe one brand is just as effective as the others."

Heat flooded Olivia's cheeks. "Oh, thank you, Mrs. Penders. I was looking for a f-friend."

Mrs. Penders gave her a knowing smile. "Right." The bell over the front door of the store rang, indicating another customer had arrived. "Let me know if you need help with anything else." The older woman hurried back to the register at the front of the store, leaving Liv to suffer her mortification in private.

After grabbing the box she'd dropped on the floor, she replaced it on the shelf and reached for the one Mrs. Penders had pointed out. Liv laid it in the plastic basket she carried and hurried to the back of the store where the refrigerators held the milk, eggs and orange juice. At the rate the three of them were going through the breakfast food, they'd be out of supplies in the next day or two.

Liv heard a loud sound as if a shelf of canned goods had been knocked over, the cans clattering across the floor.

"Mrs. Penders?" Liv stood on her toes, trying to see over the aisles of cereal boxes and laundry detergent.

"Mrs. Penders took a short break," a voice said beside her.

Don Sweeney stepped out of an aisle and blocked her path.

Liv's pulse leaped. She faced the man in front of her, while searching for an escape route in her peripheral vision. "I'll just check and make sure." She tried to step around the scary ex-marine with the unshaven face and tattoos inked across his forearms, but he moved to the side, blocking her path again.

Though she was quaking on the inside, she lifted her chin and gave the man her toughest stare. "Is there something you want, Mr. Sweeney?"

He nodded. "You to come with me. No fuss, no screaming, just come quietly."

The slither of apprehension turned into full-fledged fear. But she couldn't let it get the better of her and she couldn't let it show. A man like Sweeney would feed on her weakness. "Sorry. I have no desire to go anywhere with you." She tried again to step around him.

When he moved in front of her, she darted to the opposite side and dived past him.

For a moment, she thought she'd made it when his hand shot out and snagged her arm, gripping it so tightly it would definitely leave a bruise.

A bruise was the least of Liv's worries. If this man was a known rapist, he could do a lot more than bruise her. At twice her weight and size, he could toss her around like a rag doll and she'd be unable to stop him.

She had to use her brain and think her way out of this situation. And quickly. Mrs. Penders could be lying in a pool of her own blood. The older woman needed help.

"Let go of me," Liv said, her tone stronger and more confident than she felt. "Or I'll scream."

"No, you won't." He clamped his hand on her arm so hard, the pain nearly brought her to her knees. "Not if you want the boy to live."

She stopped resisting immediately. "What boy?"

"Your new hired hand. The Indian brat."

"CJ?" Anger boiled to the surface. "What have you done to CJ?"

"Nothing yet, but I'll kill him if you don't come with me now, quietly."

"How do I know you have him?" She glared at the man. "You could be lying."

"I caught him on the road, riding that stupid scooter you gave him." He sneered at Liv. "Then again, I'd be doing his mama a favor by taking one more kid off her hands. She'd have one less brat to feed."

Liv flew at the man with her free hand and slapped his face so hard it left a big red handprint on his cheek. "You leave that boy alone. He's done nothing to hurt you."

"He nearly shot me. That's enough reason to kill the little bastard."

"You were the one who vandalized my house!" She spit in his face. "That was my father's house."

"Yeah, and if you hadn't come home, I wouldn't need to burn it to the ground with you inside." He yanked her toward him and crushed her to his chest. "But this way, I might have a little fun first."

With her arms pinned to her sides in his iron grasp, she couldn't move to twist her way out. She kicked his shins, but it didn't seem to faze him in the least.

Sweeney strode through the back storeroom to the loading dock at the rear where a black pickup was parked.

Liv fought and kicked, knowing if she didn't break free, she wouldn't live to make love one more time with Hawkeye. She wouldn't be there to take care of the ranch that had always been her home. She wouldn't marry and have children to leave that ranch to as their heritage.

When Sweeney set her on her feet beside the truck, Liv pretended to faint, letting her body go completely limp.

Braced to fight with her, Sweeney wasn't prepared for her to slip to the ground.

He lost his grip on her and let her fall all the way to the pavement.

Once she cleared his hands, she dived beneath the truck and would have made it if he hadn't grabbed her ankle and pulled her out with one hard jerk. The ex-marine clutched a handful of her hair and dragged her to her feet.

Liv twisted and swung her arms, her fist catching Sweeney in the face.

He grunted, shoved her against the side of the truck and punched her in the jaw.

The force of the blow snapped her head back and it hit the truck. Stars swam before her eyes and pain shot through her jaw all the way back to the base of her skull. Gray fog closed in from all sides. She fought it, willing herself to stay upright, but she couldn't avoid the abyss sucking her into its void.

HAWKEYE REACHED THE door of the grocery store at a full sprint. When he hit the swinging door he expected it to open. It didn't and he slammed his forehead into the glass. He staggered backward and shook his head.

"What the heck?"

The next time he tried the door, he pushed the opposite side. Neither of the double swinging glass doors opened. He pressed his face to the window and looked inside, his blood going cold in his veins.

A shelf of cans lay spilled on the floor and a woman's leg lay sprawled across the tiles, sticking out from behind the cash-register stand.

Fear ripped through Hawkeye. The absolute certainty that something horrible had happened to Olivia filled him with dread. He turned his body and hit the door with his shoulder. Again he bounced back. The locks keeping the doors in place held true.

"What's wrong?" Garner joined him on the sidewalk.

"The door's locked and someone is lying on the floor inside. Olivia's supposed to be in there. Help me bust it open."

Ghost, Caveman and T-Rex arrived behind Garner. Together, they hit the double doors at the same time.

The locks gave way and the doors flew open.

All five men rushed in.

Garner stopped to render aid to the woman lying on the floor. "It's Mrs. Penders. I've got her. Find Miss Dawson!"

The four men spread out, each taking a different aisle to the back of the store.

Hawkeye made it there first and pushed through the door reading Authorized Personnel Only to the storeroom in the back. "Check behind the boxes!" he yelled to the others, but kept going straight for the back exit, knowing in his gut that they wouldn't find Olivia in the storeroom.

He burst through the back door to the loading dock

and ground to a halt, his breathing ragged and his heart so tight in his chest he couldn't breathe.

Black skid marks marred the pavement, indicating a rapid getaway.

Hawkeye leaped to the ground and ran around the side of the building, hoping to catch sight of the vehicle that had left the trail of rubber.

Nothing. The side street and Main Street were empty of all traffic. No cars, trucks or even bicycles moved through the little town.

Olivia was gone.

Chapter Fourteen

The bouncing and jolting motion shook Liv out of the black cloud fogging her brain. She clawed her way to consciousness, knowing in the back of her mind that someone needed help and it was up to her to get it. Her head pounded and bile roiled in her belly.

Cracking open an eyelid, she looked around at what she assumed was the floorboard in the backseat of a four-door, crew-cab truck. The smell of sweat and diesel fuel nearly made her gag. But she fought back the reflex, careful not to make a sound. She stood more of a chance to escape if Sweeney thought she was still unconscious.

Since he'd taken her out the back of the grocery store, no one would know Donald Sweeney had her. Definitely no one had a clue where he was taking her. With a thousand places in the surrounding hills and mountains he could dump her body, she wouldn't be found until some poor hikers stumbled across her bleached bones, picked clean by the numerous scavengers inhabiting the land.

Liv chased away the morbid thoughts, clearing her

mind to think of a way out of Sweeney's clutches. If she could get away, she could find her way back home.

The truck bounced along what she assumed was a gravel road until it rolled to a stop.

Sweeney got out, opened the back door of the truck and reached inside for her.

Liv planted her boot in his face as hard as she could.

The ex-marine staggered backward, clutching his nose. "You bitch!" he roared.

Bolting upright, Liv scrambled through the door and fell onto the ground.

Sweeney lunged for her.

Liv tucked her arms close to her side and rolled away. When she was far enough out of his reach, she bunched her knees beneath her and shot to her feet. She ran as fast as she could toward a white house with a wide front porch and nearly fell to her knees when she realized where she was.

Oh, dear Lord, he'd brought her home. If she could get inside, she could lock the doors, grab her father's shotgun and call for help. Then she remembered she'd locked the doors and her purse was somewhere back in the store with the unconscious Mrs. Penders.

She couldn't afford to take the time to locate the spare key and enter the house. Hell, windows wouldn't stop him from getting to her anyway. Her best bet would be to hide. In the barn or in the woods.

The sharp crack of gunfire shocked her into running faster. He was shooting at her! She couldn't move fast enough to get across the open expanses of the pastures to the tree line.

Altering her direction, she ran for the barn. Once inside, she turned and slammed the door shut. Sliding the long bolt home, she slipped the inside lock in place. Then she ran to the door at the other end of the barn and did the same.

The only other entry points were the glass window in the tack room and the sliding barn door in the loft where they dropped hay from above. Without a ladder, Sweeney couldn't get in that way.

Remembering there was an old telephone in the tack room, Liv raced for it. As she reached the open tack-room door, a shot rang out and glass shards scattered across the floor.

No. No. No.

Sweeney had found the window and would make his way inside if she didn't stop him.

Liv dared to peek around the door frame into the tack room.

Sweeney was using the barrel of his pistol to break the rest of the glass out of the window. When he pulled himself up into the gap, Liv ran into the room and jumped up, reaching for the rifle that should have been hanging over the door. It was gone!

That was when she remembered CJ had been the last one to use it. He'd carried it into the house that morning to clean and must have left it there.

Without a weapon, Liv ran back into the barn, grabbed a pitchfork hanging on a nail near a stall. She ran back to the tack room, hoping to catch Sweeney before he could clear his big body through the window.

He had just dropped to the floor when she rounded

the corner. The man glared and raised the pistol, aiming at her.

Using the pitchfork as a club, she swung with all of her might, knocking the gun from his hand.

He yelped in pain and fell backward.

Liv jabbed at the man, the tines of the tool piercing Sweeney's leg.

Screaming, he grabbed the implement and yanked it out of her hands and his leg and threw it against the wall.

Liv grabbed the door handle as she ran through the tack-room door and slammed it between them, hoping for enough time to make it out of the barn before he caught up to her.

Stormy whinnied loudly, his distress making Liv's heart hurt. If the bastard started shooting toward the horses, Liv would give herself up to save them. She had to get outside, away from the animals before one of them became collateral damage.

With her hand on the barn-door levers, she heard the tack-room door crash open behind her. It was now or never. She slid the lock to the side and rammed the door open.

Before she could take a step forward, a huge hand clamped down on her shoulder and slammed her to the ground. Her head hit hard and she blacked out.

HAWKEYE STOOD IN the middle of Main Street, shoving his hand through his hair, not knowing which direction to turn, where to look or whom to call for help.

A sheriff's vehicle pulled up in front of him and Sheriff Scott jumped out. "I came as fast as I could."

The loud wail of a siren screamed up the road toward them, heralding the arrival of an ambulance.

Sheriff Scott took Hawkeye's arm and maneuvered him out of the middle of the road.

The emergency medical technicians got out their rescue equipment and converged on Mrs. Penders, who was just coming to when they arrived.

Sheriff Scott pulled Garner aside and demanded, "What happened?"

Hawkeye swung his gaze from one end of Main Street to the other, without any idea as to which way to go. "Someone knocked out Mrs. Penders and took Olivia hostage."

"Did anyone see who it was?" the sheriff asked.

"No. Whoever it was hit Mrs. Penders from behind," Garner said. "Based on the fingerprints you lifted from the spray can and the gasoline jug, it could be one of the two men who vandalized her house last night."

"It's not Eddie Martin," the sheriff said, his face grim. "One of his neighbors found him in a ditch a mile from his house this morning. He's dead."

Hawkeye felt the blood drain from his face. CJ had fired a shot when he saw someone in front of Liv's house. Had the bullet killed his stepfather? "Any idea what killed him?"

"It appears he was bludgeoned to death with a blunt object sometime last night. The coroner will be able to tell us more when he conducts the autopsy." Sheriff Scott clicked the button on his radio and spoke. "Put out an APB on Don Sweeney. He's suspected of assault with a deadly weapon and of abducting Olivia Dawson."

Dispatch acknowledged and sent out the message to other deputies on patrol.

It was a start, but the longer the lead Sweeney had on them, the less likely they would find Olivia before he did something more drastic, like kill her.

Hawkeye refused to accept that as an option. He had to find her, and soon.

"Is there any chance he might use her as a hostage to negotiate his passage out of the country?" the sheriff asked.

"Given he's a parolee, he knows what will happen if he's caught. He'll end up in jail for the rest of his life." Garner's lips tightened. "Knowing Sweeney, he'll do anything to keep from going back to jail."

Hawkeye balled his fists, wishing he could hit something. "Where would he have taken her?"

"The sheriff is headed out to the Sweeney place."

"And what are we supposed to do in the meantime? He could have taken her anywhere." Hawkeye spun in a circle. "I can't just stand here and do nothing."

"I've mobilized the team. Ghost is going to the feed store to ask questions about Sweeney. I'm sending Caveman and T-Rex out to the area where you two were chased by the men on ATVs. Since we cleared the gang from the res, we figure the men out there last night had to be some of the Free America group."

"They were trying to scare us away from something."

"That's why I have two of the team headed out that way."

"I hope they're heavily armed. The men chasing us fired shots."

"They have rifles and handguns. They'll be looking for the caves you mentioned."

"Do you think Sweeney will take Olivia to one of those caves?" Hawkeye started toward his truck. "I should go with them."

"If you go, and she's not in one of those caves, it would take you too long to get back out of the hills to be of any help in Grizzly Pass. You should stay here in town and wait for word."

"I can't wait. I have to do something."

"Then go to her ranch. I'm sure there are some animals to take care of in her absence."

Hawkeye nodded. CJ would be getting back from his mother's by now and wondering what had happened to them. Maybe he'd have an idea where to look for Olivia.

Hawkeye almost laughed out loud at how useless he felt and how desperate he was to find Olivia. He'd even ask the teen for help.

"I'll go." He held up his cell phone. "I'll have my cell phone on me, but it doesn't work out at her place. Call the ranch number." He gave Garner the number.

Garner laid a hand on his arm. "Miss Dawson will be all right. She's one tough young lady."

"Yeah, she kept saying she could take care of herself." His chest tightened. "But Sweeney is a trained killer."

Hawkeye climbed into his truck and started the engine. He wanted to go out to the caves with the other men on the team. At the same time, he wanted to be with Ghost asking the feed-store owner if he had any idea where Sweeney hung out. But either option might be a waste of time.

Sweeney could disappear into the mountains with Olivia and no one would ever find him. His training in the Marine Corps would make him an expert at blending into the terrain. His only obstacle would be carrying a woman who would fight tooth and nail to get free.

Come on, Olivia. Get away from the bastard and let us know where you are.

He drove out of the parking lot and headed toward Stone Oak Ranch. Where else could he go?

His gaze scanned every side street, searched the nearby hills and looked into every face he passed on his way through town. Did anyone know where Olivia was? He'd just about reached the end of Main Street when his cell phone rang.

Startled by the ringing, he fumbled to hit the talk button without checking the caller ID. "Hawkeye here." He slowed at the end of town before he lost reception.

"Mr. Walsh, it's CJ." The voice on the line was so faint, Hawkeye could barely make out the words.

"CJ, where are you?"

"I'm in Miss Liv's house. You need to get here as soon as possible."

"What's wrong?"

"There's a strange truck in the yard and I heard gunfire and yelling in the barn. I found the spare key and came into the house."

Hawkeye's pulse leaped and he gunned the accelerator. "Stay hidden, CJ. I'm on my way."

"I have the rifle. I could go see what's happening."

"No!" Hawkeye yelled. "Stay away from the barn, CJ. Call 911 and tell them you have an emergency and to send everything they have."

"Mr. Walsh, is Miss Liv with you? I thought I heard her voice in the barn."

Hawkeye didn't want to answer the question, knowing the teen would want to help his new boss, no matter the cost.

"Please, Mr. Walsh. Tell me Miss Liv is with you," CJ whispered.

Static filled the line and Hawkeye lost reception.

He didn't have time to go back to town and get the sheriff. If CJ did as he was told, he'd notify the sheriff and they'd send help.

In the meantime, he had to get to Olivia before Sweeney killed her, if he hadn't already.

Chapter Fifteen

Liv struggled to the surface of what felt like a deep dark well. When she opened her eyes, she couldn't figure out where she was until she heard Stormy's whickering.

Her head felt like someone had hit it with a sledgehammer again and again, the throbbing so intense she could barely keep her eyes open.

At first she couldn't quite understand why she was in the barn, sitting on the floor, staring at the underside of the stairs to the loft.

When she tried to move her arms, she couldn't. Something anchored her wrists to one of the tall timbers that stretched from the floor to the roof.

Then everything that had happened rushed back at her like a tidal wave of memories, threatening to drown her in its wake.

Sweeney.

Movement around and behind her made her turn her head and wince.

Don Sweeney was pouring something from a jug all over a hay bale against the wall. The pungent scent of gasoline filled Liv's nostrils.

"What are you doing?" she asked, her voice hoarse, fear pinching her vocal cords.

"You're so smart—figure it out." He emptied the jug and flung it behind him. Then he pulled a lighter out of his pocket.

"So that's it? You're going to burn the barn down with me in it?" Liv knew her life was on the line and she would die in the fire, but a sense of calm stole over her. She had to keep her wits about her, if she hoped to get out of this alive. "Why?"

"What's it matter? You'll be as dead as your father in a few minutes." He rolled his thumb on the wheel and a flame lit his face.

"So my father's death wasn't the accident they say it was," she said as calmly as she could. "He didn't fall from his horse."

"Oh, he fell all right. After I hit him in the head."

Liv's stomach roiled and she nearly choked on the bile rising up her throat. "Why?"

"Why? Why? Why?" He faced her, the flame reflected in his eyes. "I'll tell you why. Because once you're labeled, your life is over. You can't get a decent job, you can't make a living and you have to work for idiots like old man Nelson, who couldn't care less that you were once the most decorated sniper in the Corps. All he cared about was how many sacks of feed I could move. That's why!" He flung the lighter at the hay bale and watched as the little flame lit the gasoline. Like a live organism, it raced around the interior of the barn, feeding on the fuel like a starving beast.

Stormy screamed and kicked at the walls of his stall.

"I did it for the money."

"You killed an innocent man for money?"

"Hell yeah. And if you hadn't decided to stay on your ranch, I would have gotten away with it."

"You would have gotten away with it if you'd left me alone."

He coughed and sneered at her. "You should have just stayed away. Now they'll know it was me." He snorted. "But I don't plan on sticking around to face any music." He ran for the door.

"Sweeney!" Liv cried out. "Who paid you?"

"Someone with a whole lot more money than you and I have. And it'll get me the hell out of this country. Say hello to your father when you get where you're going." He flung open the barn door and ran outside.

The sharp report of gunfire sounded out in the barn-yard.

Sweeney roared, cursing loud enough Liv could hear him over the crackle of the flames.

The smoke grew thicker.

She struggled to loosen the ropes binding her wrists, but they were so tight, she couldn't get her hands through. Instead, she rubbed the ropes on the edges of the six-by-six post, hoping to fray the strands. At the rate she was going and the smoke was building, she'd die of smoke inhalation before she worked herself free.

Then she heard the sound of a younger voice cry out. "Let go of me!"

CJ.

Liv struggled harder to get free. CJ was in trouble. The ex-marine would show no mercy toward the boy.

"You little brat!" Sweeney cursed.

"Leave Miss Liv alone!" CJ yelled.

Something hit the side of the barn, and the next thing Liv knew, CJ's limp body was thrown through the door. He landed like a rag doll and lay still. The barn door closed, shutting them inside with the fire and smoke.

"CJ!" Liv yelled, sucked in a lungful of smoke and shouted. "CJ!"

HAWKEYE STOOD ON the accelerator the entire three miles along the highway to the Stone Oak Ranch. The truck nearly went off the road on several of the curves, but he refused to lose control. By the time he reached the gate, his heart was racing and his lungs were so tight he could barely breathe.

Smoke rose over the top of the trees ahead.

What hell was this? Had Sweeney brought her out to her ranch to torch her home with her inside it?

He steered the truck along the winding driveway, cursing the trees in the way of his view. When he burst out into the open in front of the house, his heart stopped.

Smoke billowed up from the barn. A truck spun in the barnyard and headed directly for him.

Hawkeye slammed his foot to the accelerator and drove straight at the other vehicle. Anticipating that Sweeney would try to dodge him and keep going, Hawkeye braced himself, slammed on his brakes and twisted the steering wheel sharply to the left. The back end of the truck skidded sideways just as Sweeney's truck swung to the right.

Sweeney crashed into the bed of Hawkeye's truck, pushing him back around straight.

For a brief moment, Sweeney's truck didn't move.

Hawkeye shifted into Reverse and slammed into the passenger side of Sweeney's truck and pushed the vehicle sideways, crushing it between his tailgate and a tree. All four doors of the truck were blocked by either the tree or Hawkeye's truck.

With Sweeney trapped inside, Hawkeye hopped out of the cab and ran for the barn.

Flames leaped from the roof and the horses inside screamed.

Hawkeye pulled on the barn door, but it wouldn't open. He braced his foot beside the door and pulled as hard as he could. The door budged a little and then flew open.

Smoke billowed out, catching him full in the face.

His eyes stung and he coughed. Pulling his T-shirt up over his mouth and nose, he ducked low and charged into the barn. "Olivia!"

"Hawkeye?" she called out, her weak voice hoarse, almost unrecognizable. She coughed.

Hawkeye tripped over something on the floor.

"Get CJ out," Olivia said and coughed again.

He stared down at what he had mistaken for a pile of rags. The teen lay in a crumpled heap on the ground.

Hawkeye scooped him up in his arms and carried him out of the barn and several yards away from the building before he laid him on the ground.

Without hesitation, Hawkeye dived back into the

barn. The smoke was thicker. He crawled along the floor, searching for Olivia.

"Talk to me!" he yelled.

"Get the horses out," she said.

"Not until I get you out."

"You can't. Please, save the horses."

Hawkeye ignored her pleas and followed the sound of her voice to the space beneath the stairs.

Olivia sat with her back to a post, her arms behind her. "It's no use. You can't untie me fast enough." She coughed, the sound weak and pathetic. Then her head drooped and she passed out.

Hawkeye felt behind her, found the rope securing her to the post. He dug in his pocket for his knife, pulled it out and sawed on the ropes until they broke free.

His lungs burned and he could barely see through his stinging eyes, but he refused to leave Liv there to die.

Once he had her free, he dragged her across the floor and out of the barn, where he collapsed on the ground beside her.

Vehicles pulled into the barnyard, sirens blaring and lights flashing all around him.

T-Rex, Ghost, Caveman and Garner rushed forward with the sheriff and his deputies.

"Horses," Hawkeye said. "Four of them."

"It's too dangerous," the sheriff said.

"To hell with that." Ghost ran for the barn, followed by the other men of Garner's team.

Moments later, they led the four horses out of the burning barn and into the fresh mountain air.

Emergency medical technicians surrounded CJ, Olivia and Hawkeye.

They fixed oxygen masks to Olivia and CJ. When they tried to put one on Hawkeye, he pushed them away. "I'm okay."

"Smoke inhalation isn't something to ignore," Garner said.

"I'm going with these two to the hospital."

"Okay, but let the medical staff take care of you, too. I need you back on the team ASAP."

Hawkeye nodded. "I'll be there. Did they get Sweeney?"

Garner nodded. "Yeah, but he's in bad shape. He's unconscious right now and not responding."

"I hope that bastard dies," Hawkeye said through gritted teeth.

"Yeah, I do, too. But not before he tells us who he's working for."

At the moment, Hawkeye didn't care about anything or anyone but Olivia and CJ. If they lived, he'd be all right with the world and get on with the job of finding the people responsible for all of the problems in the area.

WHEN LIV WOKE AGAIN, she stared up at the white ceiling and wondered where she was. The strong scent of disinfectant filled the air and the sound of an intercom calling for a doctor grounded her. She was in the hospital.

"Hey," a voice said beside her.

She turned to find Hawkeye sitting in the chair next to her hospital bed. "What happened?" she asked, her voice sounding more like that of a bullfrog than a woman.

"I'm sorry, but they weren't able to save your barn."

"The barn?" Her eyes widened. "CJ?"

"He's going to be okay. Mild concussion and smoke inhalation, but he'll be back to work in no time."

"The horses?" Liv asked.

"The guys got all four out of the barn. They're in the pasture with the rest of your herd."

Liv relaxed against the pillow and closed her eyes. "What about you?"

He lifted her hand and pressed it to his cheek. "I've never been more scared in my life."

She chuckled and coughed. "You?" Liv opened her eyes and looked at him. "Scared? Why?"

"When I couldn't find you in the barn, I thought… Hell… I don't know what I thought." He squeezed her hand. "But I wasn't coming out without you."

Liv drew his hand to her lips and pressed a kiss to his knuckles. "You could have died."

His eyes welled and he shook his head. "I couldn't live with myself if I didn't save you."

She shook her head. "Hawkeye, you can't save everyone."

"No. But I had to try." He smiled. "I have goals."

"Goals?"

"Yeah. I want to give civilian life a shot."

Liv frowned. "What do you mean? I thought you loved being a part of the military?"

"I do, but I want more. I think I could be a pretty

good ranch hand for a certain ranch owner." He sat up straighter and puffed out his chest. "I've got experience."

Liv's heart swelled. "Will you ride horses?"

He brushed his lips across hers in a light kiss. "I'll ride anything she wants me to ride, if she'll give me a chance."

"I don't know," Liv said, shaking her head, when what she really wanted to do was shout with joy. "It sounds a lot like commitment to me. And I'm not so sure you and I are ready for commitment."

"Maybe we aren't, but I'd like to give it a shot." He touched his lips to her forehead and the tip of her nose. "And I could do contract work for the DHS to bring in additional income."

Liv sighed. "Hmm. Sounds like you have it all figured out." She lay back, feeling more relaxed and satisfied than she'd felt since coming back to Grizzly Pass. "I think I could use a guy like you on the ranch."

"I hope so, because I think I could fall for a boss like you."

Her eyes widened. She'd felt their connection from the first day. She'd known he could be the one. But hearing him say he could fall for her made her world light up. Despite the raspiness in her throat and the pain it caused her to talk, she had to ask. "We've only just met. How do you know?"

"Darlin', when you know, you know." Then he kissed her and proved he wasn't just fooling around.

They might not have all the answers to why someone would want Liv and her father dead. They hadn't solved the mystery of what was going on in Grizzly Pass, but they had found the answer to the most important question of all. How do you know?

* * * * *

Check out the previous books in the
BALLISTIC COWBOYS *series:*

HOT COMBAT
HOT TARGET

And don't miss the final book

HOT RESOLVE

Available soon from Mills & Boon Intrigue!

"I've lost my son."

She gasped for air. Tried to think straight, tried to remain calm, but it was all impossible. "He's two. Please." She bit back hysteria. "Help me."

"Ma'am, I'm sure he's been found and taken outside. Go outside and wait."

"Wait?" It was the second time she'd heard it and this time she could take no more. "My son is missing!" She clenched her fists, driving her recently home-manicured nails into the palms of her hands. A sharp pain ran up her arms. It grounded her, temporarily dispelled the blinding panic.

Her hands shook and her head pounded. She wouldn't give up. Coming to Marrakech had been a decision made in desperation. For it was here, in the land of the sheiks, where she searched for the lifeline that would protect her heart. Only one man could save her son and keep them both safe.

She needed to find Sheik Talib Al-Nassar. But first she had to find Everett. He was her heart, and without him, there was nothing.

SON OF
THE SHEIKH

BY
RYSHIA KENNIE

First Published in Great Britain 2017
By Mills & Boon, an imprint of HarperCollins*Publishers*
1 London Bridge Street, London, SE1 9GF

© 2017 Patricia Detta

ISBN: 978-0-263-92890-7

46-0617

Our policy is to use papers that are natural, renewable and recyclable products and made from wood grown in sustainable forests. The logging and manufacturing processes conform to the legal environmental regulations of the country of origin.

Printed and bound in Spain
by CPI, Barcelona

Ryshia Kennie has received a writing award from the City of Regina, Saskatchewan, and was also a semifinalist for the Kindle Book Awards. She finds that there's never a lack of places to set an edge-of-the-seat suspense, as prairie winters find her dreaming of warmer places for heart-stopping stories. They are places where deadly villains threaten intrepid heroes and heroines who battle for their right to live or even to love. For more, visit www.ryshiakennie.com.

When I was a toddler, you read endlessly to me and then wondered why I became a bookworm. I suppose that makes you partially responsible for the writer I am. You taught me how to read and you also taught me self-reliance. If it can be bought, it can be made. From soup to wedding veils. For my mother, who reminds me every day that nothing is impossible.

Quit just isn't in her vocabulary. To you, Mom.

Prologue

He slipped out of the back entrance of the Desert Sands Hotel and disappeared into the darkness. And, although he didn't move far away, he looked back only once, and with a self-satisfied smile. He had been in the hotel for a little over twenty minutes. It had all been too easy. He had come in through the unlocked fire exit where security cameras hadn't been installed. He didn't glance at the man at the front desk, for he knew that he had also been paid both for his assistance and his silence.

Neither of them would be here for the outcome. They only knew their parts, nothing more. He waited for the one other player in this game. She arrived exactly thirty minutes later, on schedule, as was her habit. Despite her initial reluctance, a doubling of the original sum was all that was required.

He glanced at his watch. It was five o'clock. He had ten hours before the second act.

He vanished into the narrow and twisted corridors of the Medina, where he had lived the majority of his life and where the plan had incubated. It was here where he would wait for his finale and then others would take charge. He was only a pawn in a much bigger game.

The signs of a new day merged into late morning and then followed into early afternoon. It wasn't until the day drifted close to midafternoon that the man from the Medina returned. And then he waited. There was no need to enter the hotel. Everything he needed would be brought to him, as planned.

THE FIRST SIGN of trouble went unnoticed by anyone in the lobby of the Desert Sands Hotel. The day began like any other, full of promise for business and tourists alike. The hotel was abuzz with the imminent arrival of a busload of tourists that would soon mesh with the energy of the guests already there. Times were changing and new ideas were being implemented. The hotel was under new ownership and so far, the change had been flawless. Everything was going as beautifully as the clear September day that held such promise for those eager to explore the city. Marrakech was full of places to discover, secrets waiting to be found. The city had an exotic history that was steeped in the depths of the Medina. There, the hustle and bustle in the souks, the numerous and varied shops with the merchants peddling their wares, added excitement and mystery, as had been the tradition for centuries. It was the place tourists came to spend good money and be part of that rich history. It was a special place, an exciting place. For most, it was very different from what they were familiar with. For others, it was a place of business—a place where commerce was at the center. For there was money here as well as history. There were other things, too, like poverty and crime, that lurked in the narrow alleys where he waited.

Now, near the heart of all that, the low ticking of an

explosive device went unheard. It had been placed close to where the luggage rack was customarily parked. It hid in the far corner of the lobby, buried beneath the chatter of the guests and the stream of voices that kept the hotel running without a hiccup. The deadly, monotonous beat was too quiet to be heard or seen…yet.

Chapter One

Marrakech, Morocco
Tuesday 3:15 p.m.

At the Desert Sands Hotel registration desk, Sara Elliott laid her passport on the counter. She then set her two-year-old son beside it so that she could keep an eye on him while completing the hotel registration. It had been a long flight and they were both exhausted. Despite the fact that it was midafternoon, she was looking forward to getting a snack and then getting her son bathed, and both of them having a nap. Traveling over an ocean and between continents with a two-year-old was no picnic. Only her son had managed to sleep on the long flight from Maine to Marrakech. For her, there had been no pleasure in it, but rather, only an endurance test in a flight borne out of desperation.

She had her arm around her son's waist, for a hand on his leg wasn't enough. Everett was a busy little boy. He didn't like to sit still for any length of time and now was no different, as within seconds he was reaching for the registration pen. Then he poked the edge of the registration clerk's computer while endearing himself to the older couple beside her who were checking in, as well.

After a minute of that, his bottom lip began to quiver

as he lost interest. She guessed that he was realizing that despite devouring two cookies on the ride between the hotel and the airport, he was hungry. She dug in her purse for his soother. He was too old for such a thing. That was what the latest parenting book she had read indicated, but they hadn't mentioned another option for situations such as these. The soother was immediately grabbed up in her son's chubby hand and popped into his mouth. Her nerves settled slightly. Now she had a few minutes of peace. Time to get them registered and settled in their room.

She closed her purse, using one hand to steady her son as she juggled the diaper bag that was over one shoulder, along with her carry-on bag and purse. She fisted the hotel pen in an attempt not to drop it when what sounded like outrageously loud fireworks went off behind her.

She jumped and dropped her purse onto the counter. The hand holding her son remained, instinctively, protectively, there. Someone screamed and a man shouted. The registration clerk jumped back, shock in his dark eyes. Smoke immediately began to fill the room and it was unclear what had happened.

She pulled her son off the counter, holding him tight against her side, his legs dangling. She turned to see what was going on, and one of the three bags she carried caught on the thin wooden panel that acted as a counter divider. Her carry-on twisted and wrapped around her arm, locking her in position. Smoke was billowing from the corner of the lobby, where the suitcase trolley was, and a small fire was licking at a couple of the bags. The smoke only added to the confusion because minutes earlier, the lobby had been flooded with an influx of tourists that had just gotten off a tour bus.

There was chaos in the haze, as people began to run

for the exit. They pushed through the crowded area where others stood, stunned. She could see that the window that faced the parking lot had been blown out. A bomb, she thought with shock, and then realized that it was an outrageous idea.

It was seconds before the reality of what had just happened seemed to hit her full-force. They needed to get out of here. Who knew what might follow. There could be another explosion, a larger fire. The situation was unpredictable and dangerous. She'd wasted precious seconds. Her son was in her arms, but her important documents were in the bag caught on the counter. She wasn't frightened enough to leave the bag behind, at least not yet. For without their passports and travel documents…she couldn't think of it. But she also couldn't hold her son any longer and continue to juggle her bags. She put Everett back down on the counter. His hands immediately went over his ears as he sniffled, but didn't start crying.

A woman jostled Sara and when the fire alarm began to bleat it was somehow unexpected and she let out a small involuntary scream. Everett immediately followed her example, as he always did, his soother now clutched in his chubby fist.

Darn it, she thought. But she couldn't have bit back her reaction, it was as involuntary as every other shriek that had run through the room.

"It's all right," Sara said quickly, not knowing how all right it might be. She held him in place with one hand while with the other she tried to free the caught bag. Her purse banged against her hip as Everett began to wail.

A short, thick woman pushed past her, herding a trio of children, knocked her elbow and threw her completely off balance. She staggered against the counter and noticed, while not really acknowledging, that all the staff had now vacated their posts.

A snowy-haired man with a pleasant expression and eyes that crinkled with concern approached her. "Here, let me help you." He reached for Everett. "Let's get you out of here," he said to her son.

Everett stopped crying long enough to look at the man and held his tiny arms out.

"No!" The word was sharper, louder and fiercer than she intended.

She guessed that he didn't mean any harm. Still, despite everything, she wasn't taking any chances. The thoughts ran rapidly through her mind and she considered the possibility that he might really just want to help. The offer seemed suspect, but he was from a generation where helping someone with their child was natural. The simple kindness did not place you immediately in a lineup as a suspect to potential kidnapping, as it did today.

He looked at her and moved to her other side. "I'm sorry. You just looked like you had your hands full." He reached over and unhooked her bag. "That should help."

She looked at him sheepishly. "Thank you," she said as the man nodded and moved on. And she was thankful in more ways than one, for despite the noise and confusion, Everett had stopped crying.

She lifted her son, who, at thirty-two pounds, was a good size for a two-year-old. Normally she had a stroller, but that was somewhere with the luggage, what might be left of it. She had no choice but to carry him.

"It'll be all right," she whispered to him and wasn't sure if that helped. She was just glad he hadn't let out a howl of outrage. Instead, his arms were around her in a death grip and he was sucking his soother again. If her arms stopped shaking she'd be all right. But the man was right about one thing—they needed to get out of here. The smoke was swirling through the lobby, making it almost impossible to see to the other side, where their luggage was, or to her left, where the exit was.

She moved forward. She meant to follow the crowd to the exit, when the stairwell door opened and people streamed out as they began to come down from the upper floors. The hotel lobby was suddenly not just busy but congested to the point that no one could move. Everett twisted in her arms, trying to get down, and with her arms still shaking, his squirming made him difficult to hold. The soother was gone. It must have dropped. She looked down but there was nothing but smoke and chaos. He began to cry, she imagined more from frustration than fright.

"No, sweetie. You can walk once we're outside." She tightened her grip as his cries threatened to match the noise of the fire alarm.

"Ma'am," the concierge said, taking her by the elbow. "You've got to leave now. Get the little one out of here."

"Yes," she agreed as she fumbled, the pull on her elbow the final straw to her already shaky grip that was weakening the more Everett squirmed.

"Mama!" he yelled.

"We're going, Ev. We're going." But she wasn't so sure as Everett twisted again and slid halfway down her chest.

The concierge had already moved on, unaware that his actions had loosened her hold on her son. She struggled to get a better grip on him, but he was slipping further. It was all made worse by the crowd as they jostled them this way and that. Someone knocked her left side and this time she lost her grip. She didn't have any choice but to either drop Everett, or set him down.

She placed him on the ground, her hand on his shoul-

der as she stood up. But the split second between that and
when she reached down to take his hand found her fishing for air. She looked down. In the space of a second he
had disappeared. There was nothing but a sea of people
amidst the chaos of noise and smoke. Her heart raced.

A woman screamed.

To her right, in a thick cloud of smoke, something
tipped and crashed to the floor. There was another
scream. This time she realized that it was her. Panic
threatened to engulf her. She couldn't let it. She had to
find Everett.

Through a break in the smoke, she could see that
the flames were licking one corner of the wall behind
where the suitcase trolley had been standing. Shock raced
through her at the fire and at the thought that everything
she had brought was more than likely about to be, or already was, destroyed. But the thought was fleeting, for
none of that mattered. She had to find Everett.

A man with a hotel employee jacket rushed forward
with a fire extinguisher. He blasted the flames that were
eating up the wall. Another employee attacked the flames
that were threatening one suitcase with a dripping wet
towel. But his attempts only caused the fire to move from
one area to another. Clothes were strewn around the luggage rack. It was obviously an explosive device of some
type, at least that's what her suspicious and slightly hy-
peractive mind thought. It was a strange thought, considering the panic that was filling her every second that
went by. Instead, she saw trivial details like that. Details
that meant nothing when the entire hotel could go up in
flames at any moment and her son was nowhere in sight.

"Everett!" she screamed.

To her right she distinctly heard a woman's unpleasant
voice tell her to shut up. She swung around. She was fac-

ing the opposite way that the crowd was moving. She'd been oblivious to the danger to herself, or the obstruction she was to others. It was like she faced the enemy alone, as the crowd seemed to act like one beast racing for the main exit.

She looked down, as if expecting to see Everett right there, right at her side where he should be. Instead, she bumped elbows with a matronly woman, who pushed past her, causing her to stumble. A man shoved by on her other side and as he did, he tripped and caught himself as he grabbed her arm, before he righted himself and disappeared into the smoke.

"Have you seen a little..."

She was shoved from the side as more people emerged from the stairwell and headed for the exit. Water began to spray from the overhead sprinklers.

"Ma'am," a man said. Her burning eyes could barely make out the uniform, but it was a hotel employee, and all she could think was that finally there was help.

"My son..." she began. "I've lost my baby!" The words came out in a panicked shriek. She'd lost control. She was beyond words. She had to get it together. She had to find him.

"You're going to have to leave," he said as he pushed her forward toward the exit.

"No!"

His grip on her elbow tightened. Now he was pulling her toward the exit.

"No!" This time it was more forceful and she considered that she might have to do something violent if he didn't let go, like kick him in the shins. Something. "I've lost..."

"Ma'am." He kept walking, dragging her along. "This is an urgent situation. You need to leave now. The emergency crews will handle it. You're making it difficult for the others, blocking the exit."

"What? My—"

"Out!" he said shortly, obviously losing patience with her.

She was ready to smack him if that was what it took. Instead they were pushed from behind and his grip loosened. She pulled free of him, backed up and dodged her way through the stampede.

"Everett!" she shrieked.

"Get moving!" someone else snarled as they shoved past her.

She gagged on smoke. She imagined her baby struggling to breathe. She imagined him trampled as people pushed their way out of the hotel.

She tried to call his name again but her throat was dry and tight. She coughed. He could be crushed. He was so small, too small. How had she lost him? She was a horrible mother and, despite everything that had happened, she was more frightened than she'd ever been in her life.

Someone rammed her shoulder. She was knocked off balance. She staggered, fighting to prevent herself from falling. Yet even as her hand hit the carpet, she was still frantically scanning the area. In fact here, low to the ground, she could see better, for the smoke was less dense and she was at his height, the height of a two-year-old. She was also in danger of being trampled, as she was sure he was. She swallowed against the panic and smoke that was locking her throat. Her voice was all she had—he had to hear her. For there was danger everywhere and he was alone.

Sirens were wailing in the distance, the haunting call both frightening and hopeful. Would they get here in time? They had to. She had to find him. She would find him. There was no other outcome, not one that she could survive.

"Everett," she croaked as she stood up and elbowed her way against the crowd.

Where could he be? Had someone taken him? It was another thought to cloud her mind with fear. It was a thought that taunted the mind of every parent. A fear fed by the media and that one never outgrew—the boogeyman in the closet.

But this time the boogeyman had gotten out! He had her son and her heart constricted at the thought. She bumped into a woman and pushed away from her without a second look. That wasn't her. She wasn't a rude, self-serving woman who shoved people to the side without an apology. It didn't matter. She was now. She'd be anything she needed to be if only she could find her little boy. She was bent low to the ground, not crawling, still standing and buffeted on either side by the relentless crush of panic rushing to escape.

"Crazy," someone muttered.

"Get out of my way," someone else said as a knee caught her shoulder and threatened to knock her off balance.

She stood up, saw another hotel employee and tried to make her way to him. "Help me," she said.

"Ma'am. You've got to leave."

"My son…"

She was thrown off balance as a tall, heavyset man, leading with his belly, knocked her aside as he headed for the exit.

It was impossible. She couldn't give up. She had to find him. Tears began to blur her vision and her head pounded from the smoke. What must he be feeling? She squinted in the murky lobby that oddly seemed clearer than it had only a minute ago.

She would die if she lost him. Her throat closed and smoke threatened to choke her, but she forged ahead.

Yet no matter how hard she fought against the tide of panicked hotel guests, her son was nowhere in sight. Her baby had disappeared!

"Everett!" Her son's name came out in a choked mockery of a shout. This wasn't happening! She hadn't come all the way to Morocco to lose him now, or for that matter, to lose him ever. She was here to make him safe, keep him safe. She'd given up a job, security, and now he was gone. This wasn't supposed to happen. This trip, the uncomfortable flight, all of it was supposed to result in her keeping him away from the danger that threatened him in the States. And now he was missing!

It was unbelievable. She took a deep breath and screamed his name. Smoke billowed around her and a man looked at her curiously.

"Can I help?"

"I've lost my son." She gasped for air. Tried to think straight, tried to remain calm, but it was impossible. "He's two. Please." She bit back tears. "Help me."

"Ma'am, I'm sure he's been found and taken outside. Go outside and wait."

"Wait?" It was the second time she'd heard it and this time she could take no more. Her voice was not the voice she told Everett to use on a regular basis, it was not her indoor voice. "My son is missing!" Her fists clenched, driving her recently home-manicured nails into the palms of her hands. A sharp pain ran up her arms. The pain grounded her, temporarily dispelled the blinding panic.

Her hands shook and her head pounded. She wouldn't give up. Coming to Marrakech had been a decision made in desperation. For it was here in the land of the sheiks, where she searched for the lifeline that would protect her heart. One man, who she held responsible for almost destroying her life, was now the only man who could save her son.

But now it didn't matter if she found Sheik Talib Al-Nassar. Only one thing mattered—finding Everett. He was her heart and without her son, there was nothing.

Chapter Two

Even for a car fanatic, one who had experienced the ultimate of vehicles, the BMW Z4 was a dream to drive. The car's custom paint job hinted at shades of an early morning sky. Its pearl-blue base and finishing coats were multi-layered and hand applied. The result gleamed in the sunlight. The butter-soft, smoke-gray leather steering wheel was almost erotic beneath his palm. While he'd owned and driven many luxury sports cars, this one was sweeter than any vehicle he'd had before. Just a slight touch of his hand on the wheel had the car responding. Even within the confines of the city, the vehicle was amazing. The engine purred like a satiated mountain cat. He could hardly wait to get it onto the open road and test its limits.

Talib Al-Nassar had the seat back as far as it would go, his left leg was stretched out and the warm fall air whispered across his cheek like a lover's caress. Poor analogy, he thought, reminded of his last lover. The BMW definitely scored higher points than she had. Ironically, she'd been rather like the rest, holding his attention for not much longer than it had taken to bed her. He supposed he deserved the playboy label his older brothers had given him. But the truth was that the women in his life wanted no more from the relationship than he was able to give them. It was only his brother Faisal who seemed to truly get it, but then Faisal, like him, was living what they called "the life." There was no woman to hold him to account, no children, and he wouldn't have it any other way. At twenty-nine, he just couldn't imagine being responsible for another human. It was unthinkable. And a woman… The thought dropped as he took a corner with ease and couldn't wait to get the speed up and test what this baby was capable of. He couldn't imagine a woman, no matter how beautiful or how arousing, ever matching the thrill that this BMW would give him. Only an hour ago he'd picked up the new car. He'd been looking forward to this for days. In fact, he had a road trip planned into the Atlas Mountains. He would visit an old friend and test the car's slick handling on the tight curves and bends of the mountain roads. But today he needed to stop by the hotel his friend Ian had just purchased. Ian had called wanting advice on getting the security in his hotel beefed up after a recent breach. It was only a favor between friends. It wasn't the usual kind of situation he dealt with as one of the executives of Nassar Security. The business was headed by his brother Emir and co-run by he and his brothers. It provided security and protection through branches in both Jackson, Wyoming, and here in Marrakech.

He doubted that this consultation would take any time at all as he was already familiar with the hotel's security. In fact, he anticipated that he might be able to convince Ian to go for a short test drive prior to tomorrow's excursion.

As the vehicle easily took the corner, its engine purring, he frowned.

"Bugger." He'd picked up the phrase on a recent trip to Australia and it had since become part of his vocabulary. His hands tightened on the wheel, the thrill of the car and the promise of speed and luxury it promised forgotten. Instead he was shocked first by the smell of smoke and then, as he turned another corner, by clouds of smoke filling the air.

"What's going on?" he muttered. For it looked like the hotel might be on fire, yet he couldn't see flames. What was clear was that smoke was billowing out of the door as fast as people were emerging. The fire alarm was shrilling down the street, cutting through the sounds of shouts and screams. In the distance, the sirens of the approaching emergency vehicles could be heard. He frowned as he gripped the wheel and assessed what he could of the situation from where he was. His phone was in his pocket but he hadn't received a call from Ian. That was understandable; whatever was going on, Ian would have his hands full.

Talib turned the vehicle smoothly into a parking space at the end of the block, leaving room for the emergency vehicles. He grabbed a bag from behind the seat that contained a few items that he'd often found indispensable. He pulled out one item that he hadn't thought he would need on a day where the upper-most thing on his mind was the joy of a new vehicle. The explosive detection device was more than likely overkill, but one never knew.

Talib leaped out. A few men in hotel uniforms were directing the crowd, keeping them on the sidewalk, out of the way of the imminent approach of emergency crews. Up ahead he saw one hotel employee moving among the crowd, laying a hand here, offering a word there. Another was passing out water bottles. He looked over and saw an older woman leaning against a vehicle as another staff member held her shoulder, obviously trying to calm her. Ian's staff were well trained. His friend had followed the advice that Talib had given all those months ago, when Ian had first mentioned that he was planning to get into the hotel business.

Things were chaotic but seemed under control. No one seemed to be in imminent danger—at least here, outside the hotel. It had taken him seconds to make that assessment as he strode the short distance to the hotel entrance. Now within yards of the front door, he was faced with a milling crowd that was not quite as organized or controlled as those he had just passed. He guessed that they'd just emerged from the building and were still shocked, unsure of what they'd escaped from, or what they had yet to face.

"Get away from the entrance!" he commanded, pointing to a green space just across the street. Half a dozen people followed his instruction, the rest continued to mill where they were.

He directed more stragglers across the street. In one case, he took a woman's elbow and escorted her to the curb, where she finally managed to cross the street under her own steam. He'd had a lot of experience with this as he and his brothers had built Nassar Security into the powerhouse company that it was. He'd learned over the years that people often responded like herded animals in an emergency. They lost their individual ability to think.

His phone beeped.

"Yeah," he answered, knowing it was Ian. They spoke for less than a minute. In that time, Ian told him what he knew, that they believed there'd been an explosion and that it might be linked to a suspicious-looking man seen in the early morning hours by the hotel parking lot. That information had been revealed on the security footage Ian had just remotely accessed.

"When this is over…"

"We'll get you beefed up," Talib assured him. "I'm going in now."

His friend had confirmed that the explosion had been confined to one area of the lobby. Ian had been at an outside meeting, but was now en route. From what Ian had said, he estimated that his own arrival was five minutes after the explosion and now, from the sounds of the rapidly approaching sirens, minutes before emergency crews.

Talib considered the information he'd just received. Combined with what he knew of the security and the time line, he believed that there was only one perp responsible for planting the device. It wasn't easy to plant an explosive device undetected in a public area of a hotel. The time that had passed since the explosion backed up his preliminary theory that there was only one explosive device.

Explosives were used for any number of reasons. This one appeared to be small but he would see for himself in a minute. If that was the case, there was a good chance that this bomb had been set to make a statement, or had been used to create a distraction. Since the damage had been contained and been in an area that saw low traffic, he was led to believe that whoever had done this wasn't going for a high kill rate. It could be a grudge against the owner. The explosion hadn't been far-reaching enough to provide much of a killing field. Unless there was another explosive, or this one had been a screwup...

He strode through the hotel doors, which someone had had the foresight to prop open. Inside, the emergency procedures weren't quite so efficient, as he had to weave through a lobby still crowded with stragglers.

Traces of smoke swirled through the lobby, but he was immediately able to see where the explosion had been.

Embers still burned in two ruined suitcases. Clothing was scattered everywhere. The metal suitcase trolley lay where it had tipped over. To his left, a woman, wearing only a bathrobe and flip-flops, tripped and stumbled. He was there in a flash. His reflexes were quick. They'd been honed by physical fitness and a regular baseball scrimmage with friends that occurred at least twice monthly. He had her elbow, and powered her toward the door, where he released her ten feet from the exit.

"Thank you." Her lips trembled but there was a stoic gleam in her eye. "I'm all right now."

He nodded but watched as she hurried past a hotel employee who was directing the remaining guests. He remained standing there, watching until she was safely out of the building.

He turned and scanned the lobby and saw a woman moving away from the crush and out of sight. She was wearing a maid's uniform. The dull beige material was designed to fade into the background, to provide service while flitting on the periphery. It was the perfect ensemble for what was intended, but now it seemed that blending in was giving her an advantage. The thought was one he tagged and filed away for later consideration; there were other things to concern himself with now. He was more interested in the explosion site and how someone had slipped in and out and planted the explosive unnoticed, than in the maid's uniform. He knew, from looking at the hotel plans, that a corridor led from the back of the lobby to conference rooms and a back exit. He was surprised that no one else seemed to be using that exit.

He activated the portable explosive detection device. As he moved slowly along the perimeter of the lobby with the device, he was cognizant of the rapidly thinning crowd. He was also aware that no one was acting suspiciously, but rather that there was still a great deal of confusion. People were almost spinning in circles as smoke continued to obscure the exit and the remaining staff seemed to have evacuated. So much for security measures, he thought, realizing that not everything he'd advised had been implemented. His attention returned to the device. The lobby wasn't officially clear of explosives yet, but he was reasonably sure that there wasn't another planted.

He moved away from the luggage and farther into the lobby. As he did, he looked down and saw a child's soother on the floor. That was odd. There weren't any children in sight. He didn't expect there to be. Even in chaos it seemed people managed to instinctively grab their children. He wasn't sure why, but he picked up the soother and put it in his pocket.

He looked up, thinking of the woman in the maid's uniform. She was the only one he'd seen using the back exit. His instincts, everything in his being, told him that something was off, that there was something more to this lone woman. Had she placed the explosive and come back to see the results of her work? Even as he considered that option he discounted it. Her mannerisms hadn't reflected anything nefarious.

As he made the decision to follow her, a woman's panic-torn voice sliced through both the chaos and his thoughts. It brought his attention to the lobby.

"Everett!"

The voice sounded familiar, even muted by the chaos of sounds that swirled around him. He didn't have time to analyze it. Instead, he moved deeper into the lobby, turning left and following the path of the maid he'd seen head in that direction. He turned a corner in the corridor and that's when he saw her. She was holding a small boy by the wrist, causing him to stand on tiptoes. The child's cheeks were wet from crying and he had his free thumb in his mouth. She was wearing a cream-colored head scarf and the beige uniform he'd caught a glimpse of earlier. Nothing about her seemed out of the ordinary. It appeared only that she was leading a child to safety.

But his gut told him that something was very wrong. "What are you doing with him?" he asked in Arabic. He doubted that the child was hers. No worker would have brought their child to work.

His theory was justified by the look of panic in her eyes and the way she held the boy by the wrist rather than by his hand. Clearly, she was unfamiliar with children that young, the panic obvious in her entire demeanor. He supposed his size and the fact that he was carrying an unconcealed firearm made him look official. Police, she might be thinking, although it wasn't true.

"Where did you get him?" he asked without explaining who he was. He acted on his first hunch. "He's not yours." Aggression could work to his advantage in this instance.

Her mouth tightened and her eyes darted, as if she was seeking an escape.

He strode forward and kneeled down in front of the child, who now had half of his free fist stuck in his mouth. His face was smeared with what looked like dirt and streaked with tears. His dark hair curled wildly in every direction, but his shimmering light brown eyes looked at Talib with more curiosity than fright.

Talib stood up. He wasn't sure what was happening here, but he intended to get to the bottom of it.

"A man said his wife had taken him. He paid me to deliver him to the back exit." She clasped her hands and backed up. "I…" She stumbled, speaking in Arabic.

"It was easy to take him. There was so much running, screaming."

"You took him in the confusion?" he asked.

She nodded. "I don't understand much English and that's what he—" she pointed at the child "—speaks. Although he can't speak much, he keeps saying Mama." She looked genuinely frightened and possibly even sorry. "I...something was wrong. I was going back to the desk to tell Mohammed," she said.

"Who's Mohammed?" Talib asked and made no effort to filter the edge from his voice.

"My supervisor," she said anxiously.

"How much money were you offered?"

"None. I wouldn't—"

"If you want to keep your job..." He let the threat dangle. He was beginning to lose patience with the whole situation. "Look, I assume you need the money but this kid isn't the way you're going to get it."

"He said he was his father. I needed the money. But I was going to take him back." She shook her head and looked down at the boy.

"You were doing the right thing," Talib said, strangely believing her. Poverty could cause good people to do desperate things. And in Morocco, the father's rights could still often trump those of the mother. It was possible that she truly thought she was bringing the boy to his father. Possible, but unlikely. He squatted down and picked up the child.

"I'll take it from here," he said with the voice of authority that was never questioned. "I'm sure his mother is beside herself with worry." The woman's story had rung true and odds were that she was struggling to feed a family, possibly extended family, on a maid's wages. Still, she had taken this child, and in ordinary circum-

stances he would have detained her. He shifted the toddler on one arm just as the panic in her eyes flared and
she bolted. He had no choice but to let her go.

He looked down at the child in his arms and was met
by curious eyes that looked at him in an oddly familiar
way. "You've had quite the day, little man," he said. The
toddler smiled and pushed a finger against his chin.

But as he reentered the lobby, a scream rose above
the alarms and the sirens of the emergency vehicles that
had just arrived.

A woman charged through the throng of people, heading straight toward him.

"Everett!" she screamed.

She was a petite whirlwind. She was moving so fast,
so ferociously, that there was little doubt that she was
emotionally invested, that the child was hers. There was
also no doubt that he knew her.

He allowed the child to be plucked from his arms. She
held the boy so tightly that he began to cry, but it was the
panicked look in her gray eyes and a vision from long
ago that registered with Talib. He shoved the disconcerting memory away. What mattered most was getting the
two of them out of here. Smoke still filled the area. Fire-
fighters were just entering the lobby and were already
directing the remaining guests outside.

"Let's go," he ordered. It didn't matter why she was
here or even who she'd been to him. He needed to get her
and the boy he assumed was her son to safety.

"What were you doing with him?" she demanded. Her
eyes pinned his like a thick gray mist and were the first
warning that she was dangerously angry.

It was similar to the last time he'd seen those eyes.

Except, the last time she had only recently left the bed
that was still warm from their lovemaking. He remem-

bered that she'd given him a dreamy look and told him that she loved him. He didn't like to think about that moment, for he wasn't proud of how he'd reacted.

It hadn't gone well after that, after what he had said.

She'd been proud and angry and told him what she'd thought of him, which hadn't been at all flattering. He'd said nothing, for there'd been nothing to say. Every word she'd spoken had been the truth. After that, he'd driven her home in a car that was thick with silence. He was sorry, but at the time what he had told her had been the truth. It was what he'd told every woman who'd fancied him. He wasn't ready to settle down, be serious, or declare undying love for anyone. He doubted that he ever would. Unfortunately, he'd told her that. It was then that she had tried to kill him with a look deadlier than he'd ever seen. Then, she'd managed to chip the custom paint job on that year's vehicle when she'd kicked the door with one tiny, stiletto-clad foot. To her credit, he didn't think it was deliberate. But he had his doubts. Especially because she'd done all that while telling him in a deadly calm voice that he could go to a place where it was just a bit hotter than the Sahara in midsummer.

It hadn't been his best breakup.

Chapter Three

"Sara?"

The voice was filled with that deep, commanding ring that she had never forgotten. It peeled back the layers of panic, penetrated the emotional chaos of losing Everett and her maternal fussing that she couldn't stop. For the first time that tone, that sense of self and of control, didn't grate, but instead was a life raft in a sea of insanity. The tone cut through everything and his presence broke easily through the crowd. She knew his voice like she knew her own heartbeat, would always know it, could never forget it.

He was back and he'd brought her son, when she had thought that her baby was lost. There was only one thing important in this moment—getting Everett out of the hotel.

"Are you all right, baby?"

She ran her hands over her child as if she expected to find a fatal wound, a broken bone or some injury equally as threatening. There was nothing. Only a nose that was running and eyes that were red and, oddly, a smile on his face.

She fumbled in her pocket for a tissue, pulled it out and wiped her son's nose, not slowing her stride as she headed for the door. Everett pulled away to look over her shoulder and what he saw made him giggle. At least her son was finding some amusement in a situation that was causing her empty stomach to want to heave. She clutched him tighter and walked faster.

Talib.

She could feel him right behind her and to her left. He wasn't saying anything, but his presence was insuring that there was no delay in exiting the building.

She hadn't seen him since that fateful summer almost three years ago. She'd hoped never to see him again and yet here she was looking for his help.

Despite coming here to find him, she hadn't been prepared for it to happen like this. Just his presence brought back all the hurt. She'd been afraid of that. That was one of the reasons she hadn't wanted to come here in the first place. There'd been many reasons, but that one had trumped them all. But she'd had no choice. She was here, with him right behind her. The hurt flooded back strong enough to steal her breath, like a tsunami from which she could never escape and with it came the anger.

Her heart pounded. For even after the years that had stretched between them, he affected her. He'd been a first-class jerk and one wasn't apt to forget such a man. But now there was one other thing that she wasn't apt to forget. He'd saved the most important thing in her life. Saved, found—she wasn't sure which was accurate and it didn't matter. Everett was safe.

She shifted her baby. He was heavy, even for the short distance to the exit. It didn't matter. She wasn't putting him down for anything, even as her hand shook from shock and Everett began to snuffle. She knew he felt her panic. Between that and the noise and the confusion of the last few minutes, she was surprised that he was as quiet as he was.

"It's all right," she whispered into his ear. She could smell the unique scent of the shampoo she'd used on his hair combined with the heavy smell of smoke. She ran a finger down his soft cheek, thumbing away the remaining tears. His bottom lip quivered and she knew that he was seconds away from bursting into a full-out wail. Once that happened, there'd be no stopping him. Everett's crying jags could be legendary. Now he had every reason to cry. She imagined that his flair for drama might mean she had a future actor on her hands. Or…she looked back at Talib, remembering.

She blew the thoughts from her mind. No matter Everett's discomfort or the former lover behind her, they could both wait. She needed to get her son out of this hotel and to safety.

And as she thought that a firm hand was on her waist and Everett plucked from her arms. Her heart stopped. This wouldn't happen again. She was ready to fight for her child. She turned and met the eyes of the man she had come here to see.

"Sara. He's heavy. Let me."

This time, his voice cut through her panic. His voice, like his presence, his personality, his everything, was too smooth and he was much too sure of himself. He looked the same and yet something had changed. She could see it in the depths of his dark, gold-flecked eyes. She couldn't put her finger on what it was, only that it was different, as if he was haunted by something or someone. A woman probably, she thought with scathing awareness and then pushed the thought from her mind. If she expected his help she would have to be civil and to do that she had to begin with her thoughts, and that one hadn't been fair. Whatever he was, he'd help her now. That was Talib, solid and dependable in anything that was not a romantic entanglement. Her mood dove again at that word. Entanglement. There could be no better or less flattering word for their failed relationship. And it didn't matter, for it was over—had been over for a very long time. It was another entanglement that was the problem, that was more than a problem, and that was why she was here.

He escorted her to the door, his hand holding her by the wrist as if he was her jailer. There was nothing she could do but be led to safety, to the place on the sidewalk that he deemed safe.

"Where are you taking us?" she asked.

He ignored her question. Instead he said, "You've spent enough time in this and the smoke can't be good for your little guy."

Her little guy. She sucked back relief. For coming here had been a risk. Finding Talib here today, more than lucky. Still, nothing could remove the fear. And she had so much fear. Fear for herself, for Everett, fear at facing Talib once again with the truth.

But despite all of that, she'd found him in the unlikeliest of situations. Not the most unlikely place. She'd known that he and Ian were friends, and that Ian had requested his help. That was the main reason that she'd chosen this hotel, it had been the timing that was strange. The bonus in all of it was that her travel agent had found a great promotion—everything had clicked together.

"Over here," Talib commanded and with those two words he made it clear that not only was he back in her life, but he was also taking charge, at least for now. And, at least for now, she would let him. Later—she hadn't thought that far.

This had been a journey of desperation. And now, despite having come all those miles to find him, she wanted to run—take her son with her before it was too late for both of them.

Instead she looked up at him. "I can't believe I ran into you in the midst of this. But I'm glad you were here to find—"

"What are you doing here, Sara?" He cut her off with a hint of anger in his voice.

The conceited donkey.

He thought she was here because of him. She looked at her son in his arms and that was the only reason she didn't lose it then and there. Unfortunately the truth of it was that what he was implying, what he'd left unsaid... he was right. She was here because of him, just for none of the reasons that the arrogant fool thought.

What she was here for was much more serious than any romance ever could be. And despite what he thought, and she knew very well what he thought, it was hard to deny the truth. He was a magnet for women, but he was no magnet to her. Not anymore. Those days were long over. But despite not needing him romantically, he was right about one thing. She did need him, she needed him very much.

For without him she was terribly afraid she was going to lose her son.

Chapter Four

Outside the hotel, Talib juggled the child in his arms as he put a hand on Sara's arm. It was an automatic gesture that rose out of the ashes of the past as if she'd never left, as if he'd never asked her to leave. It was strange how the truth of their relationship, how it had ended, had never been something he'd deceived himself about. He cared about her, but he couldn't be with her, not like that.

Sara owed him nothing, certainly no explanations. But the thought that she'd carried on with her life, married and had a baby, was oddly disconcerting. He pushed back the emotion, unable to face why it existed or what it meant. It was a moot point, he knew that. He had no right to question her actions and the sane thing to do now would be to push emotion to the background. Emotion did nothing in a situation like this. Still, it bothered him and it shouldn't. After all, he was the one who had broken up with her, gone his own way—forgotten about her. Or had he?

"Where's your husband?" he asked and wished he could have rephrased. The question was more abrupt, more invasive even, than he had meant it to be.

"I'm not married," she said as she turned to look at him. There was defiance in her eyes—a defiance that had hooked him on a day that now seemed a combination of yesterday and so long ago.

"Oh, I…" he spluttered, unsure of what to say. He'd fallen into a gaffe of his own making and that was completely unlike him. But even now, she pushed buttons like no one else could.

"It's okay, say it. It's not like others haven't or at least thought it."

"Say what?"

"That you thought I was smarter than that. Smarter then becoming an unwed mother that…" Her voice choked off.

"Sara…" He stopped her with a touch of his hand on her shoulder. She'd always been, in some ways, unbelievably old-fashioned. "I'm not suggesting anything. We've been apart for a long time. What you do is none of my business. What is my business is getting you to a safe—"

"We'll go wait with the others," she interrupted and held out her arms to take her son.

"Just a minute. Wait," he said. It was odd how that need to protect drew him even now. He wasn't sure what Ian had planned for his guests, but for Sara and her son, he'd make sure they had alternate arrangements. He was on the phone for a little under a minute before he had things worked out to his satisfaction. The entire time he could feel her attention on him as he juggled the boy in one hand and the phone in the other.

"You're exhausted," he said as he slipped the phone into his pocket. "I've got another hotel arranged for you. Let me get you both safely on your way."

"But—"

"It was a long flight. Get some rest and then we'll talk."

"Thank you," she said softly. "But no."

She sounded in control, calm despite everything that

had happened, yet her gaze seemed distracted, like it was all too much, and her face was pale.

"No arguments. It's on my account. You just take care of him, of the boy." He didn't tell her what he'd seen, why he was so concerned. He looked into her eyes. The look she gave him said that she trusted him and still he couldn't tell her that he'd saved her child from a potential kidnapping. He didn't know why she was here or what she wanted, but that need to protect, to not have her worry, was as alive as it had been during their relationship.

He put a hand on her shoulder. The fact that he knew the owner here, at the hotel they had only just left, was not a consideration. The hotel he was sending her to had housed royalty. It was secure on a whole other level.

"It's secure," he said as he pulled a pen and a business card from his pocket.

"I trust you," she said simply.

"I imagine you do."

"What is that supposed to mean?" she demanded. "I'm not here because of you, if that's what you're thinking." But something about her voice sounded off.

"Yet, you're here in this hotel. My friend Ian's hotel. The one I was doing security for."

"I don't know what you're talking about." Again, there was that change in tone, as if she was telling him something that wasn't quite true.

"Don't you?" he asked, trying to tone down any sarcasm. "That all seems oddly coincidental."

Her lips tightened and she wouldn't look at him.

Everything about her was the same and yet so different. The child was the most glaring change. Having a child wasn't something she'd wanted, at least not when they were dating. He knew that because when they were together she had told him often enough how she was determined to make her career in management and one day open her own bed-and-breakfast. She'd been focused and had even said she'd have a family only when she was established. With no husband and with a child, and her longed-for career obviously in jeopardy, could this be about money? He'd never have believed that of Sara, that she'd looked him up so that he could support her in the lifestyle to which she wanted to get accustomed. It had happened before with other women, women he hadn't cared much about. It was always about the money, not about him—except maybe for the good time he showed them. But Sara, she was different.

"What are you thinking?" she said and that tone was in her voice, the one where she expected he was going to toe the line. But there was no line, no relationship. He looked at her, at her determined stance, and saw the stubbornness he remembered. Still, she'd changed. She had a baby.

She glared up at him. "You think I'm here because…"

"Because what, Sara?" he asked darkly. "You need help. You have a kid now. You need help and I—"

"You always could be a jerk," she muttered, cutting him off.

"Name calling, Sara?"

She looked at him with regret. "I'm sorry. That was beneath me."

He skated over her apology. It didn't matter. She could say what she wanted but he couldn't see any other reason for her being here. And the last thing they needed was to fight in a situation like this. It was unwarranted and it would upset the boy. "You'll be safer in the new hotel," he said, as if that ended the discussion. "Let's get moving."

Instead, she was silent, as if considering something, and then she looked up at him. "Tell me the truth, Talib.

Did something happen back there in the hotel that you're not telling me? Besides the obvious—the explosion. I mean with Everett. It seems like you're not telling me something."

She was so bang on that he wanted to turn away from her. He wasn't sure what to say. So he took the safe path and said nothing.

"It's about Everett, isn't it? Where was he when you found him at the hotel? Did someone try to take him? Is that what you're not telling me?"

The tone in her voice, the words—all of it seemed to bring the heavy weight of responsibility. He wasn't sure why he would be feeling that for her, any more than he would for any other client. But she wasn't his client and there was the boy.

"No," he lied. He couldn't tell her the truth. He didn't know what the truth was. What he did know was that he could hear the edge of panic in her voice and she needed to be calm for her and for her son. Knowing wouldn't make a difference to her safety. He had taken care of that by arranging for the move. "I just want to make sure you're safe after everything that happened here. And the hotel you're going to has one of the best security systems in the city. Don't worry," he said, feeling rather low for lying to her the way he was. But in a way he felt justified for he knew she had yet to tell him why she was here and he wasn't completely convinced that money wasn't the problem.

"The security in this new hotel that you mentioned, it just frightens me that you think I need it. There's something you're not telling me, Talib." She looked at him. "But I'll let it go for now."

"I think that might be said for both of us. Here's my direct number." He handed her the business card he'd pulled out earlier—on it, he'd written the private number that few people, other than his family, had access to. "I'm available night or day at that number."

"Thank you, Talib," she said and despite the formality in her voice there was also something oddly intimate in her tone.

He hesitated. It wasn't a lover's caress that he remembered, or the stern, I'm-pissed-with-you tone. It was something else, something regretful, yet stronger than that. He'd consider it all later. For now, he had more important things to think about.

A car pulled up to the corner with one of his staffers driving. "Assad will take you there. The cost of the hotel is handled."

"Talib, no," she protested again.

"Yes," he said firmly. "I'll catch up with you later."

He opened the door and she slipped in, opening her arms for him to place her son in them. He couldn't turn away from the haunted look in her eyes and at the picture of the sleeping toddler in her arms. It was serene, so peaceful. This wasn't the Sara he remembered. This was so much more. He had to yank his thoughts back.

"Don't leave the hotel, Sara. Promise me," he said. "In fact, once you're in your suite, stay there. Order something to eat." He handed her another business card. "If you need anything else, use this number. He's a good friend and manages the hotel. Otherwise your money isn't good there…"

"Talib, no."

But her voice was quiet, resigned, as if she knew what he would say, where this was going.

"I'll be there later," he promised. This time his expression was serious as he handed her one more business card. "If you have any concerns at all and you can't reach me. Call my brother, Emir." He wanted to ask her so much more. Personal questions crowded with ones that might somehow affect this case. For now, he'd follow one of Nassar's cardinal rules—secure the innocent, regardless of whether or not they were potential witnesses.

"WE CAN'T FIGHT an Al-Nassar. As long as he didn't know, that was one thing. We could blindside him through Sara. Playing her was easy. But the Al-Nassars have resources. I don't know if they've ever lost a case." This wasn't turning out as Tad Rossi—who disliked his given name, Tadbir, and was never called anything but Tad—had planned. He knew he should have given this plan more thought, but when she'd run, he'd panicked. That wasn't what he'd intended.

"Speed will be our secret weapon."

"Secret weapon. You're talking stupid and—"

"Don't you ever call me that, ever!" The last word ended in a shout. "We clean house once and run," his partner said calmly as if he hadn't just lost his temper. "We'll be in and out before anyone is any wiser."

"What do you mean by that?" Tad gripped the phone. He was beginning to have qualms about contacting this man in the first place and definitely about calling him now. But he'd never expected Sara would run to Marrakech. And when she had, he'd become desperate. He couldn't lose her. He'd reached out to one of the few contacts he had left in that country and he'd known almost the minute he'd done it that it had been a mistake. He'd known him since public school. They'd been friends, as only two mismatched souls could be, and they had bonded together. He'd known Habib's disdain for the Al-Nassar family even then. He's also known that his childhood friend's life hadn't amounted to much except petty crime. Despite all that, they'd remained friends of sorts, oddballs thrown together by life. That was until he'd left Morocco. Then, he'd lost touch.

His old friend was someone who had every quality he required—ill feelings against the Al-Nassars and someone with no scruples. He hadn't anticipated that the grudge that motivated his accomplice was as large and far-reaching as it was. Unfortunately, now it was clear that the man would stop at nothing now that the window of opportunity had been opened. His ideas were outrageous and he couldn't believe what he was now suggesting.

"I know where he works and where he plays for the next few days. He's going to be tied to her and if he's not, he'll be at his friend's hotel. It's fairly easy, at least it is at the moment."

"Easy?" This had been a mistake and he was too far away to change any of it. "You have no idea what crap the Al-Nassars can pull, or the strings they've yanked. I wouldn't want to face one of them."

"Face? That's never going to happen." He chuckled. "That's the sweet spot. Talib Al-Nassar will never know who we are or who brought him down. He'll be done and never know what hit him. Besides, you screwed up, idiot. You're not even in the country. You've got no control over what happens."

He was right about that. Tad rubbed his thumb and forefinger together. He'd lost control and he needed to get it back. He needed to stop this thing, because what he was hearing was leading dangerously close to a place he didn't want to go—murder.

"The key to success is a clean sweep."

He knew what that meant. The only part of this plan that they both agreed on was the end, which left Sara as she had always been—a destitute single mother and of no interest to anyone, despite her model looks. That was exactly what she deserved. The only problem was that in his plan no one died. What was being proposed was nothing he would agree to. He needed to stop this before things got out of hand.

"It might only be about the money for you, but it's about much more for me." His accomplice continued, as if justifying his dark intent.

"That wasn't part of the deal."

"Too bad. But I see the biggest threat to my happiness on a morgue slab in the near future." Silence slipped darkly between them. "When that happens, money or not, I'll call it over."

He was insane. But Tad had known that before he'd contacted him. No, he corrected himself, he knew that he'd always been a little crazy. He hadn't expected this full-scale madness. He had to reel him in before his blood thirst destroyed everything. He'd acted on emotion, on panic, and reached out to the wrong man.

"This is over," he said. "I can't be part of this." He remembered how it had started, when he'd first seen Sara and been wowed by her looks. He'd only been into her for what he might get, then he'd thought it would be about sex but she'd disappointed there, refusing any of his overtures. It had been luck that had caused him to stumble on something even better than sex—money. When he'd realized who her son's father was he'd known he'd hit a gravy train he hadn't expected. That kind of luck was once in a lifetime.

"Too late. Dress rehearsal is over. We've taken the boy—"

"No!" Kidnapping wasn't in the cards—at least not what one would call a traditional kidnapping. A threat here or there, maybe. But murder hadn't been, either, and now he was suggesting both.

"You've lost control, my friend. It's my game now." He ended the call before Tad could say another word.

This was his fault, his stupidity. He'd bought time with a madman. He'd been desperate and desperate men did desperate things. He was living proof of that. But threatening to kill an Al-Nassar was insanity. Their reach and scope was not something a common man could go up against. He knew that, he'd always known that, just as he'd always known that it was Sara who was the key to everything.

And now it was Sara who was close to ruining his life, his plan—his everything. She was the path to getting what he wanted. He had to shut down his accomplice and he had to do it now. Except all he had was the twenty in his pocket. It wasn't enough for a bus across the country, never mind a plane across the Atlantic.

He was screwed unless he moved to Plan B. The thought of that cheered him, gave him hope.

If Sara wanted to play hardball, she'd be sorry. Soon she was going to learn who she was dealing with.

Chapter Five

Talib watched until the car was out of sight and Sara and the boy were out of the area—out of danger. He stood rocking on the balls of his feet, then spat the remains of his mint gum into the trash. He glanced at the No Parking sign above the trash can that was so faded, it was almost illegible. He thought of the boy. There was something familiar about him. In a way, it was like looking in a mirror. But that was ridiculous. Sara would never do that to him. She obviously liked Moroccan men and she'd made a mistake, but it hadn't been with him.

He reached into his pocket as if a pack of cigarettes was there. Stress always seemed to bring with it the need for tobacco. If nothing else, the gum took the edge off the craving and replaced a much worse habit that he'd kicked only six months ago. He'd started smoking three years ago despite his otherwise health-conscious lifestyle. It had been different then. He'd needed something, as the cliché went—a crutch. His mind flashed back to when Sara left. At the time, it seemed as though smoking was the only way to get through the pain he refused to admit he was feeling. Still refused to admit.

A senior police officer who he'd known for years came out of the north entrance, spotted him and came over. He gave the officer what information he knew.

Now, he waited as Ian crossed the street.

"How the hell could this have happened?" Ian asked, but didn't wait for an answer. "Anything new?" The frown lines carving his tanned face reflected his unspoken worry, that the explosion could have a catastrophic effect on a new opening.

"No," Talib said. "I haven't had a chance to do more than a cursory investigation and the police are still inside."

He had gone through the possibilities and checked the site before the authorities had arrived. "It all adds up to a fairly professional job, and yet, oddly amateur. I know those two images clash, but that's how it appears to have gone down. It seemed to be more a diversion than anything else."

He thought of the boy, Sara's child, that he'd snatched from the hands of a woman who claimed she was returning him. All that seemed a little much unless there was money involved. The Sara he knew had no money, but despite his assumptions, that all could have changed in the intervening years since they'd been a couple. He didn't know anything about her since their breakup. He'd been back to the States as part of his career with the family business on numerous occasions, and never had he looked her up. Mainly, he'd tried not to think about her. The end of their relationship hadn't been easy. It had been a blow to his pride, or at least that's what he told himself. The truth hurt a little too much.

He wasn't sure what to add to what he'd just said for he didn't know how the child and the maid fit in. "Of course, that's just off the top. I haven't had a chance to take a close look at the aftermath." The truth was that his thoughts couldn't focus.

Sara.

He couldn't believe she was here and he had no idea why she was. The last time he'd seen her had been in Wyoming. She'd been finishing up her last year of school and paying for it by working as a manager at the hotel where he was staying. Her appearance now was a mystery, one for which he didn't have an answer, and in the order of priorities, it would have to vie with the aftermath of the explosion and the investigation that would follow. He knew that the police would follow up with various hotel guests, but he'd pull a few strings to get her out of the fray. He'd do that because, no matter what had happened to the two of them, he still wanted to protect her. That meant making sure that neither she nor her son was any more involved than they needed to be.

"They seem to be petty thieves after money and jewelry. There was quite a bit of that taken," Ian said, breaking into his thoughts. "Three wallets and a purse are missing, but a jewelry bag in one of the suitcases holding some rather expensive jewelry was left. Odd, when it seems like a pickpocket was at work in the lobby, they miss a stash there for the taking."

One of the police officers spotted them and came over. "You were here at the outset?" he asked Talib.

"I was. I've given my report," Talib said. "Have you found anything else?"

"We've gotten all the physical evidence we can. Looks like the explosion was a diversionary ploy to commit a bit of petty theft."

"None of the rooms were disturbed. In fact, there's no evidence that the perpetrators went any farther than the main floor," he said, addressing Ian. "We'll be continuing with the investigation but we should be able to let you clean up the area later this afternoon."

"Seems a little excessive for petty theft," Talib said.

He didn't like the direction this investigation was taking. It seemed slightly off-track.

"We've seen it before," the officer said, but his tone was almost defensive. He didn't give them a chance to reply but instead moved toward where the hotel guests gathered.

He was wrong, Talib thought. The explosion as a diversion for petty theft seemed too simple. In fact, it *was* too simple. It was why law enforcement in Marrakech had recently gotten a bad name. Too many crimes had been stuffed under the rug. But the police had their own problems with ongoing complaints of conspiracy and corruption. That aside, there was more at work here and the police officer either didn't know, or wasn't admitting to.

Talib thought of the scene with the maid and the boy. He'd told no one. He wasn't prepared to divulge what he knew. Not yet, and not to the authorities. There had been too many recent issues with the police from the firing of a corrupt member, to the bungling of a recent tourist kidnapping. He wouldn't chance an error being made here. Far too much was at stake.

"We need to get your security one hundred percent in place, like I advised you weeks ago." There was an edge to his voice that only matched the darkness that seemed to fill his being.

"Talib?" Ian asked. "What's going on with you? It's got to do with her, Sara. I knew she'd booked but…"

"You didn't feel it necessary to tell me," Talib said. There was no question but only a slight recrimination in his tone.

"After three years, no. Man, you haven't been a couple for a long time."

"And it was none of my business."

"I suspected she had her reasons and if it had to do

with you, she'd let you know." He looked at Talib with a frown. "What's up?"

"Nothing," he said. "I was just shocked to see her."

"Did she say why she's here?"

"No. And I doubt if it involves a need to see the country."

"My office," Ian said, and it wasn't a question. "We need to talk and it's the only place we'll get any privacy in this craziness."

Chapter Six

Talib nodded at the police officer who was monitoring the main doors to the hotel. He held up the distinctive card with its bronze-and-black flash of color that symbolized the Nassar company logo. The hotel was under lockdown but Nassar Security was well-known in Marrakech, almost as well-known as he was. Entering a scene like this was usually not an issue.

"I'm sorry." The police officer held up his hand.

"You're kidding me," Talib began with a scowl. "You won't let us back in?" This was unprecedented.

"Do you know who I am?" Ian interrupted.

"I don't care who you are," the police officer said. "No one's getting in."

"I own…"

"Get back before I have to use force." The police officer cut off Ian's words.

"I don't believe this." Ian shook his head.

Five minutes later they had worked their way through the emergency crews and around to a side entrance that wasn't being monitored.

"Back door?" the police detective asked with an amused look as he met them a few feet from the entrance. He was in charge of the investigation and Talib had spoken to him earlier. In fact, he'd spoken to him in a number of instances on other cases in the past. He was one of the few Talib trusted. Now the officer greeted them with a frown.

"Overenthusiastic rookie wouldn't let us in," Talib said.

"I see." His grimace was half smile and half resignation. "Follow me."

"The explosive device was fairly unsophisticated," the detective confirmed five minutes later. "Looks to me like it was meant as no more than a diversion, to get what cash and jewelry they could." He looked at Talib, as if expecting that he'd provide some insight.

"Fortunately there were no injuries," Ian said. "Thanks for getting us in."

The detective gave them a brief nod. "All right, I'll leave you gentleman to it. If I can just ask that you stay away from the luggage area where the device was detonated, at least for now. They're still collecting evidence."

"This wasn't about me, was it?" Ian asked as the detective moved back into the room and into the heart of the investigation. "There's something you're not telling me."

"Get over yourself," Talib said with a smile that held an edge of dry humor.

He looked across the room. Suitcases lay scattered in the haze of smoke that hung lazily, as shadowed tendrils still drifted through the room. Talib and Ian moved past the chaos and turned into a corridor, where Ian's office was separated from the main flow of the hotel lobby.

"My hotel is attacked—my guests terrified and probably not apt to come back to the Desert Sands and you want me to get over myself." Ian laughed, a dry mirthless sound that had more edge and no light-heartedness. "What happened to a little help from my friends or at least a little sympathy?"

Talib shook his head as Ian opened the door to his office. They entered a spacious, freshly painted office. New furnishings, complete with a large gleaming mahogany desk and black leather furniture, gave a solemn feel to the room. A vibrant painting full of color and reflecting the Atlas Mountains hung on the back wall and added a touch of color.

"Nice digs," Talib said in an attempt to be casual. In reality, it was the first opportunity that he'd had to see the finished office and what he considered the hub of his friend's hotel.

He sank into one of the leather chairs. He met his friend's worried look and knew the one person who needed to know everything was Ian. After all, the woman involved was in his employ. He began to tell him everything that had transpired. Ian was not just the owner of this hotel and a good friend—Ian Hendrik had once worked for Nassar. He'd been part of their research team before ending that career path to become an entrepreneur, beginning with the purchase of this hotel.

"So you think someone may have used the explosion as a smoke screen to kidnap the child?"

"Possibly," Talib said. "I'm not closing any doors right now."

"I'll find out the identity of the maid," Ian said. "Once we have that, maybe you'll have some answers."

"None of it makes sense."

"You're sure about that?" Ian asked.

"What are you suggesting?" Talib scowled.

"Someone tries to kidnap the child. I'd say they're trying to get money from Sara or her family."

"I considered that possibility. But unless things have changed, Sara has no money."

"Her family?"

"Same." He shrugged. "She doesn't come from money. The family fishing business has never been prosperous. It supports the family, her parents and her sisters' families, but that's about it." He looked off into the distance, as if he could find the answer there. "I had the office do a quick search on the family and on Sara. She's been underemployed for a while." He frowned—that information was not in line with the ambitious, professional woman he knew. Something rang sour about all of this.

"So the attempted snatching, just a crime of opportunity, black-market adoption?" Ian mused.

"I don't know." Talib shook his head. "Seems a bit of a stretch. I suppose we can only be thankful that the maid got cold feet."

"We've got a half-dozen children registered under the age of ten." Ian ran a hand through his hair.

"Frightening," Talib said. "We need to up your security, like yesterday." He didn't need to point out that his earlier advice hadn't been followed. That the hotel had opened under Ian's new management before all systems were in place.

"You were right," Ian agreed. "Whatever the reason behind this we can be thankful that no one was seriously injured. There was no irreparable damage done, except to my reputation. I'll reimburse any of the guests who lost belongings. Meanwhile, I've done a check with my public relations people. It looks like other than being shaken up, the hotel guests, with the exception of a few, are more than happy to take advantage of my offer. A free full-spa experience and one-night free stay, and coverage of alternate rooms for tonight. Most are willing to come back for the remainder of their stay here."

"That's generous," Talib said.

"You think? After scaring them to death with what

looks like a terrorist attack." He stood up, pushing back from the desk. "It's the least I could do."

"Makes sense. You don't want to lose any business. Although, you're pretty much guaranteed to lose some."

"I don't think it will affect business in the long term and that's all that matters. That's my priority. That, and making sure that this doesn't happen again," he said with a look at Talib.

"When I'm finished, you'll have security that will make the royal family jealous," Talib said. "This time give me carte blanche and stand aside."

"You're on," Ian said. "I can't have a repeat of this. I'll have my assistant get the employee records together. Should be an hour, two at most."

Talib glanced at his watch. "I'll check in with you later."

He stood up. His hand swept through his hair as if it was long enough to get in his face. Three years ago it had been. Three years ago he had experimented with a pony-tail. Three years ago he'd experimented with a few things.

He left with a quick shake of hands and his mind already moving forward to the piece that didn't fit the puzzle—Sara and the boy.

Why were they here—why now... Why at all?

Chapter Seven

Sara shifted her sleeping son in her aching arms. She pushed back the soft dark curls that framed his face and repositioned him so that his weight lay across her, his head in the crook of her left arm. After Talib had given him back to her, in those moments of relief tinged with panic and despair, she'd seen what the future would be and she'd clung to her son. She would refuse to relinquish holding Everett to anyone, ever again. In the short time since Talib had found her, in all the chaos that had followed, he'd calmly made arrangements for an alternate place for her to stay and she hadn't been allowed to lift a finger. The arrangements had been made swiftly, silently and efficiently. She wasn't used to that. It was usually up to her, as a single parent, to do it all. Not now. The only thing she'd done was carry her son and she knew that she only had to ask and someone would do that, too. She wasn't ready to relinquish Everett after everything that had happened. She knew that after all the craziness of the explosion and evacuation, holding Everett was more for her than him. He was over it and she knew that as soon as he awoke, he would rather be on the ground, exploring on his own terms.

From the moment the car pulled up to the new hotel, the Sahara Sunset, again, everything was done for her.

Assad opened the door. The valet offered to take her bags. She refused. She didn't have much. Her suitcase had been left behind at the Desert Sands Hotel, part of the evidence in the investigation.

Everett sniffed as if he was waking up and then settled against her shoulder with that familiar yet strange little sound. It almost sounded like an old man sighing. Sometimes her son seemed older than his years, and she wondered what he would be like as he grew up.

That thought made her more determined and her fright faded into the background as she entered the hotel lobby. Nothing could stop her. She'd come all this way. Now, the only challenge she had yet to face was herself. But she knew that fear could stop her despite the distance she traveled. One sign that Everett was safe without Talib's protection and she'd turn and run back the way she'd come. But that was asking for a miracle, and for the last seven months there had been none offered through the long days, transient jobs and three states. Every one of those days had been a nightmare, highlighted by fear that any minute she'd be discovered. Now, she had little money and no place to live. More importantly, no place to hide—no options.

She shifted her purse.

"Can I take that, ma'am?" a man with threads of silver in his short, dark hair asked. He was wearing a djellaba with a gold belt around his waist. The traditional Moroccan garment had the insignia of the hotel on his shoulder. It seemed to be the uniform of many of the men employed by this hotel.

"No, I… Thank you. I have it," she replied. Even though that was a lie. She barely had it, one bag was slipping but she refused to relinquish any of her belongings. There wasn't much. Only her purse, the diaper bag and the bag with the essentials to get home or, alternatively, everything they would need if they had to run. It was an outrageous thought, but maybe not so much considering everything that had happened today.

She tried to stay focused and not be wowed by her surroundings, but it was impossible. Luxury enveloped her. The marble floors glinted across the massive lobby. The expanse of floor-to-ceiling glass circled the lobby and drew one's eye outside to the emerald green lawn and glimmering pool. There were elegantly uniformed staff everywhere. But they remained on the periphery, quietly available, slipping in to assist as needed. A massive chandelier sparkled overhead. It was only a decoration at this hour of the day, as sunlight streamed across the marble and reflected off the dark ebony trim of the registration desk.

This hotel was definitely out of her league. It felt like all eyes were on her and it was apparent that they knew of her arrival. It was also clear that she was going nowhere without someone three steps behind her. Talib's promise that she'd be safe had yet to be proven, but she was definitely feeling like she was well guarded.

She smiled and yet she felt more resigned than amused at the irony of staying in a place like this with her finances. She'd handed over the last of her retirement fund over three weeks ago and with nothing to meet Tad's demands, she'd run again. It was the fourth time she'd run; Tad had found her the other two. And on the third, she'd been in Chicago. That time, the message arrived by telephone before she could even secure a way to make a living. She'd gotten the cheap, throw-away phone to keep in touch with her family and to keep her number and location hidden from him. And two days after she'd gotten it, Tad had called in the dead of night, somehow having found her number.

The lavishness of the lobby made her want to bolt. The only thing that gave her any confidence was the fact that Talib had arranged this. Security and protection was his forte, she had no doubt that they'd be safe. But that was only part of the reason that she was here.

"Mama," Everett murmured in that sleepy, dream-time voice. He was only shifting from one sleep level to another and was more than likely not waking up. The trip had been too long and too much for him. It had been too much for both of them.

"I'm here, baby," she whispered, humming the opening line of "My Favorite Things." It was the song her grandmother sang to her as a child, taken from *The Sound of Music*. Her grandmother had sung it so many times to her. She'd sung it to Everett, in those first difficult months of being a new mother.

"Ma'am." A slim man about her age and dressed in a black, gold-trimmed suit, slightly different from the other employees, came over to her. "Can I help, a stroller for the baby, a—"

"No, thanks," she interrupted. She shifted Everett.

"Your room is ready. I'll show you to it."

Her room. Where would it be? How many floors up? Being higher up, farther from the street and possible danger, would make her feel safer. And yet, it was also more difficult to run to those same streets, to safety, should a threat lurk here, in this hotel. Hopefully it was high, but not too high.

Talib had said that they'd be safe. It was strange. After all this time and after everything that had happened, she believed him. He could keep her son safe. That knowledge had brought her across the ocean straight to him.

But she knew she might have a better chance if she was upfront with him as quickly as possible. As things stood, he didn't know what she needed to be safe from. Could he protect the boy he didn't know from a threat that he didn't know about? She doubted it. She could only hope that what the hotel's security offered to its elite guests would be enough until she could tell Talib the truth. The truth she dreaded to reveal. The truth she had vowed to tell and the truth he so desperately needed to know.

She looked to her left, where a white-haired man stood lounging in a self-possessed kind of way. He was wearing an expensive-looking suit that had a look and cut that spoke of designer as opposed to off-the-rack. The look meshed with the confident way he stood, like he was used to being in charge. The woman beside him was at least twenty years younger. As Sara watched, she turned to speak briefly to one of the staff, who nodded and disappeared. As she turned back, the red sole of her Jimmy Choo stiletto was clear.

Those around her oozed wealth. They were people who lived lives that she could never imagine, opulent lives of privilege.

Her observations only served to make her feel even more out of place. She was sure that people were looking at her, at her simple, casual dress, like nothing anyone else in this lobby was wearing. She stood out. She didn't fit. She felt like a gold digger and yet she wasn't. This was about Everett, not about her.

Her thoughts shifted. She hadn't expected to find Talib so soon. What had he been doing at the same hotel where they had registered for their first three nights? And the explosion… The thought of it made her shudder. What did it all mean?

The only thing she knew for sure was what Talib had

told her, that she and her son were safe here. That, she believed. It was words like that, that had her traveling across an ocean to a world that had once frightened her because all she could see were the differences. It was Talib's world, and it was this and other things that had driven them apart.

She was ushered into an elevator that was paneled in onyx. The walls were backlit so that the interior gleamed. This hotel was opulent in the extreme.

She shifted Everett and in the process hugged him tighter. He didn't complain. That was what she'd been afraid of, him sensing her tension. Instead, he was still sound asleep, exhausted. She was, too. Almost too tired to contemplate everything that had happened since they'd arrived. It had all been overwhelming and she needed Talib more than she'd even known. And she was frightened, more frightened than she'd been on the flight over.

She watched as the floors ticked away. Seventh floor, eighth. It was at the ninth that the elevator doors opened. The corridor was wider and more open than the standard hotel. There wasn't door after door, as there were in what she thought of as a normal hotel. They walked along a plush carpet edged in gleaming marble. Finally, they reached a door twice as wide as anything that she was accustomed to, and that shone from polish or just from the rich wood itself.

Inside, she was too overwhelmed to speak. Light flooded from a bank of windows in front of her. The ceiling soared at least twenty feet above her and the marble floor continued through the suite.

The bellhop showed her what was available and how to contact him. He took the most time going over the contents of a well-stocked bar, which, he assured her, had snacks appropriate for both her and her son. There was not just a minifridge, but a minikitchen set up to provide whatever she needed. Her mind flashed to Talib. She was both grateful and astonished that in the short time since her arrival, he'd made sure they had everything they needed. She noticed there was milk, juice and a small box of animal crackers—she had no idea where those could have been found, but they had.

As they finished the walk-through, she noted the large bathroom, the luxurious tub and the generous space so unlike any hotel room she'd ever stayed in. This wasn't a room but a small suite of rooms.

"Wait," she said as the man prepared to leave with a respectful bob in her direction. "I'll tip..."

He shook his head. "No, ma'am, you take care of the little one. The tip is handled."

"Handled?"

"Yes. If you need anything, you call me immediately." He bowed. "Sheik Talib Al-Nassar wants me to remind you that you are safe here. You are to order supper up and not worry about the cost. He will cover it. Stay in your room." He bowed again. "That is all."

He shut the door. She sank onto the soft leather couch, her son by her side. The opulence was lost in the feeling of despair she felt. Her son would be safe, but Everett would no longer be hers, he would be his, Talib's. Already, the process had started.

She closed her eyes. Everett was safe.

That was all that mattered.

TALIB HADN'T EXPECTED to be that long at the Desert Sands Hotel. But after going through the employee records with Ian, they were able to pinpoint one woman. Unfortunately, she was part-time and the address she listed turned out to belong to a cousin who hadn't seen her in weeks. Despite that glitch, he had one of the office staff tracking her.

It was dark, suppertime had come and gone. Hours had passed since he'd put Sara in the car with Assad. He hadn't had time to think of why she was here, and with a baby. None of it made sense to him, at least not the fact that she was here. She'd had a fear of traveling overseas. During the four months they'd been together and as his time in the States was waning, he'd half-jokingly said she should visit him here. She'd bluntly told him that that would never happen. She was quite comfortable never leaving the States or even Wyoming.

He stepped into the BMW, the earlier thrill of driving the incredible vehicle long gone. Around him Marrakech was lit up in its nighttime glory. It was a beautiful sight that inspired him every time he saw it. He never tired of it, yet tonight it didn't wow him as usual—he could have been anywhere. He could only think of Sara and why she was here, of what it might mean. Sara and the boy and the mystery of what had brought her to Marrakech. As well as the unlikely coincidence of finding her in that hotel in the midst of a catastrophic event. None of it added up. The hotel, he could get that. Ian had been running a blowout promotional sale that many of the tourist companies, as well as independent travelers, had picked up on. Sara undoubtedly realized she wasn't likely to get a better deal in the city, as far as location and convenience. That is, until the explosion.

In fact, he'd already checked. She'd gone through a travel agent, whose go-to hotel in the last two weeks had been the Desert Sands. There was a good chance that the hotel hadn't been picked by Sara, she'd only agreed on a choice. Her being there was more than likely coincidental. But the question was—why was she here in Morocco?

And why now? The more cynical side of him considered that it might be about the money. Why else? And yet that had never been Sara. But that was years ago. She had a kid now and he had no doubt that had impacted her career. She needed money and he had a lot of it. That fact had tempted more than one woman he'd known. They'd wanted him for superficial reasons, for the good time he could show them, for his unlimited resources. But Sara had never been the type to use people. She hadn't gone out with him for the money or the fine time he was capable of showing her. In fact, she'd begged off a number of times when he'd wanted to take her out for an exquisite dinner at an expensive restaurant. Instead she insisted on cooking for him at home, in her apartment. She'd refused to take anything but the smallest gifts from him, and even those she balked at. At the time, she'd seemed to truly be interested in him, in his company.

Was she capable of extortion or just plain begging for funds? Even if she was, she could have done that more easily than coming to Morocco. But that wasn't the Sara he knew. The Sara he knew had been hardworking—determined to learn everything she could about the hotel industry and eventually open the bed-and-breakfast. She'd been passionate about that. But that was single Sara—unencumbered, sexually adventurous…fun. That wasn't the Sara he'd seen now.

This Sara had a son and her priorities had changed. He'd gotten the search results back on her. She hadn't held a job of any importance in quite a while. Something had radically changed. And the only one who had the answers was Sara.

It was time they talked about why she was really here.

Chapter Eight

When Sara opened the door, her gray eyes were sleep-clouded and Talib was brought back to another time, and another place. But she didn't smile when she saw him, nor did she look at him with eyes rich with passion. Those days were long gone. Instead, she frowned, and then, as if to compensate for not immediately welcoming him, offered him a shaky smile.

"Come in," she said quietly and stepped back. "The baby's sleeping," she warned. The way she said it gave the disconcerting and very real reminder that she was a woman who'd been at mothering for a while.

"How much do you need?" he asked as he moved into the room. He gazed at the boy sound asleep on the bed in the bedroom just ahead of him, his profile dimly lit by the soft glow of a nightlight, saw the impression where she had obviously just been lying beside him before he'd arrived. Probably asleep, too, he imagined. And at that thought, guilt ran through him at the blunt and potentially unfair question that he'd just thrown at her. He hadn't meant to do it, to say those words, at least not in that manner. He wished that he could pull them back, as he felt the unfamiliar bitter tang of remorse.

"What do you mean?" She frowned at him, her lips

pursed, her eyes still clouded with the vestiges of sleep, and something else that he couldn't quite name.

"What are you suggesting?" Her voice was tight, contained, as if she was used to hiding her emotion.

He wasn't sure why he'd said it the way he had—raw, invasive, accusatory. But he knew that in doing so he'd opened Pandora's box and there was no going back.

"You haven't had a job in almost a year, not one of any worth, and you have a child. I can only assume you're broke and that's why you're here." They were fighting words and he couldn't stop himself.

"You…" Her voice shook and her face flushed, as it had in the past, when she was angry.

"I might not be in love with you, Sara, but I never stopped caring about you. How much do you need?" In fact, he'd wanted to compensate her when they'd broken up and he'd told her that. His brother, Zafir had later pointed out that offering money was pretty much the most insulting thing you could suggest to a woman. In fact, it was only then that he'd seen why she'd felt angry enough, that it justified scratching his car's paint with the heel of her shoe. She'd been furious and it had been weeks before he'd known exactly why. He had to admit that he'd grown a lot since then. Now he looked into eyes, which were deeper and so much older than they'd been three years ago, and waited for her reply.

Silence.

She'd traveled a long way but obviously lost her courage at the critical moment. He needed to step up and step in, and with that in mind, he offered her enough for her to live on and raise the baby, at least for a while.

Her lips tightened when she heard the generous sum he offered. He wasn't sure why—it was enough to keep her and the boy for the next five years in middle-class comfort. And plenty of time for her to get on her feet. He didn't think about all the reasons why he was so concerned about her, about another man's child.

"I…" She wrinkled her small, slightly freckled nose.

It was a habit he'd found both adorable and mildly annoying when they'd been together. He didn't like hesitation in anyone. Make up your mind and move forward. It was how he lived his life and what he demanded of others. The Sara he remembered had been a bit whimsical and, oddly enough, that had attracted him.

There were a lot of things going on here. He felt a twinge of guilt over the fact that someone had tried to take her son and she didn't know. The guilt was over the fact that he wasn't sure if he was going to mention it to her—at least not now, not right away. He wasn't sure what the motive was and he'd like to have more information before he told her. At this point he didn't know what had motivated the attempted snatching. For all he knew it might just have been a case of right age, right sex, right race. A chance to make money in the underground market, selling the child off to others desperate for a child of their own. He frowned at the idea.

The silence stretched between them.

"Where's his father?" He finally asked the burning question when she had yet to respond one way or the other to his offer. This was the question that had risen from the first moment he'd seen her and it was the question that circumstances had given him no chance to ask. Or the right, logic reminded him. But right or not, it didn't matter. He'd asked. It was out there, irretrievable.

"His father," she said and the words seemed to draw out as she backed away from him into the bedroom. There, she pulled a blanket over the boy and gently pulled his thumb out of his mouth. When she faced him in the doorway, her gray eyes were stormy as they locked with his. The connection broke swiftly as she looked away and back to her son, as if she couldn't bear to look at him for any length of time. But as he thought that, she whirled around to him, with her lips tight and her eyes sparking with a passion he couldn't identify.

"You tell me."

Chapter Nine

Sara took a mental step back, away from the anger building within her and that he'd-done-her-wrong feeling. She'd been baiting him and she had no right. It wasn't his fault that he had not participated in his son's life to date, that fell on her. But everything else was his fault. By default...

Sara yanked herself back from the pointless blame game. He wasn't psychic and yet she was treating him like he was. She should never have said what she had. She should never have set him up in a situation where he was clearly unable to defend himself. It hadn't been right and she knew she could do better. But she didn't have time to rectify any of it. They could only go on from this moment.

He'd always been insightful, slightly intuitive about everything, except, in the end, their relationship. Ironically, now, when he'd suggested that she was here for money—the thought grated, even though, for all the reasons he had yet to understand, it was true.

A knock on the door echoed sharply through the room and made her jump. She stumbled against the couch and caught herself with one hand.

"Who is it?" Talib said in a voice that was more of a demand than a question. He moved toward the door as if there was a threat, as if he knew what she had yet to tell him.

Sara's heart pounded wildly—was there danger?

She gave herself a mental shake. She was seeing shadows and demons everywhere, but considering what had happened earlier, she was justified.

Even here they weren't safe. It had been proven. Unpredictable, undefinable things were threatening her everywhere and she wasn't sure why. Although the explosion must have been a horrible coincidence. She knew that. But so much had happened that she was seeing danger lurking everywhere. She had to quit it. She needed a clear mind to protect her son and she needed Talib. He was why she was here. No, she corrected herself, it was because of Tad that she was here, that she even needed Talib.

Tad?

Had he found her? That was an outrageous thought. There were thousands of miles separating them. She shivered. Impossible, she told herself. It was more than likely a hotel employee. And yet the shadow of him finding her hung around her like a cloaking veil. Her imagination kept taking her back to that possibility. The fear had followed her on the long flight across the Atlantic and it hadn't gone away since their arrival. Her heart beat wildly and her first instinct was to move back to the bed and put her body between whoever was at that door and her son.

She looked at Talib. He was physically intimidating, intelligent and a member of the powerful Al-Nassar family. They contracted to protect and their resources were astonishing and that was one of the reasons she was here. She had to trust him.

"Emir," Talib said as he opened the door.

Her heart seemed to skip a beat at the acknowledgement the fear could be set aside. It wasn't Tad.

Talib gestured his oldest brother inside, as if his arrival was expected.

"What are you doing here?" Talib asked as he looked back at Sara and seemed to almost deliberately place himself between her and Emir.

"I was in the area. I got your message, so rather than a phone call I thought I'd—"

"Right," Talib interrupted and it was clear from his tone that he didn't believe his brother's reason for being here.

Sara moved around Talib and put out her hand. "Sara Elliott. I used to—"

"Date Talib," he said with a smile. "I know. It was a poorly kept secret."

"No secret at all," Talib said defensively.

Sara looked at him with a frown. She'd never heard Talib speak like that. It made her wonder what he'd told his brother. But it didn't matter. She had bigger things to worry about than the fact that he might have fudged the truth of their relationship, possibly made it less than it was. But what had it been? She looked back to the bedroom door, to Everett. Definitely more than either of them had expected. She brought her attention quickly back to Emir.

"Nothing bad," Emir said with a smile. "In fact we thought for sure Talib was a goner." He looked laughingly over at his brother and received a weak smile in return.

Emir took her hand and shook it warmly. The expression in his eyes matched his handshake, as if he approved of her. Yet, that was impossible, he didn't know her. They'd never met. She was an ex, and she imagined in Emir's mind, immediately bad news. She couldn't imagine what he'd think when he knew about the baby.

Everett began to cry, breaking into her thoughts as he so often did. But this time he had her full attention, for he was beginning with that soft snuffle that would escalate into a full-scale demand if she didn't stop him now.

Emir turned and walked to the doorway of the bedroom.

"And who is this?" Emir asked, interrupting her instinctive thought to go to her son.

She didn't answer him immediately, as he seemed to not want an answer. Instead, Emir was focused completely on Everett's crying.

The nightlight glowed in the room as Emir went over to her son. He talked softly to the boy and seemed completely at ease with a cranky toddler.

She frowned. He was not like the man she'd heard of in stories that Talib had told her. In those stories he had been almost legendary. There was something softer about him. Maybe love did that. She'd heard that there was love in the air between him and one of the Wyoming agents. She'd also heard that a marriage was planned. She wasn't sure if that was what had changed the man Talib had described, or if his perception of his brother was different from what hers might be. Whatever it was, it didn't matter. She didn't need Emir guessing what she had yet to tell Talib. That would only make a bad situation so much worse. But there was no stopping him. For a moment Sara's heart seemed to stop. *Please, no*, she thought. *Just give me this one break and I'll tell him.* Seconds felt like minutes as she waited for Emir to blurt out what, to her, seemed so glaringly obvious.

"You don't mind if I pick him up?" Emir smiled at her over his shoulder. "Good practice for me. Not that we have any children yet but Kate and I both…" He shrugged. "Someday."

She blew out a quiet breath as Everett smiled at him and actually chuckled when he picked him up.

"You might as well bring him out where we are. He's not going back to sleep for a while," she said as she turned and left the room. She glanced over her shoulder to see Emir following her with Everett in his arms. It was strange and the odd thought hit her that Emir, under different circumstances, could easily be a favorite uncle.

"You need a wedding first," Talib said interrupting her thoughts and Sara inwardly cringed at the words.

First comes love, then comes marriage… It was an old saying, but it was one that underlined the values she'd grown up with. The values that she'd found herself so far on the other side of. It was why she hadn't gone back to her family for help. While they wouldn't turn her away, their disapproval would be a dark shadow to raise Everett under. She wouldn't do that, because it would mark the man he would eventually become. She hoped eventually that her family would come around, become more open-minded. Now, it didn't matter. Since she'd run, she had kept in touch with them via private messaging on social media. Because, no matter what their feelings were about the situation, they'd come to accept it. Ironically, in the past months of long-distance communication, it was clear that while they might not like that their daughter had given birth to their grandson as a single woman, in the end they loved both she and Everett and, because of that, they worried.

"He's good with kids," Talib told her. "Most likely because he's the oldest."

Sara was at a loss, grateful for the size of the room, because in a normal-size hotel room these two vibrant

Al-Nassar brothers would have overwhelmed her. Power seemed to emanate from them. It was a self-assuredness that she would like to have said was more pronounced with Talib, but that wasn't the case. They wielded their authority with ease, but in different ways. Even here, Emir was larger than life and Talib even larger than that, at least physically. She sank down on the bed as Emir handed her son back to her. But the look Emir gave her was like the moment of truth. She could see it all in his eyes. He knew the truth that had yet to be told.

The hand that he put on her shoulder, as brief as it was, spoke of support and solidarity. As she met Emir's ebony eyes, she sensed he knew. He had seen the truth in her son's face. Even he couldn't help but see how closely the boy resembled Talib.

Talib had the power to take her son and offer him the life she could not. Running from the blackmail rather than turning to Talib had been a bad decision. It wasn't until she'd run out of places to go that she'd been willing to turn to the one man that could help her: Talib. But seeing Emir and Talib together terrified her because it reminded her of everything she stood to lose. Everett was one of them in a way she never could be. The Al-Nassar family had the power and the might to run roughshod over someone like her. They had the resources to claim Everett and raise him as their own. And the head of all that might was making this room just a little too crowded.

The nightmares that had awoken her so many nights in a cold sweat, trembling with what she imagined the future could be, seemed so much closer to becoming a reality. Emir had squeezed her shoulder, as if telling her he was on her side, not to worry. Or maybe all of that was wishful thinking. It would be nice to have one member of the family on her side. But was he on her side? The

Al-Nassar brothers' loyalty to each other and their sister ran deep. But the look that was now on his face confirmed not only what she already suspected, but that he also guessed that Talib did not know.

"The hotel's secure?" Emir asked as he turned to Talib.

"It is."

"I heard there was an explosion…"

"Handled," Talib said shortly. "Look. Can we talk later?"

"There's a case I want you to take." Emir looked at his phone as it beeped a message. "Take care of whatever you need to, tonight. And I'll brief you in the morning. If you're not needed here…" He let the words trail off, but his eyes were on her and not Talib as he nodded and exited the suite.

"What was that about?" Talib asked as he came over to her. "I thought you'd never met Emir."

"I didn't."

"Then what was with the look between the two of you?"

"Sit down," she said, indicating the bed, where Everett had again fallen asleep.

She'd run out of time. But this wasn't how she'd meant to tell him.

He didn't sit down; instead he strode away from her. He stood distant and alone, looking out at the night sky of Marrakech. A minute passed, then another.

She stood up and followed him into the sitting area where she stood for a moment, watching him, as she contemplated what she needed to say. She took a breath. She'd wasted enough time.

"When we broke up…" *I was devastated*, she thought. *And you couldn't have cared less*. Instead she said, "A few weeks later, I…"

He turned from the window. His emotions were hidden in the unreadable look that had frustrated her so much throughout the span of the last few days of summer that led to the breakup. Before that, it had been a magical time.

This was so hard.

"I'm sorry about your car," she said, thinking of how she'd deliberately scratched the paint with the heel of her shoe. It had been so long ago and yet she'd been sorry about it ever since.

"My car?"

He frowned and something in the way his brows drew together reminded her so very much of Everett. Who was she kidding? Everything about him reminded her of Everett.

"Never mind." She shook her head. "It's irrelevant." She felt stupid having said it, but it had been one of those involuntary things that you just spit out and regret later. The car was now long gone, or at least she assumed so, and would have been replaced by a newer, more exquisitely expensive sports model. That was Talib. Some things never changed. She twisted her hands together and considered how to begin even though she'd gone over this a dozen times.

"You came to see me," Talib said quietly, as if encouraging her to continue.

She wasn't ready. She turned the words around in her head.

"In Wyoming, you never wanted to break up. I regret all of it now, at least how it ended. I didn't want you to leave that way. I should have known how you felt, I should have…" He broke off as if gathering his thoughts. "It was me and…"

Her jaw tightened.

"Things have changed, Sara, but I'm still the man you remember, I…"

His words were a low rumble in the back of her thoughts as her disbelief seemed to mute the sound of his voice. What was he talking about? He couldn't possibly believe that she'd come here to beg to be back in his life? He couldn't possibly. But he'd always been an arrogant son of…

There was no time for such thoughts. She combed her hair with splayed fingers, then dropped her hand. She had no defense. He was right. She had come to see him and as difficult as it was, she had to remember why she was here. Tell him, the voice of reason inside of her screamed. And then figure out how to tell him why she'd hidden this from him for so long.

"Everett…" she began.

She couldn't do it.

Her next words were going to change everything, and the neat little life she had built would crumple around her. Who was she kidding? The neat little life had been blasted into oblivion by one stupid move months ago. One date that turned into a half dozen with the wrong man. Now she was in a corner and there was nothing she could do, other than the one thing that would protect her son. The one thing that would destroy the world she had still hoped she could return to.

His eyes seemed to hold shadows, as if he felt her pain, as if he knew. She saw the promise of courage and strength that mirrored the passion he lived by. They were eyes she could drown in if she didn't stay strong.

She took a breath. She'd flown halfway around the world. She'd dodged a madman for months and arrived here in desperation, willing to lose what she loved most in exchange for the promise of his safety. There was no more delaying.

She met his scrutiny, and it seemed to hit somewhere deep inside of her. She didn't have time to wait for courage and she no longer had an excuse for keeping it secret. She'd determined that when she'd bought the plane ticket for Morocco.

The truth needed to be told. It couldn't wait another minute longer.

She looked up, met his gaze and with all the courage she had—held it.

"Everett is your son." She blurted out the words before her doubts took over once again.

This time the silence hung heavy in the room.

"My son," he finally said.

"Yes," she whispered. "Everett Talib." She said his full name, as if that confirmed everything. And in a way it did. The second name referenced the fact that Everett belonged to the Al-Nassar family. One day she'd fully intended that he would know his father and claim the heritage that was his right. But one day wasn't supposed to be until Everett was older. One day was when he was able to make his own decisions. When he was safe from being ripped out of her arms by a man who had more power than she could ever imagine.

Circumstances had worked against her.

"And you thought now was a good time to tell me," Talib said, turning a question into a statement, and the statement into an accusation.

The moment that followed seemed to tick like a retro alarm clock between them. The silence was full of recrimination on his part, and fear on hers. He didn't look at her but instead walked away and stared out the window before turning again to face her.

"Why, Sara? Why now? Two, three, if you count pregnancy, years later." His voice was low, in that way of his when anger was brewing just below the surface.

She didn't say anything. Seconds ticked by and turned into a minute.

"And why would I believe you? How can I believe that there weren't other men, that…" He ran the palm of his hand across his chin and his gaze never quite met hers.

She was shocked. He'd actually insinuated that not only had there been other men, but that there also might have been many men. There'd been Tad, but that had never been physical. She couldn't, not after… Her thought dropped off. Somehow, of all his possible reactions, she'd never thought that he wouldn't believe her, that he would think so little of her. "I don't expect—"

"Don't say anything, Sara, please." He swung around. "I've sensed from the moment you arrived that money was the issue. I didn't want to believe it. That was never you."

She should be angry. She should tell him where to go, but shock and desperation seemed to act as a wet blanket to any outrage she might have felt.

Instead, she wanted to deny his accusations. She wasn't a gold digger. She'd starve first, but that was herself she was talking about, not Everett. Her stomach clenched. Now, to admit the truth was to admit that he was right, it was about money. For it was only money that could save her son.

"So, why now, Sara? Did you think this was adequate punishment for the breakup?" He shook his head. "Keeping my son from me. That is, if he is my son."

"He is," she said. "Look at him." For it was true. Everett was his father's son. He had skipped over her fair complexion, gray eyes and light brown hair streaked with blond. Instead, he had his father's thick, black wildly curly hair, although in the sun it was a softer curl that framed his olive-toned face. If he was awake, you could see the warm eyes that had so many times reminded her of the man she'd loved and left. Or, more specifically, asked her to leave. And if he looked at his hands, he would see that even as a baby, Everett had extremely long fingers, like his father. "I meant to tell you eventually. Just not now, but—"

"Do you have a birth certificate?" he said, cutting her off in a voice that had a dark edge.

"You're not on it," she admitted softly and this time she couldn't look at him. It was an admission that had been a long time coming and one that drove the final nail into her betrayal. But he was his son and he needed his father and it was that fact that had her standing her ground.

Silence beat accusing wings around them.

He'd stood with his back to her, now he turned to face her.

"We left on bad terms, Sara, but I never thought you'd do this, keep—"

"Is that what you think?" she interrupted, struggling to keep her voice low, so as not to awaken Everett. "That I kept your son from you so that I could punish you? You arrogant son of a donkey," she whispered. This conversation had to end. It was not something to discuss around a baby, sleeping or otherwise.

"I can't believe this," he said. "My son," he mused, as if saying the words made them more palatable.

A minute passed, as if he needed the time to absorb it all.

There were things she wanted to say and she said

none of them. Instead, her bottom lip quivered and she knew that she had to tell him everything and soon, before it was too late.

Chapter Ten

Talib ran a hand along the back of his neck, like he was too hot, but the only thing hot was the situation. He stood there for a minute, maybe two. Neither of them said anything. It seemed like there was so much to say and yet all of it ran too deep.

"I'm sorry, Sara. I know I'm not dealing well with this. I…" He shook his head. "I'm not sure what to say. I believe you, he's my son and I'll do right by him, but I need some time."

She looked at him with a frown. "There's more I need to tell you. Everett—"

"Not now," he said shortly. He knew she'd heard the edge in his voice. He could see that in her face. He couldn't help that. It was all too much. He was overwhelmed. He needed time alone to figure out what he felt, but the doubt wasn't about the boy or about being a father to him. That was a given. It was about the lost time, about Sara and her deception.

"Keep the door locked. You're safe here. Despite that, don't open it for anyone. I'll be back."

"When? This is important. I—"

"Tonight," he interrupted. "The hotel is secure. You'll be safe. But for now, stay in your suite."

She frowned.

The door of the suite shut with a finality behind him. It made him remember that other door shutting almost three years ago. Only then the door had slammed, brutally closing in conjunction with words that told him where to go. In a way it had been like their relationship, high-powered and unpredictable. And yet, he'd never forgotten her.

It was all too much and he was furious with Sara. Whatever her reasons, one more minute in that room would have had him doing something juvenile like put a fist through a plaster wall. It was a thought that in real life he doubted would give one any satisfaction. But the fact that the thought was there had frightened him. What he needed was time and space before he said something to her that no apology would ever repair.

His heart pounded and he wasn't sure what he wanted or needed to do. He wasn't thinking logically. The familiarity that had immediately struck him between Everett and himself... He had blown off believing that Sara would never deceive him about something that important. Now, the truth of her deception took his breath away. He only knew that he needed to get out of the confines of the hotel and get some air.

He'd been deceived on a scale that was unfathomable, by a woman who he thought incapable of such a thing. He clenched his fist and his jaw twitched. He pushed past the uniformed bellhop and past another man, who looked at him oddly. He needed to get it together, but first he had to get his emotions under control.

If it was true, that this boy was his son, he'd missed so much. He wasn't sure what it all meant or how this could have happened. They'd used birth control. They'd been careful, but obviously not careful enough. It didn't seem possible and yet he knew she hadn't lied. He strode through the lobby, heading through a side door and into the parking lot.

"Why now, Sara? Why the hell now?"

IT HAD WORKED beautifully and still it had failed. Tad Rossi rubbed his thumb against his index finger. His teeth were clenched and his back molar ached. He'd have to get that fixed one day. Except that he had no money even for emergency dentistry. He'd maxed out what little credit he had and borrowed everything he could from what little family he had. But they'd long since closed the door on him. He'd been scrounging ever since—living off his good looks and the back of one girl or another.

He needed to get to Morocco and he needed to get there without delay. But he had no resources, that had been the reason behind all of this. Sara had been a lucky find. The fact that she was hot enough for any man—a bonus. She was nothing now. He'd drained her of everything, at least everything monetary, or so he'd thought. Then, she'd surprised him. Getting more money out of her should have been easy. She should have done what he asked and she had, and then she'd stopped.

"Damn," he snarled. The plan was now far bigger than terrorizing one resource-limited woman. Al-Nassar had money, more money than he wanted to contemplate. But that had been his first mistake—sharing that part of the plan. He'd set something in motion that he wasn't sure he'd be able to stop, at least from here.

Sara and the boy were nothing. Neither of them mattered. Despite his initial interest in her, like any woman, that hadn't lasted long. Sara had been pleasant enough and the child mattered not at all. Although he'd threatened kidnapping to encourage her to get more money, he didn't want the child for any longer than it took to get his mother to comply.

He couldn't believe she'd run. That had been a major oversight on his part. She'd run before, that was true, but it was also true that it had been in the United States. She'd been easy to find. A computer-geek friend, an app that easily fished information out of a social-media site and he was in business. The bonus was that she was conscientious about contacting her parents through social media. In a private message to them, she'd left a contact number each time. He'd followed that trail with ease. But Morocco was another story.

He was losing his touch. He couldn't believe that this had happened, that he'd read her wrong. She wouldn't have chanced it if she wasn't desperate. He'd pushed her too hard.

He remembered the moment like it was yesterday. He'd picked up his phone and punched a number that had been on his contact list for over a decade, spoken with someone he hadn't in years. But it was a man whom he'd always felt was a kindred spirit.

When the call had ended, they'd reached an agreement. One that hadn't made him happy, for it had been no agreement at all, only demands. He had to fix what he'd put into motion before he screwed himself out of the money that was his. He needed to get to Morocco and take control of his own scheme, but to do that he needed money.

Everything would have been fine, if he'd kept a level head. But it had felt like his world was falling apart. He panicked, unable to think of how he would come up with the funds to even purchase an airline ticket to get there and get control of his own game. He'd been desperate. It was the quick rip-off of an elderly woman at an auto teller that had been his next mistake. He hadn't expected the woman to not only fight and knock him off balance with a kick to the shins, but also yank out a shrill whistle and blow it again and again.

He'd turned to push her out of the way, but she still had the whistle. When he'd decided to give up and run, he'd been waylaid by a punch from an overexcited do-gooder.

And all of it ended in a humiliating choke hold as the curtain fell on his plan. Instead, the plan was radically changed by the glaring flash of the lights of a police cruiser. The memory of being roughly frisked and read his rights and then a forceful hand on his head that shoved him into the dark interior of a police cruiser.

Now there was no stopping the force of the Pandora's box he'd opened.

For him it was over, for Sara...it soon would be.

Chapter Eleven

It felt like the breath had been knocked out of him. Talib had never imagined what it would feel like to learn that he was a father. He only knew that this wasn't how it was supposed to be. This wasn't how most people might feel to become a parent. But most people didn't become a parent in this manner. In a way he felt robbed. And what he knew for sure was that he was feeling too much. He needed to get it together and figure out this mess. He had to shove the emotions into boxes that they just didn't want to squeeze into. He hated the feel of this, of being overwhelmed with confusing feelings for another human being.

That had only happened once before. It had been Sara who had precipitated that confusing melee of feelings as well, but that time it had been in a good way. In the first blush of new love, in the hot demands and passion of a series of firsts. He'd broken up with her when the need for her had become too much, when it was all he could think of. But she'd gotten one up on him. She'd taken his son with her. He wasn't sure if he could ever forgive her for that.

"Damn!" He smacked his fist into the palm of his hand.

Only his parents' deaths had made him feel anywhere

close to this betrayed. And their demise hadn't been accidental—it had been murder. The emotion he felt now was different, but just as intense.

He stood at the door to her hotel room for a full five minutes before he could bring himself to knock.

When she opened the door less than an hour after he'd left, neither of them said anything. Instead, he looked beyond her to the bedroom where the boy slept, but there was only a small hill beneath a blanket in the middle of the bed. The outline of the child was there and now, instead of the nightlight, a small bedside light was on so that the boy wasn't in the dark. The living area was dimly lit by one lamp on a desk and the blush of city light coming in from a window where the blind was partly up.

"I expected more of you than that," he said as he strode past her.

Seconds ticked by and the silence deepened.

"You expected…" She said the words softly, as if she couldn't quite fathom the meaning of what he was trying to say. "More of me? I wanted more of our relationship. I expected more."

"You could have told me. I would—"

"If you couldn't handle our relationship, how were you going to handle a baby?" she interrupted.

Silence pulsed through the room.

"Why are you here, Sara? Why now?"

"I never wanted you to know," she said. "At least not now. Not while he's so young."

The words were like a razor slicing skin. It hurt like few things could. He knew the boy was his son. He didn't think she'd lie about that. He'd seen the similarity as much as he'd wanted to discount it. It was what she had done, or more accurately, what she hadn't done that bothered him most of all.

"You had no right," he said through clenched teeth.

"Didn't I?" She paused. "You were the one who walked out on me, not the other way around. Would you have come running back if I'd told you?" She turned away.

That she thought he would walk from such an epic responsibility was inconceivable. He wanted to shout at the injustice of it all, but the source of his upset was sleeping not that far away from them.

Silence ticked between them as she waited and he fought for control.

He couldn't look at her. Instead he turned his back to her and to the view of Marrakech, the city he knew so well and, in this moment, couldn't care less about. He wasn't sure who he was angry at—her, himself, or fate. Her words were valid. Three years ago, he hadn't been ready for a relationship. But a child, that was different.

Minutes passed.

He went over to her and stood just behind her, hesitant to come any closer.

She slipped past him, moving back into the living area.

He followed her.

"I wanted him to see where his ancestors came from," she finally said.

"At two?"

"It's never too soon," she said.

"You're not the adventurous type, Sara. Travel wasn't your thing and definitely not with a toddler." He came over to where she stood, looking small and vulnerable, one shoulder against the wall. She wouldn't look at him. He needed her to look at him. He put a thumb under her chin, nudging her to look.

"What's going on, Sara?"

But his gut already knew. It was about money, like he'd already so ungraciously said. Her evasive nonanswer had been answer enough. Even though that was so unlike her. Even though he would have said with some assuredness that never would such a thing happen, now it was the only explanation that made any sense. All of it, her being here with the boy, at the hotel that he, at the moment, had a vested interest in—all of it stunk of desperation.

"Damn it, Sara," he said with a sharp edge that seemed to knife through the room.

She shook her head and a tear rolled down her cheek.

"I'm desperate or I wouldn't be here." She met his gaze with a half smile that was no smile at all. "I'm being blackmailed," she said bluntly. "My ex-boyfriend. We didn't go out long and we never…" She shook her head. "Never mind. That's none of your business." She was quiet for a minute, collecting her thoughts. "He didn't like Everett. Actually, that's not true, he just didn't want anything to do with him. Because of that, I broke things off. Actually, it was because of a lot of things."

A minute passed, then two.

"It turned out that he wasn't interested in me. But he was interested in any money I could give him," she added and a sour thread ran through the words.

"A man leaching off a woman," Talib said with disdain. There was nothing wrong with a strong, independent woman. That had been Sara. But there was everything wrong with a man who couldn't support himself.

"He was a stockbroker, at least that's what he said." She paused and wiped the corner of her eye. "It wasn't true. He was only a two-bit con man who gambled his money away in the stock market."

She looked at him with wide eyes, a look that would have had her in his arms all those years ago. Instead he stood there and waited, prepared to wait for as long as it took for her to tell him the truth, all of it.

"He went through my things one day when I was in another room changing Everett. I'd written out a list of instructions, in case anything happened to me. I wanted Everett to know who he was, where he came from. He saw your name." Her eyes met his. "And your family, what I know of them. He saw it and…" She bit her lip, her fingers lacing through each other. "He knew who you were."

"How?"

She shook her head. "I don't know. He was Moroccan, but… I don't know how he knew who you were or, more importantly, that you had money."

"And he's the one who blackmailed you?"

"He threatened to tell you…about Everett." Pain seemed to lace each word, as if saying the fact again was more difficult than the first time she'd said it.

"What was his name?"

"Tad Rossi." The name was stilted, without inflection. She folded her arms across her chest and turned away.

She was silent, and he waited. This was on her. Her regret, her mistake.

He waited until she turned around again to face him, but the pain in her eyes broke his resolve.

"I could have protected him, and you."

"I know," she whispered.

"You should have told me," he said and he couldn't filter the anger from his voice. "If I'd known from the beginning, nothing like this would have happened."

"I was afraid," she said softly. She'd moved to the couch, flopping down as if her legs would no longer hold her. "You're my last resort. I've given him all the money I can. Now, if I don't give him all the money he's demanding." She shook her head. "I don't know how this is going to end. I'm scared that he might take Everett exactly like he threatened."

"Over my dead body," he snarled. "That will never happen."

"They've found me everywhere I've gone." Her cheeks were flushed and her eyes were filled with pain. "I've moved to three different states in the last seven months."

His fist clenched at the thought of her running, frightened and without resources.

"Everett in his hands for even an hour is incomprehensible." Her voice trembled.

Never. Not while I still live, he thought. And as far as the creep that had been stalking his girl, he would put an end to that. The thought stopped him—Sara was not his girl, not anymore. Then he remembered something else she had said, maybe just a misplaced pronoun, maybe something more.

"You said *they*. Who else is there, Sara?"

"I don't know if there's anyone else. It's intuition only," she said. "What I know of him. Some of the things he's done are out of character. It's like he's getting advice somewhere else. And at the Desert Sands Hotel— I almost felt like whoever it was, whoever was helping him, was there. But that's crazy and there's no reason to believe anything like that. He didn't have the resources to travel. He gambled away everything he had."

"From what you've said, it's been a while since you've seen him. What resources he might have now is pure speculation. He could have found what was needed to come here, to follow you."

"Talib, you're frightening me."

"How are you contacting your family?"

"Through social media messaging."

He grimaced at that.

"What? I… I don't tell them much. Give them the new mobile number to reach me. It's safe, it's…"

"There are apps that can hack that without problem, Sara," he said. "I'm not saying that's how he found you, but that's definitely one way."

She shook her head. "I can't believe it. I used disposable phones so they couldn't get to me. The numbers are changed out regularly." She frowned. "I messaged my parents with the new number every time."

"On social media. That wasn't the smartest move."

Their research team had recently briefed him on another case, showing him how information could be mined from the web. One of the easiest places to fish for information was through social networks and their messaging systems.

"I…" Her words choked off. She was clearly overwhelmed as she realized the mistake she'd made. She had chosen to avoid calling her parents because she wasn't ready to answer the questions they would ask or the demands to come home that they'd already made. Both had been more easily evaded in writing than by telephone.

In another time and in another place, he might have apologized. Not now. She needed to be on guard. His gaze went to the bedroom—there was too much at stake.

He thought of the scene in the first hotel, the maid holding his son, her claim that she had been paid to bring him to a man who waited somewhere outside. He thought of how close he'd come to losing his son before he'd ever gotten a chance to know him, and the thought of that was incomprehensible.

"I can't lose him," she repeated. "I'll pay you back, Talib. I promise. If it takes me my entire life."

She would never pay him back. He wouldn't allow

it. But he told her none of that. Instead he asked, "How much, Sara? How much do you want from me?"

She flinched and he knew that it was because of the way he'd worded that last question. He felt like the biggest jerk, the biggest bully. He'd worded it that way to make her feel uncomfortable. But now, seeing her discomfort, it didn't give him any pleasure. In fact, looking at her, he was afraid he'd broken her.

He was relieved when she drew her shoulders back and looked at him with stoic eyes. Even though her lips still quivered, she was giving him attitude, backbone—she was far from broken.

And then she told him what she needed.

At first he didn't know what to say. The figure she mentioned was large even by Al-Nassar standards.

"We'll get this fixed. He won't get away with this and you don't need to worry, Sara. Not anymore. I'll handle whatever demands they have directly." No matter what she had done and how she had deceived him, Sara and his son would have no worries from here on out.

His fists clenched as he paced the room.

There were questions that needed to be answered, two years to catch up on and so much more that he hadn't addressed. But in truth, he couldn't look at her or his son another moment. For she only reminded him of the deception and the sleeping child reminded him of all that he had missed. He needed time and space, they both did. The morning would come soon enough.

"Get some sleep," he said. "I'll be next door."

SARA'S PHONE RANG at exactly 3:15 a.m.

Her heart stopped.

This was the time when all the calls had come in. It was the exact time that Everett had been born. She'd forgotten to tell that important fact to Talib, but their conversation had been so overwhelming.

She debated not answering, but she didn't want to wake Everett and she knew that he'd call again and again, until she answered. They would not give up. She'd purchased a disposable phone again, as she had every time she'd run. And he'd found her again, as he had every time. It was like a never-ending story that one might read to a child before bedtime, except this story threatened a very bad ending. She remembered what Talib had said, about the app that could track her and she cringed.

She pushed Talk with a shaking finger.

She didn't say anything. She couldn't bear to say more than necessary. Just to think that this man had once kissed her, that she'd allowed certain liberties—all of that made her queasy. The only good thing that hadn't happened, consummating it—she would always be thankful he had never been the man in her bed. The thought of that made her want to hurl.

"He can't protect you," a snide, almost robotic voice said.

"Who are you?" She frowned. This wasn't Tad. Not only was it not his voice, but Tad wouldn't play such games. He would speak to her directly, as he always had.

"Next time we'll take the boy and he won't be able to stop it."

"What are you saying?" And who is *we*? she thought.

"You don't know?" A dry chuckle followed—it was more creepy than humorous. "If not for your boyfriend, we would have taken the kid before the fire was out at the Desert Sands."

"What?" Her breath caught in her throat.

"Preventing that kidnapping was only luck on his part.

Next time it will be real. Nothing except money will stop the inevitable."

The call broke off and Sara dropped the phone like it contained poison that might seep into her skin.

Her mind went back to the hotel, to the smoke, the panic at losing Everett. It had been Talib who had found him, maybe even saved him, but saved him from what? Was the caller just playing with her emotions or had something happened that Talib had failed to tell her?

She looked at her watch. Fifteen minutes had gone by.

She couldn't believe that Talib hadn't told her that her son had almost been taken. It was typical Talib, the need to protect, to shelter. But he'd been wrong. She needed to know about all threats. There was no way to protect Everett otherwise.

She sank down on the couch, her head in her hands. Who was she kidding? She was here because she couldn't protect her son. She needed Talib, but his deception of silence was not acceptable and she would tell him that immediately. But it wasn't just him, there were things that she hadn't told. No more secrets, she promised herself.

She went over to the desk and grabbed a blank piece of paper and a pen, and began writing it all down, everything that had happened, from the beginning. For there was more to all of this than even she knew. She was sure of it. Something far darker and more deadly lurked and she was putting her trust in one man, believing that he would know what to do. She trusted that he would find the truth and would be fair. For in doing this, trusting him, she stood to lose her son to the power that was Al-Nassar. He could take Everett and there was nothing she could do about it. It broke her heart to think of it, but considering everything, it might be best for Everett and that was all that mattered.

No matter how much it would break her heart to let him go.

Chapter Twelve

Talib ran a hand through his hair.

In a suite beside Sara's, his work had only begun. He'd just ended a call from Barb Almay, who headed office research in both their home office and their Wyoming branch. She'd traced Sara's movements from the past several months. He wondered what resources the boyfriend had hired here and where he'd gotten the funds to do so. From everything Sara had told him, the man had no funds. He ran a hand through his hair, thinking about what he did know. A trace on Sara's accounts had made it clear that she'd been telling the truth. Her last withdrawal was enough to get a flight here. After that, she was living on fumes. She had no money to give to anyone. But it was clear the amounts she had told him had been the amounts withdrawn, at the time she'd said, the last over two months ago and then she'd run. It was exactly as she'd told him, the states she'd fled to, the mindless menial jobs, all of it. He felt rather low to be doing this, but he didn't have a choice. The stakes were too high. He would not jeopardize either his son's life or Sara's for her feelings. She might feel compromised or, more than likely, angry when she found out, but that was the risk he needed to take.

He ran through the facts. There were too few of them

and nothing was making any sense. From everything he knew, Tad Rossi had never entered Morocco. Someone within Morocco had to be involved. Someone with expertise, as they'd been able to rig the explosion in the hotel and almost carry off the kidnapping of his son. He had to get to the heart of who was running this toxic little scheme.

His thoughts were interrupted by a banging on his door and a woman's voice.

Sara.

He strode to the door, opened it and looked down at her slight frame almost completely hidden by the blanket that was draped over her shoulders and around their son. She was struggling with the weight of the boy. He took the sleeping toddler from her arms.

"Why didn't you tell me?" she demanded.

"Tell you what?"

If anyone hadn't been told anything, if anyone had the right to be angry, it was him. He said nothing, just watched her as she pushed past him, leaving the door hanging open. He closed it and followed her, baffled at how the anger he had been feeling had suddenly shifted to her and, more intriguingly, seemed justified. He was in an emotional sandpit. Instinctively, he lay the boy down on a beige leather couch that sat on the reverse wall of the one in her suite.

"Someone tried to steal Everett, kidnap him?" Her voice was high, almost on the edge of hysteria. "What else aren't you telling me?"

His mind went back to those moments in the hotel. It was something they needed to discuss, but he wanted to have a clearer idea as to how it all fit before they did.

"Who told you?"

"That's not important, not right now."

She had a point. He'd felt wrong and justified at the same time about keeping the information from her. "I wasn't sure what had been going on. Until I did, there was no point saying anything that might get you unnecessarily upset."

"Unnecessarily upset," she said slowly, drawing out each syllable. "And you think that it wasn't wise that I knew as soon as possible so I could be more aware—prepared."

"You're right," he admitted. It was a fact that he'd struggled with and was only justified because he felt he could keep them safe here. But maybe knowing the truth would help her accept the boundaries necessary to keep them safe. Her suite within this hotel was the boundary.

"Sit down," he said, pointing to a chair.

She ignored his instruction and sat down on the edge of the couch by their son.

And then he told her everything he'd seen in the lobby of the Desert Sands Hotel. When only twelve hours ago fate had thrown them together and meeting his son meant that he had to save him first.

He came over to her, kneeled down in front of her and took her hands, squeezing them. "Sara."

"Don't." She shook her head, pulling her hands free. "This isn't about us."

Us.

That had all been so long ago and in the end, so regretful.

There were times in their romance that he'd acted more playboy than responsible lover. He had never denied that, but a relationship hadn't been what he wanted, no matter his feelings for Sara. He'd toyed with her and for that he was sorry. But none of what he had done justified what she had done.

"I get a call regularly at three fifteen in the morning," she said, breaking into his thoughts. "It's always been Tad on the other end. But not this time. The voice was robotic, like something generated by a computer maybe, but the tone, the message—all of it was the same."

Talib shook his head. "What's the significance of three fifteen?"

"It was the time that Everett was born."

In the early hours of the morning she'd given birth to his son. Regret ran through him, not of the boy's existence, but of so many other things that he didn't want to acknowledge. He looked at her, her slight build, her peaches-and-cream complexion and the honesty and hope mixed with fear that shone from her eyes. And in that moment he hoped it hadn't been difficult. He didn't want to think of it much more than that, for any consideration to those facts brought a tsunami of emotion that was overwhelming.

"What does he say?"

"It's rather the same each time," she said.

"Tell me," he said shortly. He didn't know what she believed but what he knew was that they didn't have much time. It sounded to him like her ex-boyfriend had just lost control and tipped the scales in favor of an unknown entity who was here in Marrakech. At least that was his best guess. How it had all come together was unknown. The unknown needed to be removed. For, it was the unknown that got people killed and the unknown that was his job to clear up as quickly as possible.

"He called to remind me that I owe him and that I'll lose my son if I don't come through. But like I told you, what he wants now, I can't give him." She shook her head.

"Until now," he said.

She didn't look at him at first, and when she did her

eyes were full of such anguish that it almost broke his resolve. Despite the betrayal he still felt, he had an over-whelming need to protect her and now it was loaded with a surprising emotion, one that he couldn't quite identify. He pulled her up, taking her into his arms, feeling her soft curves against him. He'd thought once that letting her go had been a mistake, now he knew that it had been more than that. But so much had happened, so many life-altering things that she had gone through without him. Regret was beginning to overshadow his anger. Neither emotion was relevant or productive to attaining the one goal he needed to focus on—keeping their son safe. He ran a comforting hand along her shoulder before releasing her and stepping away.

"There's a lot of hurt in the past for both of us."

She looked up at him with surprise.

He offered her a smile that held more regret than humor. "I know, that's not what the old Talib would say. But I'm three years older and hopefully three years wiser. I hurt you…"

"It was a long time ago."

"It doesn't matter how long ago it was, what happened was monumental and now we have him." He had her hands, squeezing them as if that would reestablish a con-nection or help either of them understand what had bro-ken between them.

She pulled away from him and he realized his mis-take immediately. He'd used the word *we*. In her mind Everett was her son, he knew that and it was a point that he'd never concede. He might have missed out on over two years, but now Everett was as much his son as hers and he planned to make up for lost time. But all that was something they would hash out later.

"We," he said firmly, despite his thoughts. "He's my

son and it will be a while before I forgive you, if I ever can," he warned. "But going forward I'm an equal parent."

"Equal," she repeated and there was a smile that was almost relief.

He didn't understand it. He'd just told her that he was in her life whether she wanted him to be or not.

A strand of hair flipped across her face. He reached with one finger to push it back and she jerked away from him.

"Sara!" He took her shoulders, squeezing them. She cringed and took another step away.

He frowned, dropping his hands and feeling outrage and shock at the same time. She was acting like a woman who had experienced physical violence at the hands of a man. That wasn't the Sara he knew, either. "Did someone…did he lay a hand on you?"

She didn't say anything.

"Sara, tell me. Please."

"Once. We broke up after that. But I would have, even if it hadn't happened."

He didn't curse despite choice words that mixed with the rage and boiled hot and furious, wanting, needing an outlet. He was only thankful that the man was an ocean away from him, for at this moment he would have killed him.

"He threatened you," he said thickly. "He laid a hand on you. I'll kill…" He put a hand on her shoulder. "Not literally, but I'd make it painful for him to function properly for a good long time."

"Thank you for that," she said softly. "But no, Talib. Don't ever. It could ruin your life."

"I won't murder the son of a—"

"Donkey," she suggested with a wry smile.

"Thank you," he said with a grin that was only half-sincere. Unless opportunity arrives during the investigation, he thought, but it was a thought she didn't need to know about. "One thing is sure," he said through tight lips. "He'll never touch either of you again."

"Be careful," she said softly. "He'll get what he deserves, legally."

"How did you meet him?" Even now, after hearing his name, he had no desire to say it.

"Tad was from Morocco, like you," she said, not sensing his withdrawal. "I went to a travel show on Morocco."

"Why?"

"Why do you think?" she said softly, glancing over at Everett. "I wanted Everett to know his heritage."

"You wanted to keep the baby in touch with his roots?"

"Don't look so surprised. He was living in America but eventually he needed to know his heritage. I was looking for safe options."

"Safe?"

"Never mind, Talib. It seems a long time ago. Anyway, I met him there."

"So there's a good chance he has family, friends, at the least, an acquaintance here," he said thoughtfully. The scene played out in his mind. His son in the arms of the maid, her words. It wasn't something he wanted to discuss with Sara. She'd given him all she could. It was clear that she knew little of her former boyfriend's connections. All of it was stressing her, he could see it in the taut lips that had once been full and the new line in her once smooth brow.

She handed him a piece of paper. "I've written down everything that's happened, anything of any significance that might help you end this."

He scanned her notes. Some of the information was

new, none of it earth-shattering enough to provide any clear clues or motive. He looked up, met her eyes and was hit by truths that disturbed him.

She had few funds and everything she had was going into their son. That was clear in the weight she'd lost and the hollows under her eyes.

He would protect them with his life. The burden wouldn't be shared. It would become his. Only once before had they had a case that had threatened those he loved. It involved his sister, Tara, and had happened almost a year ago. But this wasn't the same, he didn't love Sara, but his son... His thoughts dropped off. He didn't know what he felt. He'd never felt so conflicted, so emotionally off-kilter.

She shook her head, her mind clearly going back over their discussion. "I can't believe that Tad would do this—hire someone to kidnap him, if he even found the funds. I just can't believe it."

"I don't think it was a kidnapping as you're thinking of it. Not that that makes this any better."

"I don't understand. They were in the process of—"

"Kidnapping." He shook his head. "No. Making a child disappear for a few hours. Making a point. I've seen it done before. The other option, that is if Tad hasn't left American soil, is that the incident isn't related. That it was a crime of opportunity, nothing else."

"Thank goodness you were there." Relief softened her features. "You saved him. Thank you. You've already done so much, you've been investigating..." Her voice trailed off and she bit her trembling lower lip.

"I have my research team on it. In the meantime, we can protect you better at the family compound."

"No!" She shook her head. "I won't go there," she said with a note of finality.

He'd heard that tone before and knew that she was prepared to stand her ground. In her position, he wasn't sure he wouldn't do the same. The family compound was ideal but he'd known it was a long shot for her to agree to go. The compound was also the heart of his family. While it wasn't true, he knew that she'd feel like she'd given up her last bit of autonomy. But that was Sara, fiercely independent. He'd offered the option and hoped but he'd prepared for her refusal by securing her suite here.

"Sara." He went to her, taking her face in his hands, looking into her troubled eyes. He only wanted to comfort her. Instead he bent down and tasted the softness of her lips. As he remembered the passion of their romance, he claimed her with all the emotion that ran conflicted through him.

Her hands were on his shoulders and she pushed him gently back, brought him to reality.

"I'm sorry, I…"

"It won't happen again," she said softly. "Promise me."

"No need," he said as he turned away from her.

Chapter Thirteen

"I'm going to meet with Emir," Talib said and the words broke the silence that had hung in the room for the last few minutes.

"Now?" She frowned.

"I know." He gave her an off-kilter smile. "It's almost four thirty in the morning but he starts his day at five, sometimes sooner."

They were both wide awake. And while he was sure sleep was at least another day away for him, he doubted if it would be any different for her. The only one getting any sleep was the boy and a thought struck him that maybe it would be nice to have her company. He would cut short his trip to see Emir and then take her around to the family compound, maybe sway her mind to relocate there. It was an argument he wasn't ready to drop.

"Come with me. You can bring the baby."

"You said I was safe here," she said. "I'm not leaving, Talib. Just tell me it's safe."

"You are," he assured her. No matter how much he'd rather she go to the compound, he couldn't lie. He'd prepared for such a situation and now that she'd made it clear by refusing once again, that it was a done deal, it was time to tell her. "In fact what I haven't told you is that I've hired a twenty-four-seven guard duty. There'll be someone patrolling this hallway at all times. So if I'm not here and you need anything, anything at all—even…" He looked over at the boy. "Cookies or biscuits, whatever…"

"Biscuits," she said with a small laugh.

"You know what I mean, Sara. You have round-the-clock protection. The man who has the day shifts will be Andre." He went over to a desk in the far corner of the room and picked up a sheet of paper. "Here," he said as he handed it to her. "It has their names and shifts and a picture so you can verify their identity."

"You're frightening me."

"No, Sara. It's nothing to be frightened of." He leaned down and gave her a chaste kiss on the cheek. Yet he wanted to turn her to face him and kiss her hot and wet on the lips. He took a step away and turned to grab his keys off a small stand. "It's a necessity until we catch your blackmailer."

"I don't need a babysitter," she interrupted with determination running like steel through her voice. "I just needed you to know. To be on board with this. To…"

"Protect him." He nodded. "I know. And you need money, too, I'll have some wired to your—"

"Talib, no. You make my head spin. This is too much. The money I mean. Thank you, but I won't accept unless this is a loan."

"No loan," he said. "Get the information to my assistant and she'll facilitate the transfer. I insist on not only protecting you and my son, but supporting him, too." He looked at her and ran a finger gently along her cheek.

He met her questioning gaze.

"I wish I could say no, but…"

"It's all right," he said. "My assistant will contact you."

She shook her head.

"You can trust her. Give her Tad's contact information and she'll get the money to him," he continued.

Her eyes were bright with tears. "I'll pay you back."

"Sara…" He touched her shoulder. "Let me do this. And as far as the blackmailing piece of camel dung, trust me, he won't get everything he wants—not yet. Only enough to buy some time."

"I don't understand," she said with a frown. "If he doesn't get what he wants he'll…"

"Do nothing," Talib said. "There's nothing he or whoever he is partnered with can do. Trust me, Sara. Holding back money may make him careless."

"Buy time," she murmured.

"Exactly," he agreed.

Enough time for him to take him down and have him drown in his own blood, he thought. They were words he would never say to her, in front of his son or otherwise. "And, it goes without saying when this is over, I'll be supporting my son."

Silence hung between them. If he was reading her emotions right, he would say she was stunned or possibly just in a state of disbelief. He wasn't sure what he expected, but it didn't feel right to think that she might have, in some way, expected the worst from him.

"And maybe you can get a few hours' sleep before I get back. You're right, you're probably better off here than trailing along after me. Besides, that would wake the baby."

She looked at him oddly.

"His name's Everett."

"I know," he said thickly, but the name stuck in his throat.

He picked up his son. Somehow he was able to think of him in terms of a relationship, as an entity but not as a name, an individual who somehow made their situation all too glaringly real.

"I'll walk you both back to your room." He gazed down at the bundle in his arms. He looked at Sara and circled her shoulders with his arm, drawing her along with him to the door.

She smiled, a rather tired effort, as she reached to open the door.

"As far as your blackmailer..." He met her eyes as if delivering a silent promise. "Like I said, we'll deal with him. I promise you, Sara, this will work out. No one will hurt either you or the boy."

She nodded.

He realized that again he hadn't referred to the child by name. He thought of him as his, but the name, somehow, in an odd way, meant acknowledging his son's mother. Because Everett was a name that he knew Sara loved. She'd once mentioned that if she ever had a boy, she'd call him by that name. Saying the name felt like he was accepting what she had done and in doing so, forgiving her for not telling him. He wasn't ready for that.

"What's going on?" Emir asked as Talib slouched down into one of the leather chairs that had been his father's and his grandfather's before that. The leather sank beneath his weight, yet not so much that it still wasn't providing support.

The office was a place that he considered the heart of the family compound. It was a place that reminded him of the strength and loyalty of his family and where Nassar Security had begun.

"You look terrible, Talib," Emir said. "Something on your mind besides the obvious? I'm betting it's not the breach of security and the explosion at Ian's hotel either."

Talib looked at his brother and for a moment wondered why he was here. There was nothing Emir could do or say that would change any of it. Not the part that haunted him, the boy—his son.

"You know, don't you?"

"Sara came here with your son." Emir nodded.

Talib's eyes met his older brother's. He ran a hand through his hair. "It was that obvious?"

"I guessed," Emir said. "Am I right?"

Emir smiled in that all-knowing older-brother way that, through the years, had been nothing short of infuriating. This time there was too much on his mind to even think about it.

"That the boy is mine." He nodded. "That's what she says."

"What do you say?" Emir asked, his dark eyes clashing with Talib's, challenging him.

"How'd you know?" Talib asked instead.

"A blind man could see that, T. He's like seeing you when you were a kid."

"I can't believe she's here. That she never told me, that…"

"What are you going to do about it?"

He lurched to his feet, as if sitting for another moment was just too difficult. "I'll take responsibility."

"A given," Emir said easily. "But that doesn't answer my question."

Talib paced the room before turning to face his brother. "She's in trouble."

"I assumed as much," Emir said as he leaned back in his chair and folded his arms, his dark eyes fixed on him. "You mentioned once that she didn't like to travel. And yet, here she is halfway around the world. You two are no longer a couple—so why is she here? I couldn't think of anything else other than the fact that it's your business to protect and she needs help. What else could it be?"

Despite his oldest brother's look, which could be disconcerting at times, this time it didn't faze him. His brother was bang on as usual.

"She's in trouble alright, in more ways than one," he said, thinking of the boy who was innocently caught in the midst of it all. He went on to tell Emir what he'd learned from Sara.

"Tad demanded money at regular intervals. Sara met them all until she ran out of money. It looks like he's not alone and they've upped their demands in the time since then and when she arrived in Morocco. I plan to give them a quarter of what they're asking. If whoever is at the helm of this in Morocco is outraged enough they might slip up. I've already set up a transfer of funds to meet part of the demand," Talib added.

"We've used the strategy before," Emir said.

Talib nodded. "I'm hoping it may flush them out."

"I'll assign another agent to that case I mentioned earlier," Emir said. "You need to stay focused on this. Has our office found anything?"

Talib went through what he knew. "I'm going back to the Sahara Sunset this morning."

Emir nodded approvingly. "You couldn't get a more impenetrable security. A crown prince or two has been known to stay there."

"You're telling me it was a good choice," Talib said with a self-deprecating smile.

"I don't need to," Emir said. "Old habits…"

"Never die," Talib said, referring to Emir's need as an older brother to give advice to his siblings.

"Have you considered moving them?"

"To the compound," Talib said. "Yes, in fact I already suggested it. She won't go."

"Probably not an issue. From what you've said you've eliminated, or at least controlled the possibility of any danger at the moment."

"Exactly. They're safe where they are. It's secure."

"But you're considering this as a temporary measure. Depending how long it takes to contain the danger?"

"If anything changes, I'll move them immediately. But the security there is every bit as tight as at the compound. And I know the security team well."

"Agreed. Is there anything I can do?" Emir asked.

"I'll let you know," Talib said as he moved to leave. He hesitated at the door before turning around. "Thanks," he said. "Sara's ex is a small-time crook but he's got someone contracted here that has me worried. Mainly because he's an unknown entity. I'll feel better when I have an ID on him. But one thing is clear—he has more resources than her ex-boyfriend."

"So who is he? Any ideas?"

"The ex-boyfriend's name is Tad Rossi and he has Moroccan roots. I'm assuming it could be anyone he had connections with here. It might be a deeper dig to find them then I thought."

"Really? The boyfriend was Moroccan too?"

"Apparently she has a type."

"A type?" Emir frowned.

"You know dark-haired, exotic—or so I've been told," Talib said with a grin. "Or maybe it's just tall, dark and handsome." He shoved his hands in his pockets. "Seriously, she met him at a Moroccan travel presentation. It appeared to be coincidental, but I don't believe in coincidence."

"She was singled out."

"It's a possibility I considered," Talib replied. "Despite that theory, he seems like a rank amateur. It won't take much to bring him down and close this case. Then I'll be available."

"Will you?"

"What do you mean?"

"Aren't you forgetting something?" Emir asked softly.

Talib met Emir's gaze and somehow he couldn't acknowledge the obvious reference his brother was making. It was all too big and too incomprehensible.

"You have a son, T," Emir said gravely. "Our family has an heir. Getting to know him might take a bit of your time."

An heir to the Al-Nassar wealth and history—it was inconceivable and he'd been treating it all so lightly. He frowned. When this was over, and only then, he needed to rethink his position, because he knew, as Emir had implied, that his son needed to be here—with him.

That wouldn't go over with Sara, but he'd have time to bring her around.

In the end, he knew she'd do anything to protect their son.

And he'd do anything to protect his family—even if it meant his own life.

Chapter Fourteen

"What do you have?" Talib asked as he answered a call from his youngest brother, Faisal. He wasn't surprised to hear from Faisal, considering that the trouble had originated in America. Faisal headed the Wyoming office of Nassar Security. As a result, he was their go-to person for most things relating to the United States. They'd worked through the night on this one, no different than any other case.

"Barb Almay contacted me," Faisal said, referring to their head researcher. "She was doing some research for you and hit a sticking point. Tad Rossi was placed under arrest, but she couldn't get any more information than that. So she called me."

"Under arrest." Talib frowned. "And?"

"I pulled some strings here and discovered that the man you're looking for is now out of the picture."

"What do you mean?"

"Tad Rossi was arrested yesterday for assault of an elderly woman at a banking machine near the state border of New Hampshire and Maine. The woman fought back and with the help of a passerby, he was restrained and held until police arrived."

"Good Samaritan?"

"Exactly. You'll be interested in this—he had a newly issued passport on him as well as a small bag."

"Needed money for the flight over?"

"My guess," Faisal said.

"So now he's, at least for the time being, in a jail cell."

"Not exactly. He was killed early this morning. Attacked by another prisoner while being transferred from the police holding cells."

"You're joking," Talib said, but it wasn't a question. Faisal would never joke about something like that. "Do you have anything else on him?"

"Not a lot. He's been in the States for the last twelve years. Any ties he has in Morocco reveal nothing from this end. You might have a better chance of uncovering something where you are."

"Thanks, bro," Talib said as he disconnected. He flipped the phone in his hand as he pondered the situation. Before this news he'd hoped to interrogate Sara's ex-boyfriend and find out who he'd contracted here. Now, they'd lost that connection. Whoever was here was working alone and the danger had escalated drastically, for the threat was now not only anonymous, but also connected to no known entity. It was reduced, as Sara had described, to a robotic voice on a phone line.

THE DARKNESS WAS just beginning to thin as Talib pulled into the parking lot of the Desert Sands Hotel. Shadows shifted across the lot, where only four other vehicles were parked. He knew one was Ian's—the others, he could only assume belonged to upper management, security, or other, similar such people. He didn't envy his friend being dealt such a massive hand of trouble, but Ian would persevere and succeed. He always did.

He got out, giving the car door a light push as it closed with a slick precision that didn't make a sound.

He glanced around.

He was alone. Everything was deadly silent.

There was no parking lot attendant. He frowned. There should have been at least a contracted guard considering everything that had happened.

A breeze ran through the lot. The shadows seemed to shift and then everything was still. He looked around. There was nothing. He was jumpy. Like this was his first case, his first assignment. It was a poor analogy for he'd never been jumpy before, even then, in his youth—in the beginning of his career. He wasn't sure why he was jumpy now.

He stopped, caught in his own musings.

He had a son.

It was incomprehensible.

The kid would be the first of the next generation in his family. And he'd missed over two years of his life. Something shifted. The shadows seemed to move around him. And, on the horizon, a streak of sunlight cut through the dawn sky, tantalizing, in a way teasing with the fact that soon it would take back the night. But his mind was occupied with other things and he didn't hear footsteps until he was swinging around, swinging into danger.

He was aware of it immediately, and too late. He should have dumped the thoughts and pulled his gun. That was his first mistake. To say he was overwhelmed was an understatement. But that was no excuse. His mind told him to reach for his gun, his fingers moved as if in that direction. He would have done it, given another second.

He only had enough time to duck as he tried to make out the blur, the shadow of a man coming at him. It was not only too late, but also not enough. The only thing the move did was make sure that the bat his attacker was wielding caught him on the edge of his shoulder instead of the side of his head. He was thrown off balance and had to fight to keep on his feet. The pain that ran through his shoulder was sharp and immobilizing. He could see the bat coming down again. This time he had an arm up as he grabbed the man's wrist, but it was again too late to stop the bat and he was only able to slow its progress. The bat connected with his upper arm and pain rocketed through him. He twisted the man's wrist with everything he had, ignoring his own pain, pushing to hear a snap of bone.

But the snap didn't come and he was in too awkward a position. He let go, unable to hold on any longer. He lost his balance, but caught his fall with one hand—his right, the injured arm. The pain ran up his arm into his throbbing shoulder.

He looked up as he struggled to stand.

Dark hair, wiry, a half head shorter than him but thick and wearing a soft, camel-colored jacket. They were all facts that his brain registered in the muted light that hung somewhere between day and night.

He was sure his attacker didn't have a gun. He would have shot him by now if he had. That spoke volumes. A small-time crook, a street hood. Quick money. He was being taken out by what appeared to be a rank amateur. But there was little time for pride. Instead, the thoughts were quick and automatic as he struggled to pull his gun.

Again he was too late. The man got a second wind and rushed him. Talib's hands weren't as skilled or as quick as usual. His dominant right hand was bruised, temporarily crippled from the earlier blow. Otherwise, he would have taken him down at the outset. Instead, he grabbed his attacker's arm with his left hand, making him drop the bat, grimaced at his own pain and plowed through it. The bat fell to the pavement and rolled out of reach.

One of the blows had hit the side of his head and he was seeing stars. He had to get it together. He pulled himself upright with a willpower that had seen him through a stint with the Royal Moroccan Army.

This was inconceivable and unthinkable, but the truth was that he'd had his guard down. He deserved all of this and more for his own stupidity. But he needed to get out of this.

But even realizing that, something else occurred to him—he had to fight harder or he was going down. He had let it go too far. The advantage of surprise had been everything for his attacker.

Sara depended on him. The truth of that had him pushing to stand upright.

He managed to get in a few blows of his own and his attacker was struggling. If he could just get control of himself, he knew that he could come out the victor. He didn't keep himself in peak condition to lose to a street hood. The hours he'd spent in the gym wouldn't be wasted. His head spun but he forced himself to stand up.

He had an advantage. He was armed, his fuzzy brain reminded him. His attacker wasn't. The bat still lay a distance away on the pavement. He reached for his gun. That's when he found himself grabbing air.

This was outrageous.

Then he had his gun in his hand and then somehow he didn't. It was on the pavement and he wasn't sure how that had happened, but his hand was stinging like it had been hit. He had no weapon. This was a fight using hand-to-hand combat.

He looked up. He couldn't have been more wrong. The

gun and the bat were still out of reach on the pavement, but his attacker was no longer unarmed. The morning sun was clearing the darkness away, sending streaks of light across the pavement and reflecting off the knife in his hand that glinted for a split second, almost blinding him.

A switchblade.

The realization seemed to change everything. It was like the last push in his army survival training, only it was more immediate than that. This was life or death like he'd never faced before.

Suddenly his head cleared, and the stars were gone. He had one chance here, one chance to live or die. There was no more time for anything but the skills he had and the gut instinct to move in the right direction at the right time. To be offensive or defensive, to make the best choice of either of those options. His weapon was his bare hands and the power of his mind.

The man was rushing him.

He twisted left, away from his attacker, who was swift and lethal despite his smaller size. He was wearing a hoodie and dressed in black, his face indistinguishable from so many others on the street. Talib bent low and came up with the edge of his hand on the man's already injured wrist.

The man grunted—he'd scored a hit but the switchblade was still tight in his hand and coming at him again. The morning sun was streaking across the pavement, reflecting off the knife in his hand and off his face. There was a hard look in his eyes and an unfocused look in one of them. The glint lasted a second, shifted and almost blinded him.

The man glared at him, the eye connection was brief, a millisecond, no more. But in that look a challenge was laid out. He could see the pain behind the challenge.

He'd injured him badly. Still, he held the knife. Now, the switchblade came down again, close, slicing his shirt just below his rib cage as his hand caught the man's wrist, sending the knife short of its target. The man snarled as he pushed him off balance. That was all the time that Talib needed to gain the advantage.

This time, as the man came in for another attack, he was ready for him. He came in from the side as the knife sliced through air. He had his attacker's wrist. He twisted and felt a bone crack as the man grunted in pain. The switchblade dropped and Talib's foot came down on it. At the same time, a knee hit his groin slightly off center, but still sending him reeling. His palm touched the pavement and he saw that his gun was just to his left. He reached and had it.

But his attacker had had enough.

He was already running across the parking lot, holding one arm against his chest. The man was too far away for Talib to have an accurate shot.

"We'll take your son!" the attacker shouted hoarsely, before he disappeared past the fringes of the lot and into what remained of the night.

The words seemed to echo over and over through the parking lot, or maybe it was through his shell-shocked brain. A son and a threat all at the same time. He ached where no man should ever have to ache. He was immobilized. He lost track of the minutes before he was on his feet and ready to walk.

He was alone. His entire body was bruised and he knew that he would feel the effects for a while. He hadn't been bruised up this bad in a long time.

He looked around, getting his bearings, making sure that he wasn't going to be assaulted again in a surprise attack. Nothing moved.

He stood there for a moment just taking breaths, combing the shadows as if somewhere on the edges of the pavement his attacker still lurked.

Chapter Fifteen

"What the hell happened to you, man?" Ian asked as Talib came in through the service entrance.

Talib tried not to favor his left leg, where his attacker had kicked him, or his shoulder that had also been clipped. They were what pained him most; he wouldn't think of what else hurt.

"You need to see a doctor."

"I'm fine. Looks worse than it is."

"You're sure?"

Ian's look of concern almost made him laugh.

"Definitely. Besides, there's no time," Talib said impatiently. "Was the surveillance camera on the guest parking lot working this morning?"

"Of course," Ian replied. "That was one of the first security measures I put into place. Exactly as you recommended."

"I need to see it."

Ian frowned. "You're not saying…" His dark brows drew together. "This is more than a security issue." His gaze roved over him. "Someone messed you up good, my friend."

"There was no one in the parking lot, Ian. No security."

He looked at Talib as if he'd forgotten the initial state

his friend had been in, as if the shock of first sight had only now been addressed. "What happened?"

"I was attacked in the parking lot. Guy with a bat and a switchblade."

"Sweet mother," Ian muttered. "That's why you asked about the camera. I can't believe this. You were right all along that I should have steered clear of this hotel. Purchasing it might have been premature."

"No. You might have led too soon off the block with opening but otherwise..." Talib shook his head. Bad move, his head was aching...deeply. "Do you have an aspirin?"

"Yeah, sure—give me a minute." Ian disappeared and returned a few minutes later with a bottle of pills and a glass of water.

Talib swallowed a couple of the painkillers and drained the glass before putting it down and turning to look at his friend.

"Crap, you look bad," Ian muttered.

"I've been worse," Talib said. There had been the time when he'd crashed a Ferrari and ended up three days in a hospital and with a scar that ran the length of his right thigh. That had been worse. This time he was still walking, although the pounding in his head was difficult to ignore. There was no point dwelling on it. His body would heal in its own time. Unfortunately, he didn't have that time to waste. He needed to keep moving and protect Sara and his son. "Let's run the footage and see if we can pin an ID on this piece of camel dung. He had his first and last run at me or anyone I care about," he said, thinking of Sara and the boy.

Fifteen minutes and a few calls later, they had a lead, and the name of a Moroccan national. He was a man with a long list of petty crimes and with no obvious link to either Sara or his son.

"Interesting," Talib said. His headache had calmed to a dull roar. He looked at the name he'd scrawled on a piece of paper along with a few other bits of information they'd dredged up. It was a name that meant nothing to anyone. Hired by someone to take him out or, at the least, ward him off.

The question was, who had hired him?

It HADN'T BEEN EASY, but Habib finally got the information he needed. He knew where she was, where the kid was. For a while it had seemed like the whole scheme had fallen apart, but now it was moving forward.

He gritted his teeth. To think he had started life as one of them. Rich like all the rest. He'd attended the same privileged primary school and then, because of his father's foolhardiness, they had lost it all. He remembered the school-yard taunts. Kids could be cruel, but what he remembered the most was the fact that Talib's father, Ruhul Al-Nassar, could have saved his family from the financial and social ruin that followed. Ruhul could have been a silent partner in the financial opportunity that his father had presented to him. If Al-Nassar had invested in the oil company his father had had a chance to partner in, they would have been rich once again. But Al-Nassar had refused. He'd said the investment wasn't something he was interested in. In fact, he'd hinted that his father wasn't capable of turning the business into a lucrative enterprise. He'd even pointed out his past failures. Listening silently on the other side of a closed door, he'd heard it all. His father didn't have the money to do it alone and the opportunity had slipped out of his hands almost as quickly as the life of luxury they had known disappeared.

Instead, the mighty Al-Nassar had offered his father a job and, worse than that, his father had taken it.

He'd hated the Al-Nassars from that moment on. He could have gotten over the school-yard taunts for those few remaining months at private school. He could have skated over the public school education for his last six years. But he'd never forget the chance that was lost to his family because of an Al-Nassar. His father was dead now and so was Ruhul Al-Nassar. The grudge had been carried to the next generation, to Talib, the man who, as a boy, had once been his classmate. He'd always secretly blamed Talib. He was sure that somehow, in some way, he had influenced his father's decision. He'd never know but he'd go to his grave believing that. He hated them all but he hated Talib most of all. Now, he finally had a chance to get it all back.

He considered his options. The idiot Tad had been wrong. Kidnapping the child was exactly what he needed to do. Just short-term. He didn't need the kid longer than that. Al-Nassar had to know by now that the kid was his and he'd do anything, give anything, to get him back. He knew about family loyalty and he knew all about them. They fought for what was theirs. It was a trait that he would use to his advantage.

He lit a cigarette and took a drag. The thought of what all of this could do to those who had made him feel so inferior ran through his body, in a shiver that snaked down his spine.

Tad had told him they only needed a fright and he'd initially agreed to that.

But he was having doubts now. They already knew the kid was the key to everything. This time he would be successful. If they thought money would save the kid, then the Al-Nassars would throw money at him. It was a brilliant plan and surprisingly simple. Once he had the money it was game over and the desert was pretty unforgiving. If the kid was hardy, maybe he'd come through in one piece. He didn't really care how that turned out. He'd handle the kid next time and it would be serious, a real kidnapping. Meanwhile, Al-Nassar had moved her and the kid, and it had taken him until now to find out where. By this time tomorrow he'd have the kid and be long gone and Al-Nassar would quit playing games with him and give him every dime he demanded.

In fact, with Al-Nassar in the game, it was going to be a challenge, but that just upped the fun. The Sahara Sunset was one of the best as far as security. But no security was impenetrable. He'd gotten most of the information he needed—now all that was required was time and an opportunity. In a career of crime that he'd honed over the last decade, he'd learned that there was always a weak link. There was always someone who could be bought and whose skills could be used. It had taken him less time to find the hotel than it had to find that link that could be bought. Only an hour ago, the necessary money had changed hands. Now, he just needed to set the plan in motion.

Chapter Sixteen

"The police caught and lost your attacker," Ian said in that quick way that was unique to him. He tended to get straight to business and avoided any pleasantries or time wasters, as he liked to call them. It was what worked for both of them. "I just spoke to the detective on the case."

"What do you mean lost?" Talib asked.

"The bugger slipped police restraints as he was being transferred. Had him on a minor traffic violation and it was only your mention of the lazy eye that had our officer frisk him and find the switchblade." He gave Talib the name of the suspect, but it meant nothing to him.

Talib returned to the Sahara Sunset later that day with a feeling of relief and of coming home.

He knocked on the door, not wanting to scare her.

"It's me, Talib," he added for good measure.

The door opened and her smile of relief almost melted his heart. "Talib," she said. "Where have you been?" And that was followed by an immediate gasp. "What happened to you?" Her hands were on his cheeks, as she gently ran her fingers down his bruises. "Who did this?" she asked in a tone like she was about to launch war on the perpetrator. She had his hand before he could answer any of that and dragged him over to the couch. In truth, he followed willingly, rather enjoying the attention.

"You need ointment, bandages…" She tsked.

"I'm fine, Sara, really." He patted the seat beside him. "Sit down with me. That's all I need right now is you."

"I can't believe it. What happened?" she asked as she sat down close beside him. Her bare arm rubbed against his and the thought of his bruises went to the back of his mind.

It was like being met by a wife's loving scolding. He'd never thought that of a woman, never thought he'd want to be in that position. The words were oddly unromantic and yet they made him feel as though his world just turned around.

"Talib," she said, shifting on the seat so that she was turned sideways to look at him. "I was worried."

"I would have been here sooner. I had a bit of a scuffle."

She brushed his arm with her hand. "I'm so sorry, Talib. I should never have come. I've put you in danger, disrupted your life. I'm sorry."

"The only mistake you made, Sara," he said thickly, "was not finding me sooner."

Thirty minutes later, as they sat together over coffee, there was rustling in the bedroom and the sound of their son's voice chattering in his version of English and baby talk. The mix was uniquely his own.

Sara stood up. He touched her arm with gentle fingers. "Please," he said. "Let me. I've never gotten him up from a nap."

Something in her face broke, like she might cry. He leaned down and kissed her. "I didn't mean that as a jibe. I really meant that I want to make up for lost time," he said.

"I know," she said softly.

Later, they ordered supper, a pizza, and enjoyed it together as a family. They were moments they would all remember. He stayed with her through that night, spooning her, feeling her soft curves and realizing that restraint was more difficult than he thought.

But he knew that he had to get moving. He didn't have the luxury of hanging around a hotel suite. It was his job to keep them safe.

His phone rang early the next morning and he answered to hear Barb's voice. "The suspect was last seen leaving one of the seedier areas of the Medina the evening before the attack." She gave him the address that they both knew housed more criminals than upstanding citizens.

"Possibly where he lives," Talib mused. "Or there was some sort of business dealings, or a myriad of things." He considered the options. "Not a great area," he said. "Anything else?"

"Still working on it. This is a tough one. There isn't much information easily available."

"None of your research is easy, Barb," Talib said with a laugh. "You're the best. Keep digging."

"Always."

He disconnected. There was only so much that could be found by their desk-bound researchers. He needed to get back in the field and check the address out.

"I've got to go," he said to Sara who'd been awakened by the call. It was just after 6:00 a.m. "Are you going to be all right?" he asked.

"I'm fine, Talib. We'll be fine," she reiterated. "Everything is secure. You do what needs to be done to make sure our son is safe." She hesitated, then took his right hand in both of hers. "Be careful. Don't do anything risky," she said. "Promise me."

He couldn't do that. Instead he leaned down and kissed

her, wanting to pull her into his arms and offer more comfort than that brief kiss. Instead he left her with the promise that he'd see her soon.

Thirty minutes later Talib stood outside a run-down apartment building on the edge of one of Marrakech's oldest souks. Unlike the other areas, this particular section didn't have the vibrancy that drew the tourists and locals alike. Much of what might once have been heritage buildings were now weathered and broken. He passed a small, gray, rectangular building, which was wedged between two bigger buildings of a similar style, before arriving at his destination—a decrepit, four-story brick structure.

Farther down an alleyway, two white-haired men were smoking and talking. Both of them were too far away to ID him and neither of them paid any attention to him. He could slip in and out. A check with the super had confirmed that the tenant worked an early morning shift leaving well before six in the morning and returning to the apartment later in the afternoon. Hopefully, there was evidence in the apartment of who he was, who he knew and, better yet, who he might be associated with.

He jimmied the lock on the main door and slipped inside. He was met by a rush of stale, hot air that made him want to breathe as little as possible. The smell of something rancid, like cooking oil, wafted through the air—it was an unwelcome stench. There was no one else around. He took the concrete stairs, one at a time, with caution. The staircase was steep and narrow. The apartment was at the end on the second floor and as he stood outside of it, silence seemed to tick around him.

He put his ear to the wooden door. No sound. A door banged shut on the floor above him and his hand jerked back from the knob. He looked around. There was no one, nothing near him. Minutes later he was inside. The room was meager. Directly in front of him was a cot and to his right, a small television. There was a bathroom to his left, the only other room unless you counted a closet and an open-area kitchenette. He stepped farther in, moving around a stack of travel magazines.

"Going somewhere?" he murmured. The possibility was there—if this was their man, that he was picking the next destination where he could take the money and run. But there were no answers from a stack of magazines.

He stepped deeper into the room. Despite the fact that clothes and paper were strewn across the bed, they were arranged in an oddly organized way. It was a contradiction and yet it was clearly a pattern. He lifted a magazine from the bed.

A piece of pale yellow note paper slipped out from the pages of the magazine. There was a name on that paper. It was a name that wasn't unfamiliar to him. It didn't necessarily mean anything, but he'd gone to primary school with a boy by that name. It wasn't a common name. And there was a phone number. He grimaced at the thought of calling the number out of the blue, and saying what? What did Habib Kattanni have to do with a two-bit criminal who had fled detection? He frowned. His mind went back to the fact that Habib had gone to school with him. It was years ago and he couldn't imagine what the connection might be now. In fact, logically he'd like to say there was no connection, but the evidence seemed to be hinting otherwise. That gave rise to the question that the man might have the same name as the boy he'd gone to school with, but there the similarity stopped. Same name—different person. They were all things that needed to be followed up on. He thought back, remembering the boy who had been there for a term, maybe two—he wasn't sure. And then he'd left. There'd never been any explanation. What he remembered was his father saying something about the disgrace of it all. His father would have known for he'd employed Habib's father for a brief time after what everyone referred to as the scandal. Unfortunately, his father was no longer around for answers.

Talib looked at the paper and tried to dredge up any memory of the man. But there was nothing. It had been a long time ago.

Habib.

The few memories he had weren't good. He remembered that he was a whiney, unlikeable kid, but that didn't mean anything. Kids were a lot of things before they matured and became who it was they were meant to become. He couldn't see anyone he had gone to school with sinking to this. But why was Habib's name here, in this apartment? Was it a case of same name, different identity?

He stuffed the paper in his pocket and did a thorough check of the room. Whoever he was, he'd left in a hurry, but he'd taken almost everything of importance with him. None of it was matching what the super had said. The evidence he saw was looking like the tenant wasn't coming back. Ten minutes later, he was finished. He'd found nothing except the one name that led him into the shadows of his past—to when he was a boy.

He paused in the doorway as he contemplated the abject poverty so in opposition to the homes that anyone who had gone to his primary school had come from. Had the unsub contracted this man to attack him? And how was Habib linked into all of this, or was he? Had Habib hired someone to attack him? That made no sense, but if he hadn't, who had? What motivation did he have? The connection, the link, was the dead boyfriend, Tad. But dead men didn't talk.

He left, closing the door behind him, making sure to leave no evidence that he'd been there. Despite his belief that his parking-lot assailant was gone, he made sure that no one saw him as he left. But there was no one around, the cramped, age-greased corridor was as silent as when he'd arrived.

Outside, the narrow street was crowded with people and the occasional donkey. A slight man on a Vespa wound his way slowly through the throng.

Talib slipped into the crowd. His clothes were as worn as anyone else's in the area. He'd made sure to haul out the clothes he used to do some of the mechanic work on his vehicles. This wasn't an area where designer clothes and pressed shirts would fit. He wasn't much of an actor and he knew that how he presented himself was different than the working class that held the majority in the area. If someone questioned his appearance... But it didn't matter much anyway—the man he was after had already run.

He passed another alley, and saw a man of average height and build, and in faded jeans and an olive-green T-shirt watching him from the shadows.

Then the man motioned to him.

What the hell? Talib thought as he watched the man jerk his head to the alley, as if indicating he should follow.

The man disappeared again into the shadows.

He moved into the head of the alley. There was no one around him. He had his gun in one hand and yet it seemed like overkill. But he wasn't taking any chances. The man seemed to have disappeared. He could go forward or back out—this could be a trap. Just as he decided to back up and return to the busy shopping area behind him, he felt the presence of someone. He had no time to turn or duck.

The blow came before he could react. It was silent and even more lethal because of it. As Talib fell he could only think of one name—Sara. He had to get up. He had to go to her. Instead he kept falling, down, down as if the spiral was out of control and would never end. It finally did end as consciousness left him.

Chapter Seventeen

Sahara Sunset Hotel
Thursday 1:30 p.m.

Sara looked at her watch and gritted her teeth—her stomach clenched and she felt sick. She hadn't heard from Talib since early this morning. She'd counted on him and somehow, in some way, he was letting her down.

She kept thinking the worst and it was making her crazy. That and the fact that she was trapped, imprisoned by a promise she'd made to Talib to stay in her suite. There was nowhere to go and no one to talk to. It was maddening.

Talib hadn't called as he had promised and he'd been gone for over seven hours.

"Where are you?" she murmured. Her worry and boredom were building in conflicting degrees.

She told herself that she shouldn't be worried, Talib knew what he was doing. She shouldn't be bored, either. She wasn't being held in a barren cell. She had every amenity. And if it wasn't available, whatever she might need was only a phone call away. There was a bodyguard, security Talib had called him, who, although not at the door at all times, was usually in the vicinity. One of the men that Talib had assigned, Andre, was the only one she'd seen so far. Andre knocked on her door at regular intervals to ensure that they were fine and that they weren't needing anything. He didn't lurk in the hallway, but she knew that he was always somewhere close by. He was amiable enough and she'd even teased him about a girl when he'd taken a call that was clearly not business. He had an easy smile, dark cropped hair, intense dark eyes and a physique that would deter most villains. He looked exactly like what he was—muscle for hire— unless you got to know him as she had. She'd learned that there was a soft spot with Andre and it was children. It was only with Everett that he turned completely to mush. His smile softened as he spoke baby talk to the boy and made him smile with his exaggerated facial expressions. Some were so absurd that Sara even found herself smiling.

But the visits from Andre were brief and the confinement was driving her crazy. She took a breath and then another as if to calm herself, or at least to redirect her thoughts. But there was no getting around it, the suite was claustrophobic despite what initially had seemed its expansive size. They'd been here too long. While there was no lack of things to watch on television or games that had been delivered to her room, everything had been toddler-centric. Despite Talib's company last night, she was alone now and feeling it. She was about to go out of her mind.

If nothing else, they needed to get out of this room. They were both restless and with Everett that meant his mood was going south fast. In the last five minutes he'd gone from whimpering to tears and she knew that a screaming fit wasn't too far away. The terrible twos had hit and sometimes there was just no calming him.

Soon, she was desperate to stop his screams and tears.

He hadn't had one of these fits in weeks and really, she'd experienced this kind of meltdown only a few times in the past. What she knew was that without diversion, this was poised to become epic. Everett was stubborn, as toddlers can be, and was testing the edges of his world and his own sense of autonomy. She knew she'd been lucky so far. Thanks to the long trip, the strange environment and her own stress, she knew Everett was on edge. She was surprised that this hadn't come sooner.

Everett shrieked louder and higher, and then gulped, more than likely gaining energy for his next howl, and within a minute she was right. She needed a solution fast. This hotel might be luxurious and well-built, but insulation only blocked so much noise. In a regular hotel, someone would already be pounding on the walls for them to be quiet. She was betting it was only a matter of time here.

They needed a break from this suite. The hotel was safe, Talib had said so himself. She wouldn't do anything foolish, like step outside or stray from any areas that weren't well trafficked and secure. Her thoughts broke off as she smiled at that. Talib had told her that the hotel had security cameras on every floor, and in every area. Add to that a security team, one of whom she was on a first-name basis with, and there was no reason to worry. Besides, she wasn't planning to be gone long—ten, maybe fifteen, minutes. Just enough to calm Everett and regain her sanity.

There was no one that she needed to tell where she was going or what she was doing. Andre was on a late lunch break and it would be another thirty minutes before he returned. He'd knocked on the door only fifteen minutes ago to see if there was anything she needed. She'd assured him everything was fine, but it was the calm before the storm.

"WHEN DID YOU speak to Talib last?" Emir asked one of their office staff, and her answer had him concerned.

"The police had an identification on the man who attacked him at the Desert Sands parking lot. From that I found an address. Barb gave the information to Talib just after six this morning and we haven't heard anything from him since. I left a text for him to call four hours ago, but I haven't heard anything." The dark-haired, petite woman was their latest hire. Rania had turned out to be quick and efficient, digging up information in record time.

Emir shook his head. He didn't like the passage of time. That was a problem. He expected their agents, brothers or not, to check in when flying solo on a case. Especially one where he really should have been assigned backup. It was only Talib's request and the nature of the case that had him holding back from assigning another agent.

His brother had been out of communication for over seven hours. Again, considering the nature of the case and the fact that it was contained within the city limits of Marrakech, a lapse in communication was troubling. As a result, his senses were on alert. If everything was going right, then this didn't happen in their business, not on a case like this. They were all too well-trained, too conscientious. There was only one reason for this and it didn't bode well—something had happened.

Rania gave him the address that Barb had earlier given to Talib. He was pulling on a bulletproof vest as he headed out the door. He reached for his gun to make sure it was tucked in place under his waistband, ready at a moment's notice.

Chapter Eighteen

When Talib woke, the banging in his skull made him want to close his eyes again. He didn't have that luxury. He needed to stay awake, stay focused and figure out where he was and what kind of dung pile he'd landed in.

The pain was blinding.

He gave in and briefly closed his eyes, but only in an effort to get control of the pain. When he opened them again, he could see nothing but darkness, or at least that's what he initially thought. His eyes were barely open, not enough to get a good visual on anything—light, dark, nothing. He took conscious breaths, closed his eyes and opened them again. Wherever he was, he was in a place that smelled of dirt. Graveyard dirt. Bad image, he thought. Must, he was smelling must and lying on something hard. There was a flicker of light overhead. Where was he? How long had he been out and was he alone? They were questions that all needed to be answered before he made a move.

He remembered bits of what had happened. The man, smaller than he, had come from nowhere. He hadn't had a chance to get a good look at him. He could have been the same man from the parking lot attack, or someone totally different. Because before he could turn and confront him, he'd been hit on the back of the head. It was only his earlier injuries that had slowed him down and allowed this to happen. After that there had been nothing, until now. He wasn't sure how much time had passed or where he was.

He should have asked for backup. That was his oversight.

He reached up with his bound hands to where the thin line of light sifted into his prison. A board was what was over his head. He could feel the wood. From what he could piece together, it was the floor just above him, some sort of trapdoor over a shallow storage area. Had they decided that taking out the father was better than the son? His mind whirred with possibilities. Were they just taking him out, out of the way so that they could take his son next? He bit back pain and panic. He needed to get control of both his emotions and the pain.

He lay still, trying to get his bearings, trying to figure out his next move and how he was going to get out of here. He was used to thinking on his feet, but not with his head thumping the way it was. He took a breath and then another. He'd learned a long time ago that in a crisis one should get a plan together. He couldn't burst out of his prison not knowing what lay on the other side. A thin shard of light grazed across his arm, bouncing off of broken tile just to the left of him. It was like someone had begun a cellar and then stopped and what remained was a shallow hole beneath the floor. It made no sense unless one had planned this in advance. Or was this a temporary prison? But that made no sense, either.

He stilled his thoughts, listening. There was no sound. There hadn't been any sound in the minutes he'd been conscious. He was fairly certain that wherever he was, he was alone.

He let his thoughts shift from his current predicament to his greatest worry.

Sara. He had to get to her, to warn her. More importantly he needed to protect her, for this was much more deadly, much more immediate, than he had thought. She was all that stood between their son and danger. He knew that she'd defend him with her life. He couldn't allow things to get to that point.

His thoughts were clearer now. They knew who he was. That was the only explanation. It had taken two attacks but their intent was to take him out. It was his own fault that they were close to succeeding. He'd let emotion fog the case and in doing that he'd underestimated the opponent. He needed to get back in the field to protect what he cherished most—his family.

"Let's go for a walk," Sara said to Everett, who was sniffling and red-faced. She spoke to him as if he was an adult. She often did that, speaking as if he understood the idea that walks often calmed him down. Her thought was to go to the hotel gift shop, maybe even a snack shop. Whatever stores were available here, she didn't know, as she'd had no time to explore. She was like a prisoner within the opulence of her suite. Somehow she'd never thought her visit would turn out like this. For that was all it was, a visit. She hadn't thought beyond that. It had been a flight of desperation, a cry for help that was turning out far different than she could ever have imagined. But she hadn't changed plans, this trip had an end date—return tickets booked and no resolution to her problem in sight. She pushed that thought from her mind.

"We'll go to the store," she said. In all probability they would be stores selling high-end products and designer goods. Even that would be helpful. Oddly, Everett always liked shopping. He was distracted by all the different things he saw on the shelves. It often made it a challenge for her, but it was exactly what she needed now. She imagined that the shelves might be filled with expensive trinkets. Shiny things that would only cause her grief as he reached for them, but would, more importantly, provide a distraction for him.

"Cracker," he demanded, waving his chubby hand. He hiccupped before bursting into a fresh bout of wails.

The fridge had been restocked, but crackers hadn't been included. She could phone and they'd be brought up immediately, but that wasn't the point.

She smiled at Everett and he snuffled and rubbed his eyes with the back of his fists. He was in a lull. Right now, his mood could go either way.

Five minutes later they reached the main floor without incident. There, the lobby was a pleasant surprise. The staff was courteous and willing to help, and directed her to a small snack shop that carried the animal crackers Everett loved. She also found a few shops that were entertaining enough for a small boy. She let Everett walk. She held his hand but her attention was fixed on everything around her. She watched for danger, trusted no one and paid attention to her environment. Someone had tried to kidnap Everett once and she wouldn't let it happen again.

Twenty minutes later they were heading back to their room. It was a different elevator ride than their earlier one, where Everett had hiccupped and sobbed the entire descent to the main floor. Now, he was smiling and she had managed to relax somewhat although she would never—could never—tone down her vigilance.

She stepped out of the elevator and turned to her right, heading for their suite. She passed one door, the carpet no less soft and luxurious beneath her feet than it had been the first time.

Twelve feet from her room, she stopped.

"No," she murmured.

"No," Everett repeated with a smile.

"Shh," she said as she put a finger to her lips and juggled him in one arm.

He nodded his head and smiled. He was slipping from her grip. She boosted him higher and his smile broadened. He put a finger to her lips.

She left his finger there, barely noticing. Instead her gaze was caught by what she saw in front of her. She took a step backward.

The door to her hotel suite was open.

She'd shut and locked it.

Her first thought was that it could be hotel staff.

She knew that didn't fly even as she thought it. There was no reason for them to be checking her suite. The maids did the rounds in the morning and no maid visited their suite unless requested. One had yet to be requested.

Sara started to move backward, away from the suite, away from the possibility of a threat. She was being overly cautious, but considering everything that had happened, she wasn't taking a chance.

She looked at Everett and winked while mouthing *shush*. She was grateful for the silly game she'd created in the hours they'd spent alone. She had taught Everett how to play spy, and how to be extra quiet while doing so. She'd done it because of all that was happening, just in case. But to the boy it was a fun game. Now his striking, light brown eyes sparked with the anticipation of playing his new favorite game and he clamped his lips with a tiny finger on them.

She shifted him in her arms. He was almost too heavy,

but she had to soldier through. She couldn't chance putting him down. Whoever had been in her room could still be there. She'd hung a Do Not Disturb sign on the door. From what she could see, it was still there. She had all her important papers with her, she always did. There was nothing for them to steal but the clothes, baby things and some cosmetics and toys that Talib had had delivered early yesterday.

Something scuffled, like a footstep sliding over paper, making it rustle, and it was coming from their suite. She remembered the newspaper that Andre had brought her earlier this morning. He had laid it on a small table by the door and only an hour ago, Everett had thrown it off. She didn't remember picking it up, she'd been distracted and...

Her thoughts broke off.

She backed up faster, smiling at Everett, being careful not to frighten him. He was still clutching an animal cracker and seemed more fascinated by the fan that turned slowly over their head than what she was frightened of. She backed away from their suite quietly and headed for the fire exit. She'd slip down that way. The elevator wasn't a thought. The last thing she needed to do was get trapped in an elevator or caught while waiting for one.

A bang behind them made her jump as it echoed down the hallway.

"Mama!" Everett squawked.

"Shh." She was terrified that they'd been heard. Terrified that whoever was in the room would be out here in seconds, threatening them, snatching her son from her arms.

She turned and ran.

"No," Everett cried as he was jostled in her arms.

"Shh."

She glanced frantically over her shoulder and her worst fears were realized. There was a flash of movement, a bulky person, a man exiting their suite. There were seconds before he would see them, come after them. To her right was the fire alarm. Should she do it? It seemed rather extreme. She looked frantically behind her and now there was clearly no choice. Briefly she met the distant look of the man who was just leaving her room. It was clear now that he was wiry rather than bulky and it was also clear that he was a threat. He glared at her before he began to move in her direction. She didn't wait to see the distance between them being eaten up. She couldn't run as fast as him and carry Everett. She didn't chance another look, but swung around and pulled the fire alarm.

Chapter Nineteen

The alarm bell was ringing loudly through the hotel.

Sara fumbled with the emergency door with one arm, struggling to get it open before finally turning and ramming it open with her butt.

A door slammed to her right and she could hear excited voices.

The fire exit opened and a rush of cool air seemed to sweep around her. Compared to the opulence elsewhere, the cement and steel almost made her stop. Almost. They had to get out of here. Within a floor she was joined by others. People kept streaming in and the flow slowed with each addition. Soon she was caught in a wave of panicked people who were now moving at a crawl. Caught in the middle of the pack, she was out of sight. Everett was silently sucking his thumb. His eyes were wide, fascinated or frightened, she wasn't sure. It seemed he was more shocked than she.

She couldn't believe this was happening again. It had been a mistake to come here, to come to Morocco at all. She'd thought that she'd run away from trouble and now she only was finding herself caught in something far worse.

She shifted Everett in her arms and marveled at the fact that he was still quiet. It was the only bit of luck that was coming her way. It was up to her to keep him safe. How had she thought that it would be any other way? It had always been about her and Everett. Her son was not a responsibility she could ask anyone else to share, even Talib.

"Mama," Everett said.

"Shh." She pressed a finger to his lips.

She concentrated on keeping her footing in the crowd and putting distance between them and the intruder, and what was clearly danger targeted at her and her son. A twinge of guilt ran through her at the thought that by pulling the alarm bell she had involved not only other people, but also a whole hotel.

She'd begun the evacuation of a hotel, pulled the fire alarm when no fire existed. Behind her a woman's bag pushed into the back of her legs. She stumbled, caught her balance and reached for the railing. Her heart was pounding and her mouth was dry.

The cool stairwell was beginning to heat up from the waves of people joining at each level. Finally, they were on the main floor and bursting into the flooded lobby, where hotel staff were organizing people as they emerged. Rather than the chaos of the first hotel, this one was calm and orchestrated. No one looked anything more than slightly flustered or, in one case, put out.

She had to admit what she'd done, stop what she'd unintentionally put into motion.

She hurried over to a man with the telltale gold braid, but whose uniform indicated he might be security. He was directing people as they emerged from the stairwell. "Someone has broken into my room," she said in a hurried breath.

"We'll send someone up."

"He may be armed."

"Just a moment, madam," he said as he moved toward the desk.

"No, wait." She didn't need anyone hurt, but she needed the emergency crews called off. "I pulled the fire alarm. There is no fire."

"No fire." His eyes darkened and he picked up a phone. "You?"

"Yes," she said firmly and swallowed a ball of fear.

She was in deep trouble. She couldn't imagine what the penalty might be for a tourist falsely claiming an emergency. But there was still the threat, somewhere here in this hotel. She needed to get Everett out.

"Remain here. For the authorities." He turned to the desk and spoke rapidly, words that she didn't understand.

A voice came over the intercom, asking for calm, stating it had only been a practice run. That there was no emergency. Excited voices swirled around her.

"Don't move," the man behind the desk instructed her.

She pulled out her phone and called Talib.

No answer.

Within minutes an intercom again repeated that it had been a false alarm and promised refreshments for those remaining in the lobby. A form of compensation, she supposed. She put down Everett, never letting her hand leave his. She tried Talib again with no success. Five minutes went by and around her, the rush of the crowd was nothing like it had been in the first hotel. Instead, hotel patrons milled about chatting and laughing. Staff moved among them, offering the promised cocktails and other refreshments.

She could see a pair of men in suits. They looked big, almost bulky and definitely intimidating as they huddled together in a closed discussion. One looked up and glanced over at her.

She moved away, out of their line of vision, and sat in an overstuffed chair in the midst of a group of older, well-dressed men and women. They were chatting, enjoying their drinks and not paying much attention to her. She hoped that their numbers and loud voices might, for a minute or two, shield her.

Her eyes shifted around.

Someone had been in her room, had come after her and was more than likely still looking for her. The danger wasn't gone, at least not for her, and more importantly, not for Everett. Was the intruder connected with the hotel? He'd worn a similar jacket to hotel personnel. But there was something different in the way he had looked at her, the way he had acted. Plus, he'd worn a T-shirt beneath the jacket. That alone screamed fraud. She wasn't sure who to trust. She needed Talib desperately and she needed him now.

She remembered Talib telling her that if she sensed trouble and she couldn't, for any reason, get a hold of him, to contact his oldest brother, Emir. She had yet to follow that advice, but she hadn't been in a situation such as this. She pulled out her phone and the card he'd given her.

Emir answered with worry evident in his voice.

She frowned. That was odd. The worry was almost an omen, for it was so unlike the man she'd met, or the stories of him that Talib had told her. Something was going on but she was in no position to ask what.

"Where's Talib?" she asked shortly.

"Sara, what's wrong?" he asked instead of answering her question. His voice sounded rather stressed and there was a rush of traffic noise, a car honking in the background.

She didn't ask about any of it. She only explained what was happening.

"You were right to call me, Sara. I'll be there in five minutes. I'm actually just a few blocks away. Never mind, I'll talk to you when I get there. Stay where you are, where security can see you. And no worries, I'll handle that situation, as well."

She almost smiled at that, if smiling was even a possibility considering the circumstances. Security wasn't detaining her but she could feel their unsmiling looks burning into her. They weren't about to let her out of their sight and although it was for a different reason, that fact was oddly comforting. She put her phone into her pocket. Then she pulled out a toy car for Everett out of her other pocket. She could see two brawny security men now moving in her direction. They were well-dressed but their broad shoulders and unforgiving faces told her clearly who and what they were. But before they could reach her, the elevator doors opened and Andre rushed out.

"Madam," he said. It was the title he'd always referred to her as and it had always seemed like he was giving her the respect offered an older woman. But at twenty-five, it had seemed odd. Hearing it now was comforting. Seeing a familiar face was a relief.

"You're all right?"

"I think so. The security…"

"Won't touch you," he said. He turned to Everett and took the chubby face in his big hands and then pretended to take his nose, making the boy laugh. His dark eyes met hers. "You left the room," he said in an accusing voice.

She nodded. "There was a man leaving my room. We ran and I pulled the alarm." She didn't bother to mention her earlier infraction, the one that put them in the hallway to begin with. He didn't push the issue. She imagined with Talib she wouldn't be so lucky. But that was later.

Where was he? She picked up Everett. "Mama," he whined, struggling to get down.

She held him tighter as she turned her attention back to Andre, realizing that he was still speaking and she'd missed what he'd said. "I'm sorry. I was distracted and didn't hear what you said."

"It's all right," he replied. "I was saying that I suspected something like that when I saw you were missing. I've had the hotel locked down," he said gravely. He glanced behind them. "They know you pulled the alarm?"

She nodded.

"I'll handle it." It was a man's voice behind her. The voice was distinctive and one she'd heard only recently. She turned to see Emir and felt relief, while at the same time her heart sank. The arrival of Talib's brother only made his absence so much more noticeable. Where was Talib?

"Stay there," Emir said as he motioned to Sara. "Andre, come with me," he said in a voice that was easy and yet commanding at the same time.

Everett poked her lip with his finger and squirmed to get onto the ground. Her arms still ached from carrying him down the stairs. If Talib had been here, he'd take him from her. In such a short time, she'd gotten used to that small act of chivalry. She'd gotten used to a lot of things. She was here under the name Al-Nassar, under Talib's name, his protection, and she needed him desperately.

What would she do if she couldn't find him?

Chapter Twenty

Talib had been working the rope on his wrist, worrying it with his teeth and rubbing it back and forth on the cement edge to his right, and he was finally able to break it. He didn't consider why his attacker hadn't just killed him when he had the chance. One didn't question good luck. But the penalty for death was a lot tougher than one for assault and forcible restraint. Penalties and justice, of course, depended on one getting caught and there was no doubt in his mind that this piece of camel dung was going to get caught. Caught and tried and convicted if he had any say in it.

Bugger, he mouthed, afraid to make any sound in case there was someone above him. If he hadn't been banged up from the earlier attack, this never would have happened.

He moved his ankles, working to restore his circulation. Then something changed. He could sense that he wasn't alone.

There was a rustling above him.

That was new. There had only been silence in the time he'd been awake. How long had he been here? He wasn't sure. He'd drifted in and out of consciousness. He was fairly certain that he'd been drugged. It was the only thing that made sense for he estimated he'd been out for hours.

It had been questionable before, the sound just a whisper, a hint of movement. Now he knew that he wasn't alone. Now there was a clear scuffing noise unique to the sound of the leather soles of traditional Moroccan shoes.

He wasn't alone. But it wasn't clear who was above him.

His attacker?

Whoever was above him, he could almost hear them breathing, as if the person was kneeling on the door that trapped him. Talib was silent. He didn't need to know he was conscious and free and ready to unleash his rage on whoever had done this to him.

Sara.

He needed to get to her. He moved his legs, quietly, clenching his fists, turning his ankles, getting the circulation going again. It was all he could do to be as quiet as possible and not break the wood above him and burst through. He would let his abductor think he still had the advantage and then take the bugger down.

Open the door, he thought, and fought his impatience.

More shuffling and then there was a thud and clunk of metal as whatever was holding the door down was shoved aside. He didn't have much time to consider what it might be before the door opened upward. Light spilled into the dark dungeon-like space he'd been trapped in. He remained still for a second, then two. He was barely breathing. His eyes were closed and every one of his senses was on alert. Then, on an inhale, he opened his eyes and bellowed a war cry meant to throw off the enemy. He lunged at his captor, moving up and out and flattening the man with the surprise of his attack and his greater size. His fist crunched the man's jaw even as his other hand sank into his midriff. In a few minutes it was over. The man was bound and thrown into the same dungeon Talib had been in. A look at the man told him that it was the same one who had accosted him in the parking lot.

Who had hired him? Had it been his old classmate? And yet none of that made sense. But there was no time for answers to any of those questions.

Urgency pulsed through him.

He remembered other things he'd heard through the hours of his captivity. Random voices that had filtered in and out as he'd struggled for consciousness. He'd heard another voice, a man's, and a mention of the Sahara Sunset. More than one man was involved in this and he'd only trapped one. Worse, they knew the name of the hotel where Sara and his son were staying.

Sara's safe place had been compromised.

He pulled a cell phone from the man's pocket. This piece of filth would be under lock and key within the hour and not just the makeshift one that Talib had tossed him into.

"Have a nice life," he said sarcastically as he slid the metal rod across the door, locking the unconscious man inside. It was two o'clock in the afternoon. He'd been held captive much longer than he thought.

He emerged out of what had only been a shanty of a room in the basement of the apartment building he'd so recently visited. He limped down the narrow corridor and burst out into a silent alley. The circulation in his legs was coming back, in tingles that made his gait more unsteady than smooth. But he didn't have time to think about that. He needed to get to Sara and the boy.

"Where are you?" Emir asked as he took the call from Talib.

"Not relevant," Talib said shortly, thinking of the hours he'd been held captive. How much time had passed? His watch was gone, so was his gun.

"Very relevant, Talib. What the hell is going on?"

"Surprise attack. I'm okay," he said before Emir could ask about his well-being. He could feel the sweat on his forehead. It seemed like it had taken forever to get here, to where he had parked the car. He was lucky to be alive, he knew that. But he had more important things to concern himself with. He needed to make sure Sara and the boy remained safe. "Look, we have a situation. I need to get Sara and the boy out of that hotel and to the compound as quickly as possible. I have one of our suspects restrained." He gave him the location and briefly told him what had transpired.

"We need to get a tail on Habib Kattanni. I went to school with him as a kid. Family went hard up and somehow it seems he's involved in this. We need to know where he is and what he's doing now."

"I'll handle it," Emir said. "In the meantime, there's a situation at the Sahara Sunset."

"What the..." He broke off, already running in a limping gait for his vehicle.

"Fire alarm went off. There was no fire."

"No fire. Sara and the boy?"

"Sara pulled the alarm, T." Emir went on to explain what had happened. "I'm at the hotel with Sara now."

"He was there. I know it."

"Who?"

"Habib. I'll be there in ten, can you wait?"

"I'm not following, but yeah, I'm not going anywhere."

Talib moved out of the silent alley and into the noise and congestion of the souk. The narrow, walled corridor was filled with people, merchants and chaos. To think he'd been trapped so close to all this was ludicrous. To think he'd been attacked at all again, and by who—unthinkable.

Somehow his school days, which he had once remembered as a time of innocence, now seemed a breeding ground for one boy to turn to corruption and evil. And now that evil threatened his family.

He blinked. The light hurt his eyes.

And he didn't consider how the idea of family had so quickly and easily evolved to include Sara and Everett.

SARA WAITED AS Emir spoke to the hotel officials. Andre stood like a shadow to her right, not letting them out of his sight, and somehow his stoic presence only reminded her of the mess her life was in. Then she saw Talib striding through the front entrance. She hurried toward him. But she was stopped as a security officer seemed to emerge from the shadows and placed a hand on her upper arm. He was followed by a second security officer.

"Ma'am, a word," the shorter of the two said, but what he lacked in height he made up for in muscular girth.

"Please, I…"

"Let her go," Emir's cool voice demanded beside her.

Andre stood just behind him, his silent and equally intimidating presence backing him up.

Everett slipped and she would have dropped him, but strong hands had him out of her arms and she was face-to-face with Talib.

"Yes, I'm sorry, Mr. Al-Nassar."

The security team looked at the two brothers, who now flanked Sara. The men eased back, each gave a small bow and they moved away.

Everett took that moment to begin to snuffle, his face red and clearly ready to launch into something more epic. Talib put a finger on his lips and offered him a smile, which seemed to calm him.

"Are you all right?" Talib asked with a look of concern that made her want to sink into his arms. Her hands shook and her head ached and she looked up at him with relief. But that relief disappeared when she saw his face. He'd been banged up before but now he was much worse. One side of his face was entirely black and blue and he seemed to favor his left arm as if it was in pain. His hair was dull with what looked like dirt. All in all he was a mess, not the pulled-together man she knew. It was only the determined look in his eyes and the proud stance that was the same. Otherwise he looked like he'd been to hell and back.

"What happened?"

"It's not important," he growled.

"You were beat up," she persisted. "What happened? Where have you been?" she asked, not meaning to sound accusatory.

"I was in a situation or two," he said with a smile.

She couldn't help herself, her finger ran along his cheek. There was something more, something he was hiding. "What aren't you telling me?"

"Let's just say for now that I was broadsided, unexpectedly. I expect now, he looks worse than I do," Talib replied.

"You're sure? That you're okay," she said.

"I'm fine." His left arm was around her waist as he held their son in the crook of his other arm.

"Talib?" Emir said. "I don't mean to interrupt but we need to get some things sorted out."

"Wait here with Andre," he said to her and strode after his brother.

Sara sank down into a nearby chair, ignoring the big man by her side, her gaze following Talib as he walked away with Everett. The three were similar in so many ways, two men and a boy—family.

Something caught in her throat. Already, it had begun.

Chapter Twenty-One

"Where have you been?" Emir asked. "What happened?" he added before Talib could say anything to the first question. "Details this time."

"I was broadsided. I can't believe this, the second time..."

"Same unsub?"

"The one I've detained, yes. He's not going anywhere."

Emir nodded. "I didn't get a chance between your call and Sara's but I'll get the authorities on it."

"I was jumped from behind, thrown into a storage area that was hidden beneath the floorboards and left. I didn't get a visual on that one but I'm assuming it's the same guy. At some point, I heard him talking to another man. Don't know who he was. But before that I found a name on a scrap of paper. Here's where it gets strange. Like I told you earlier, I went to primary school with this guy. The guy whose name was on the paper. Like he was some kind of contact. I'm not sure what the connection was."

"Son of a..." Emir shook his head. "I was worried, I never thought—"

"But you were going after me," Talib interrupted as he eyed the bulletproof vest.

"Of course," Emir said.

"I'll get the other situation, your man in the cellar,

cleaned up." Emir looked over at Sara. "In the meantime, we need to get Sara out of here. As you said, the man behind all this knows she's here. And you and me need to talk. I've got the office on alert, this case is moving to code red."

They looked at each other, both of them knowing that a code red meant their agent needed backup. It was the most dangerous case, unlike white, which was the one least fraught with danger.

"I think it's contained," Talib said. "At least in the short term, if we can get Sara and the boy to the compound they'll be safe. At least for now."

FIVE MINUTES LATER the head of security shook Talib's hand. "This breach in security is troubling. We've checked camera footage and it appears there was an intruder. He slipped in through a delivery entrance. This has never happened before." He shook his head. "He's left the building. We've verified that and we are in the process of beefing up the defective area. That doesn't change what happened." He looked at Sara. "I'm so sorry. We pride ourselves on the safety of our hotel. Can we offer you an upgraded suite or…"

She shook her head. "No, thank you." She couldn't imagine anything more luxurious than what she already had.

More effusive apologies went on before it was only the three of them.

"What happened, Sara?" Talib asked. "I know you told me the short version but I don't understand, I mean I got how he came in, but you weren't in the room. How did he know that? Was he watching?"

She shook her head. "I don't know any of that. I'm just glad we weren't there. I don't think he expected us back so soon." She looked at him. "He could have planned to hide in the suite and take Everett."

He didn't mention that there was no need to hide. He only needed to overpower Sara, not a difficult feat. A chill ran through him at the thought.

"Why did you leave the room, Sara?"

She shook her head. "Everett was bored. We were both going stir-crazy."

"That's no excuse. You could have taken Andre."

"I thought it was safe. It's not Andre's fault," she said quickly. "I slipped out, it was stupid."

"Beyond foolhardy," he said darkly. "Promise me you won't do anything like that again."

"I promise."

He put his palms on either side of her face and leaned down and kissed her. "If something had happened to you…" He looked over at Everett. "Or him. I don't know what I would have done." He pulled her down onto one of the lobby couches. "Tell me what happened."

"When I realized that there was someone there and that they might come after us, I knew I had to do something. So I pulled the alarm when it looked like he had seen us. We were going to head down the emergency exit and he—he…" She stopped as if to catch her breath, gather her thoughts. "He was headed toward us. All things considered…"

"You're out of here." He hadn't meant to present the idea so bluntly. That was how he spoke to his brothers but this was Sara, the woman he… His thoughts broke off.

"What do you mean?"

He could see the panic run through her in the way her face went from pale to white.

"You're walking?" she asked in a small voice.

"Walking? What are you talking about?"

"I know we're in trouble and…"

"You think I'm washing my hands of you?"

She nodded.

"Are you out of your mind? I didn't say I was out of here," he said with disbelief. "I said you're out of here. And I meant you'll be going with me." Leaving her was the last thing on his mind. Leaving his son, never. "There's no choice now, you need to go to the family compound, where we can control access. I don't want—"

"You're getting no arguments from me," she interrupted in a voice filled with relief. "Let's go." And with a frown that seemed as much pained as determined.

"We'll end this," he said with gritted teeth, conscious of the boy in his arms.

"Let's go," Sara repeated as she slipped her hand tentatively into his.

And it was with that simple gesture that his decision was made. It was time to play hard ball.

Chapter Twenty-Two

The elevator door opened on the ninth floor.

Sara looked up at Talib. He could see the relief in her eyes. They both knew that after all that had happened she couldn't stay here another night.

"You can't stay here. The Nassar family compound isn't so bad," he said as he followed her out into the spacious hall.

"Just get us to safety," she said in a hoarse whisper. "I won't argue. And with any luck I won't be running..."

"You won't have to run from anyone ever again," he interrupted.

"I knew this was no life to live even before I got on that plane."

"You should have got on that plane a lot sooner than you did," he said.

"I know," she whispered.

"You'll be safer at the compound. Until we get this thing sorted out." He looked down and pushed a curl of hair off his son's face. "I planned to move you there first thing in the morning. Now I don't have to convince you."

"I know there's no choice," she said. "I wish there was..."

"The game has shifted players and the last thing I need to be doing is worrying about you," Talib said.

She looked at him with a frown.

There were so many things unspoken in that sentence. For by refusing to go to the compound, he knew that she blamed herself for his attack. She'd said as much.

He went to put his arm around her shoulders and winced as pain shot through his injured arm.

"I'm so sorry, Talib. It's my fault."

"It's not your fault, you did what you thought was best."

She shook her head. "No. Going there, to your family's compound. It wffas like a line in the sand. I couldn't do it. I thought I'd lose Everett to you and going there sealed the deal."

"Me?"

"The Al-Nassars." She wiped her eyes with the back of her hand. "I should have realized sooner that none of that mattered as long as he's safe."

"He's safe and no one is taking him from you, Sara. You're his mother. You'll always be his mother."

She looked up at him with gratitude and something else shining in her eyes. He didn't want to acknowledge what that might be for it frightened him and she looked away so quickly he thought he might have imagined it. It was a look that said that he was still her everything. Maybe that was only what he wanted to see. He pushed the thoughts away.

Instead, he thought of telling her about Tad. That he was dead and she didn't have to worry about him, but something stopped him. It was a time crunch and Tad's death didn't eliminate the threat to her. He needed to get moving, put a stop to this. And the other reason was he didn't want her to let down her guard. He'd rather have her vigilant and worried than... He couldn't think of the alternative.

"Damn," he said as he swung around. He needed to tell her. It wasn't fair otherwise.

"What's going on, Talib?" Sara asked, reading the look on his face like she seemed to do so easily. "Whatever it is, I need to know," she said softly.

She was right. She was strong enough to handle anything. She'd handled months on the run, raised a baby by herself and kept the two of them from starving. She'd done a lot before she'd come to him.

"Sit down," he said softly, directing her to a set of chairs in an alcove near her room. He'd held this news to himself for too long. It was time that she knew that the originator of this horror was no longer a threat.

"That bad?" she asked, but she sat.

"Tad Rossi was arrested in the States on assault charges. He ripped off an elderly lady at an ATM."

She put her hand to her mouth, her eyes horrified.

"I don't know how to put this. There's no way to soften it."

"Just say it," she said.

"He died in police custody."

Silence sat heavily between them. Her lips were parted and her wide gray eyes were shocked. She didn't move, it was almost as if she couldn't breathe.

He hugged her with his free arm. The embrace was brief.

"It's not over, remember that," he said. "I need you to be vigilant. Promise me."

"I promise," she whispered, but there was the first hint of a real smile on her face.

"We'll get your luggage collected and delivered to the compound." He put his free hand on her shoulder. She felt so small, so fragile. And then she looked up at him and concern was in her eyes and the way she ran her finger gently down one bruised cheek.

"You got this protecting us."

There was no answer to that statement. It was true and he knew he would do it again. "If they breach those defenses, it'll be the last thing they breach," he said ominously. "No worries. There isn't a safer place in the city, or even the country."

"I know," she said softly. "It's why I'm here. I was just afraid."

He looked at her as Everett ran his thumb along his earlobe as if that was normal, as if he'd done it forever. The soft feel of that tentative touch as if the boy was making sure he was real made it hard to focus on what was important.

She stood up.

He followed.

He looked at Sara and saw tears in her eyes.

His hand was on her waist. "You're okay?" he asked.

She backed up.

"You're afraid? No one will hurt you. You know that."

She shook her head. "I do know that. I'm sorry, Talib I'm just…"

Shock ran through him. "You're afraid of me. Is that it?" He couldn't believe it. "You're his mother, Sara. Nothing will change that. I just want a chance to know him and be his father."

She smiled but the smile didn't quite meet her eyes.

"Wait here. I'll make sure the room is clear."

A few minutes later he emerged from the suite. "It's safe. Get what you need and let's get out of here."

She headed into the suite, looking back once, and he gave her a smile of encouragement but turned almost immediately to his phone. There was work that needed to be done and he was learning to do it one-handed with his son in his other arm. He needed to put the pieces in place that would keep them safe. Whether she knew it or not, this was no longer her game. It never had been—it was his.

"THIS HAS NEVER been anything but personal," Talib said with a low growl in his throat. "He wants money and he wants to bring our family down."

"He's become more resourceful over the years," Emir said. "From two-bit crime to possible kidnapping—"

"Never going to happen," Talib interrupted.

"We know that," Emir said impatiently. "As I was saying he's evolved to kidnapping and blackmail."

"On our side he may be more desperate," Talib said. "From what we've discovered when he was contacted by Sara's ex, he saw a cash cow."

"The ex is gone and Habib has lost many of his men. Poor planning on Habib's part, it seems everything was just dashed together. So now we have a desperate man ready to do anything. Is he still in Marrakech?"

"There's no guarantees. The only thing we know for sure is that he didn't take any kind of public transport out of the city. I'll get Sara settled in Tara's suite at the compound."

"He's smart enough not to rent anything in his own name."

"You're right about that," Talib agreed. "I'll get research to run some aliases."

"That's not enough."

"I know," Talib agreed. "I've put in an order to get a paper trail that takes Sara and the boy back to the States. With any luck, he follows that and the police can make an arrest."

"And if not," Emir said, "Kate and I are out of town

on the weekend. There's no getting around it. A friend of Kate's from Montreal is getting married here in Morocco. They're both geologists and are fascinated by the Sahara. Anyway," he said with a look of concern, "we're the only witnesses. But I think we have time. And our new hire, Khalid, is just off his first assignment. Don't hesitate to use him."

"I'll be fine, Emir. I'm a professional."

"Watch your back T, and don't get cocky."

Talib rubbed the back of his neck. "I think I learned that lesson a few hours ago."

Chapter Twenty-Three

Talib was on his phone again when Sara returned, his other arm holding their son, who was smiling and pulling his father's earlobe.

He disconnected and asked what had been taken.

"Nothing," she said. "I'm packed and ready to go." The clothes she had were all new, purchased and delivered in the hours when she'd first arrived at the hotel by someone in Talib's office. Like Everett's toys, everything had arrived without her mentioning the need.

He looked at his phone as if considering what he should or should not reveal.

"What's up?" she asked.

"The police arrested the suspect two blocks from the hotel. Looks like he slipped in while a delivery was being made. Hotel security is all over that breach."

"Who was it?"

"Not who I expected," he said bluntly.

She stopped and turned to face him. "Who did you expect?"

"I know who is behind this," he said. "It wasn't him, but we'll stop him before this happens again."

Everett was clinging to Talib's pant leg and chortling as Talib shook his leg slightly, making his son cling harder and laugh.

"You're not telling me everything," she said. "Including what really happened to you." She was quiet for a moment. "You'll tell me when this is all over?"

"Promise," he said, his attention focused on her despite his leg antics for his son. "I promise I'll tell you a lot of things when this is all over. All of them good."

He bent to kiss her. She hadn't expected that and she didn't pull away and couldn't as his lips parted hers and she only wanted to melt into him. But he'd always had that effect on her.

She took a step back.

"No, Talib. Not now." What was she saying? Not ever. But she wasn't so sure about that. She wanted Talib. She always had and that was where the problems had all begun.

"Leave the bags. They'll be picked up and loaded before we get downstairs," Talib assured her.

She looked at him and one thought seemed to overwhelm her. The return date on her airline ticket was burned into her memory, but Everett didn't have to go home. It was unthinkable and yet he'd be safe. She turned away as tears burned her eyes.

"Sara." He had his hands on her shoulders as he turned her to look at him. "It will be all right. I'll find the bugger and he'll pay. No one will hurt you again."

She clung to his last statement and hoped against hope that the "no one" he referred to included himself. And she never told him the other fear, the dread that ran deep and aching through her being. It was nothing she could fix and something she had to learn to live with—life without Everett.

Talib picked up Everett and said something that made the boy laugh. A bellhop waited with a cart to take their bags and within minutes they were in the main lobby.

The lobby had returned to calm elegance. The chaos of the earlier alarm had been quickly swept away and only cultured sophistication remained.

"I'm going to miss it here," Sara said with a laugh. "My last stay in high-end luxury. Wave goodbye, Ev," she said, but pain clutched her heart at the thought that it was more than likely not her son's last stay in such luxury. For him, it was only beginning. And while it made her happy to know he'd have opportunities she'd never know, it was the thought of letting him go so he had that chance that was killing her.

"You may be surprised," Talib said dryly.

"Are you suggesting more luxury?" she said with a teasing note in her voice despite her pain.

"Much more," he replied.

Five minutes later they were making their way through Marrakech. The hotel had been on the edge of the Medina. It was where the tourists flocked for a taste of exotica, to barter in the souks and soak up the culture. It was where the locals came to get the necessities of day-to-day life. Within minutes, they were on a busy freeway. High-rise buildings, both commercial property and penthouse apartments, bordered the freeway. To her, Marrakech was just another city and she'd seen too many in recent months.

She looked back where Everett was secured into a brand-new car seat. She glanced at Talib. His attention was on the road, but there was a small quirk to his full lips, like he was smiling.

"You're happy?"

"Relieved," he said and he glanced at her before returning his attention to the road. "The two of you are safe and I can focus on getting this threat behind bars."

Again, guilt washed over her. It had been her stubbornness, her need to have her son to herself and her fear that had drawn this out longer than it ever needed to be. She should have told Talib the truth months ago.

"I'm sorry this happened while you were under my protection. I should have been there…"

"You were investigating, finding the threat. Who else would do that if not you?" To her, the question was only proof that no apology was necessary.

"Still, it was my fault, if I had been there—"

"No, it was mine," she insisted. "If anyone broadsided anyone, it was me with the news of Everett. You weren't on your game and it was my fault. I'm sorry. If I hadn't overwhelmed you, you might have been more prepared, and the attacker wouldn't have injured you like he did."

"Ouch," he said. "You're also psychic?"

"I didn't mean that in a derogatory way," she said softly. "You're everything I've always known you to be and more. I wouldn't have come here otherwise. There's no one more qualified to protect our son."

He looked at her with surprise in his eyes and something seemed to soften in his face. But he didn't say anything about her pronouncement. Instead he returned his attention to the road as a comfortable silence settled between them.

"I'm sorry I've been so much trouble. You'll be relieved when we leave."

"Leave…" The word trailed off as if he'd never considered the possibility.

"Our flight home," she replied, dodging her earlier thoughts about leaving her son. It was a consideration that no mother wanted to contemplate and not one she wanted to admit yet. "It seems trouble has only followed us here. We may be safer at home now with Tad gone."

"No."

"No?"

"Definitely not," he said.

And they drove the rest of the way in silence, both of them deep in their own thoughts.

Chapter Twenty-Four

Sara was glad for her son's silence. It gave her a chance to take in the full effect of the Al-Nassar estate, to let the opulence sink into her reality. It was majestic. The grounds alone were overwhelming. She could only imagine the mansion, which sprawled in the distance. Palm trees lined the drive and on the left she could see the beginning of a glistening infinity pool. The city of Marrakech seemed to have faded into the background, even though Talib had assured her that the compound was well within city limits.

"It's huge," she breathed. They'd just passed through a security check, a one-roomed stucco cabin that was just at the entrance. At that gate, Talib conversed with a middle-aged man with a rock-hard physique and an equally intimidating AK-47 over his shoulder. The conversation ended and the iron gates opened and they moved on.

"Five acres," he replied. "We've beefed up security. There are cameras 24/7."

"Everywhere?" she said in a voice that sounded small.

"Inside and out."

"You expect trouble?" she asked and her voice sounded worried even to her.

"We upped the security for exactly the opposite reason. To prevent trouble," he said. "You're safe here. Safer than the hotel and definitely safer than on your own in the States. There are sensors in the wall monitoring activity on either side of the wall."

Her eyes followed the sweep of his arm, where a cream-colored masonry fence surrounded the entire complex. She knew about some of the high-profile cases Nassar Security handled from what Talib had told her when they were dating. Between that and the family wealth, security was a priority. Ironically, it was security that they'd founded their business on.

She nodded. She could only hope that he was right. But she'd placed her trust in him and so far, despite the threats, he'd done just that—protect them. But seeing this, his family's home, only confirmed what she already knew. He was out of her league. He proved that now and he'd proved it before. And he always had been. Maybe that was why the romance had faded, at least for him.

Their lives were polar opposites. This was the life that Everett would inherit. This world wasn't hers. Things would change, she knew that. She'd have to learn, at worst, to share Everett. He was no longer a secret and deep in her heart she knew that he never should have been. But she wasn't ready to admit that, not now—possibly never.

Because of Everett they had to find common ground to make him a home where their differences equated only to a shared love for him. It was a lot to think about for a woman who'd only celebrated her quarter-century birthday three months ago. But since she'd become pregnant with Everett, she'd grown up fast. She'd set her mind with the same dedication she had to her career, to parenting her son.

She looked around, admiring the grounds as if she was a tourist dropped into an opulent resort. His world.

So very different from hers. They'd just passed four men with guns strapped across their backs. Now they were passing a more bucolic scene.

No guns, no Tad to worry about, just a peaceful and luxurious landscape. The endless sweep of emerald-green lawn, the elegant curve of the drive all fronted the massive home in front of them. She couldn't believe it was almost over. In her mind it was, it was only Talib that wanted to make extra sure.

She folded her hands together, glanced back at Everett, saw that his attention was caught by something and relaxed. He was safe and a good part of the trouble had shifted to Talib's shoulders. She felt guilty at the relief that ran through her, but she'd carried the load alone for so long. She also felt guilty about being relieved about a man's death. But that's all she felt about the demise of Tad. In fact, knowing he was gone almost made her smile. That was so wrong and yet her world now felt so right. She had Everett and Talib together, at least for a time. It was heaven. Or at least she could pretend it was so. She glanced over at Talib. She didn't delude herself, what she felt for him wasn't what he felt for her. She knew that. She loved him, she always had.

Talib braked for a peacock that strolled across the road. "Darn, I wish they'd keep those things contained." He glanced over at her. "Tara's idea," he said. "We have three of them. Noisier than hell at odd times of the day."

"Beautiful," she said with a smile. The bird's vibrant feathers were folded in as he moved along the side of the road and over to where a hedge was manicured into the shape of a small pyramid.

"The hedges?" she asked, wondering which of his siblings had come up with the idea and knowing it wasn't Talib.

"Emir's idea," he said. "Seems my siblings are turning this place into the Al-Nassar Disneyland."

She smiled.

Two minutes later, they got out of the car at the entrance of the mansion that stretched out on either side of them. The white tiled entrance gleamed. Soaring white columns rose on either side of a massive, arched set of doors. It was opulence on a level she'd never seen.

Inside was every bit as awe-inspiring as the outside. Twenty-foot-high ceilings stretched out on either side. White columns like those outside, only slimmer, more elegant, ran the length of the hall. The ivory-colored, tiled floor seemed to wink in the well-lit vastness that stretched endlessly in front of them. She'd never seen anything like this. Even Everett was quiet as if he, too, was overwhelmed by the size and scale of everything.

The pictures of ancestors dating back generations, lined one part of the expansive wall. All of it was luxury like she had only glimpsed at the hotel. This was so much more. This was a side of Talib she hadn't known. She knew that he was wealthy. She knew that he had the resources to save their son, but she'd never quantified what exactly that might mean.

Ten minutes later they stood outside one of the largest doors she'd ever seen in the interior of any home. A heart insignia made from what looked like gold was on the panel of each door.

He looked back at her with an impish smile. "The old harem quarters."

"Talib," she giggled, and for the first time there was a lighthearted humor between them like there had been when they first dated.

"Tara's apartment," he said with a smile. "She got a

laugh out of living in the harem, but she's done it all up so it doesn't look anything like the old days."

"I think I'd like your sister," she said quietly.

"She'll be here in a few months for a break."

In a few months she herself would be long gone, she thought, and wondered if he'd just realized the same.

"It's where you'll be safest," he said as he turned to look at her. "Tara no longer stays here much. You'll be secure here and there's a suite just over there." He pointed just behind them and to her left, where a smaller door was almost hidden. "Servants used to stay there," he said with a grin. "I'll be staying there. It's not far away from your suite. In fact it's just out the door and to your right. You'll be safe."

She skated over the safe part, caught on the luxury he was showing her. "Me?" She stopped in the middle of the doorway. "Here?"

"You," he said confidently. "Like I said, I'll be nearby. I'm not leaving you alone. Not again." He looked at her in a way that made her want to melt. "It's safe here and until this thing is resolved, I won't be leaving you for any length of time. Estate security will be on extra alert."

He turned his back to her as he entered the code and the majestic doors opened in effortless silence.

"State-of-the-art electronics," Talib said with a shrug. He pulled a key out of his pocket as a smaller door was revealed.

"Extra security," he said as he unlocked it the old-fashioned way.

Inside, the apartment was sleek and modern, like the penthouse apartments she'd seen on television.

The ivory tile that had been in the hallway continued into the suite.

She walked through the gleaming kitchen to a sitting area that looked out onto the expansive infinity pool. Palm trees moved gently in a breeze that had come up as the afternoon waned.

"Wow." It was all she could think to say.

She moved around the kitchen to where a sitting area with a wall-length bookcase was offset by a soft leather yellow sofa. She thought of Everett and grimaced. To her left was a teak desk that looked well-worn and loved.

"There's plenty to keep me entertained anyway," she said. She scanned the eclectic collection of books, including a row of children's books, from picture books to classics. She wondered if that had been a new addition, put there for Everett.

He looked at Sara. "You'll be safe here," he said. "That's the important thing."

His phone beeped.

"I need to take this." He held up his hand. "Just a minute."

"CAN YOU MEET me at my office?" Ian said. "The maid who returned Sara Elliott's son is scheduled to work this evening."

"And you think she'll show up?" He realized there was a big chunk of information that Ian didn't know and he wasn't about to fill him in. At least not yet.

"Fifteen minutes. Can you be here?"

"I won't miss it," he said dryly as he thought of the bouts of bad luck he'd had with the other suspects.

"Listen, sweetheart," he said a few minutes later as he held both of Sara's hands in his. "I've got a lead on getting this resolved. I won't be gone long. You'll be safe here and if you need anything just buzz. There's an army of servants and a security team that would make your White House proud. Don't leave the apartment."

She laughed and squeezed his hands. "We'll be fine. Ev is napping and I'll just read a book."

Ten minutes later he was in Ian's office and a minute after that they had confirmation that the maid had shown up. They weren't the only ones waiting for her—a plainclothes police office was also on site waiting to interview the woman.

In fact, it was the police officer who escorted the frightened woman into their office. It wasn't very long before it was clear that other than a description of the man who'd contracted her, there wasn't much she could tell them.

But from the description it was clear, at least to Talib, that the suspect who was in collusion with her was not Habib nor was it the man he had disabled a few hours ago.

In the end, the maid told them not much more than they already knew. That aside, she wasn't free to leave, either. She was still an accessory to an attempted kidnapping and was taken into custody. Talib felt for her, but even his influence couldn't change the course of justice.

Chapter Twenty-Five

Talib made sure that the estate was locked down and that Sara and the boy had everything they needed before retiring to his own suite of rooms.

He'd returned early enough to order their supper and give Sara a rundown on how things worked. He had to smile at how blown away she was at the idea of having three servants at her beck and call. And by the fact that she didn't need to prepare a single meal, despite a kitchen that any chef would die for.

But that bit of lightheartedness aside, his thoughts were on more life-and-death things. He'd thought of arming Sara, just in case, but when he mentioned that alternative her face had turned white. He'd immediately backpedaled on that suggestion. He hadn't realized what a pacifist she was. The subject had never come up while they were dating.

There were many things he hadn't realized about her, but he was learning quickly. His ex-girlfriend, the mother of his son, was deeper than he'd ever imagined in those long ago days of going out. Then it had only been about the fun and the passion. Now it was about reality and a threat that should be part of no one's reality. But all Al-Nassars were familiar with threats. Wealth was a siren call that attracted the opportunists, a double-edged sword that the family had wrestled with over the years.

He'd told Sara to stay inside for the next day at least, as at the hotel, and she'd agreed. Unlike the hotel, this time he was sure she'd follow up on her promise. She'd learned the hard truth of safety breach consequences. He'd assured her that it wouldn't be for long. There were upgrades to the security that needed to be done and he planned to get them done by the end of the next day.

Sara.

She was exceptional. He couldn't ask for a better mother for his son. Yet, a streak of anger and even of hurt ran through him at the thought that only desperation had allowed her to trust him. Only desperation had given him his son.

The next morning, he stopped to check on them before heading out for the day. It was time to get some answers. Already the police would have finished their interrogation and he wanted to hear what they'd learned.

Twenty minutes later he was in police headquarters. He strode past the counter and through a door made to stop anyone not in uniform. But he wasn't just anyone. His family name opened doors—combined with his reputation, he knew, with no degree of false pride, that no one in this building would stop him.

He reached his destination on the second floor and entered a large, rather sparse office.

"Talib." Diwan Zidan was a large man with a rich chocolate complexion who stood a quarter of an inch taller than Talib's six foot three. Now he rose and held out his hand, leaning across his desk and smiling an undeniable welcome. "It's been a long time."

Diwan was a detective Talib had worked with often. Despite the problems in the police force, he was among a select few that Talib trusted completely. Over the years they'd shared tips, one helping the other to close cases. It was an informal relationship, a friendship that had begun with their fathers and moved to the sons. Unfortunately, both their fathers had died too early. Both in what were originally labeled traffic accidents. Diwan's father's death had been an accident. His parents' accident, and resulting deaths, had unfortunately not been. That had been a long time ago. But it had changed the family's world.

"It's been a while."

"Thank the stars for that. Every time I see you it's bad news," Diwan said with a smile, before looking down at his computer. He then scrolled through what was on the screen. "I assume you're here because of what happened at the Desert Sands Hotel."

"You've had your ear to the ground," Talib said with a chuckle.

"My job," he said shortly. "You were attacked twice by the same man." He shook his head. "Hard to believe that one."

"I'm pretty banged up," Talib said in his own defense.

"I've seen you look better." He pulled out a file.

"The maid wasn't able to give us any information. She was exactly as you thought, an opportunist who had a change of heart." He gestured to a chair on the other side of his desk. "Have a seat."

He opened the file and pulled out a picture, turning it around so Talib could see. It was a picture of a thirty-something man with a sullen expression.

"The guy who attacked you." He looked up. "Twice."

Talib bit back a scathing remark birthed out of his own embarrassment.

"Just a small-time crook. We've got him in a holding cell. He's refusing to talk." He sat down before continuing. "We brought him in and had him interrogated by one of our female investigators. Sometimes that's more effective than men." He shook his head. "Not in this case, though. He was still pretty tight-lipped but he did give us the name of the man who contracted him. Here's where it gets interesting. The man who contracted him knows you, Talib. Not just knows of you, but there's a family connection." He opened another file and pulled out an old newspaper article. "Back in the day, before most things were online, his family made headlines."

Talib looked and saw a face that rang a bell, but didn't bring anything immediately to mind. But he knew who Diwan was going to say. Coming here today was only adding to what he already knew.

"He went to the same primary school as you, same class. Wealthy family. Scandal involving gambling on borrowed funds and some suspicious stock market trades." He looked up. "But you know this?"

"Some of it," Talib admitted.

"The family left Morocco over fifteen years ago."

"And fast-forward to today," Talib said impatiently. He was trying to move the story along.

But Diwan had a love of telling a story and when he had a handle on a good one, he wasn't about to be hurried.

"Not quite, my impatient friend. So you remember him, Habib Kattanni?"

Talib nodded. "The question is how did he hook up with Sara Elliott's ex-boyfriend?"

"Tad went to public school with him. When Sara came here I'm betting he panicked. He needed help fast. Who better then Habib, a small-time crook he was once friends with who is living in Marrakech to help regain control of Sara? Especially with the ante upped—I mean your family's wealth and all."

"Son of a..." Talib's curse broke off as his fists clenched.

"There's no known address on Habib. Wherever he's living, he's keeping low. We'll get a report filed on him and hopefully he'll be picked up."

They looked at each other and neither said what they were thinking, but it was clear that they both had the same thoughts. That he was more violent and unpredictable now as his resources ran out.

"Watch your back, Talib," Diwan said. "I'd send some extra men your way, but with the recent attacks on the outskirts of the city and a flu bug running through the ranks, I'm low on men. Anyway, Habib has made a relatively successful life of crime. He's the one you need to watch, Talib. The others were disposable."

Talib shook his head. Everything he'd heard was typical of so many career criminals.

They shook hands and four minutes later he was back in the BMW heading for home and Sara.

HABIB KATTANNI NEVER thought that Al-Nassar would get away. He should have guessed that he would. The family lived on luck. It didn't matter what tragedy they had to deal with. They came out smelling sweet. They always had.

He hated them and he hated Talib the most. But none of that mattered. What mattered was getting the money. He'd been an idiot. He'd tried for revenge and he'd failed. Talib had gotten away. He wasn't sure how, but he had. If he was here he'd kill him with his bare hands.

He gritted his teeth. That was impossible, he knew that. Without an advantage, Talib could take him down in an instant and had on that horrible day in primary school when they'd both been ten years old. It had been one of the most humiliating experiences of his life. The worst had happened the next day, when his father had publicly declared his bankruptcy. He'd been removed from the school where other children of wealth and privilege went. Al-Nassar had given him a bloody lip when he was a boy and he'd set his life for failure ever since.

Now he had a chance to put his life back together and get the final revenge. This time when he took the boy, he'd make sure that no one ever saw the little brat again. This time it wasn't Talib Al-Nassar he vowed would die, but his son.

He'd hired out with his last attempt at the Desert Sands and two of his hires had been caught. The other had blown the simple job he'd been hired for and hadn't been heard from since. But Habib wasn't in the business of being screwed around. He'd had to step in himself, it was the only way to get the job done.

The only thing that had been accomplished at the hotel was to frighten the woman. She wouldn't be staying there a moment longer. It was the only logical move, to get her out of there and take her and the boy to the safest place possible. There was only one place safer than a hotel that housed royalty and that was the Al-Nassar estate or compound, as they'd always called it. He'd hated the term. He'd hated everything about them.

They thought it was so safe, so impenetrable. And it was. Not just anyone could breach the well-protected grounds. But he wasn't just anyone.

He had an in that they wouldn't expect. He had friends in all kinds of places and it was about time he looked up the one he had at the Office National de l'Electricité. He was sure something could be arranged to let him slip by the security, it didn't have to be a long power outage, just one at the right time.

Chapter Twenty-Six

"I've bad news, Sara. You were right in assuming that Tad had connected with someone here," Talib said. "You might want to sit."

She looked reluctant but sat on the edge of the sofa just off the dining area. She laced her fingers together, her hands on her lap. "Tell me."

"The little worm he's hooked up with went to primary school with me. It was only for a few years. I wouldn't remember him except there was a scandal and his parents pulled him out." The memory of that for a moment diverted his anger. "I remember they moved. I never considered where they would have gone."

"Go on."

"The game has changed, Sara. We've found out a few things that surprise and concern me. Appears your boyfriend…" He wasn't sure why he tagged that on, but he knew it pissed her off like nothing else he could say would. Unless, of course, he said something derogatory about the boy. But he would never do that, couldn't… The boy was perfect in the way that only one's child can be.

"He's not—"

"No matter," he said, cutting her off even though he knew he'd said it that way to anger her. It was stupid. One of the childish things one does in a relationship to provoke the other. In this situation it was uncalled for because for one, they weren't in a relationship. "I'm sorry," he said and he truly meant it. He had to get his emotions under control.

"I only remember him, the man Tad partnered with, because at the time, what happened to Habib's family was so dramatic that the adults talked about it in front of us."

"What happened?"

"Bankruptcy," he said, the word stark and as bare as its meaning.

"You remember things like that," she agreed softly with a troubled look on her face.

"His family lost everything in the stock market crash. His father unwisely invested everything, diversified too little, probably trying to recoup prior losses. Instead they went from wealth to selling their properties in order to survive. They emigrated to England. After that, I heard nothing…" He made a note of another line of investigation that needed to be followed. "Apparently he's back and has been for a while. He also leans toward petty theft and a lot of unsavory acquaintances, but other than a couple of brushes with the law he's a free man."

"So what's changed?" Sara asked, a puzzled expression on her face.

"Since Tad contacted him he's hooked up with some other unsavory types. He was responsible for ramping up the kidnapping threats. The others are in custody." He covered her hand with his. He didn't mention the one hood still at large. He wasn't a threat, as he wasn't directly after Sara, but instead more of a threat to society as a whole. He'd leave that one to the police. "You're safe here. I wouldn't worry. We have decoys out to make him think you're leaving Morocco. With any luck we'll be able to catch him before he realizes that the decoys are just that."

"How do we end this?" Sara asked.

"There is no *we*," Talib said. "We have to put our son first. That means you staying here so I can protect him, and you."

He could see the anger flare in her gray eyes, and in the way she frowned at him.

"What do you think—"

"You've been doing the last two years...is that what you're going to say?" He squeezed her shoulder. "You've done a fine job of protecting him. Now it's my turn."

"But—"

"There's no choice, Sara," he interrupted. "If we want to keep Everett safe, no choice at all."

She looked at him and something softened in her look as they both realized that for the first time, he'd called his son by name.

Chapter Twenty-Seven

"Sara."

His tone was soft and yet strong and unhesitating. It carried a world of strength, the strength she'd run so far to come to. The strength she now feared. He could protect and destroy everything that she had. He was the devil and her savior, and he held her destiny in his strong, sun-bronzed hands. It was terrifying, it was…

It was as if he knew what she thought. And she wasn't sure how it happened, how she ended up in his arms. All she knew was that she didn't want to be there and couldn't move away.

As she looked into the passion sparkling in his eyes, she was drawn like she'd been so long ago. She ran a finger along his jawbone, wanting him, needing him as she always had. This time when he bent to kiss her, there was something different. Maybe it was the life they'd lived in the interim, or the boy they'd created. But the kiss was more intense, more passionate than anything she'd remembered before.

She tentatively reached up, her fingers threading through the curls that framed his face. It was an odd combination, that sun-bronzed, masculine face and the curls that seemed so soft in comparison.

Everett.

She pulled away at just the thought of her son. This was all too much, too inappropriate. It didn't matter that the boy was in another room or that he couldn't hear them or that he was asleep. None of it mattered.

She pushed him back and turned away from him, her arms folded beneath her breasts, her breath coming fast and her heart pounding.

"Sara," he said softly. "I'm sorry." His hand was on her shoulder as if that might make her turn around and face what she couldn't admit even to herself. It wasn't just about Everett anymore. She loved Talib and yet a relationship between them would never happen. She knew that. He'd thrown her to the curb once, she wouldn't allow it to happen again.

His hand was gentle but firm on her shoulder and she turned with the slight pressure. She saw the regret in his eyes and it was her undoing.

"That shouldn't have happened," he said softly. "I'm sorry."

Something inside her died at those words. Somehow, despite everything or maybe because of everything, she had hoped. That had been ridiculous. That hope had been a child's dream not that of a grown woman, especially that of a woman fighting to save her child. It was no longer about her. It hadn't been for a long time. Yet, for a moment back in Talib's arms, she had hoped.

"No worries," she said briskly as if the issue at hand was nothing more major than a broken dish.

She walked away from him and stopped at the window, where she could feel the solitude of the compound as it lay edged in darkness.

She'd only been here a short time, yet she hadn't gotten used to the silence.

"Sara," he said, interrupting her thoughts.

She turned slowly, reluctantly, as if facing him would reveal what she really felt, the feelings that she didn't even want to admit to herself.

"You're not making this easy," he said.

"What…" She wasn't sure where he was going with this. He'd been so clear three years ago. It was only now that she'd muddied the waters coming here, bringing Everett, that he seemed to have more on his mind.

"You do things to me. You always have."

She couldn't look at him. She didn't want him to dredge up feelings she'd never fully buried. "Don't say it."

"You don't know what I was going to say."

"Yes, I do. You don't want me. You want…"

"Sex?" He shook his head. "Is that what you think? It's not…"

She came over to him, drawn as she always was, as much as she tried to resist. She traced his cheek with her forefinger. "It's what I want." The words were soft and a surprise to both of them but especially her.

"Sara."

The blouse slipped off easily. He watched her. And knowing that, even without looking up, meeting his eyes, he made her hot, made her want it more. The shoulder strap of her camisole slipped down as her thumb casually looped under it. She shut down the evil little voice in the back of her mind that told her to remember what had happened, despite protection, the last time. And with everything and all she'd been through, she wanted this—one last time.

"Sara." There was a thickness to his voice, a gravelly edge that wasn't normally there.

She moved closer.

"For old times' sake," she said and wondered where those words came from, whose voice that was. But heat ran through her and she only wanted him and she wanted him now.

He stood there as if she was no more interesting than any of the other pieces of furniture in this expansive room. She took another step and her breasts lightly touched his chest. The other strap dropped and the camisole slipped, revealing a lacy pink bra.

"Sara," he said again, as if her name was the only English word he knew, and he sounded slightly choked.

"Kiss me," she said softly as she reached up, taking his face in her hands, bringing him down to her as their lips met, soft, tentative. Everything inside her, the logic she refused to listen to, was screaming at her that this was insanity.

This time she didn't wait, she pulled him, unresisting, to her. She deepened the kiss, tasting him, feeling him hard against her before his arms tightened around her. This was what she wanted, what she knew they both wanted.

This was wrong, not the way it should be.

"No," she murmured, her hands moving to his shoulders, pushing him back.

He looked at her with troubled eyes.

She wanted him and yet she didn't. She wanted him for a short time and was terrified that her heart would make that a long time. She couldn't stand the heartache of losing him again. And she was fooling no one, herself least of all. She loved him and there was no going back.

She kissed him, hot and openmouthed, her body tight against his.

"I want you."

"You're sure?"

She didn't say anything, instead her hands slipped under his shirt and felt the silken skin and the sleek lines.

His body was as hard and toned as she remembered. "I couldn't be more sure," she whispered.

It was hours later. She'd fallen asleep in his arms and now moonlight streamed across the bed and awakened her. She looked over to see him watching her.

"Sara." His voice was seductive in the waning hours of the night.

He leaned over and kissed her hard and deep. His hand was hot against her nipple. And passion eclipsed them again as his tongue worshiped her body and she begged him to enter her within minutes and end the sweet torture. They slept spooned together for what was left of the night and it was only the sunlight streaming across the room that awakened them.

Chapter Twenty-Eight

Talib left early that morning. She knew that he hoped to find a lead, to end this as soon as possible. In fact, he'd said as much. He'd been brisk and businesslike, but the kiss he had given her when he left had promised so much more.

Despite his absence, she knew that they were safe. Talib had made sure of that. When he wasn't there, there were trusted servants only a call away. There were three that she now knew well. Tazim, a middle-aged man with an easy smile, was the one she saw most frequently. In the last few days, he'd made a point of bringing a special treat for Everett every time he'd arrived. The fact that he checked on them three or four times a day and often dropped to his knees to briefly play with the boy had Everett chortling happily now at the sight of him.

After Talib had left, she'd been consumed with thoughts of what things might be like after this was over. Would she return to the States and take Everett with her, separate him from his father? Could she do that? She knew now that her fear could not shadow her son's life. He needed to know his father. She wasn't sure how she was going to make that happen. Could she endure months without her son while he was here and she was in the States? Not possible. He was too young to be wrenched from her in that way. But she couldn't fathom moving here, either.

She needed to get out, to get some air. Despite the vastness of this apartment—Talib had told her that it was four thousand square feet—she was restless. Her life was on hold. Her once busy days were now reduced to caring for Everett and worrying. It wasn't enough to keep either her mind or her soul occupied. It hadn't been for a long time. When she'd been on the run in the States, she couldn't use any of the management skills she trained for. Instead her drive and ambition had been reduced to a collection of menial jobs—salesclerk, a waitress at a bar and others she hardly remembered. Waitressing had been the best job as far as money. As long as she could handle the lewd comments and the fact that some drunk man was ogling her generous breasts, the tips were good. It wasn't the drunk trying to feel her up as she went by that ended that career. That one she handled with a well-placed elbow to the face. The one that ended it was the drunk who tried to accost her on her way to her car and scared her to death. The assault had been prevented by the intervention of an observant bouncer and had her turning in her waitress apron. It had been that job that had brought her to the brink and eventually here, when she realized that she couldn't run anymore.

She pushed away the thoughts of the events that had brought her here. She'd thought the whole process out one too many times in the planning and in the long hours in the hotel and now here. She had nothing to do but wait and it was driving her crazy. She'd ventured out of the suite of rooms that Talib had given her and Everett only a few times, and then only into the main quarters.

In some ways it seemed like they'd been here much longer. She was homesick but she had no home. She missed what was familiar. She missed the old life she'd once had in Casper, Wyoming, where she'd met and dated Talib.

That was all so long ago. In fact, months ago she'd given up the lease to her apartment. She'd done that when she'd first fled and put her things into storage. The items most important to her, she'd left with her parents. She'd contacted them regularly, which was how Tad had followed her. She'd stopped that once she'd learned from Talib how the app worked. Talib had given her access to a secure connection that had allowed her to let her family know that everything was fine. Interestingly, her mother had even been pleased at the fact that she was with Talib. But her mother had always liked him and she knew she'd secretly hoped, especially after the birth of Everett, that they'd get back together.

She thought of other things, of the tragedy of Tad. That just made her sad. That he'd turned bad, that he'd died, all of it. And thinking about it, she was angry, too. He'd had no right to do what he had done. But if none of it had happened she wouldn't have run to Talib. She wouldn't be here now knowing that she'd never stopped loving him. She wouldn't be here wondering if she had a chance.

She shivered as she looked out onto the lush grounds. It was a beautiful day, not too hot, not too cold. She looked back at the bookshelf. The books had spared her sanity. She'd thumbed through more books in the last hours than she could remember looking at in a long time. Maybe, at some point she'd have time to read them. Talib's sister had an eclectic taste that matched her own and she'd flipped through fiction and nonfiction with equal enthusiasm. Other than the books she'd felt awkward living in an apartment among someone else's things. And now, she felt like she was going stir-crazy.

It was early afternoon. Lunch was over and the day stretched out and with no clear objective to complete, it seemed endless. Everett had fallen asleep in the middle of the story she was reading him.

She settled down with a book but she couldn't concentrate. Her thoughts were everywhere. She wanted to be free to move around. She needed an objective, something to do. She was restless. One could only stay locked up for so long. She wasn't sure how zoo animals survived. But then she'd never believed in either the fairness or the rightness of locking another being up—even another species. That was why Everett had never been to a zoo in his young life, nor would he if she had any say.

Any say.

She put the book down, the words she'd just thought haunted her. It was the fear that one day, in her pursuit of her son's safety, she might give up her say in who he was and who he might become. One day, she might have no choice. It was her worst fear. It was why she'd kept him a secret when her heart knew she should have told Talib a long time ago. She didn't want to think about that. Instead, she forced herself to concentrate on other things, on the book she'd spent fifteen minutes selecting.

A little while later she nodded off.

"WE'VE GOT YOUR suspect who set the explosive device," Talib said as he leaned against the wall of Ian's office. "I just spoke to the police and they've made an arrest."

"That's a relief," Ian said, but he looked at Talib. "But it's not over, is it?"

"No. The suspect was hired by a man named Habib. No last name, at least not one that's available. I'm fairly certain it's the same man I've been investigating the last few days." He didn't go into details. Ian was a good friend, but there were some things he couldn't share. Something so critical to the investigation was one of them. In a way, keeping the information close to his chest protected everyone's best interest.

"I assume he's been arrested?" Ian asked.

"He has. I think Habib will be, too. It's only a matter of time. A very short time," he said.

"What about Sara?"

"She's safe," Talib replied.

"You're pretty closemouthed about this. But I get it. You're deep into a case." He stood up. "Look, they're upgrading some of the surveillance cameras this afternoon." He held out his hand. "Thanks for arranging that."

"We'll have you rock-solid by the end of next week," Talib said as he engaged in a brief handshake.

"Odd," Ian said. "Five days ago you were planning a joyride into the mountains. Now…"

"Everything has changed," Talib said.

"Everything," Ian replied. "But you'll make it right, man. You always do."

Chapter Twenty-Nine

"T," Emir said as soon as Talib answered his phone. "There's trouble at the compound."

"Damn, I'm nowhere near." Talib's jaw tightened. Emir was out of town. Because he was handling a code red case on his own Emir had compensated by continuing to field office calls. This call had come from their administrative and research backbone. If this hadn't been a code red, he would have taken on that duty in Emir's absence.

"The alarm just came in," Emir said. They had the security alarms feeding directly to the office. There, staff would immediately relay necessary information to Emir and any other relevant agents. It was a relay system that took mere seconds. Security was top priority. It was their livelihood and a service they sold. Their reputation hinged on the fact that it was as tight as it could be. But no security was airtight.

His grip on the phone tightened until he was threatening to break the plastic.

"The power's out, T. It went out exactly forty seconds ago. It appears there was a break in the line just outside the main fence, cutting off the entire compound. The generators should be cutting in immediately, but..."

"Even a few second delay is enough to breach the security," Talib said. This was unbelievable. They had considered every angle except this. "I'm five minutes away. Get the guardhouse on alert. Get them to secure…"

"I tried. There's no answer," Emir replied. "Drive like a sane man, T."

They were the last words Talib heard. He'd disconnected and was testing the limits of the BMW as he navigated the obstacle course of cars. He needed to get onto the freeway and make time. Five minutes away. It had to be less. He had to make it in four, three even. A truck pulled out in front of him.

He laid on the horn and the driver seemed to take that as a challenge and slowed slightly as a car passed him on either side, preventing him from pulling out. Finally, in what seemed like minutes but was only seconds, he was able to pull out and pass. He didn't bother giving the driver a look, a blast of the horn, anything. His concentration was solely on the road and on getting to the compound. And in all that time his mind could only think of Sara as he'd last seen her and Everett.

He had a son. He'd had little time with him and the fates couldn't be so cruel. Wouldn't be that cruel that he would lose him now. He'd get there on time or he'd die trying.

SARA WOKE WITH a start. She'd been napping like the very old or the very young, having fallen into a sleep that was deep and uninterrupted by dreams. The kind of sleep that had you waking up foggy, wondering where you were and how long you'd slept.

But something had awakened her. The book she'd been reading and that had slipped into her lap while she slept fell to the floor. She picked it up and set it on the small table beside the couch. She was still, listening, wondering what it was that had awakened her. There was no sound from down the hall, where Everett slept. But she knew it hadn't been him. It had been something else.

"Is anyone there?" she called, wondering if one of the servants had come to check on them or even if Talib had come back.

Silence.

Yet something wasn't right. She could feel the change in the air, like it was real and tangible when in fact there was nothing. She couldn't take any chances, especially considering all that had happened. Her instincts were on alert. Something was wrong. She couldn't see or hear it, but she could sense it.

She tiptoed to Everett's room and opened the door to peek in. The room he was in had no window. He was sound asleep. He was safe. Still, something wasn't right.

She went back to the main area. Again she heard something, a whisper of sound against the window. It was closed, but she knew something was off and she didn't like that she couldn't identify what it was.

It had to be one of the servants. She was just being paranoid, but despite how logical and safe that sounded, she was unable to convince herself. Her heart pounded as her imagination amplified the danger. She was backing up, putting herself between whatever her imagination was conjuring and her son.

"Hello?" She had to fight to keep the quaver out of her voice.

She knotted her fists and scanned the room, grabbing a tennis racket from a shelf at the bottom of the bookcase. It was out of place, something she'd meant to put back and another thing that had been rearranged by her busy son.

Everett.

She began to move more determinedly backward, toward his room, her eye remaining on the door. Should she call out? It was probably nothing. But the longer this went on, the more real it seemed to become.

Silence reigned. The seconds ticked by. She barely breathed but the sounds she heard just a few moments ago didn't repeat. It had been her imagination. She blew out a sigh of relief but still stood where she was, just in case.

Bushes rustled just outside the terrace doors.

She wanted to rush to Everett and yet something told her that would be the wrong thing to do. She was basing the thought purely on instinct. And other than the tennis racket, she was defenseless. But the logical side of her mind told her there were at least twenty-five people in this compound at any given time. The sheer numbers, never mind the security that was in place, made her feel safe.

It was nothing. She was being ridiculous. She looked over to where there was a call pad to page one of the servants or the guardhouse. It was usually lit up. She went to pick it up—nothing. It was dead. She grabbed her phone. She'd call the main number for the guardhouse. They might think she was crazy but she didn't care. Everett's safety was her main concern.

She had the phone in one hand and the racket under one arm when someone grabbed her around her neck and she was yanked back. The phone clattered to the tiles. Whoever it was, he was male, his arm thick and hairy. His hand was over her mouth and she was dragged through the apartment and down the hall that ran on the other side and away from Everett's room. She didn't scream, not wanting to awaken him, grateful that the danger was moving farther away from her son.

"Your boyfriend is a fool." The man's breath was like the rancid smell of rotted fish guts on her parents' dock.

Something hard knocked against her temple. She could only assume that it was a gun.

She almost choked but instinct told her that would only enrage him. It took all her willpower not to.

"But then he always was, even when we were children."

He took his hand away from her mouth. "Who are you?" She struggled to regain some control, to stand up straight and take some of the pressure off the painful tugging of her hair that was caught beneath his arm, making her eyes water. Between that and his foul breath and the fear racing through her, she couldn't think. She needed to think, to get herself out of this jam and keep Everett safe.

The apartment was so large and initially, with Everett she liked to be close to him, and not being so had disconcerted her. Now she was glad for the distance. Everett couldn't hear what was going on, he wouldn't cry and bring attention to his presence.

But the moment she thought that, she heard him call her.

No, no, no, sweetheart. Ev, please no. Her head hurt as she tried to send the thoughts to her son. But she knew it was useless, she wasn't psychic and neither was her son.

"Your boy?" he asked almost pleasantly and went on without her answer. "Let's go get him," he said.

Instinct told her to play coy, to buy time. "Who?"

"Al-Nassar's heir."

"I have no idea who or what you're talking about."

"Your kid." He yanked her head back painfully by her hair and her eyes watered.

"He belongs to me."

"Tad said otherwise," he said. "I don't have time for this. Move." He pushed forward, not releasing his grip on her and making her stumble. "Give me the boy and I'll let you go."

Never, she thought. Play along, her sane, less panicked side told her. Buy time.

She heard scraping, what sounded like the murmur of voices—she wasn't sure. It was too faint. Maybe it was only her imagination. The door was old and heavy, the construction of the entire mansion such that sounds didn't travel well through closed doors.

Then she did what she told herself would only enrage him, but she needed to do something, because maybe in some way it would buy her some time.

She dug her nails into his hand and the grip around her neck only tightened and she choked.

In another hallway, yards away from her, Everett wailed.

She had to think. It was on her. She needed to get them out of this and she had no idea how.

Chapter Thirty

Talib's finger had been poised to ring the bell to the suite. This was Sara's home for now and he wouldn't invade it. Before he could press it, he heard his son crying. The baby monitor was hanging from his belt, where he'd put it yesterday and where it was whenever he was in the compound. He'd taken no chances with security, or so he'd thought until the power had gone out. Another minute and he knew it would be back up. It should have been back up already.

He frowned at the sound of his son's cries. Because the child wasn't crying at all. Instead they were shrieks of anger and frustration. Something was going on that he didn't like. He expected to hear Sara's voice comforting the boy. She never let him be upset for any length of time. She'd told him that she didn't think it was healthy.

Everett's cries escalated, but he heard nothing of Sara. Something wasn't right.

"Son of a…" Talib had his fingers on the keypad and unlocked the outer doors. But the key wouldn't go into the inside door's lock. It was jammed. Alarms were ringing in his head. All of this was pointing to something very wrong, something very bad. His family was in danger.

For a moment he was blinded by rage, but he soon had that under control and shifted into combat mode as he'd done so many times in his life. His family was inside and he was not stopping until they were safe and again under his watch.

Driving a shoulder into the door would do nothing. He knew that the door wouldn't budge. It was that well-built.

He pulled the Glock from his hip and stood back. He used his forearm to cover his eyes and as much of his face as possible as he stood slightly sideways and fired once, twice. He blew a hole through the lock and flipped the knob, bursting into the room.

He could hear voices in the corridor to his left, away from the boy. Relief and rage collided. The boy's room was in the opposite direction. He might be safe. Was Sara?

He had his gun in both hands and he led with the weapon as he turned into the corridor.

The man Talib faced was not the boy he remembered. He'd obviously lived a hard life in the interim, hard and bitter from the looks of the deep lines and the hateful twist of his mouth. But it was who he had by the neck that terrified Talib.

"I didn't expect you," Habib said, the gun he held to Sara's head not wavering for an instant.

"I'm sure you didn't," Talib said calmly as he lowered the gun.

"Give me the money and she lives," Habib snarled as his eyes met Talib's. "You gave a quarter of what I asked. What do you think I am, a fool?"

"Certainly not," Talib said carefully.

"Certainly not," he replied, mocking Talib's careful diction. "Quit making bloody fun of me. You and your rich-kid attitude."

It was like he was slipping back into childhood and using terms he might have used as a boy.

"I would never make fun of you," Talib said. "I'll get the money…" He met Sara's eyes. He wanted to give her a signal, tell her that it was all right. That he'd make it all right no matter what it took. She and Everett would be fine. But he couldn't say any of that, he could only try to communicate some of it with a look.

She blinked, slowly, carefully, as if telling him that she understood.

"Certainly, I can give you money. How much? I'm always happy to help someone in need. Even though I have no tie to the kid."

"Certainly, nothing," Habib said in a raised voice that had a snarl edging through it. "I'm taking the boy, there's nothing you can do to stop me. You can have him back when I get the money."

He met Sara's eyes. There was something sparking in them that reflected more determination than panic. Habib had her by the throat and he could see the red handprint on her cheek where he'd hit her. Down the opposite hall, Everett continued to scream for his mother.

It was a horrific scene. His family was on the edge of destruction because of a madman. He needed to think his way out of this. But options had been eliminated. There were no guns blazing, no hand-to-hand battle. The mother of his son stood between those two options.

"Take him. Take the kid if you want," Talib said and Sara looked at him with horror. "I was willing to help once. But twice." He shrugged. "It's not like my heart's in it."

He tried not to meet her eyes after that. He could only hope that she'd realize what he was trying to do.

"What are you saying?" Habib scowled.

"I don't want him. He was born out of wedlock. Did you know that?" He put his gun back in its holster and ran a hand through his hair as he attempted to look put out and casual. "There's no guarantee he's even mine. In fact, I have serious doubts…"

"Shut up!" Habib screamed. "Just shut up. He's yours."

"I'm not on the birth certificate," Talib said calmly, but his heart beat at an insane rate. He couldn't look at Sara, could only hope that her silence was confirmation that she realized what he was doing and was playing along. "Besides that, any kid of mine wouldn't be that ugly."

"You're playing me."

"You're the lucky one, Habib. You got out of the establishment. Away from the users like her."

Silence was heavy between them. He kept eye contact with Habib. It was one of the hardest things he'd ever done.

"Don't make me repeat it. If you want the kid, take him. As you can hear, all he does is scream. I want nothing to do with him. Take her, too." The words stuck on his lips. They were the most difficult words he'd ever said. But they were having an effect, he could see the doubt on his opponent's face.

"You want me to take the kid?" Habib scowled as if what Talib had been saying was finally registering. He wasn't holding Sara as tightly against him as his face reflected his doubts.

Talib shrugged. Finally, he looked at Sara, saw the tears that shimmered, but her lips turned slightly up. It was a signal that she was with him. "Why don't you show us that birth certificate and prove once and for all that you're just another conniving gold digger?" Talib said to Sara as he glared at her and mentally begged her to stay strong.

She didn't drop her gaze, only the slight smile was gone. "I needed the money," she said softly.

"Sure you did," he snarled. "I'm sick of her. Take her if you want."

He looked at Habib. "You know I envied you. You never had these problems with women like her. I don't know if any woman ever liked me for me. Seriously, this one's a doozy, the kid really is uglier than sin."

He looked at Sara. "Get the birth certificate, show him," he demanded in a voice that was lethal. "If nothing else, get the brat's passport."

Sara's eyes met his and something—an understanding—passed between them, almost as electric as the passion they'd so recently rediscovered. It was brief, and as quickly as they disconnected, she sank her teeth into her captor's forearm and, at the same time, pushed away from his grip. It wasn't much. There was a split second of time that was all it would take for Habib to regain control.

It was all Talib needed. He pulled his gun. He aimed even as he said that one important word to the woman he knew he loved. "Run."

He didn't have to say more. There was only one place for her to run. Straight to their son, where she would protect him with her life.

He only had an instant, but it was enough. One shot took out Habib.

He couldn't let his thoughts stray any further than that. Habib was down and he wasn't moving. Blood pooled around his head. He strode over, pushed him with his foot, then leaned down and put the back of his hand under his nostrils. Nothing. He checked his pulse for good measure.

"Dead," he said with satisfaction and pulled an afghan off the back of the couch and dropped it over the body. It wasn't a matter of respect but rather an act of protection. He didn't want his son's innocence destroyed by the sight, or the woman he loved traumatized any more than she already had been.

This kind of thing was his world. For a short time, it had been theirs. It was up to him to make sure it never happened again.

Chapter Thirty-One

"It's finally over, sweetheart," Talib said to Sara. It was a few hours later. The police had completed their questioning and the body had been removed. In the midst of all that, Everett had been placed under the watchful care of Andre. When she'd last checked, Andre had parked the boy with him in the kitchen, where the staff were being entertained by the toddler's antics. There were more volunteer guards and nannies in that kitchen than a state prison. Even if there was a threat, Talib had no doubt that it would be handled.

"What do we do now?" Sara asked.

It wasn't about the two of them. They both knew that she asked because of their son. He was the one unspoken agreement between them. They'd both do whatever it took to protect him and that meant giving him what was best for him in all things.

"You'll want to see him."

"Of course," Talib said easily. "But I want to see his mother, too."

"What do you mean?"

"I love you, Sara. I think I always have. I..." He paused and rephrased his words. "We should never have broken up."

"It was your doing." She shook her head as if remembering the experience. "Although, I think I might have had my moments."

"No, you're right. It was my fault. If I'd hung in there, we would have been a family. I wouldn't have missed…"

"I'm so sorry, Talib. If I could do it over—"

"I know," he said, cutting her off. He put a hand on her shoulder. "There's so much more I know about you, sweetheart, and oddly about myself that I've learned since you came back into my life."

"Can you forgive me?"

"Not that long ago I would have never forgiven you," Talib said darkly. "What you did was incomprehensible. At least that's how I would have seen it even a year ago and how I saw it when you first told me. I see it a little differently now. I guess, I see your side, or at least some of it."

"I wouldn't forgive me," she said softly.

"You're not me," Talib replied. "I'm willing to forgive if you are."

She stood up, her hands twisted behind her back. She couldn't look at him. She didn't want to admit the real reason that she'd kept them apart. Her fear had been that great. They couldn't reach an agreement if she wasn't honest with herself, with Talib.

Fear. That's all it had been, but it wasn't such a small thing for it had stolen two years of a father's time with his son. It was unforgiveable and in an odd way she thought she might feel worse about it than Talib.

"I was afraid."

"Were you that afraid of me?" Talib asked darkly. "What did I do?" He stood up, his hands opening wide as he made an expansive gesture that seemed to include her and the empty room at large.

"You didn't do anything," she said softly, although

she thought of the breakup and realized that that wasn't completely true. She'd harbored some resentment toward him over that. But that wasn't the reason for everything that came down after that point. "It was about who you are. Who your family is."

"My family?" His dark brows drew together and, for a minute, there was silence between them. "You mean our wealth." It wasn't a question. They both knew that was part of the problem. He hadn't needed to ask.

"Part of it," she said softly. "Your influence. All of it."

"Everett is part of that."

"I know. And I planned for you to know of him someday. I just didn't want…"

"This is about custody, isn't it?" He scowled. "I don't believe this. You thought…"

"It wasn't like that. It—"

"You came here believing that you would lose him," Talib said in a soft voice that was underscored with a steely determination. Somehow he had closed the gap between them and now he stood just to her left, behind her, too large, too imposing, too close.

His hand touched her shoulder, heavy and solid, as he turned her around to face him, closing the last bit of safety, of distance, between them.

"It was a reprehensible thing you did," he said softly.

Her heart broke at the words.

"But it took real courage to come here." He cupped her face between his hands. "Your sense of right won over."

"It was what Ev needed," she said quietly. She looked up, met his eyes. Usually so guarded, they now seemed to reflect a piece of his soul. "It was what you both needed."

"It was what *we* needed," he said in a thick whisper. "Everett needs to know who he is and where he comes from. He needs to spend time in Morocco."

"With you?"

"Exactly. But not by himself, of course," he quickly assured her. "He's too young to be without his mother."

"What are you suggesting?"

He took both her hands in his. "I want to try again, Sara, with us. I want us to be good parents to our son. Together—here, in Morocco."

"My career?" She blushed. They both knew her management career had dead-ended in the States along with her dream to own a bed-and-breakfast, as she'd fled from state to state.

"Ian is in desperate need of a manager. Someone who knows the business. I mentioned…"

"You didn't?" She felt a sudden sense of relief.

"I did."

"I don't have a work visa," she said, realizing the silliness of such a comment. She was speaking to an Al-Nassar. She didn't doubt that paperwork would not be an issue. They lived in a different world than other beings, it had been part of what had torn them apart.

"I love you," he said simply.

"I've never stopped loving you," she said.

"You've never said that before."

"I was afraid you'd never say it back," she replied. For it was true—what did she have to offer an Al-Nassar? She had nothing that he wanted but his son.

"I'd marry you whether you had Everett or not," he said. "In fact, I'd have married you three years ago if one of us hadn't botched things up."

"Talib." She punched him lightly in the chest.

He leaned down and kissed her, hot and hard and passionately, and it told her everything she needed to know and everything he felt. She melted into him and into the promise of that kiss, knowing that the future would be much different than she'd imagined. It would be a future, that, once, so unbelievably long ago, she'd dreaded.

Epilogue

Three months later

The move had been less difficult than Sara had imagined. She'd never considered traveling anywhere. Not in her previous life and definitely nowhere as exotic as Morocco. She'd never thought of living anywhere other than Wyoming. Since becoming a mother, the focus of her thoughts had been what was best for her son. He needed his father. The events of the last months had proven that. More importantly, both her son and his father had roots here. It was a pull that was undeniable. It was a land that belonged to both of them and, as a result, belonged to her, as well.

But Talib had rocked everything when he'd announced only a few days ago that he wanted to join his brother Faisal in the Wyoming branch of Nassar Security.

After everything that had transpired, she'd been ready to stay in Morocco for a while, even for the duration of Everett's childhood, if that's what it took to make their family feel whole. But Talib had insisted that while his son needed to know his family, he was fine with raising him in Wyoming with visits to Morocco. Sara was overjoyed—Wyoming was where she grew up and, truthfully, the thought of returning was something she'd never anticipated and filled her with joy. Morocco had been an experience, a place she was willing to stay for the good of her son, but Wyoming was what she knew and, before she met Talib, what made her feel safe. Going home was the ultimate gift.

The time they'd spent in the compound had, in an odd way, been like a trial marriage. But it was the patient wooing that Talib had done, the thoughtful dates that always factored in what her interests and passions were, dates he'd arranged over the weeks when the horror in their lives had finally ended. When life calmed down he'd also spent time alone with their son. Taking him out on what he called boy trips, which Everett loved. Sara also enjoyed the time alone. He was thoughtful in every way, a natural father. But it was as a lover that he totally won her over. Not, if she really wanted to admit it, that he needed to win her over. She'd always loved him and even after everything that had happened, she'd always trusted him. He'd been who she'd turn to in what had looked like her darkest hour.

It had been a surprise to learn he had felt the same.

But it was the ring on her finger that early winter evening over a private supper that had convinced her more than Talib's words. Even though his words meant everything.

As his lips met hers, she knew that it meant everything to Talib, too.

"It's not official," he whispered against her lips. "But the three of us are a family.

"Sara Al-Nassar," he whispered.

"Elliott," she whispered back. "I'll save Al-Nassar for you and the baby."

"As long as you're mine," he said.

"Deal," she whispered back and his tongue opened

her lips with a gentle caress and they both knew that the name meant nothing and everything.

"Unless you wanted to argue now and make up with a little loving…"

"Talib," she giggled and curled up against him. "Al-Nassar and Elliott, that's a lot of family."

"A whole lot of family," he agreed.

* * * * *

Check out the previous books in the
DESERT JUSTICE *series:*

SHEIKH'S RULE
SHEIKH'S RESCUE

And don't miss the thrilling conclusion in

SHEIKH DEFENSE

Available soon from Mills & Boon Intrigue!

Join Britain's BIGGEST Romance Book Club

50% OFF your first parcel

- **EXCLUSIVE offers every month**
- **FREE delivery direct to your door**
- **NEVER MISS a title**
- **EARN Bonus Book points**

Call Customer Services
0844 844 1358*

or visit
millsandboon.co.uk/subscriptions

* This call will cost you 7 pence per minute plus your
phone company's price per minute access charge.

CB3